For my parents and grandparents.

In memory of Shadow and Wilber.

In memory of my relatives that have passed on.

Hondor

Edited by: Aaron and James Dalzell

Copyright © 2015 by Aaron J. Dalzell

ISBN: 978-0692446676

Other Works Include:

Forgemaster (2013)

...by Candlelight (2014)

Trail of Flies (2014)

Off Road (2014)

Conflict (2014)

Hondor

by

Aaron Dalzell

"Beware Kandarius...when his time has come...

he will be hunting you down,

searching for the blood...that you take from me...!"

-Naumokron,

Possessor: Part X

Prologue:

"These Ancient Words"

~

It's dark. Too dark to see, too opaque throughout the furthest reaches of the midnight brood of luminescent clouds that swirl above like cyclones with a powerful breath, a wind so powerful and vast, it draws those swept within its grasp, the talons of the air, and pushes them over into the darkness below the cliffs. It's far too dark to see, without the strike of lightning, the electric serpent that lights abound the very colossus that looms above with its poisonous essence of electricity, of light for which the darkness is allergic to, the darkness of the mountains of cumulus stacked upon one another throughout the vast atmosphere of Aura.

The rocks and crags are high upon all sides of them, barely a luminous glow in the clash of thunder which roars, and the thunder serpents continue their illuminating encirclement. Their culminating charges that illuminate more and more with each strike of their fangs, the rocks avalanche and shake with the thunder's hellish, daemonic roar that rings out like an echo within the hollow bowels, the ribbed hallways of Wom's stomach.

But the darkness beneath them is thicker. The opposition of the ivory light swirls round beneath their feet, far beneath in fact, deep within the Great Divide. The yawning black abyss, swallowing downwards into the spiral of a clockwise vortex, where the many gears and leavers of natures wind takes precedence. Yet, the many of Aura shall never understand, except for the ones whose time has passed, and join in, becoming one with the darkness, prisoners of the eternal voids.

For them to reach this place, Glasgar Vor`, the Gormon standing several feet above Duul`ak the winged Asyndian, in height; they had to climb the highest summits at the very edge of the Great Divide, the vast pit, the crack which separates the land of Aura from Raukmar.

The storm around them, however...isn't anywhere near being as horrid or terrible as the one that's approaching, the storm of fates, the storm that shall take in many, and let none escape. The storm...the unstoppable force that is *"He!"*

Another strip of lightning illuminates, flashing across the sky like a nude harlot performing her dance, distracting them for a moment, breaking their concentration by her scream of terror that carries on the winds from the valley below. The sky serpent briefly lights their pathway, ahead of them. Glasgar notices a vast pathway, a road that has been dug up, devoid of its once marble bricks and ancient mortar to hold them within their bonds. However, this pathway leads to nowhere, at least nowhere in particular...for they still do not see their destination in sight. The road leads to the edge, overlooking the Divide far beneath, for the gaping maw is so vast and huge, they are unable to see the boundaries of Raukmar further beyond the way, across the seas of darkness and the waves of black beneath.

Glasgar and Duul`ak stand at the edge of the high cliff to gain a further survey of their surroundings. Glasgar is very confused and dumb-founded, while the curses of Duul`ak echo aloud across the dark skies around them, enraged and upset by their failure...their failure to follow in their master's path. The winds are far too strong, for Duul`ak is unable to fly up and take a look from a higher point of view.

'Damn it! Where is this lair of his!!!' Duul`ak shouts. Glasgar furrows his brow, grabs a nearby chunk of rock and tosses it out into the voids.

'We followed the trail...followed the signs! Where is this place!' Glasgar shouts at Duul`ak. He looks down at the Asyndian. 'I thought you knew where to find the master!'

'The master chooses to go where he wants , and do what he wants! It's almost impossible to track him!' Duul`ak retorts.

Glasgar growls.

'It's luck Glasgar! Luck! I thought you Gormons could see in these dark places! I don't hear anything coming from you, or that big mouth! Why do you think I released you from your prison?! To be your friend? No Glasgar, I use what tools I can to find the master...you are only a tool to me, as well as the master.'

'I ought to tear your wings off, you damn Asyndian scum! My father always said your kind were nothing more than aristocratic tricksters! Even worse than the Civilian dung!'

The two prepare to fight, and Glasgar leaps at Duul`ak, but the Asyndian leaps away as he smashes through a large boulder.

'You Gormons are so hot headed...hmmm, I guess that it makes up for your cowardice, for that is your reason for going into battle...because someone stepped on your thick boot, as thick as your moronic head!'

'I'll shove my boot up your ass...! And Glasgar charges again, this time drawing his gargantuan mace, clumped with blood and hair from previous battles.

'Please do! Come and try it, you'll only be smashing rocks with that useless cudgel you brandish!' Duul`ak replies.

Glasgar swings the mace about him wildly, and as Duul`ak foretold, the Gormon was only hitting rocks in his blind rage, as Duul`ak danced about and away, laughing at Glasgar. Duul`ak stood atop a giant monolithic crag and looks down at the raging Gormon, still laughing wickedly, amused by Glasgar's anguish and hate.

'Are you finished playing around yet?! We still have much work to do!' Duul`ak yells down.

Glasgar's eyes glow red, filled with fury, and with a final charge, he rams straight through the thick wall of rock and mineral, and the structure crumbles down around him. Duul`ak lands upon the ground, but turns to see Glasgar as he rolls over the edge, and tumbles down to the valley, his armor and bones making a crunching noise as he hits the bottom upon impact.

Duul`ak looks over the edge, and cannot see the bottom, nor any trace of Glasgar. Then, from the darkness beneath, he hears the loud grunt of a sore and injured Gormon. Duul`ak extends his wings, and hovers down to the bottom, the winds shifting him, and rocking him to and fro. Then his talons scratch against the rocky earth beneath.

'I congratulate you, being the imbecile you are, you've managed to get us back on track. Perhaps you are more of a useful tool than I thought.'

Glasgar lets out another grunt, and gets to his feet, shaking his head, and dusting the rubble from his long white beard and black armor. His dark-blood colored cape flutters with the winds exhaling from the valley and the dust blows off. Glasgar notices a large crack in the cliff face ahead of them, some sort of opening by the looks of it.

'There...through there.' He walks forward towards the opening, and Duul`ak follows behind, keeping an eye on Glasgar, now that he has insulted the heated Gormon criminal.

On the other side of the vast chasm, they enter into a valley of monstrosities, where the sickly creatures native to this region grumble about and thrash their spiked tails through the ashen shrubs and tear down trees by the thick roots, not living trees, but ancient trees, sick trees...trees that have seen the beginning of time, and have been around long enough to bear witness to its many encounters with the end. Their roars echo through the rocks and carry upon the supersonic belch of the wind's deafening speech, the ear-bursting howls.

They trudge through, they shuffle onwards, making their way across the makeshift path through these depressing woods, and if they do come across the dying roars of these decrepit beasts, they slay them where they stand. There is no warning, no countdown, its kill on demand...or be killed. Further upwards, upon the breach of the hill of bones and rotting carcasses that pile upon an ancient tar pit, Glasgar's sharp eyes notices a bright yellow eye hovering in the sky, and upon closer inspection, the eye is part of a body, a body of stone and dull gray bricks...for a tower lays before them, or above them would be the more correct term to use.

The lower they traverse into the valley, the harsher the wind breaks against their armor. Duul`ak can barely keep his wings closed, as the winds push him back. And Glasgar, even being the tank he is, is having trouble keeping upon his feet in this section of the valley. Duul`ak loses his footing and is carried off. He clutches onto a nearby tree. Glasgar turns around and looks at him for a minute, laughing out loud at the Asyndian, laughing because of all the insults he drove upon Glasgar, now it seems he's getting his due. Glasgar trots back a few paces, and clutches Duul`ak by his head-feathers and drags him along. Duul`ak yells out in pain, cursing the Gormon, but Glasgar pays no heed.

The touch of lightning upon the high cliffs ahead, sends a massive, hulking boulder spiraling towards the ground with a roaring pummel as the mass strikes the dirt.

'Smash the damn thing!' Duul`ak yells.

Glasgar positions himself in front of the huge rock, brings his fist back, and with a huge massive drive forward, ramming his fist through the stone, letting out a chugging roar, as the boulder crumbles down into nothing but tiny, miniscule pieces of debris.

They continue onward, Glasgar walking the long miles ahead of them, still dragging Duul`ak, as the winds get more and more powerful with every mile. They approach the base of the tower's epicenter. The black, grayish tower is now in view of them, as they discover the source of this voracious wind that drives the directions of the dust and soot about upon their vacant quest without any destination in sight, no destiny at the end.

Below where the massive tower floats, circles a huge cyclone, vast in its width, yet static for it does not shift its direction to move, it only stands in one location and belts its screams and animosity outwards, standing as the guardian to this tower that floats above as its crown.

Glasgar stands in front of the cyclone, the cause of these degenerating winds that howl across the Divide and

6

pierce the blackened air and mists that swarm about the area like diseased locusts in massive clusters, the armies of legion that patrol over these grounds. He holds up Duul`ak to bear witness to its magnificence.

'This...this is it... we have to step into the winds, we must...'

Glasgar tosses Duul`ak into the vortex like some sacrificial offering, and watches him fly upwards. Then Glasgar walks in, and the swirling winds take him as well.

The cyclone takes them skyward to the fifteenth floor of the tower, for half the structure is missing, only the top portion remains hovering at the tip of the vortex's gaping maw.

Glasgar grabs hold of the railing at the middle of the spiral stairwell, while Duul`ak embraces the essence of the winds, and the true Asyndian comes alive deep within him, as he spreads his wings and soars to the top. He looks back down at Glasgar who is hanging on at the bottom.

'Hurry...get up here!' Duul`ak screams with the echo and sharpness of a falcon in his vocals.

'Not all of us have wings!' He retorts at Duul`ak with an angry grunt.

Glasgar makes his trek up by stairs, not wanting to fly any higher, he takes the rest of the way by foot, till he reaches where Duul`ak waits.

Glasgar reaches the top, out of breath and wheezing, a scratch trebles in his throat with each and every gasp. He makes his way over to where Duul`ak is seated with his legs crossed, hovering in the air in deep meditation, concentrating upon the fiery jewel near the window, the very eye Glasgar saw from the distance, back where they started on their way to reach this place.

Glasgar gets closer to this mysterious flame near where Duul`ak is seated.

'So good of you to join us...' Duul`ak says in a sly whisper.

'We...is the master here?' Glasgar replies.

'BE SILENT! If you shut up...and listen...you too, will hear him speak...'

Glasgar drew nearer, now standing next to Duul`ak, and he said nothing, not a word...and then, at that moment, he too could hear the whisper, the voice of the master which Duul`ak has spoken of, had promised Glasgar that he would meet for his pardon...is here. Was this voice inside his head, these could not be the words of Duul`ak, for his lips do not move. No, it was coming from the eye, the bright yellow jewel that hovered within the center of the room.

Curiosity overcame Glasgar, he had to see this master for himself, with his own eyes, and he walked closer, and closer, and closer...until, a hand reached out and gripped his wrist like a deadly vice. Glasgar looks back, and it is Duul`ak holding him in place, clutching him.

'You dare! Get your claw off of...!' Glasgar yells, but Duul`ak silences him.

'Do not get any closer...the master is almost ready.' Duul`ak says. He motions over to the window where Glasgar notices thousands of tiny Mig-like creatures with stingers upon their abdomens and snapping claws stretched ahead of them as they move, they scale the wall, crawling out the window with an eerie clicking sound their tiny steps make scratching against the flaking mortar. The last few of them crawl out the window...and then an ominous blood-red light flares outside against the blackened sky, as a ghostly visage enters within the tower, striking the eye, and becoming one with the flame.

The crystal explodes, the great eye ruptures, and the flames blossom outwards like the falling petals of a dying flower. They encircle Duul`ak and Glasgar. Before their eyes, the color's change, not a spectacle of the magnificent rainbow after a spring rain, nor the respectability of being primary, but bursting forth colors that would ooze from the dying carcass, green and yellows like puss, blood that runs red, and the fiery charred embers of a cadaver's ashes after a funerary pyre, a pyre of a very other-worldly and undivine sort.

And that's when they see, they witness the very horrors of the unsacred pit, the gurgling gaping stomach of the darkest place, the bowels of Wom...the Hexagus realm and the empty thrones without the Lords upon them, gracing them with their apocalyptic presence no more. Only the visage of one...a forthcoming shadow in the swirling mist, a silhouette within the embrace of the swirling colors and fog.

The flames erupt and shoot outwards and sear the walls. From the pit of embers at the center of the tower's pinnacle, arising from the marker, the Hexagus symbol that has been tattooed upon the floor with the explosion, drawn from the ashes of the Hexagus Lord's, their bones...from this, a shadow rises up, a pair of huge black wings spreads outwards as far as the tower in width, and the dark being stands almost to the tower's ceiling. The flames dance and shiver, reflecting off his outline of opaque feathers, silhouetted among the fires live a looming overcast of black storm clouds, for the essence of Naumokron hovers in their wake, returned from Wom's ethereal plane, appearing in a corporeal representation of his former dignity.

9

The shape of Naumokron says nothing, not a word. He only looks down upon then, Duul`ak in particular. Naumokron holds out his arm and, within the grasp of his index finger and thumb, squirms one of the mig-like creatures. He releases the creature and Duul`ak opens his hand and catches it before it hits the ground. He looks at the mig, then back at Naumokron, and without words, he understands, he knows the answer to Naumokron's actions.

Duul`ak raises his arm up, and holds the creature up high, he opens his mouth and lets go of the mig, as the creature falls from his clutches into his mouth. Duul`ak closes his beak, and the crunches from his chewing echoes in the tower's dome. He swallows the remaining pieces, and that's when the event happens, the sudden flare of a red light erupts upwards from Duul`ak's stomach, a bright volcanic surge bursts upwards, he grasps his throat and begins to choke, gasping for air, he opens his mouth wide once more for a gasp of air, pleading to the shadow looming over him. Glasgar looks on, but is unable to move, his eyes blinded by the red lights that flood the room.

Duul`ak lets out a gasping scream, a terrorizing holler, a cry of merciless torture. His red eyes widen, he is lifted into the air by the pulsing surge, his wings open out by electrical energy and reaction, then within a moment, his body convulses and then closes up into a fetal position, he forces his head up, and looks to the sky through the hole in the tower ceiling, he grasps his heart and then...he does not fall from grace, but is forced to the ground by the rampaging assault upon his body.

Glasgar uncovers his eyes, and the light is gone, all has fallen silent, and the shadow of Naumokron that haunts over this tower...has vanished from this realm once more, for the eye is now a dull, opaque stone sitting upon the center of the floor, and just nearby, is Duul`ak's body, laying there in front of Glasgar, limp and lifeless.

Glasgar walks over with caution, and briskly kicks at Duul`ak's body. The Asyndian doesn't respond.

'Duul`ak...' Glasgar speaks in a low tone. He kicks at the body once more, thinking he is dead, for his sharp ears listen...there is no heart beat, nor breathing. Glasgar thinking of a way to get out of the tower, turns to abandon Duul`ak to his fate...when all of a sudden, at that moment Glasgar heard a thump echo across the walls, then a moments silence, and then another loud thump. This was no collapse about to occur. He turns around, looking at the vast space, a dark space of night and stars, faint flickers of red candles scatter about the vast open nothingness, as though he were standing within another plane of some ominous existence, another world. And again, the loud thud, echoes into the night realm.

And out from the dark space of this eternal twilight, screams a hurricane of deadly wind, and all the stars, the candles, go out...and Glasgar is left here, standing in the darkness.

Out from the abyss, walks Duul'ak, he looks the similar Asyndian, yet his eyes are much more sinister than before, as though there is someone else in there with him, and his feathers are darker. Glasgar looks around him, wondering how he came to be in this place. He wasn't sure why, but he felt nervous, this dark place, this...empty space so to say, doesn't feel right. His eye twitches, and he feels a nip upon the back of his neck. The prisons of Stonehaven were one thing, but this place...he feels suffocated, as though he cannot breathe, and his sight is darkening.

Duul'ak's shape gets closer, it seems like he isn't even walking, but hovering across the gray mists that swirl about his feet.

11

'Duul…Duul'ak…what is this place? Why are we here? What happened to the master?!'

The dark side of the Asyndian comes to a halt in his glide across the mist, only a few feet away from Glasgar. Duul'ak's face is hidden in the shadows, only his eyes can be seen. Those black pupils, those lifeless doll's eyes glare upon Glasgar, almost piercing deep within him, into his mind, as well as his hulking body. Duul'ak's laugh echoes throughout the darkness, and the whirling winds go silent.

'Duul'ak! What is going on here? What is the meaning of this?!' Glasgar roars with fervor and rage, trying to fight to keep to his feet, but his struggle is evident.

Duul'ak laughs once more, but more of a sinister giggle, but when he speaks, it seems as though there is an echo in his throat…as though two of him is speaking. 'I told you Glasgar…you are nothing more than a pawn, a means to an end. You have an important use to us! You are about to serve your purpose, for your fate awaits you…'

And the room seems to spin around Glasgar, everything seems to darken about him, and without any warning, his body loses all control, all feeling, and he collapses to the floor, as the rest of the lights go out around him.

Glasgar goes through several rooms, several hallways of a high and mighty citadel, a palace upon the far away mountains that lays across the other side of Aura, far beyond even the regions of Raukmar and the Great Divide. The palace is built of some form of ethereal essence, the likes of which no being has ever laid eyes on, except the creator… the one who conceived this place, the one who used and destroyed lives to construct this place and then silence their tongues and blind their eyes so they may never speak of its location.

Glasgar holds up his hands to see them, yet he cannot see flesh, only the blurred shadows that make out the silhouette shapes of his left and right hand. He looks down at his body, but there is no form, only a hovering shadow, a shadow that pulls itself through this nightmare, this ominous dream, for that is what Glasgar is appearing as now…a something, a shapeless apparition, neither flesh nor armor graces his bones, but there are no bones, for he is able to see the hovering mist upon the floor looking through himself.

He comes face to face with a door ahead of him, a fire-breathing door, a door that sprays blood through the creases, and beyond he can hear the cries of something suffering, the pale white face is cut along the middle of the seam of the door, bleeds from the mouth, and the eyes begin to melt, as the flames gush forth. The face screams and the door begins to open outwards, and Glasgar can see the insides of the face, the brains, veins, as well as tissue and muscle, everything is revealed to him.

The gateway is open, and before him…stands a huge being, much larger than even his Gormon stature can compare to. The hulking figure has no features, it only stands a ghostly shade against a fiery-green flame behind that dances and claws at the putrid air, giving off poisonous fumes that smell rancid. The figure goes into a crouching stance, leans its head forward, and in the flick of a clashing lightning strike off in the far away distances, the being charges full force at Glasgar, without faltering, without showing any sign of slowing down.

Glasgar reaches for his mace, but his weapon does not exist within this realm of putrid green lights and rancid flame. He has nothing to protect himself against this charging force. The charging force is just before him, and Glasgar does what every Gormon refuses to do, what every Gormon would not admit to, even when the fear takes hold of their body…he raises his defenses, he feels fear, empty as the feeling may be, feeling so artificial like it's not even real, yet the fear is there, fear that would shame his ancestors, his brethren. Here he is, a Gormon who stood against legions of soldiers, surrounded by armies, was about to be taken down by this one foe, yet a foe that bears the strength of many and all. A strange imaginative sensation, a hallucination pours into his thoughts and out through his very being...for a moment, he could see that day...that day all those years ago, he felt his body stretch, and the time rip apart, as the being blurs and obstructs his momentary reasoning and conscience of his very essence....he could see himself, like a reflection into the mirror of the past, a looking glass of sorts.

Glasgar stands upon the wet soil, soggy from the cold rain, freezing like the touch of the blade, yet the drops and splashes upon his hands and face is warm. He opens his eyes wide, so he can see, so he can look upon the derelict scene before him. About his feet, are...bodies, the bodies of many, the victim's lay around...dead, the faces are unrecognizable and the corpses...butchered meat, like cattle, simply victims led to the slaughter, the slaughter of the two axes within his hands, the blades of the axes covered in blood, the crimson tide flows beneath him into a nearby stream that flows off into a vast canyon beneath. About the area and horizons surrounding him, are the charred remains of a massive city complex, and the stones and skeletal remains of the buildings cascade downwards into nothing more than charred dirt. Surrounding him from all sides, a vast army of thousands of soldiers charge at him upon hofts fully clad in dull cobalt armor, along with armored soldiers upon them, and at the base of his mighty stature, frontlines of soldiers throw spears and archers fire arrows from behind the row of pikes and centurions.

He is taken by surprise of the attack, he recognizes them as Civilian and Gormon soldiers of Runegard, he realizes they are trying to capture him, and hand him over to the Gormons, to be taken back to Fausengard. But he does not

14

understand why he killed so many, for he never killed on purpose, it was in defense, who were these people that fell to his weapons, and whose axes are these, for his weapon of choice is a mace…but there was no time to think or hesitate, these bastards of Runegard wanted a fight, well, he would give them one, and would not go quietly, even though it seems, judging by the blood-thirsty glare in their eyes, and the sound of retribution in their cries…they do not plan to take him alive.

Glasgar raises the two bloody axes in front of him, he raises them high above his head, and…as the first wave attacks, soldier upon soldier, he cleaves them back, body piles upon body, piece upon piece, the blood splatters and soars with the wind, covering the vast waves of armies and soldiers. Their screams of war strike without fear, yet their retreat with cowardice echoes back to each wave, for the pain of being splayed in two, dripping their own guts, and swallowing the blood shower of their comrades is too much to bear, Glasgar sees him standing there in the distance, the young general forces a retreat of his soldiers.

'Flee…flee this monstrosity, we are no match! Save yourselves!' He cries out to the screaming men.

But Glasgar isn't going to let them escape…they started this fight, and he's going to finish it. He cleaves the wounded away, and steps upon the ones who crawl, some with only a single arm, many without limbs, a pathetic nub trying to crawl away from battle, an insect with a bad wing, and broken legs, smashed under Glasgar's immense steel boot, covered thick with mud, blood, flesh and hair.

He chases them all down, catching them as the twin axes eat away at their armor, driving their way to the core, down into the blood-enriched skin, and beneath, churning their way to silence the beating heart within the soldiers' chest. He carves his way through the masses, making his way to their General.

The General draws his blade, raises the steel broadsword high above his head and begins the charge. The general casts no fear to war, but to face the mass eradication of his soldiers...is unbearable to hold that weight upon his shoulders, for this...is General A'deon's first war under his command. A'deon had taken over command after General Gabriel II had withdrawn from battle and retired his blade, in exchange for the ceremonial golden helm that all Grand General's receive after their retirement. He named A'deon his successor...and it is now the young general's duty, to protect against those who would threaten Runegard, in the name of she, the Daughter of Runegard.

'Fall back! Fall back everyone...leave this threat to me!' A'deon, mounted upon his hoft, charges with brisk speed, he pushes the steed further on and on, faster and faster, as fast as the hoft's four legs will go, leaping over body and fallen debris in its path. A'deon was not looked upon as a hero, nor a great general, he has not proved himself, and he knew by the looks of all his men, and their lack of devotion to him, they held no respect towards him, not to the degree they respected Gabriel II, a general who led their armies into a post golden age for all of Aura. But he would gain their trust, he would gain their respect...even if it meant losing his own life.

The great black steed charges, leaps over the hordes of fleeing soldiers, their eyes look upon him in awe and wonder. The hooves hit the dirt, and A'deon continues his charge full force. Glasgar raises the axes into an X formation in front of him. A'deon raises the blade, and...at that last moment, he lowers his head, he brings his arm across his eyes, and falls from the horse, he...he cannot bring himself to do it, to face such a gruesome death, but he hears that horrible cry, the shrill scream of the hoft, as Glasgar's axes chops the beast into pieces, leaving only a puddle of chunky blood and a splintered horse cadaver. Shards of the reins and saddle lay within the massacre, hacked away like the bones and limbs.

A`deon can't bring himself to look, for he is ashamed, a cowered he still remains. He looks away, and towards his soldiers, a few still remain, yet most have fled, and they look back with horrified eyes, he can hear the heavy thrump, the heavy shuffle and trod of footsteps, one after the other. A`deon looks back, and the huge shape stands above him, eclipsing him within the horrid shadow. The massive figure reaches down and picks up A`deon by the neck, and holds him up for all to look upon, to look upon the cowardice of their failed general. The monster grasps A`deon's face and his leg, the bestial figure lifts A`deon over his head and wrenches and contorts the general's body, his bones pierce flesh, as his cry of unbearable pain and agony holler into the storm. The blood pours with the rain. The figure releases his face, and slams A`deon to the ground, spraying mud and blood across the plains.

A`deon lays sprawled and lifeless, his eyes begin to close, as all around him…goes black, a shadow that lingers as an unforgiving dream, as the curtains close upon this nightmare. He looks up to the sky, at the towering monstrosity...for that's what he is, this figure, this beast is a monstrosity, an atrocity. A`deon looks upon the monster, his lips barely quiver, and with his last breath, can only whisper, can only discern one word, one simple word, yet so simple as it may be, it resonates a chill a gut-wrenching feeling within any who hears it's syllables.

Glasgar looks down at the broken figure. He speaks to him, laughs at him, yet he cannot hear his sentences, he cannot decipher his own laughter, or even pass it off as his own voice.

"What...who is this that speaks...what is the meaning of this...for this is not even language, this is noise, just noise of a being that can barely even speak right!" These are his first thoughts to himself.

He sees the broken figure of the general sprawled in the mud before him. His breaths wheeze with each inhale and exhale, a trickle of blood runs from his nose and smears and spreads out over his lips like a puddle gaining in size with more and more rain. The rain clangs and runs down the general's armor, his limp broken hand is slung over the Civilian's Crest upon his breast-plate, as though he were protecting his heart and his country, he is doing in near death...what he could not do in life, for he failed his duties, yet he tried, he tried so hard to be a different, more responsible man, just like Gabriel II, his predecessor before him, for A`deon had large boots to fill, and he did so, ungallantly, or could it be, could this act be seen as having a shed of bravery.

Glasgar continues to watch the general as he slowly passes from this life, and fades away to follow the golden road leading to and beyond the realms of Arla. He also keeps his eyes about him and his surroundings, watching the other soldiers as they slowly peek their heads up, and creep over the hills and from around the burning ruins, some hold their sliced arms and limp upon their broken legs and backs, some carry their swords and spears with shaking arms, as they grip the weapons close to their chest.

But Glasgar can see by their broken bodies and dead eyes that are haunted by fear and the catastrophe around them, that they have no fight left in them, no more can they defend themselves, for Glasgar would be able to, with the stroke of his arm, and whip of his hands and quick reflexes, stomp the rest of them out like the tips of the thumb and index finger smothers out a flame. He then focuses his attention back to A`deon, as the general begins to twitch and convulse, with a horrific gag, he spews up a gut-full of blood, and whines with agony as the movements of his body jerk and causes his shattered bones to move around, as immense pain swarms over his body like a nest of angered hornets that sting and puncture the flesh.

A`deon's eyes now twitch and flicker as he opens them up to the darkness of the world around him. He looks up to the shadow which eclipses over all of Runegard. The pale flame in the distances encircles him and blurs as his sight once more darkens. The flames dance like the lines of Baldushan maidens in a line ready to sway their way into the maw of a vast volcano as a gift to Abhor's essence. The lights entrance him into time and twists his thoughts about as memories seem as current as the past, and the future unravels before his present, as the boulders of his life crumble down and spiral from the dizzying heights of a colossal mountain top.

And that's when his focus overcomes him for that brief moment, and his time passage hones in to the now, something shakes him while he's lost within his dying thoughts, something...some instinct grips hold of him and shakes him into coherence, and he again retains focus of the gargantuan shade of a monstrous being standing upon him with lifeless, empty eyes...the eyes of horror.

A`deon thinks for a moment...as he feels his life fade more and more as the minutes pass by.

"...for I must name my pain, for I must give a subject and a title to my demise...for this...this thing, this monster, he is a beast of ancients old and legends far past, for the coming of the Wom would bring into this world, a slayer, a marauder, a beast of apocalyptic and genocidal proportions...and he would be born from the flaccid, empty gut of Wom's domain, where once, the Hexagus suckled upon her darkness...and in their place, this creature would step forward from the shadows and bring the decay to Aura, that the Hexagus were denied!

For I admit...I am a coward at heart...I covered my eyes when I needed to see...I commanded legions of brave soldiers into a cowardice retreat, instead of defending to the last drop of blood...even my own...but, I think even with a brave general...that could lead these brave men and women into battle...I...believe would have ended up being a butcher...leading his stock...to the slaughter, for this being shows no mercy in his attack, he shows no remorse with his two axes...the left axe domination, and his right axe...annihilation! For now...I know of the name I think of...a name that has soaked many bloody lips with dread, as they cough up their own blood, when screaming his name in horror...there is one name that is left within the blade wound of every corpse that fell by his axe...there is only one name that spells the terror and butchery, a description for the bloodshed and conquering of a battlefield...yes...there is a name of this...caliber, of this...magnitude...for we all thought Maz Dregor was the destroyer...but, if they only knew...if they only knew what Destroyer really meant...Yes, the Gormons had a name for it..."

A`deon looks into the eyes of his demise, and utters a single word, a single name.

'... *Hôɳdoʀ*!'

Glasgar listens to this word, as A`deon spits it from his blood-filled lips... *Hôɳdoʀ*...he's heard this word before, he understood what it means. He drops the two axes, and holds up his hands, looks at them, and watches as the crimson splashes dry upon his palms and in between his finger tips. He watches as the time seems to slow, and the blood swirls together, and then he hears that voice, a distant voice echo in his head, echo within his thoughts, a dark void feels as though it opens up far within the dark recesses of his mind.

A loud booming thud overpowers him, it sounds as though a large explosion rips through his conscious, and Glasgar feels his body weaken. He clutches his head, he wraps his hands around the helm upon his head, and tries to take it off, tries to rip it off, but he cannot, he cannot undo this trap that hold's his breath in. He falls down to his knees, and his body becomes a sliding scale, drifting more and more into a direction of vulnerability, a feeling of helplessness.

The whispers grow louder and louder, until the speech sounds as though the being is standing next to his ear, and shouting these words to him, leaving him ready to fall into the darkness that begins to surround him. Glasgar feels his consciousness begin to slip away. And that's when he feels the rip and the tear, not of his body, but he feels as though his veins are being torn away, his body turns hot and feverish, and a jerking and tugging at his very insides consumes him with pain. The skeletal structure of his body is being ripped away and separated from him. Something is manipulating him, pulling at his very being, and Glasgar tries to fight back.

He grips his body, and this realm, these battlements he kneels before, seems to almost become transparent and vague to his mind, as though he were continuing an odyssey through a strange point of being, continuing to the next and leaving this nightmare behind, to become absent like an old memory better off forgotten.

And those words repeat themselves over and over again, quickening in their dialect, melding all together, yet they speak of the same thing. Glasgar can barely discern them, but the language is familiar, yet so old and distant, for this language has not been spoken by any beings in a millennia.

As to their purpose...he does not know, but they seem to almost hypnotize him, fill him with a bitter sweet feeling of control...and they make sense, yet he cannot understand them, but he must obey, he must follow in the footsteps, in the echo of these words, as they resonate upon the walls of this misty fortress, of this plane of existence within his mind. And, with one final tear at his body and mind, the huge shadow returns, bursting forth from his insides, yet this time, the shadow is more clear, more of a fully, fleshed out figure than before, yet still not all the way, comprehendible, much like these words, they are there, yet unintelligible.

The grayed figure reaches down and grips Glasgar by the neck, trying to choke and exhaust the Gormon of his life, yet Glasgar fights back, trying to hold off the attack. And as this is going on, all the soldiers wonder...wonder why this invader, who tried to do them in, almost slaughtered every man, woman and child, as well as their soldiers...they stared and contemplated, what was causing this monster called Hondor...to now attack himself?

Glasgar could see himself fall to the ground, yet his conscious was still awake and alive. The surroundings fade once more to that far away, misty fortress, where Glasgar continues his skirmish with this figure, he pulls the shadow away, and the figure leaps away from him, and raises his guard. Glasgar notices that not only has the figure become more defined, but so has this fortress that seems to almost keep Glasgar a prisoner here. A sense of stifling and suffocation comes over him, and the figure pounces once more at Glasgar, who again, holds the figure back, he...he can now grasp the figure, which he could not do before, the figure is now a tangible shape. Glasgar bashes the brooding shape away, and ascends the stairs behind him, for the floor below his feet begins to break away, and enter into an endless abyss below.

That's when he hears it...he hears that familiar voice again, yet this time, he can understand the words and recognizes Duul`ak's voice...he listens carefully to the omniscient, echoing voice of the Asyndian, for there is another, another being speaks as well, it is the master. *"It has to be...!"* Glasgar says to himself. The voice speaks to him.

"Rise...rise to the top Hondor...rise to the pinnacle, where the power is strongest...where control over all is infinite, and being in control of all..is purest, for none shall falter, none shall stray...no more wars will falter us...and no more bloodshed, shall fray the brittle streams of a world that has seen its dark times, return to an altered light...a true light that will protect under the iron fist, where none will falter, and none shall stray, no wars will fray...become the Destroyer, the one who was born to unite all under one...and all who will not bow before you...they shall be disciplined as seems fit..."

"NO, I AM NOT! This Hondor they speak of...Me? No I am not this monster...that is not who I am!" This lost and confused Gormon thinks to himself, fighting these many voices of the master.

Glasgar covers his ears...and he notices something...his hands, his hands look different, his hands are not his own...he gazes in horror at what is happening. He turns around, and looks back down to the shadowed figure at the foot of the stairs. Surrounding the figure, is the frame of a huge mirror, a mirror bearing obsidian thorns and the color as empty as a night full of sorrows and despair, and sees the swirling abyss beneath as he floats over the crumbled floor, and the figure looks up at him from beyond the looking glass, returning the glare of hatred...the figure, as Glasgar can see, bears his hands now...and there's something about his eyes as well, that seems all too familiar.

The mirror begins to ascend the steps and gets closer and closer to where Glasgar stands at the very top. He walks slowly to the mirror, and can see more and more of his reflection looking back at him, a sight all too familiar to him, yet so foreign. He sees a Gormon he barely recognizes anymore. He begins to reflect upon his own past, and his own ways, and the images almost seem to pass before his eyes, as reflected within this mirror.

The figure begins to fade away out of existence, and the smoke and colors within the darkness begins to swirl, as the silhouette of an opaque figure walks forward once more, the shape of feathers and black wings becomes clearer and more visible as Duul`ak walks towards Glasgar. And the voice overtakes the Gormon's mind once again, he tries to resist as he did before, but this time, it is stronger, and as hard as he tries to cover his thoughts and strengthens this shelter to protect his mind, he cannot, for he hears them, he hears those words, those words he cannot decipher, cannot understand, except for he knows he cannot disobey. The syllables, sound so much like a quaint lullaby, and his eyes begin to close, he takes a step forward, his hand held outwards, as he steps towards the mirror, and enters beyond into the realms of places where terrors are born, and the light goes to die, as it is swallowed away into a black-lit, endless night...where shadows dwell, and the slaughtered of the past memories, are played over and over, to never be forgotten, where the hopes in the death of many coming to pass...remains alive.

A`deon watches as the invader collapses to the dirt. And he feels, just as well, he feels the long, drawn out sleep coming over him. Is this the shadow of death that hovers over him, or was it someone else, that looms in his wake, setting a vigil over him, just as he is about to die. Has his soldiers come back to retrieve him, are they to hold him up high, and praise his name in memory, to immortalize him into legends like in the days of old? Or will his cowardice have shown through, and he be mocked for letting the enemy bring him down and breaking his body to pieces? What was his story...his legend in for, he wondered. What would be his legacy, the legacy of a hero, or a legacy of hate to a general that no one respected, and was shadowed by a living legend in Gabriel II, the ancestor, the great, great grandchild of Cezius Cabriel and Shoranna Cabriel, the last of the Drog Riders, he was *"one who communicates"* with the beast that fought by his side. Gabriel II was renowned for going into battle on wings and not hoft like most soldiers do.

Yet, A`deon was not a drog rider, he was not of Cezius's blood, he was a close friend of Gabriel II, and usually kept to his shadow, basking in his deeds, in his fame. A`deon did not have his own ties, his own adventures, and many knew this, and detested that the greatest general of all of Aura, would choose someone who had nothing going for himself, nothing to back himself on. Yet, now he would have a testament, he would have a place in Aura's history...as the general who covered his eyes at the enemy, and fell in battle for it, maimed beyond repair, and would die alone, abandoned by his fellow Civilians, the Gormons, as well as the Asyndians.

So who would come back to see to him, to watch over his essence, as he passes over to the realms Arla, for where he knew he would only be honorary as a street urchin under the tall, vast ivory buildings, and sleep upon the golden streets and back alleys of the lighted city. Who knows, maybe he could bask once more, in the glory of his general's reputation, maybe those of Arla, had not yet picked up wind, of A`deon's failure. Maybe they would not know, that he is a hack.

But, maybe there is someone who saw that he tried, bared witness to a small hint of courage within his heart, for he did try, they could not deny that he did try, he attempted one last charge, he wanted to give his life bravely, but instead covered his eyes, and refused to see how gory and brutal his death would be for him and his hoft that road with him, his hoft who deserves more fame than he does. For it was his hoft that kept going, where he did not, for General A`deon did in fact fall from his horse in disgrace, not from a rough hill, or an inconsistency in the dirt, the horse did not slip in the mud, it was he, by conscious, the wit of a general that was supposed to be brave, who by his own volition, abandoned that conflict, and tried to save himself the gory death at the hands of this invading monster, the monster he calls *Hôŋdoʀ*.

But who, who would reach out their hands to him? Who would try to help a Civilian, whose time has come, who was at the end, not just of his dignity, but of his life? There was nothing they could do for him, for he did not want help, if he could, he would muster a defense and refuse to be moved from where he lays.

He did not want to be bothered, he simply wanted to sleep, to be left to his demise, for he accepts his fate, because there was nothing else he had to go further, move forward. This was to be the last ride, the final hour of General A`deon, Civilian of Othetica, and general of Runegard. He, in shambles and shaking, holds up his hands and looks at them. He sees the hands of a man, a man who has tried his entire life, yet has failed, a man who has taken under the wing and shelter of someone else's reputation and name, yet failed to hide it miserably.

"Why...why me? Why was I given this task of yours? What do you think of me now? What would you say, when the messenger rode up to your home on the hill of green, under the illusion of daylight, and he handed you the scrawled note of my demise...of my failure, of what I did? Would you mourn my death, or feel betrayed...that I damaged the decision of a man who has a legend, who has a name for himself? What would you say now?"

A`deon asks this question of himself, while his thoughts still allow him to do so.

"...whose...whose hands are these? I wish they would not try to touch me, just leave me be...I want them to, let me pass, let me lay where my corpse may diminish..."

Yet, the hands reach out to him and his body goes into shock, and once more, he fades into twilight.

Part I:

Catacombs of Midlo`v

~

Do you remember... in ages gone by, a time when the Auroras and the Asyndians kept a close eye on events, a careful watch over this land of Aura, the beacon of the Galakaos, the light of enticement whose freedoms invited us, welcomed us in? A time when a sullen warrior traversed these foreboding roads and dark forests when the time seemed to darken, and the skies gray as ash during the rebirth of the black phoenix, when this warrior fought across time and dimensions, and under his eye and guiding blade, we were at peace.

Do you remember those days...those days which now seem so long ago and have passed in the blink of an eye? The Dregor are no more, only but a legend to be told, folklore for the old, fairy tales for our young...but it seems even those pages have been torn out and burned like the hearts of the dead, and held in *HIS* clenched fist, slain, body, soul and mind...all in harmony before *HE* came, before one figure, one...beast if you will, one who would see our land of Aura, our jewel wiped away, taken deep out beyond the rims of the crimson sea, and drowned under the tides of the blood spilled from millions, by a genocidal maniac!

Do you remember…or do you simply shake your head in agreement? For how could we remember good days? How could our merry times surpass anything he has done?! For when the future comes, who will be left to remember! Who will carry on that which we have accomplished and established and fought for, for hundreds of years!

"And all bones will shatter! All flesh will melt away!

For when Hondor comes…there will be none,

to stand in his way,

to oppose him, for none…he obeys!"

Within the wide chasms and tunnels beneath Runegard, the Civilians, Gormons, and Asyndians are spread out across the rocky soil, lying upon makeshift beds, eating scraps, and anything they can get their hands on. The children's faces are filthy with dirt, the women's hair tangled and brambly like worn and tired thorn bushes, and the men are sore and driven to death by heavy labor, and everyone wears rags of clothing that have been collected and pieced together by wiry thread and rotten cloth. Some of the stronger and the guards and soldiers as well, must explore the caves to hunt for the rodents that scuttle about the crevasses and dark bowels, but they dare not go far, for there are other fowler, and more horrid things which lurk in the dark places of Aura.

The many who have survived the brutal attack and slaughter, those who have escaped, have suffered through the many days and sleepless nights. The Daughter of Runegard does what she can to maintain morale among the many that lay sick and weak, the healers and the Asyndians who have the gift of knowing medicines, seek for cures of ailments and the diseases caused by the rodent and insect bites, and keep the guards able to do their duties and keep their strength, for the rodents, reptiles, and insects have a taste for the fresh blood of

29

these prisoners, those who hide from the deadliest of all monstrosities that destroys and slaughters above. Every now and again, these fiends of the dark will creep out while everyone sleeps, and will carry off the smaller and weaker, mainly the children, or the other unfortunate victim who is not able to defend themselves, for survival has no bias...for everyone is a victim during starvation.

The guards have been able to build a crude palisade around the people, which has slowed the attacks, but somehow, many still manage to disappear. But the main problem..is Zed, an eccentric who has caused problems and has stirred unrest amongst the Gormons, Civilians, Asyndians, the guards and soldiers, one and all. He even claims that there is a Hexagus Lord hidden away in the darkness of the caves, and many blamed him for the predator attacks. Zed came to the conclusion that at least once a day, one amongst them must be sent into the darkness to appease the blood lust of the Hexagus Lord, and that is the only way they will remain safe from further attacks. The guards have kept Zed locked away in his cell for months now, so he did not try to proceed with his plan for sacrificial blood. But there are still those who are restless, tired of these caverns, tired of the stale air, tired of the eternal darkness and the only light is the flickering of torches, for this cavern has turned into a small deadly space, were many keep close to those they love, and many, talk to their own shadow, and to the dark, just like old Zed did.

'For how long are we supposed to hide under these catacombs and tunnels?!' An old scavenger of the Civilian descendants cried aloud. 'We have not seen the light of day in months! How can one...just ONE Gormon cause all this terror and destruction! My children starve, my wife lays up there...her blood soaking into the soil and her corpse can't even feed the vultures and the scavengers, for he has killed all, everything that moves, man, woman, child, beast...it does not matter to him! He has no pulse, he does not breath! He is an inhuman monster, a monster like the fowl things that live in these caves, and stalk us in our sleep...but I will persevere to see his neck hacked in two by the executioner's blade!' The man causes quite a stir amongst the scared and fearing Civilians and Asyndians which cower and hold onto their young and their loved ones.

'Why don't you be silent?!' An Asyndian woman screams, whose young son starts to cry. 'Why do you rage and holler so? We know he's there, up there, constantly hunting for things to kill, for blood to spill and flesh to hack! Can you not see the fear in our eyes, and can you not hear yourself?! Your taunts and threatening observations help none of us! You sound as mad as that maniac over behind those bars.' She coddles her child, a son she calls Hrend. 'It's okay child, it's going to be okay! That scary man is going to stop...' She flashes him a glare to agree with her.

'Ah, and why do you lie to your child? Why sweeten the tongue that poisons his ears? I know, and you know just as well, and all of you Civilians, Gormons, and Asyndians know! Even old Zed knows, that once he finds his way into these tunnels...you know what our fate will be!'

One of the soldiers approaches the Civilian and shoves him to the ground in a rather harsh manner. The man falls to his side and cuts his leg upon the rocks. The man crawls and gets back to his feet, fists raised at the guard ready to fight. 'How dare you! All you guards do is push people down around here because you can! That uniform is a symbol for what you truly are, and what this land means now, for you are all the scum of Aura, and the smashed slug under Hondor's boot!'

'That'll be enough out of you sir!' The guard yells back, warning the eccentric man to calm himself.

A brawn Gormon with a mighty gray beard jumps to his feet He is Roúgsver, a dedicated servant and guardian to the Daughter. 'I warn you Civilian, I've been sitting here, I've had to listen to your wretched tongue for some time now, and I've had it! The Daughter has had enough, as well as everyone else down here...and I dare you to call that beast up there a Gormon again! I dare you insult the Gormon once more, do it!'

The Daughter attempts to silence her guard. 'Please Roúgsver, no more yelling.'

'I saw him with my own two eyes, he was a Gormon! He bore the sign of Tul Ra`; they are kin, for Tul Ra` was a blood-thirsty Gormon Warlord, a genocidal maniac! He tried to exterminate the land, just as this fiend, for Hondor follows in the footsteps of his brother!'

'Tul Ra` was not a true Gormon! Tul Ra` was a monster like *Him*!' He points towards the surface above. 'My ancestors fought his troops till we were almost all but vanquished! We saved your lands from his black malice, his will to destroy.' Roúgsver falls back and sits back upon the rock he was rested on, across from the Daughter of Runegard. 'Of course, we had help...*"those were the golden days"* my grandfather told me, golden days that were covered in a river of blood, when the Sentinels flew across the skies, and the Auroras protected their domains, before the black times, that was even before the Grey Age.' Roúgsver finishes his reminiscing.

'But I heard rumor...that one of your Auroras still yet lives. The Soldier if I am correct. So tell me, Gormon, why does your Aurora hide, why does he not come and put an end to Hondor? Why does he not fight for what the Auroras once believed in, after all this is their land, or let me correct myself, was once their land. Why does he not defend it?' The man grins with a sinister tooth at the worried look upon Roúgsver's old face, for he can see that the Gormon thinks the same thing. *"Why does Agonan not come to our aide?"*

'I'll tell you why your Aurora does not come; I'll…TELL YOU…just why your Aurora is a coward! Let me enlighten you, as to why your Auroras lay dead, why they gave up on all of you, and why we now…rot in these slime covered, vermin infested caves…!'

The guards raise their spears. 'We're warning you, don't. We will lock you into the cells.'

'Lock Me?! Lock me in the cells like old Zed eh?' The man begins to laugh like the chattering stark cry of the hyena beasts that roam the vast southern deserts of Isa. 'You…and I thought the Gormons were stupid, you have got to be joking with me?! Look…AROUND YOU, we are ALL in a prison, and we are all in a tomb! Grab your hammer and nails, because we are going to be buried here, there will be no funeral, no flowers upon our caskets, for we are going to be slaughtered here, for these are our graves, this rock is a butcher's block, and we are nothing more than the corpse that has been wretched from its coffin to be hacked into pieces!'

He grabs the spear of the guard and holds it to his heart and slightly presses his chest against the tip. 'Go on! DO IT! For then I will be free and…HA! And the rest of you…will be little tiny prisoners, you'll be dolls, yes all of you! Will be dolls, unstitched, undone, all crammed into those tiny little cells these guards of truth and justice threaten us with, your toy chests, were Hondor will pull out your cold dead corpse and hack it up! Oh how he will play with all of you, he'll butcher you all, and then roast your flesh over his fire until your skin blisters and sears, and your tender enough to eat down to the bone!'

'Mother…make him stop!' Hrend cries.

'Stop it! That's enough!' The female Asyndian cries out.

Roúgsver pushes aside the guards and tackles the man to the ground, were he proceeds to hammer his fist down upon the man's face, the same way the hammer pounds upon the molten blade to shape the steel.

'Roúgsver...that's enough! Guards break them up!' The Daughter cries.

The guards attempt to pull the Gormon away, but he fights them off as though they were flies pestering the mighty bull. But they keep grabbing the Gormons arm and yelling, "Release Him! Let him go!" but to no avail, for the Roúgsver just keeps pounding and pounding, until there, laying upon the rocks, is nothing more than a withered, bruised head, spitting blood, and a purple welt the size of a rock-hard fist, indented into were his eye once was, but is now swollen over by pain and inflamed skin.

The man slumps over and several fragments of teeth fall to the ground, once a yellowish enamel, now a deep crimson buried in a puddle of spit and bloody saliva. Now the guards hold their spears at Roúgsver. The battered man, with his one good eye, slowly turns and looks upon the sight.

'See...' He coughs up blood. 'I told you these...Gormon...are...dangerous.' He laughs as more blood is spit and vomited up from his throat.

The Gormon looks around at the frightened refugees, their eyes wide and in tears, men and women, child, young and old alike, horrified by the brutality of both the Civilian and Gormon.

'Please, lower your spears, I am sorry, for I did not mean for it to go so far. I am sorry. To the Daughter and to all

34

of you.' Roúgsver tries to apologize, and several guards lead the Gormon away to the other side of the cavern. The remaining soldiers pick up the limp Civilian and drag him over to the cells, unhinge the latch, and open the door, keeping an eye on old Zed, who sits over in the corner, hunched up and gripping his legs, holding himself in a fetal position, and staring off towards a cave, and from the cave emits a dank, and putrid smell. They look upon Zed curiously, for he has been rather quiet all day, and has not said anything, he only sits there, and isn't moving.

'What's the matter Zed, you've been quiet? Has your Lord stopped talking to you, has he found out that your nothing more than just another fanatic, like everyone else that has believed in the Hexagus Lords?!' The guards laugh, but Zed doesn't reply, as though he did not hear anything they just said to him, and they lock the door behind them and walk away, back to their posts to continue overseeing the area.

The Civilian spits at the guards as they walk away. He then turns and looks at Zed, who still stares at the darkness. He is a bit nervous, for Zed is unstable, and unpredictable, and he wonders if that blood lust still resides upon Zed's mind, if he would be Zed's sacrifice that he has promised the darkness. Zed twitches, and the man becomes terrified and worried, then Zed begins to speak to him.

'Are you afraid, Civilian?'

This question startles him, and he doesn't know what to say, or how to respond. But before he even thinks of an answer, Zed, without even turning to him, seems to pierce his skull, and delve deep into his thoughts and feelings.

'You are afraid...aren't you? But let me ask you this, are you afraid of me, or are you afraid of the red eye that looks at us from the darkness.' Zed points his finger to the cave, and sure enough, a piercing lens, a pupil recedes into the blackness and shadows. The man falls back and presses firmly against the bars of the cells, and his fear increases tenfold, for now he sees, he sees what Zed sees, it is really there, the beast in the darkness that this eccentric has spoken of.

'What...what kind of monstrosity is that?!' His voice trembles, barely able to get the words out, stammering and stuttering. 'Is it *HIM*...Has he found us?!'

With the most sinister look, of a red-eyed, crooked man, Zed slowly turns his head, and smiles with a sinister grin at the Civilian. The look of Zed, turned the man white, and seemed to sway and almost faint, his flesh turning cold, and almost blue as ice from the fear sucking away his color.

'He is here...He has...smelled us out!'

From the other side of the cave, the man hears the others fall silent, and then the voice of the Daughter begins to speak. She gathers everyone around to her as she speaks to them, making an announcement.

The Daughter of Runegard stands and calls to all. The hopeless, and washed out eyes of all Civilians, Gormons, and Asyndians look upon her.

'Everyone, everyone...please listen to me...'

The caverns go silent from the echoing voices of the masses.

'Our brave soldiers have fought valiantly, and sadly many have fallen, but I am proud to say, they have secured the underground oasis ahead, and we will no longer have to tread dangerous areas to get our water, for we will soon reside alongside it!'

Everyone stirs; many are relieved by the news, they hug their families and loved ones, but they still wish they were leaving these deplorable caves for good.

'I know these last few months have been excruciating upon us all, for we are all miserable, we are all plagued by famine and thirst, for our fate down here, I am sorry to say, is a slower death, than compared to death by *Him*, the one who hunts above, *He* who kills all that moves, all life he comes across! There is no other choice I can make, and I will not see my people, nor the Gormons or Asyndians, butchered without mercy or without any hope!' Tears begin to fill her eyes. 'At...at least down here, we can remain alongside those we love, and be with those whose final days have come, and we can look upon the faces of our loved ones, instead of in the eyes of... That Monster! That...that...Beast who has killed families...their husbands and fathers...their wives and mothers...and children...sons and daughters!' She falls to her knees and weeps, as her maidens console her. Roúgsver walks past the guards to be by her side. He helps her to her feet, and they sit down upon a nearby rock until she is calm.

The captain of the soldiers gives her a moment, and then he performs his duties and gathers those, and organizes these denizens together, and prepares to move them out. All is going smoothly, until they hear a scratchy voice cry out from the cells far in the corner of the caverns.

"Far beyond this raging sea...I witness the inferno,

for Runegard burns, as her people are put to sleep,

buried under dirt, and the bodies that bleed..."

'Go...Ha! You have nowhere to go! You can never leave! That which dwells in the darkness will never let you go, and he watches all day, and all night!' The voice of Zed, the raving lunatic within his shackles screeches and cries, echoing through the cave, his turn makes the children cry, and terrorizes their flesh and feathers with a cold, deathly fear.

One of the guards faces the Daughter. 'I don't know why you let that scum live...we should just execute him and be done with it.' He shouts. 'The food we waste on him could be seconds for those who need it more!'

'We are not like those barbaric Skahljah! We must look after our own...no matter how wretched they may seem, that was the way of my ancestor, King Edrin, a being who treated all with dignity and respect, he even showed it to his enemies, or else they would have attacked him from right under his nose. He kept his friends close, yet the knowledge of his enemies, he kept closer.' She replies to the Civilian guard.

'He's a monster, that's why he's locked in a cage like one, like the beast that roams above...you show him dignity if you want, but he will get none from me, neither of them!' He storms away and tends to the rest of the denizens within the cave.

She turns to Roúgsver. 'What do you think?'

'I don't care for the wretched smell of that Civilian my lady. But I knew King Edrin and you do him proud...you show great patience and courage in these bleak times...' He replies.

She smiles. 'Thank you Roúgsver...go now and help get the others together, we must move out, and with haste.'

He nods, and tends to his orders.

'Look at all of you...you call yourselves civil, a bunch of Gormons, Asyndians, Civilians...none of you are any better, no different than *He* who storms and terrorizes above! Once your little river is dried up, your fishes and plants all gone...what then? Huh? Oh, I know! You will...eat each other

38

alive! Tear at your own flesh…just as It will do, for your lives will rest within his belly!' He stirs silent for a moment, with that wicked grin upon his cracked and blistered lips. Then, he speaks once more. 'Can you hear that, the child of darkness comes! What a sweet song he will sing as you grovel in pounds of flesh, within his gut!' Zed lets out a deviant cry of laughter.

Indeed they do hear it, something grotesque approaches. The denizens and refugees of Runegard hear the roar as something stirs in the darkness. Mothers and fathers grasp for their children, loved ones clutch each other wildly, as the exodus of Aura citizens rush in a mad panic through the caves. They push and shove through the northern exits as the guards lead them onwards. The only ones who remain, are the Daughter and Roúgsver by her side, a few guards, the Civilian prisoner, and Zed, both who are still locked within the cage. The Daughter looks upon them, she does not want to leave them, for the guilt fills her heart, and she is far more fearful of the thing that approaches their way, more so than a raving lunatic and a fearful, panic-stricken Civilian. She has to decide what to do, and fast, for whatever it is that comes, is approaching, coming closer and closer, crawling and writhing its way through the crevices and caves, reaching for that smell of blood that lingers in the air.

The Civilian, bruised and battered, his broken hand reaches out to her. 'Please, I did not mean what I said, I take it back…I'm, I'm so scared! I was afraid for myself, for all of us…I have despaired…I am sorry, please get me out of here…set me free…Hurry!'

Something grabs hold of the Daughters arm, it is her guard. 'Please my lady, we have to leave here!'

'The Civilian screams to her. 'Please…you cannot leave me here! Let me out!'

Zed simply laughs at them.

She watches the Civilian slam his broken bones against the cage, hollering and crying, as the torn ligaments rip in excruciating pain as he is trying to escape. But he would rather suffer from a torn body, than the horrible fate which approaches, like a hen sensing the fox approaching, but unaware of when it will strike.

A roar echoes from the abyss.

'PLEASE! LET ME OUT!' The Civilian cries louder, tears stream from his face.

'My lady, let's go!' The guard shouts, trying to get her moving in the direction of the others that flee.

'He is right my lady..it is too late, we have to go!' Roúgsver replies.

"But was Zed right? If we leave him to die…are we no different than that monster? No different than the monstrosity that resides above our coward heads?" She asks herself.

'Please, it's getting closer!'

They can hear its body scratching against the rocks, its saliva melts through the ground with a sizzle of acid.

The Daughter turns to her guard, and tears her arm from his grasp. 'Give me the key!' She demands to him.

'You're mad! You're going to save them?!' He replies.

'I will not leave them, they will have to face their punishment another day. Now, give me the key!'

'But, but they may…that thing is…!' The guard stammers.

'Just give it to me, I command it!' She shouts.

The guard fumbles with the chain, and takes off the key ring, then hands it to the Daughter, as she rips it out of the grip of his fingertips.

'Go on, and show them your dignity, but I will not die for them!' He yells back to her as she rushes for the cage.

'My lady, please don't go...it's too dangerous!' Roúgsver calls to her, but she does not listen and bolts for the cell.

The Daughter struggles to fit the key into the lock.

'Thank you…thank you so much, please hurry!' The Civilian says to her.

But before she can undo the lock, the cave falls deathly silent, and the Civilian sees her slowly looking up towards something, and that's when he hears its breathing. An unsettling presence lingers in the air.

Roúgsver rushes in and grabs her by the arm, and pulls her away from the cell door, and she drops the keys just short of the cage. 'I will not risk my life for them, but I will see to it that I get you out of here alive!' Roúgsver cries, and he pulls her away, and they rush off with the rest of the fleeing refugees.

'No, I can't leave them!' She cries.

I'm getting you out of here! It's my duty to protect you!' Roúgsver throws the Daughter over his shoulder and rushes away as fast as he can go.

They can hear the Civilian crying back to them. 'Come back, you can't leave me here like this!'

He hits the ground and scrambles for the keys, but he cannot reach them. He can see the horror upon their faces, and he slowly turns, the tears stream from his eyes, as there behind him, he gazes upon the two red eyes glowing in the darkness in the vast cave beyond. The Civilian backs against the cold bars, and sinks down to a crouch and begs...begs for some kind of salvation to come his way.

Out from the night of the caves, the red piercing fires of the monsters pupils shines forth like death bound to strike forth, and the creature emerges from the darkness, the suction of its tentacles and slimy secretion from the worm body oozes from the crusty jaws, and the rancid breath from its mouth swelters the air with a rotting odor that causes the Civilian's eyes to water and tear up from disgust and sickness.

The Civilian turns to the old, decayed Zed. 'What...what sort of creature is that...which oozes from the scars of Aura like puss from an infected wound?!'

Old Zed laughs, the whistle in his throat sounds like the sinister, creaking of an ancient, corroded iron gate in need of oil.

'Heh...heh...that...is....reckoning...my...young...friend ....reckoning!'

The Civilian turns once more to the beast, 'What do you mean...?' But then looks back to Zed, only to find, that he has mysteriously disappeared.

The Civilian, bruised and bloodied, helpless, is now trapped within this isolated prison...alone, prey to the beast, food for this creeping terror of the black abyss. Outside of the cage, he hears Zed's laugh, but it was no longer Zed, but something else, for Zed was not as he appeared, for he was never a Civilian, but is that odd little creature that looks like an old man, but with a bestial torso and tiny clawed fingers and toes, for Aumon was now laughing and snickering at him. He turns to see the Daughter of Runegard and her Gormon lackey leaving the cave, not looking back.

'Curse you...curse all of you! I hope Hondor gives you a fate worse than the one you abandon me to! Curse you all!' He shouts at them, and they disappear through the cave.

Then, two long and slimy grey tentacles emerge. They sense around the area, and feel the cage. The tentacles coil tightly around the bars and squeeze to get within and catch their prey.

'No, stay away! Please no!'

He swipes at the boiled grey fatty flesh that jiggles as he punches them.

And so the Daughter returns, only to see as the tyrant monster rips through the steel bars, and rips the Civilian to pieces. Roúgsver comes back as well and watches from over her shoulder. The man's bones are crushed and his skin ripped and chewed away in a bloody slaughter.

'I told you...we can do nothing!' Roúgsver says.

And the scene is left in gore. The Daughter covers her eyes, wipes her tears, and Roúgsver consoles her, as they walk away to rejoin the others. And she vowed, within herself...she would not let anyone else behind...if she could help it!

But nobody sees, the little impish figure of Aumon, as he vanishes in a wisp of smoke and electricity.

As they rush back to the cave with the others, a scout approaches them with a vast grin across his face, and he is out of breath, there is excitement in his voice, but they are not prepared for the news they are about to hear.

'My lady! Oh Daughter of Runegard! I bring news…I bring news from above!'

'What news?! She asks.

'They've done it, A`deon and his men have done it…in all these months, I never thought I would hear such news upon my ears!' The Asyndian scout whirls around in the air and cries aloud.

'What…what has happened, you will tell me this instant, what is this wonderful news you bring to me!?' She demands the scout to speak at once.

'It has been done, the impossible…they have captured him…Hondor has been subdued!' The Asyndian cries with the utmost joy.

And the Daughter and the guard…are left speechless, for they have no words, for such an occasion has never been made ready, for there has never been any hope, in the shadow of Hondor. But, they feel that the echo of the refugees that cheer from the caves up ahead, would suffice to suit what they feel deep inside themselves.

Part II:

Aumon

~

Somewhere...in a realm far across the edge of all the Galakaos, at the center of the Astral Rift, where nothing more remains...except the lone islands that aimlessly float through this empty space...these landforms constructed from the dust, the remains of the dead Aura, Kathaxes...

The harsh dry wind full of debris and a chalky substance, the incinerated bones of the ancient Aura Kathaxes, decimates over the rugged dunes of glassy sands and razor-like pieces and fragments of sharp bone remains jutting from the sands. In the distance, way far off, a flicker of purple light sparks from within the realm, not a huge glow, but one that is very faint and miniscule, only visible by the most acute and sensitive eyes.

The spark strikes and chars the ground with a small black dot being left over showing where the flame scorched the sands. The light disappears, then it reappears, only this time, the spark is closer into the foreground, closer to its destination. This time the spark seems to almost emerge from some form of rip, a tear in the space of this world, this realm, and the gap opens wider and wider, revealing an ominous black hole, and a faint mist spews from this abyss, and from this rip in time, emerges a familiar being, one who reemerges from a fate all were certain...was death.

Aumon, a figure from ancient Aura history, with a small body of a child, furry like an animal with a tail, and the face of an old man with pointed, long ears. Aumon emerges from his transport, his rip in the fabric of space he uses to transport himself across the realms, to spy and to see everything for his Master to see.

The portal closes behind him, being swallowed up in a puff of smoke and a bright cosmic burst of the purple light. Aumon looks about his surroundings, searching intently for something...or perhaps, someone. He has journeyed far and a long way from Aura, but his final steps have lead him all the way here, to the center of all being, the vortex of the Astral Rift, where all creation emerged, and now, only a graveyard of dead planets and islands engulfed in space now exist. The island Aumon now walks upon, is possibly the furthest know mass from Aura, for this desert is cold, the atmosphere is a blizzard of storms and cyclones, constantly attacking the surface and annihilating the already weak and miniscule atmosphere that still lingers about this cosmic territory.

This place has no known name upon Aura, but if it did, it would be called Ur` Maur, or *"Isle of the Suffering"*. Habitation upon this planet is impossible for no life could ever survive, cultivate, or reproduce. Yet, though it is not meant for life, it does have a purpose... Ur` Maur is here for one reason and one reason only...this is where the ancient being, the Blade Wielder, the one who was destined to be the true Hero of Aura, the one who was baptized by the Dregor in an ocean of chaos and war, the redeemer of the Grey Age, the hands of darkness who summoned the Lords from Hexagus...Kandarius Lockmore, the once master of Aumon.

Aumon travels some distance, some miles, passing vacant mountains and empty hills where only the blackest of nightmares howl and twist, until he reaches his destination. Ahead of him, standing some thousands of feet high reaching vast altitudes far into the noxious atmosphere, is the severed head of Kathaxes, buried deep into the ground where it impacted many, many eons before. Aumon notices the right eye socket is empty, yet he looks off into the sky, and the eye of Kathaxes orbits this island much like a moon orbits its planet. The eye twists in an erratic orbit, swaying to and fro upon a crooked, elliptical rotation around the Aurora's bones. The eye does not keep guard, for the eye has long decayed, and blindness cripples and covers over the orb in a thick film similar to the crust of a planet. However, the film slowly each passing day, melts, and a drop of fermented liquid falls like a tear to the surface of Ur` Maur, the only moisture this barren waste receives.

Aumon examines the structure of the head, and at its base, tied by the Aurora's veins within the gaping mouth, is a figure, a figure of a once powerful stature, but is now lithe and skeletal, his flesh is a pale violet color, almost pink in complexion, with heavy bruises and burns covering his body, yet the body seems very transparent and see-through. The thinning black hair hangs down in tangled knots over his face and strands of a beard are tangled into the hair in a clumped mess. This...is the disposed of figure, what remains of Kandarius Lockmore. The right leg is gone, the nub is bound by a thick root of the veins tied around his knee. From the Kathaxes's teeth, drips a painful acid that eats away at Kandarius's flesh, day after day, for the last two hundred years, since he fell to the Hero of Ages. Kandarius's neck is broken, his head simply droops over and points to the floor, as he screams in pain every minute, as the acrid, burning liquid drips upon his shoulders and runs down his back, eating away at his spinal cord, paralyzing him so he cannot escape from his eternal prison.

Aumon follows the unbearable screams, and step after step, with every patter of his feet, gets closer to the pitiful being of Kandarius.

Kandarius hears something getting closer, his speech is slurred, yet he is still able to speak.

'Who...who approaches?!'

He wrestles around with his shackles, yet can barely move, another drop of acid falls, and he screams more from annoyance than pain, for he has had enough of this suffering.

'Who are you?! Whatever you are, you have not come to this place without a reason...are...are you here to release me!? Please, I beg of you, I can repay you in any way, I have much power to offer!' Kandarius pleads and begs.

He listens and hears the squeaking and gruffles of Aumon's familiar noises.

Acid drops, and Kandarius screams, yet he feels overjoyed.

'Aumon...Aumon is that you?! I knew you'd be able to find me here, for truly, the Dregor blood flows in your veins!' Kandarius says ending with a sinister laugh. Yet, he chokes himself as weak as he is, not speaking to anything for so long, except for himself, bound here for all time.

And then, something happens that Kandarius did not expect, something that has never happened before.

"Why, yes master...Dregor's blood, blood of power that you desperately need to further exist, power that you need to escape this prison, the power you need...to become whole

again, for the last of your life...exists with me. You need me, to
make you whole, or else those drops will eat at you for another
two hundred, maybe five hundred years, maybe forever...until
your nothing more than a puddle of melted slime and the very
essence of yourself, is no more."

Aumon, has spoken, yet he speaks to Kandarius within
his mind.

'Aumon...?'

'You see Kandarius...I not only possess half of your
power...for you must remember, I came to you by the will of
Maz Dregor, I was created from the blood of each Hexagus
Lord. Now, I could help you, I could sacrifice my life-force
and join with you, abandon the rest of my power to you so you
can become whole again, but...if I take what is left of your
miserable essence, which doesn't look like much, then I will be
the one, who commands the chaos and the power to control
thoughts and minds, to build my own agenda for Aura the way
I see fit. Now, doesn't that sound like a much grander plan, for
I have some interesting things of my own that I'd like to do?
Well...what do you think? Should you remain the master...or
will I supplant you, and then I'll be the master, for I will carry
the essence of all chaos, Dregor, and all the Hexagus Lords!
I...will be the Destroyer anew...he will live again!'

'You will help me...I am your master, Maz Dregor
demanded you serve me!'

Aumon snickers, then when he speaks, his voice drops
to a deep, grovel, a roaring pitch that shakes all of Ur` Maur,
'...and, just as you were going to betray US, you tried to use
that blade, Azalir, to end OUR reign, to reclaim all of Aura and
return it to chaos!'

Aumon's eyes glow a deep red. 'You and Naumokron
were worthless, weak...that is why you where destroyed so

easily...my servant here, he has lived on, survived...he is the one who will reclaim our kingdom, rebuild our world! You see...his will is MY WILL!'

Aumon leaps upon Kandarius's melted shoulders, grips his head and pulls back his broken neck with a harsh jerk.

'No...no, you can't do this to me! Please...!'

'Without our power, you have reverted back to your weak, pathetic self, the way I found you when you were a groveling, little child! Nothing more than a lamb for the slaughter!'

The deep voice of Aumon, of all the Hexagus Lords roars with ferocity. 'And now, your essence...now belongs to me, no more will you exist, for you now belong to US, to the legion of night...you shall be digested away, in the bile of our mother Wom! Take his heart Aumon, and eat it! We will be done with this insignificant dust once and for all!' And all the fires of Wom ignite, and the voices of the Hexagus, have spoken!

Aumon takes the razor of his claw, and slashes a long cut down Kandarius's ribs and stomach, he then cuts across the shoulder blades, and splays him open. Bone by bone, Aumon tears away the rib cage of Kandarius, and when all the bones and veins, as well as the lungs and arteries are cleared away, Aumon grips the black, corroded beating heart of Kandarius, and tears it away with a harsh pull, and then a wrenching tug. The heart is held up like a piece of rotten fruit that is alive with a thump and a beat, the rest of the blood is pumped out through the major artery.

Kandarius's head falls back, and his eyes roll into the back of his head. His last sight, is that of Aumon biting into that clump of muscle, ending its beat, and pulling his mouth away, revealing those tiny sharp incisors as they chew and rip apart the fat around it and the valves within.

Aumon leaps from the dead essence of Kandarius as the corpse just hovers within its confines, and a bleeding hole ripped into the chest, now an empty cavity, as hollow as the call of the dying winds that scratch and claw, and tear away at Ur` Maur's surface.

The familiar, now his own master, leaps to the ground and taking chunk after chunk out of this piece of meat, he swallows each morsel, briefly hacking up and choking on every mouthful, and then he takes the last bite and finishes.

Aumon's body begins to glow and react with sparks of lighting and ominous flashes radiate from his eyes and mouth, bursting outwards like a hideous spotlight burning through the dead clouds and toxic atmosphere. There is a sudden burst of energy as Aumon's body begins to undergo a metamorphosis. The ground shakes and begins to crumble all around, the core of this dead realm goes into overload, and a deafening explosion rattles across the entire Galakaos.

As the rubble clears, and the bones of Ur` Maur have been turned to ashes, now a shower of soil in this dark abyss, a figure remains, a figure wrapped in long robes and materials, his claws are now hands, his walk and stride are intimidating and will be a sign to all who perish before his power, as he walks across their conquered lands. His face, is the face of someone others can trust, his eyes are stern and hair as black as midnight. Aumon, is transformed, molded into a new power.

Aumon looks out across the entire Galakaos and surveys the Astral Rift, he examines all that needs to be done, and to start...there is unfinished business upon Aura, for he feels something, senses something familiar has been awakened, summoned back into this realm. It is a presence that is close to

Kandarius, and he himself feels it overcoming his consciousness. Ahead of him, the black stirs and all the stars off ways seem to shift and move, re-orbiting and changing their alignment and their positions. He feels the omniscient eyes, breech into his very body, and warm him, relax him...the Hexagus blood within him settles and is at peace. The darkness of space...is becoming darker, a force is casting the very edges of the universe, in shadow.

Aumon closes his eyes, and takes in the power he feels, all the power that encompasses within him stirs with excitement...for she...has come!

Aumon opens up his eyes, and before him, a huge line is forming, splitting the Astral Rift in half, and the line is growing longer and getting thicker, as though something is opening up onto the Rift. The line, soon turns to an oval, and as the mass expands more and more, reaching dizzying levels of awesomeness, for neither colossal nor titanic can describe the size of this thing, this object. The sizes is greater than any planet, more vast than the sun or the largest star, for Aumon is no more than the size of a speck of sand compared to it.

Aumon gazes upon its magnificence, the shape has a glare off its glassy surface, and at the center, is a vast pupil, connecting to large veins the size of roads that would connect a thousand planets hundreds of times over. Aumon...is gazing into an eye, the largest eye of all time and space that has ever existed. Then another opens up further away, and then another some light-years away peeks open. He can hear the heavy breathing of what sounds like a long, drawn-out explosion, and below, way below this pupil, a wall, millions of miles long, of rows and rows of razor sharp fangs shows itself.

The exhilaration Aumon feels is like a shot of ecstasy that cannot be compared to any other feeling of power. He

gazes upon the awesome sight, and can only utter a single
word.

'... ..... WOM!'

Part III:

Aftermath & Ruin

~

The Daughter of Runegard escorts her people along the underground tunnel, her guards lead ahead, just by a few paces. Ahead, they see no light, but they feel a bitter wind on all their faces. A voice cries from the back.

'Is it the exit ahead of us?!'

The rest of the crowd stirs, excited to finally walk on the surface, to start a new existence. They have spent month after month hidden away far beneath Runegard, and they were ready to walk on the surface again. Runegard can be rebuilt, the lost and the dead will be mourned, and a new sun will again rise. Hondor has been apprehended, soon he will be no more, he will be tried, he will be executed, slaughtered, just as he has slaughtered them, just as he has tormented and destroyed them, so will he be, though such a beast could never be tormented, they will see to it he is destroyed! *(Or can he be?)*

The Daughter can feel the heat blow through the caves, coming from the west of their current location, beneath the mountains. The air is scorched from the flames which rise from the walls of Runegard. The soldier in the lead looks back at

54

her, she sits quietly and listens…then she nods her head to the soldier, who then looks back at one of the scouts and commands him to go on ahead to take a closer look at what awaits them on the surface.

'Do you think it's really safe, my lady?' Roúgsver asks.

She shakes her head. 'I guess we'll find out…won't we…' She replies.

The scout treks ahead, and scales up the rough terrain of the throat of the cave. The further he gets, the stronger the smell of smoke is on the wind, and the closer he gets to the surface, he hears the whisper, the smoldering crackle of flames, and the heat against his face is strong. Once outside, he looks about his surroundings, and all seems clear. He gives the whistle, and the two guards, the Daughter of Runegard, Roúgsver, then the rest of the Civilians, the Gormons, the Asyndians, and all their children and loved ones follow. They reach the surface and the wind, they wish would be a comfort for them, but the heat in the winds seems to almost scar their dirty faces, covered in soot and dirt, that fell from the ceiling as Hondor decimated their homes and slaughtered their livestock and their families unfortunate enough to be caught within range of his twin axes.

Over the western hill, the sky is polluted by smoke, swelling into thick clouds that swirl into the air, the faint flicker of the dying flames as they drown into embers, smolders down, and the highlights dance across their faces, mocking them, taunting them, as the large exodus of denizens pass through the forests and under the thick Ashwood and Oak trees which loom overhead, covering their movements in the rising dawn.

They exit from the forests, and cut cross-country for a stretch, until they come to the main road. After about a mile or so, the main gates to Runegard is in their sights. The crowds get closer and they see what was only the beginning of the destruction which occurred. The gates where the monster burst through, are collapsed inward, the hinges ripped away and the outer wall around the gate, has crumbled inwards. Most of the towers have been torn down, there is a huge break in the eastern wall, the homes of Runegard, where one and all have lived for many years, have been annihilated, torn down, destroyed, decimated, now nothing more than piles of brick, stone, rubble, and straw from thatched roves and all has been blanketed in charred, black ash from the flames. The roads and crosswalks of the city have been torn up and ripped away, and titanic footprints are left imprinted in the rocky soil. The urchins that have returned from the catacombs, all embrace and hold each other, hanging on only by the sadness of a memory of this beautiful, lush land they loved and called their home.

The Daughter looks far ahead to the palace upon the hill and bolts forward. Roúgsver and her guards chase along after her. The soldiers that have returned from the battlefield hug and embrace their loved ones that have been hidden away. The other guards and centurions collect the dead and place them at the center of the town. With each passing hour, more and more bodies are found. Many, are nothing more than limbs and pieces. They cover them with rags, blankets…whatever they can get hold of. The others go around to claim them as their family, friends, and spouses…even children.

The Daughter runs up the hot marble stairs towards the front of the palace, which lays empty, a collapsed, hollow shell that has been charred to a black crust, for the outer bricks and marble have disintegrated and the skeletal exterior is left exposed. She falls to her knees and sobs, and Roúgsver kneels next to her. They are approached from behind by a calming voice.

'We searched the remains and found nothing of anyone…I am sorry, fair Daughter.' A centurion officer says as he places his hand upon her shoulder to console her grief.

She looks out over the city, she does not look at anyone as she speaks. 'Where…where is the general…where is General A'deon!'

The centurion does not reply right away, not knowing for sure what to say. She repeats her question.

'Where is he…I need to speak with him!'

'The general…is gone! He vanished from the battlefield!' He replies.

'Disappeared?'

'After the battle was over, we went to collect the wounded, and when we searched, he was not there, missing…nowhere to be found!'

'Did anyone see anything?' She asks.

'I heard some say, he may have defected…ran away, most told me as he rode in to strike at Hondor, he coward away, and fell from his horse, many say he was beaten and broken, left for dead…and that was the last anyone has seen him.' The centurion replies.

'And what of Hondor…how did you stop him?!'

He looks at her again, she can see the blank stare looking at her through his mighty bronze helmet.

'I don't know how they stopped him, my lady.' He replies.

'You don't know?' Roúgsver asks with impatience at the centurion not answering the Daughter's questions directly.

'Our soldiers have been fighting this battle for months, dying, being cut to pieces and having their bones ripped from their bodies...and you mean to tell me you don't know how he was captured?!' Her voice raises to an echoing shriek.

'I tell you both, I...don't know how to explain what happened! I was simply told that he...stopped, he just froze like a dead corpse, a statue...and then he fell, collapsed. At that moment, they bound and chained him so he could not move...I don't know what happened, neither does anyone else!' He replies.

'Where is Hondor now, where is the monster being held?!' The Daughter asks.

'The Asyndians came and he has been taken to Yuldurian to stand trial.' Replies the centurion.

'Trial...? We should just kill this bastard before he wakes up!' Roúgsver scowls.

'My people are dead because of him, my kingdom has been decimated...I'd spit in the scum's face now if I could!' She curses at him with rage.

She unsheathes a ferocious looking, royal dagger of cobalt, blue steel and the royal insignia chiseled upon the crest of the handle and a luscious ruby at the base of the hilt.

'I'd drive this blade straight through his heart...if he but had one!' She cries out.

'I...pardon me for saying, but I don't think that would do any good.' The centurion says.

'What are you saying?' Roúgsver asks, confused by the soldier's statement.

'From what I understand...he had several blades driven into his chest, several spears to the throat, as well as a battle axe embedded into his spine, which he simply reached around...and yanked out as though it were a mere bee sting!' The centurion claims, implying that her blade would have done nothing but cause a simple flesh wound.

'I don't know what that beast is made of, but he is not of any race or denizen that I have seen walk upon Aura!' He says.

She sheathes the blade, and whips her hair back with the wind howling furiously about. Roúgsver and the centurion stand at attention awaiting what will be her next order for the situation at hand.

'We will see...when the judgment has been made...we will see!' She whispers to herself, but the centurion hears her words. She turns around, the centurion to her back, and she looks about at the destruction and the ruins of her ancestor's lands and cities across the landscape, for the top of these stairs she has ascended are high up, and grant her view over much of her surroundings. She cannot go higher for the sentinel tower of the city, the highest point of Runegard, was torn down and ripped into pieces of debris and crushed brick, and disintegrated mortar.

Across the seas of dying grass and plains of smoldered embers, upon the fields just outside the city, bodies litter the entire battlefield, and off to the right towards the farmlands, dead livestock and destroyed homes are scattered around in puddles of blood and pieces of flesh and the remains of masticated bones from where Hondor had feasted upon sheep and pigs, cows as well as hofts and smaller poultry beasts.

'...what can one say...about such destruction? What can I say to these Civilians, these Gormons and Asyndians, who have lost everything...?' The Daughter asks aloud, hoping the answer is on the wind, or will fall from the sky, or strike her in the form of a bolt of lightning mumbled from the thunderous tongue in the mouth of the clouds.

'Be strong, my lady, and speak strong...speak to your people as a stout leader...as one who is strong enough to see through these shadows, and make it through this dark day...lead your own to reach the daylight of tomorrow...if they feel you can make it, so will they, they will try to make it as well.' Roúgsver responds, trying to lend her some form of comfort.

She turns and looks at Roúgsver with a stern look in her eyes.

'That, my lady, is the look of a woman, who is going to make it through this...' He walks closer to her. 'Let your people see that look, let them feel the strength you hold in your eyes. It's not always words, but our actions that show what we truly are, what we feel inside and out.'

They hear something swoop down from the wind and land upon the cobbled stairs. In the corner of their eyes, they see the shadow of a wide set of wings that fold back, and an Asyndian stands to his feet, his talons dig in deep to the stone from the impact of his landing.

The Daughter and Roúgsver turn to face the Asyndian. He is clad in scaled-bronze armor, and brandishes a long spear tipped with a curved silver blade. The sash wrapped tightly around his waist blows in the wind and his feathers ruffle about.

'My lady...Daughter of Runegard...'

He bows to her presence, then raises his head, and waits for permission to speak.

'Go ahead...' She commands.

'I have come by command of Yuldurian, High Judge of the Court and Ruler over all of Thylesian! He sends his condolences for what has happened here at Runegard, and is glad to hear you and your own have returned safe from the catacombs.'

'Thank you, and I wish to thank him for sending his brave Asyndian guard to aid my soldiers here on the surface, and am sad to see your brethren killed in battle against that monster... but they fought bravely and did not die in vain! Now that we will see justice brought to this monster!' She nods to the Asyndian and he nods back.

'Thank you for your condolences my lady, you are most gracious, even after all that has transpired to yours of Runegard...you keep the despair your own, and not spread it.' The Asyndian replies with a grim smile, as he takes notice of the Asyndian bodies that lay sprawled about with the Gormon and Civilian troops.

'Please tell me, how can I serve Lord Yuldurian?' She asks.

'He wishes for you to be present during the trial and the final judgment. I am to take you immediately to Thylesian as soon as possible, for the trial will be starting momentarily. The beast is being escorted to the halls of judgment as we speak.'

This is music to her ears, but she has a responsibility to her people. She looks around at the sad faces and miserable denizens as they shift about the ruined streets, crying and mourning over their dead. Roúgsver sees the concerned look upon her face.

'Do not worry, my lady...I will stand charge in your absence. Myself and your most loyal guardians, we will look over each other, we will guard the weaponless and the helpless with our lives, should any threats return while you are gone. I know this is important for everyone, for all of Runegard and all of Aura...you do us all a service by representing us at the trial, and being our voice of justice that will be served...go my lady!'

She nods in understanding.

'Thank you Roύgsver.' She walks down the stairs and across the walkway and central market area where the remains of shops and merchant's carts once flooded the streets. She is going to speak to them.

'Everyone...please can I have your attention!'

The crowds of people turn to her, to listen to the words of their leader, the Daughter of all their land.

'My citizens...my brave Civilians, Gormons, and Asyndians! I have news, for the trial of this monster is about to commence, and I have been summoned to represent our wonderful land to face this foe, and finally see him run through for the pain he has caused us!'

She maintains her composure, she does not falter in her words or standing as she continues her speech.

'We may have been dealt a severe blow...we have lost many we loved, friends and family, homes and land...but we will rebuild, we will remember our lost in memory and smile when we think of them...we will make it through these dark times and see the morning light when it peeks over the eastern hills, and the shadow that looms over us, will be alleviated from our shoulders! So please...take this time, embrace these hours to be with those who you love, mourn the loss, but let the weeping cease...and never...never forget to smile, laugh, and live!'

The crowd looks at her with tears in their eyes, yet they try to hold them back, they feel obligated, as though they should not let their grief show in the eyes of a woman they feel has the strength, the strength to carry them through this.

She feels the vibes of the crowds radiate over the streets and through the ruins. The feelings of all her own, seems to strike her in the heart, but she does not falter, she does not let her legs buckle, she...does not, but turns and moves to the Asyndian who awaits her, to carry her over the skies, and go north to the city beyond the clouds, to Thylesian where her presence is expected.

'...you will take care of them?' She asks Roúgsver.

'I will not let them loose their strength.' He replies.

She turns to the Asyndian. ' I am ready.'

'Then let us be off, this will not take long..' The Asyndian replies to her.

The crowds watch as the Daughter is hoisted onto the Asyndians back, she holds on tight as he spreads his mighty gray wings and catches the wind, and he flaps his wings and they rise up vertically, higher and higher. She turns around and looks down upon the city, the denizens look like tiny dots and the buildings fade more and more out of focus and into the vast distance below them, the higher the Asyndian goes. He hovers momentarily, leans forward a bit, and pushes off with great force, soaring across the clouds and through the channels of wind and air with terrific speed.

She closes her eyes, for what only feels like a moment, and then she looks down, the fields and mountains zoom by in blurs of green and tints of gray.

The pass is quick, but she notices something in the corner of her eye, she see what looks like the ruins of an ancient city.

'Below us...is the remains of what is left of Athilnovia, our ancient city before Thylesian was built!' The Asyndian calls back to her in a shout to talk over the roaring gusts of wind that shakes them around in the atmosphere.

'What caused it to fall?' She replies.

'Over two-hundred years ago...when the Twelve Altars of Y`nahlia were destroyed by the Dregor...the city lost its power and fell! Thylesian was built in its place...!' He answers.

'Look...Thylesian is straight ahead!' The Asyndian points directly ahead of them with his spear.

The Daughter can barely make out anything when she looks ahead, the wind gusts across her face are too powerful to see past a squint.

'I cannot see..this wind is too strong!' She cries.

With that, she feels their speed start to slow down. The Asyndian goes from a steady soar, now to flapping his wings at a slower pace.

'You do not have to slow down for me to see...time is of the essence!' She says to the Asyndian.

'I am slowing down...because everyone, at least once, should gaze upon our beautiful city in the clouds...from this altitude, from this position, at least once. For the days are growing darker...and this may very well, be the last morning sun, in which Thylesian...basks in!' The Asyndian replies with pride in his voice, for his pride sounds genuine, this is the pride she needs more of, for pretty speeches can hide doubt for so long, but sooner or later, that doubt will come back, like a dark past creeping up from behind, an old ghost once thought exercised.

'Look! It's a sight that will take your breath away!' The Asyndian calls back to her.

She looks forward, and the Asyndian...is correct. She casts her eyes upon the city in the clouds, far up over the mountains and all the lands of Aura, the crown of this land, the diadems, the towers of marble and the surrounding homes for all the Asyndians as well as the Civilians and Gormons who have taken up residency here, are marvels to behold, and the golden trunks and leaves of the trees sparkle with a faint glow in the sun's rays which manage to pierce the thick wall of clouds and the morning dew trickles from the branches into puddles that form upon the marble streets are absorbed within the patches of emerald green grass.

They pass through the clouds, and more of the city opens up, and she gasps as she looks off to the north, far across this empire in the sky, she looks to the range of white mountains that line the horizon and she lays her eyes upon the mighty fortress where Yuldurian resides and follows the white tower as it rises upwards and disappears far above the city in dizzying heights miles and miles high.

'So...what do you think of our great city?!'

She takes in a deep breath and feels the soothing cool air fill her lungs, then she exhales. She answers with the tone of the most excited, wide-eyed curiosity of a child, that the Asyndian has ever heard within an adult.

'I have heard the legends, the tales of the mighty city of Thylesian...it has gained the reputation for being the crown of Aura...for this place has earned its title, for I have never gazed upon a sight more beautiful! And to walk upon her streets and within the halls of a palace so mighty, so handsome in its architecture and foundation of a lavish cascade of mountains and surrounded by a twilight of clouds and mists which radiate the magnificent colors of a thousand jewels and stones of the most precious kind! Why, t'would be an honor! For let this day be known...today, beauty slays the beast...!'

'That it will, my lady...that it will!' The Asyndian replies. And she tightens her grip around the Asyndian once more, as he once again, increases his speed and heads for Yuldurian's fortress.

Little did they know, that the shadows were closing in around them, the curtain was being closed behind them, for it seems the morning was transforming itself into twilight. The black clouds loomed in the distance like the shadow of a cat, a killer in the dark to destroy the daylight, for something is upon them, and the darkness senses, that its time has come, the storm is brewing, the waiting is over, and the pieces on the board, are once more moving, configuring... and waiting for their chance to strike.

Yet, the Asyndian could feel the moisture in the wind, a storm...was indeed coming.

Part IV:

The Trial

~

Upon mighty golden hofts that fly through the clouds with golden wings that glimmer from the molten hurricanes upon the Aura star, soldiers and guardians ride, with golden bronze armor to match and in their gauntlets, are clutched long pikes tipped with a glowing essence of flame, and within the dancing fire, is the ancient eye, the symbol of the once mighty Airical who watched over all of Aura from the ancient, fallen city of Athilnovia.

Now, these mighty steeds fly to a higher bastion, a city even brighter, even more of a spectacle to gaze upon, than any other civilization that has preceded it within Aura's ancient past. Now, burning outwards from the solar heavens, is the realm of Thylesian, that lays in wait for the steeds to approach, for the steeds glide by, and they pull thick chrome chains and upon those chains, is the awesome Dungeon Galleon, a wonder of the skies, a flying battleship with an impressive five hundred foot length, with no sails, and no oars steer her, only the mighty, flaming steeds at the helm. The galleon has a massive hull that makes a drastic curve under the stomach of the ship, and over the vast deck, is a covered dome of the purest diamond and mineral welded together by solid titanium bars, thus forming and impenetrable fortress of the sky.

And at the center under the dome, chained and bound, clad with a helmet of golden spikes and shackles of rebar thickness, is the monster in the flesh, chained and crucified to this titanic X of metal at the center of the dome, is Glasgar...but to those in Aura, every lip is shuddering *"Hondor"*.

Surrounding him in a vast circular pit that surrounds the stand where Hondor is chained are vicious, barking hounds with snarling teeth, gagged by leashes of thick hide and chain. These beasts are held back by centurion guards, heavily armored soldiers in bronze armor, and above Hondor, are legions of crossbowmen, with their missiles and bolts aimed straight for the monstrosities heart, or should I be more clear, and say, that all want so badly to fire, and kill the beast who is responsible for so many deaths. They want to put him down, but there is one thing holding them back...they take all these precautions to transport this beast, but could they truly harm him if he awakens? Could their insignificant bolts, truly pierce his thick skin, could they muster their trigger finger, as it shakes from the terror, as he rushes for them, to tear them to pieces? Could he be killed? If they shot now, would he die, could such a thing be killed? Is such evil possible to be destroyed and done away with? Many witnessed what happened to Runegard and her armies...they know just how damn-near immortal he really is.

Up ahead, upon the wide and vast open space of marble causeway, thousands and thousands of Asyndian soldiers await the approaching fortress, for the first row of golden hofts are in their line of sight and the Asyndians know the danger that awaits within the vast dome barge that is pulled by the many flying hofts.

The Dungeon Galleon descends upon the vast landing of Thylesian, and a mighty boom and roar echoes outwards and rumbles the entire field of the city, along with the vast dome of the sky around them, the vibrations nearly send the staunch line of soldiers and guards off their feet, an unbalanced stance, which throws them off their guard.

Earlier that evening, before the arrival of the prisoner, the representatives of the Civilians of Othetica and several Gormon war-master's, mighty soldiers and leaders from Otoni and Fausengard arrived by Asyndian escort, for word has spread across the realm of the Gormon's capture, and the other regions were invited to witness his trial...and his judgment to pass. For the Civilians of Othetica, Lord Rolom attends with his aristocrats that follow closely behind, as well as several from his personal guard, heavily clad, muscular Civilians branded in solid steel armor, brandishing hefty bronze claymores wielded by two hands. He is attending the trial while his younger brother, Tolm the Steward, is in charge of the lands in his brother's absence. For the Gormons, there is the Oldgaur Clan, seven brothers, the sons of Rolg` Oldgaur, ruler and overseer of the Gormon cities across the north of Aura. And now they too wait, they look on as the prison galleon approaches, lands...the doors are opening.

The doors to the haul open outwards in the form of a massive golden and silver riveted draw bridge with many steps leading up to the vast open entryway, and attached to the chrome steel chains, controlled by a mechanism of steaming metal and churning gears that hum and roar in the deep darkness of the haul. The door comes to a halt, and the onlookers watch and wait, terrified, the fear churning and ripping apart their bones, but not even near as worse as to what Hondor's axe would do to their flesh and bones, for the beast is about to be presented, he will be making that long trek down the cobbled stone and marble walkway, off to where the trial will be held, at the far end of Thylesian, within the tall ivory and silver fortress far, far in the distance, upon the highest peak above the bright and majestic city, connected along a winding walkway, the Midnight Stair, which looms above a vast and deep abysmal pit below, and then, they will cross the Eternal Bridge. To the Asyndians, these structures are called Mildoyaun, the Stair of Midnight, and Ethera, the Eternal Bridge.

Everyone stands at the ready, all are silent and tremble, only the murmur upon the lips and beaks are heard. There are not only Asyndians upon Thylesian, but Civilians as well, and their teeth chatter and skin shivers, afraid of what might come out of that ship. And so...they wait. *("What if he gets loose?! What if...")*

This was the primary question on everyone's mind, aside from...*"How...how did they do it? How did A`deon and his soldiers...subdue and capture Hondor?"*

The first wave of guards march forth from the haul, heavily armored and wielding mighty claymores and heavy flails, and thick whips that are wrapped around their arm like a snake. They take their positions, and the second wave of guards march forward. This battalion carries mighty, double-bladed battleaxes and iron-bound shields as thick as the stone on a heavily fortified castle wall. Then the third wave emerges, these Asyndian guardians carry crossbows armed with poison and flame bolts ready to fire, again...if *"He"* tries to break loose from his confinement. And then, the fourth and final wave of soldiers and guardians emerge, pulling the thick chains which bind Hondor to his imprisonment.

At last, upon his crucifixion, bound to the bloody-nailed X of metal, Hondor is brought forth, pulled upon a cart by hulking, dino-like beasts called Durzurs, horned and grunting. His head slumped forward, held down at a tilted angle by the immense weight of the massive helmet over his face, with each

70

spike upon the helmet bearing the same weight as a full grown adult drog, and the helmet itself the same weight as a pregnant mig, who is bearing her thousands and thousands of eggs upon the back of her abdomen.

"He...looks like a Gormon...Hondor, is a Gormon?"

This threw puzzlement to those watching on, as to how one Gormon could do so much damage. Now Gormons are known for their battle prowess, but not even the seven of the Oldgaur Clan could take down an entire army of ten thousand strong. Never the less, this confusion did not make them feel any less fearful of him, for the blood of soldiers upon his arms and across his chest, was evidence enough of his brutality.

Following behind Hondor, two pale beasts emerge, with white flesh-colored scales, pale eyes, and a thick mane of hair covering their draconic, lion-like features, and a mystical light flowing about their golden wings, and upon their back rides a soldier of Asyndia. These sacred beasts are called Mataru`, sacred forms which emerged from the fallen light of Lota's ancient city of Athilnovia many, many years before, during the Cleansing, the Reich of Dregor Worship. The Mataru` are used to protect and keep watch over Aura where the Asyndians can't be, similar to the ancient clan of Drog Riders. Mataru` are the carriers of the stars, and on this day, they are protecting all within Thylesian from the black and murky dread that emanates from Hondor's blank, sleeping stare beneath that helmet.

The long line of marching guardians watch the way, as Hondor is moved slowly, for they are careful not to disturb or even slightly cause a collapse of this contraption which stands between them and a bloody, gory death, for the monster is in some form of catatonic state, a twilight, he has not moved since his capture, as though he is lifeless, but the blood, the vile thick blood still pulsates within his jutting, bursting veins of his limbs, neck, and chest.

The crowds stare in silence, with clenched jaws and tight lips bitten, turning blue and purple with the pressure placed upon them, as though they were suffocating themselves, to keep from screaming in terror of Hondor's presence. They dare not to shout, or to even make a sound, as not to aggravate or disturb the beast or throw debris to disturb the meandering nightmares the creature's mind follows deep within his trance, or else they shall invoke the monstrosities' wrath, worse than the darkness of the Hexagus born from the black sludge that drips from Wom's stomach. The only sound that is to be heard, is the dead, howling screech of the northern winds, cold and icy, from the peaks of Mirym and the Glorial Mountains.

The soldiers keep looking back, shaking, terrified within themselves, though they dare not show the feeling of their legs wanting to buckle, or the beads of sweat pouring from their body, for every bump upon the marble tile, every rustle of the chains to and fro, of the cart which bears *"Him"* along, they keep looking, peering over their shoulder, because the fear keeps biting at their neck like a vampire, a parasite to take away their bravery, to bleed them dry of courage, and they will be nothing more than empty husks, cowards. And those empty husks, will shatter like the breaking of stone, the collapse of a sturdy bridge, a brick fortress that has stood the test of time for thousands and thousands of years, as they feel the earthquake beneath their feet, feel the shaking of the ground, and the tremble of the fear strikes full force to their will and being, all they have trained for will be for not, when they turn back, and see Hondor standing there, gnawing at the white limbs of the sacred Matarus', as the crystal blood runs down his chin and corroded, parched lips, long without the taste of the elixir of life, for blood of all creatures, is his drive, to lap the bottom of the goblet filled with the blood of Auroras.

At his back, will be a pile of bodies, not just the soldiers and centurions, but the bones of the men, women, and children of Thylesian. No Gormon, Asyndian, or Civilian will have survived, fists covered in guts and feathers, from him bashing down the Gormons into nothing, and leaping into the sky to catch the fleeing Asyndians, and a mouthful of Civilian bones. For there is no remorse, no regrets, only an instinct deep within him, within the dark pits of his gut, and the back of the abyss of his thoughts and mind, a deep, primitive instinct...to kill. Oh, the gates seem so near...yet so far away to them, as they appear over the horizon, across the causeway in the distance, passed hanging gardens, of lush vegetation and grass upon all sides, and tall golden buildings, which seem to be the color of a dull bronze, as the eye of Lota in the sky has been eclipsed by the dull, grey clouds above.

They arrive at the main entryway, the duel double-doors of the tall ivory archway stands before them, which opens inwards to lead them along the path to the mountains ahead of them, not just a simple path, but a long winding marble road, across a bridge over a thick cloud of mist, and after that, the road turns upwards, and now the trek into the mountains begins. And so, they all look upwards, and above on the highest peak, standing as a sentinel, a guardian of the winds, and a serpent of the clouds, is the mighty tower, perfected in all its architecture and creation by its builders, standing upon the mighty bastion of the palace of judgment, were the justice of all Aura waits, and where the beast, where the judgment, the trial of Hondor, will commence. The building, which once seemed to burst with light, reflected from the golden camaraderie above, a brotherhood of millions of burning arms, and rays of golden sun, now seems, just as the other buildings and structures within Thylesian, dull and lifeless, as though the dark cumuli above has stripped the life from her, and all the inhabitants which stand in the gloom and doom, of Hondor's shadow, with long dark spots under their eyes, and lithe pale skin milked away by that same fear that's within the heart of every guard.

Far above, atop the highest pinnacle of the ivory tower, a brawn, white Asyndian, with a great flowing robe, and a ruffle of feathers, and mighty wings, impressive in their span outwards, the diamond glint in his eyes looks down upon the approaching rank of soldiers, appearing as nothing more than a hundred miniscule dots, from his point of view, but he knows of their arrival, he knows why the soldiers are here, why they come. One of them leaves the ranks, and the silhouette approaches from the distance, one of the Asyndian guards draws near.

The Asyndian lands upon the balcony, wrapping his talons around the silver railing, his voice radiates and echoes out from his bronze helm in a deep tone.

'Honorable Yuldurian Mha`, the prisoner has arrived, the gates are ready to be open on your command.'

Yuldurian Mha`, the great Asyndian, the Judgment of Thylesian, a descendant of Y'nahlia, the high priestess and wife of Airical, looks on, and after a moment of silence, gazing out below into a stare, bracing himself, preparing to confront and come face to face with this moment he has long dread, yet at the same time, has anxiously awaited, nods to the guards below and the vast golden gates to the valley open, the lush valley heavily guarded by Asyndians and watch towers, lines the high and mighty walls of rock along the way, until they come to the foot of the palace itself. As careful as the army has come, they continue along the road with just as much caution, just as much worry, and the Asyndian guards above their heads, watch and wait, to see what happens, keeping their keen eyes upon every step of the Gormons and Civilians, as the other Asyndians lead them along, and their eyes turn with a swift jerk, to the giant "X", and the bestial figure that is chained and nailed to it.

That's when true terror strikes at the heart, of every brave Asyndian warrior.

From the doorway of Yuldurian's quarters, several Asyndians stand before him. The white Asyndian turns as the others bow to him and his majestic presence. They wear flowing robes of many colors and patterns according to their hierarchy. They each also wear a helm with a particular pattern and made of its own precious metal, one wears an iron helm, the other wears bronze, there is copper, as well as titanium, silver, and nickel. Yuldurian wears a helm of solid gold with silver hoft hair flowing from the crown, braided down the back, with a faint sparkle in the dim sunlight peering through the clouds, as well as an assortment of feathers on the back of the helmet, and the tips...are stained with his mother's blood, for this is the headdress of Y'nahlia.

'My lord...?' One of them steps forward.

Yuldurian turns from gazing out the window of the vast, open room. The sun dims, but it's still not dark yet. He looks amongst his flock.

'He is here...prepare, the time for the final judgment has come. This...beast....this monster, the one the Civilians and Gormons call Hondor, will pay for his atrocities towards Aura and all her people, all Gormons, Civilians, and Asyndians...all those who have died...will have justice this day.'

'But, lord Yuldurian...why do we not just kill Hondor? Why must we hold trial for such an uncompromising monster, without feelings or compassion, no regret for what he has done, he just kills!'

Yuldurian turns and glares at the Asyndian. 'That is the logic of barbarians, of the blackest sort...that was the ideology of Kandarius and the Dregor! And I will not hear of it! Then we would be no different than that monster if we just slaughtered him! He will be tried, and a sentence will be administered by the power invested within me!'

The Asyndians simply bow to Yuldurian in acknowledgement and leave the room.

Yuldurian looks back out to the open window and watches the grey clouds roll over, turning from clumps of thick cotton, and twisting... morphing into the faces of tormented souls. A cold wind slivers across his feathers. A cool damp air will be out tonight, a storm approaches, for the twisted souls above writhe with warning as they crawl across the sky, crawling up from the south, as though they were running from the black clouds approaching close behind, dark like smoke from a funeral pyre, charring the flesh to ash, and the rain...the tears. A bellow of thunder roars across the atmosphere, the serpent's tongue of lightning strikes the mountains in the west, those who dwell within the streets and courtyards of Thylesian, take shelter in their homes. The Asyndians take to their towers high above the other buildings and architecture.

Yuldurian makes his way to the courtroom, walking through the archways and taking the mighty trek through the breezeway, and beyond the two double mighty doors, opened outwards before him, by two bulked Asyndians holding fierce halberds, and wearing golden armor of ceremonial design. The other judges, the jury, and citizens of Thylesian that have been invited to attend the trial, all await Yuldurian's arrival. Rolom and his Civilian aristocrats take their seats, and upon the far side, the Oldgaur clan take their seats as well. The time has come, the trial is about to begin.

Outside of the palace walls, those within the court hear the patter of the rain on the windows, a slight drizzle at first, but as those thick, black clouds reach overhead of this ivory palace, the sun slips, and the light falls to the merciless, brooding darkness. The rain grows heavier, the storm is thick to wash away the small creatures that roam about the streets at night, and causes the sects to flutter away, taken by the harsh winds that blow. The candlelight extinguished, and the flame torn from the wick of every candle within the windows of all those who go to close their shutters.

The silver doors open upon the highest balcony of the courtroom, and from above, Yuldurian flies down from above onto his place at the head of the court. Along the far window at the far side of the vast room, filled with hundreds in view, as well as the twenty or so jury members, are the seven floating shapes wrapped around in a semi-circle, mystical triangular projections, chiseled and crafted to perfection without flaw, that spark with a blue electricity, an aura of force that holds them aloft, and upon these mystical floating stands, are perched the seven judges of the court, seven judges including Yuldurian. All within the courtroom rise to hold honor to them, and Yuldurian motions for them to be seated as he makes the opening statements for all in attendance.

He raises his arms up high. "In this hour...we hence forth, pass the final judgment. We condemn that which would seek to destroy us, my fellow Asyndians...as well as all Gormons and Civilians alike.

As my duty, as well as the duty of my judges who sit upon this trial of Aura law, we abide by the power invested in us, passed down from our ancestors before, by the lady Y`nahlia and Airical, the mother and father of Athilnovia, we will bring forward now this monster, this beast born from the unfathomable depths of Wom, and we will bring him forth, and strike down upon him our law that we hold sacred, a law that preserves us, one and all and protects us...when we feel our wound is open and vulnerable to no forgiveness and shown no mercy.'

Yuldurian stands upon the perch of his platform.

'Now, let us commence with why we are here…we are here to place on trial…the beast called Hondor…for crimes against all Runegard and the slaughter of thousands…Civilians, Gormons, and Asyndians. In addition to the slaughter of countless Runegard denizens, where the body count still remains unknown, for many of the remains recovered…were not whole, but in pieces!'

Yuldurian raises his hands.

'Bring forth…the perpetrator!' He calls out, and the other judges rise at his back. The doors leading into the courtroom crack open, and a large line of soldiers walk in double lines, arms drawn, just as they were when they stepped off the prisoner vessel. They march with brisk speed and space out into the vast room. The members of the jury and the Civilians, Gormons, and Asyndians in attendance stand to their feet to see. Behind the soldiers, the Durzurs drag the captured Hondor across the marble floor and into the room. There is an uneasy restless silence that falls and ripples across the room in waves, except for the squeal of the cart wheels. Not even these great, hulking beasts are marveled by the crowds, for it is Hondor that captures and enraptures the denizens in a grip of fear.

The cart pulling Hondor stops, the wheels shrill and squeak to a halt. The echo of the sound is jarring and pierces like crystals and crying glass in everyone's ears.

Eyes look on in terror…many of Thylesian have not laid eyes upon this monster, only those who fought against him, were almost slaughtered by him…they are the ones who have seen it…the true horror, the horror of mangled bodies and a splattered blood-spilled mess, not just of Hondor's brooding appearance and stature…it's his actions they need to be afraid of. Two of the soldiers release the beasts from the cart and lead them back out of the courtroom to the courtyards just outside where they will wait until called upon, lead by their handlers to where they need to go.

'Before we begin, we wish to thank the one who brought this monster to justice and would now bring him before us. Bring him forth...the one who is responsible.'

Yuldurian looks to the large double golden doors at the far end of the aisle at the entrance of the room. Yet, nothing happens, no one answers.

'Where is the one who I must thank for saving our lives, for saving the lives of all! I command them, if they would show themselves, to come forward!' Yuldurian speaks in a commanding force.

Again, much the same, nothing happens, no one enters or moves within the room. Then, someone stirs off to the side, a young soldier stands to his feet, holding his helmet, cradled within his left arm and his mighty sword is slung over his back. His dark black hair is brushed across his right eye, and is combed neatly to the side at the top. He is clad in a full plated set of armor bearing the insignia of a captain upon his helmet, and the Civilian Crest upon his breast-plate, the same that was on A`deon's armor. This soldier is of a normal stature, yet well built, with two strong sword arms to wield the mighty claymore upon his back. He makes his way from his seat, descends down the stairs near the aisle he was seated, and crosses over the marble floor to stand before Yuldurian and the other judges.

Yuldurian's guards stand on edge as they watch the soldier's every move and every footstep. The soldier kneels before the judges of Thylesian and bows in respect, waiting to speak.

'Guards, stand down. Can you not see by his helmet he is a Captain!' He looks over to the soldier. 'You! Captain of

Runegard...please, speak! Tell us your name please, for I fear with all that conspires I fear I am not up to date with the operations of the armies throughout Aura, and I do not recognize your face.' Yuldurian commands, but in a pleasant voice.

The Civilian bows. 'I am called Kale, I am in service to Runegard and of the fair lady, the Daughter of Runegard. Both my great grandfather and my great uncle fought under the command of Grand General Cezius Cabriel during the Grey Age War over two-hundred years ago, and through our lineage, I have come into the service of Aura.'

'And your station?' Yuldurian asks.

'I was stationed along the borders near Fausengard. I was there during the prison break several months ago, and we attempted to locate the escapees, a Gormon and two Civilians. The Gormon vanished with an Asyndian, and the trail of the Civilians ran cold. With the call of the battle that has taken place here, I was relocated by my superiors. I told them of what has transpired, and they ordered me to attend and report on the trial.'

'And...are you the one we have to thank?'

'No...alas I am not, that honor would go to all the soldiers who stood their ground on the battlefield,' Kale raises a stern finger into the air, '...ALL, except for one!' He replies.

'And who would that be?' Yuldurian asks.

Kale lowers his hand and paces to and fro at a slow pace with his arms tucked behind his back. He speaks in a loud, stern voice, a voice that will sink into the minds of those who bear witness around him.

'That! My Lord Yuldurian...would be the defector himself, General A`deon! Leader of the Runegard armies!'

The room gasps, then all falls to a quiet murmur and whispers pass amongst the room, even the judges delegate to themselves. Yuldurian takes a moment to contemplate this thought. He raises his hands to silence everyone.

'Order! Everyone, be silent for a moment!' He shifts his attention to Kale. 'And...you've seen this?'

'Yes! With my own eyes, ask any here who stood by on the battlements, they will tell you how the general coward away from dealing the death blow to Hondor, and once the monster was subdued, he walked away with two of Aura's most wanted criminals, Diin and his sister Nilta! You know of who I speak, the ones who escaped...the ones who were set free, along with this Gormon, the one you call Hondor, this is Glasgar...the one who has mimicked and taken on the guise of a horrid legend, the legend of the battle-clad Hondor. They are working for a monstrous Asyndian by the name of Duul`ak! They are all in league with each other, splitting up so we would lose track and never find them...but it appears the Gormon was stupid enough to come back for more...foolish creatures they are!'

The Oldgaur clan stand to their feet and roar at Kale's mocking of their race. Yuldurian silences the room to maintain order.

'What proof do you have this Gormon is the same one you seek, the one called Glasgar?' Yuldurian inquires.

'The markings upon his left arm, the white hair beneath that helmet, remove that helmet, and I will show you!' Kale moves closer to Glasgar, to grasp the hulking mask. As he gets closer, something catches his eye, he sees something small, something move across the Gormons shoulder. He moves in closer to the bound prisoner, the restrained animal. The other's see this, including Yuldurian. The tension in the room swelters, and the panic rises, making the air hot and dense with anxiousness.

'Kale…what do you think you're doing?!' Yuldurian cries.

The guards grapple with Kale as he struggles to break loose, driven with madness, trying to reach Glasgar, to see what it was that moved, to rip off that mask and see for sure though he was certain, he knew it was him, the Gormon he was after, who he hunted, that is why he was here, the suspect those in Runegard captured, bore the same similarities to Glasgar, though the fighting style, he must admit, seemed different, the tactics more polished, more honed. He must have trained himself…or was it something else that gave him power…and there was something after all, to this whole Hondor idea that the Asyndians and Civilians spoke of.

'What is the meaning of this Kale?' Yuldurian asks with intent, standing from the center podium he has been perched upon.

'I…I want to see his face, I was going to tear off that mask…but then, something moved…something moved…I must know!' He cried, the guards still holding him back.

And the then, the court erupts into a panic, and the grand exodus begins, Civilians and Gormons leap from their seat and rush to the closed doors of the courtroom, pounding, trying to force their way through the door and force their way down the grand, vast halls to the front doors, blind with panic. But they are locked, none can get out. Even many of the guards drop their weapons and try to flee the room, terrified of what will happen. Yet, in the middle of all the chaos, Hondor still remains there, motionless as he has been for these past hours. It was something else Kale saw move, a quick shadow, tiny and insignificant creep over the muscle and tendons.

Yuldurian could not keep order, though things were starting to settle down, in a loud booming voice he cried, forcing all to return to their seats. The guards from Othetica had Rolom surrounded and protected, and the Oldgaur Clan had their battleaxes and hammers ready to fight their Gormon brethren and kill him if they had to...*(if they could)*. The bravest...or should I say, the most foolish of the guards, held their ground.

Yuldurian surveys the situation. He then throws a blazing gaze of fire to Kale. 'What is the meaning of this Kale...I should lock you away for this scare, what is wrong with you? How dare you disrupt my courtroom in such a way! If I say we must take off the Gormons mask, then I will be the one to say so...you keep your distance, make another move and you will be imprisoned for many years to come! Do I make myself clear?!'

'Have your guards release this hold on me...I will not go further...' Kale replies.

Yuldurian motions for the guards to let Kale go. He would not be able to get any closer and catch what he saw. *"What was it?"* He thought... Kale fixes his cape and straightens his gauntlets, then gives the guard and Yuldurian a wicked, insulted look. The guards return to their positions, as do those who are in attendance, the jury, and all the others in the audience return to their seats and calm themselves to be able to keep themselves seated, but their legs won't stay still, their minds still filled with the dark, ominous thought that he had awakened, that the monster was back from the nightmare he was trapped in, ready to make them a part of that nightmare by tearing them to pieces where they are seated.

'Kale...Now...I demand an answer!' Yuldurian cries aloud.

'I...I must be jumping at shadows, I got too anxious, and didn't think of the consequences, please...Yuldurian, members of the jury, please accept my apologies.' He replies, bowing his head, feeling humiliated.

'Guards....escort...escort the captain away! I do not want to see him within my halls anymore!' Yuldurian commands.

Kale puts up his hand to stop the guards from handling him again. 'There is no need, I can see myself out...your guards better stay to keep an eye on our prisoner here.' He says in a snarky, aristocratic voice. Then he turns and walks down the outstretched hall and one of the doors crack open, held ajar by one of the guards that watches the door. He leaves the court behind him, Yuldurian watches Kale walk away, and at the end of the hallway he almost seemed to disappear past the shadows under a mighty archway before the grand entryway and the palace doors, outside into the pouring rain where his hoft awaits to take him back to Runegard or wherever he may go, Yuldurian did not care.

Yuldurian returns to his former concentration, a judges focus, now that he has rid himself of the young captain who has caused upset to the decision at hand.

'Now...I must ask, did the captain speak true? Did the general indeed, desert and flee away with two convicts...is this so? Is there anyone from the battlefields, any at all who can testify to this? Were his words lies...or words to be believed?' He asks, eyes closed, rubbing his temple feeling a severe pain amassing within his brain.

An injured soldier stands to his feet.

'I was there, I can't explain exactly what it was I saw, but I know the general did indeed cower away from Hondor...but...!' He chokes for a moment as though he just swallowed a large gulp in his throat, he starts to cough and he grabs his head. He recovers himself to speak further.

'I apologize, your honor...as I was saying, while we were binding that monster's hands and legs, a small force went to recover the general's body, thinking he were dead...they reported back and he was indeed seen leaving with what looked like a Civilian man and woman! From what Captain Kale stated...it had to be them!'

'Any other witnesses?!' Yuldurian asks.

There was nothing at first, then another soldier begins to cough as he stands up. 'I second this story! For I was one of the scouts who went to recover the body!'

'...and I as well!' Another soldier stood up.

Yuldurian fell silent, he could not believe what he was hearing. Then, he himself felt the tickle in his throat as he began to cough. He wondered where the Daughter was. Then, from his seat, Lord Rolom stepped forward with a ferocious intensity. After hearing the testimonials, he would speak. Two of his guards followed behind him.

'I have listened to this long enough, and I know what is going on! For my oracles in their towers see the many events that occur within Aura, and they tell me, report to me of these situations. The return of this Gormon as Hondor, the criminals Diin and Nilta escaping north...you know who these two are bound to...don't you?! You know they are bound to the Asyndians in the northern wastes...these Asyndians you know all too well! Diin and Nilta are in league with Dregor Worship...as is General A`deon! The one the captain spoke of...this Duul`ak! He is NOT their leader...it is an Asyndian called Arctalus who is behind this! You know this is true, you know deep down all too well that there is something else here at stake that is bigger than anything that has transpired before!'

Rolom points at Hondor. 'The return of this Gormon, is a sign of something else, he is a warning, a red flag that we must keep a closer eye on...he does not simply sleep...he is waiting, and if we don't finish with this trial...there will be no more waiting...remember the Gray Age..' His voice ends in dread monotone.

Yuldurian feels the air leave him, and the clutch at his throat is too strong. He grasps his heart.

'That...is a word, that has not existed for hundreds of years...' He replies to Rolom.

'Not uttering a word...does not kill it! It only hides it in the shadows, until its time comes again, to strike when it means to!'

From above, the doors burst open, and from beyond the Daughter of Runegard enters. Yuldurian looks to the balcony.

'My lady, it is good to see you have returned from the caves safely. And your people?'

'Sadly many did not return from the caves, but those who have...are well, though their hope has waned greatly, for much destruction has occurred these last months.' She replies. 'I apologize for my lateness...' She continues.

'Do not worry, we were just discussing the fate of General A`deon...' Yuldurian explains.

Her ears seem to lift with eagerness. 'Yes! What of him...'

'One of your captains, Kale, *(a name I will not forget...)*, He growls to himself, 'has been explaining to me, and proven by several eye witness testimonies...'

Rolom bursts into the conversation. '...ah, the Daughter of Runegard...how nice to see you again! I've heard of your plights in the caves...how unfortunate. I bring my condolences from Othetica with me from myself and all my people.' He smiled.

'Hello Lord Rolom, I see you have been able to pry yourself from that ruin you call Othetica...tell me, does your people still eat their own bread off their own plates...or do you take that from them too...and replace it with lies?! What sweet words and promises do you feed them?' She asks in a smart, crude way, despising the serpent tongue of Rolom and his hideous, sneaky politics, bringing the vast civilization of Othetica to its knees under him and his brother's iron fists, stealing the supplies from his people, leaving them nearly poor and vulnerable, at his mercy, even in some cases, taking the wives of the soldiers, and making them his own, because of war debts these brave soldiers have been unable to pay. Having affairs with the women while their husbands' are away in far off lands, wooing them with riches and power. The Daughter...after certain "circumstances arose" removed her people from Othetica, to escape the reign of Rolom and Tolm, taking half the army, those who were loyal to her, and escaped to the refuge of Runegard, where the dying lord accepted her as a daughter, the child he never had...and at his passing, she became the Daughter of Runegard, the ruler of the western lands of Runegard.

'My lady...that is enough...we have a common interest here and an enemy that will be judged by us all... we must stay on the same page, whatever politics stand between you and Lord Rolom...can be settled later as you two see fit...but for now, I will not have these arguments and insults take place when more important things are at hand.' Yuldurian put her in place, and turns to Rolom, warning him to keep his mouth shut, or he would do to them both, what he did to Kale.

"You bitch...how dare you!" He shoots her a fiery glare, she returns the same look, staring at each other eye to eye as the trial continues, they then turn their attention to Yuldurian as he motions for the trial to continue. 'General A`deon...' Rolom interrupts Yuldurian.

'Your general A`deon, is a deserter...a coward! When he was supposed to be leading your armies and protecting your people while they were hiding in caves...he has turned his back on you and your own!' Rolom explains.

The Daughter takes a stern stance. 'I have heard of what my general has done...but my soldiers cannot clearly explain what happened to...'

'...your soldiers have already spoken, they have taken their stance in front of this court and have claimed with all honesty of A`deon's guilt!' Rolom interrupts.

She turns to Yuldurian. 'Is this true...do you believe these testimonies?'

'With all the witnesses and all proof against him...I cannot think otherwise.' Yuldurian replies.

The Daughter of Runegard intervenes.

'Enough of these words...for I have heard enough about what the general has done... I also know him and my armies have stood up to an impossible foe, and have won the day, and there he is, bound before you. If they did not, we would still be in those caves, rotting away, suffering until this monster found us, to finish us off...but to believe General A`deon is in league with such horrible enemies, I will not!' She pounds her fist upon the banister. 'I don't know where General A`deon went, nor what his motives were, but I will send those who I can trust to find him, and bring him back to Runegard. If, Yuldurian will permit?'

Yuldurian furrows his brow. 'I don't like the idea, he sounds like he may be dangerous, I fear for the safety of you and your people being exposed to any further attacks...' The tingly feeling returns, and Yuldurian feels an itch in his throat. '...but he is your general, he is under your...jurisdiction.' Sweat begins to bead under his feathers, and trickle down his forehead. He turns and looks upon Rolom.

'Do you disagree?' He asks.

'The Daughter may do as she sees fit, but I stand by what I have said, that A`deon is dangerous and a threat to all Runegard and Aura. As dangerous as this monster that stands trial before us!' He bows his head in respect to her wishes. 'But mark my words...the general will, and I warn you...if you live long enough to bring him back and unless he is punished...he will do so again and again, he will run, he will flee, he may kill, he may pillage and slaughter. You will not recognize the general if you do find him!' Rolom decrees.

'As long as I have clearance from the high court...that is all I need. What does occur after that...remains to be decided, but if he must be tried, then he will be, I will say no more of the matter.' The Daughter replies to Rolom's disgust of the idea. His eyes simply roll at the matter.

'My most loyal will help me. I will track down the general and get to the bottom of what is going on.' The Daughter says.

'Very well, but when he is returned, he will be tried.' Yuldurian replies. He turns to Rolom. 'Is there anything else you'd wish to add?'

Rolom says nothing as he bows his head, as he and his guards slip back to their seats.

The Daughter of Runegard looks down upon him in terror, sweat pours from her forehead and she is engulfed with perspiration as though she has awakened from the most horrid nightmare imaginable, but she is awake, and Hondor is no nightmare, he is a awakened evil spell-bound into a dark, ominous comatose-state, a slumber he could awaken from at any moment.

She fears this, as do others within the high courtroom. Just as those on the outside, they know, something inside tells them, a little voice, a cry for help, like the instinct of an animal, something is warning them, that those thick chains will not hold the monster back, that brawn helmet will not hold back from the mastication of their bodies, for Hondor preys upon the weak. *"And all bones will shatter! All flesh will melt away! For when Hondor comes...there will be none, to stand in his way, to oppose him, for none...he obeys!"*

'Bring him center!' Yuldurian says, motioning to Hondor. The largest, strongest of the guards push the cart closer to the center court, and the bound Hondor is left in front of all, still surrounded by the army of soldiers that pack and line across the courtroom. The trial has seemed to almost turn into a spectacle to behold, to be entertained, an event within an arena.

'I think everyone here in witness knows what the verdict will be, but then why, why hold trial? Why not kill what should be killed, what should be executed?' Yuldurian takes a deeper breath and prepares to speak.

'I say we butcher this bastard and be done with it!' The eldest of the Oldgaur family stands up and shouts aloud to the judges. 'You Asyndians waste your time with traditions and trials, when we need to just kill him and be down with the matter!' The rest of the clan hoot and grumble in agreement.

Yuldurian motions for him to be silent and sit back down.

'First, we are not barbaric, we are a civilized race, all of us! Asyndians, even Civilians, and even you Gormons...now act like it!' He points to the Oldgaur Clan. 'We are not a mob of low-life scum like those that dwell in the east, we are higher, better than that, we are evolved, and it is our laws, our customs and our system of the way order is run, that we avoid chaos, we avoid complete and utter ruin of us all! And like a civilized group, we will hold trial and we will pass judgment, for without law...we have no order.'

He holds up his fist and continues. 'And, I will point out, that a legion of the best soldiers was placed against this...this one foe! And he would have slaughtered all of them, for this monster came from a war with nothing but a few cuts and deep gashes, yet all who opposed him either came back a corpse or they still lay out there in front of the ruins of Runegard...dead! The few who have returned, and have made it here to join us..I thank you from us of Thylesian and all of Aura for your courage and sacrifice.'

Yuldurian can hear the cries of those loved-ones of the deceased who have come to this place to witness justice be served, begin to cry from Yuldurian's words.

'I want to show my sorrow for those who in witness grieve for their loss.' He comments.

'Now...without further speeches, or delay, for we can afford none...' Yuldurian looks down upon Glasgar, the one they call Hondor, the Gormon's eyes are still closed, his head limp, and the binds still hold back his arms and legs against the X as tight as when they were placed. "How is it he cannot be killed…what kind of unnatural blood…flows in this monster's veins…?"

'Jury!' He cries atop his lungs, pointing attention to the rows of Asyndians perched off to the side of the courtroom, they raise their hands. 'All are in favor of guilty...!'

And the judges agree, the decision, to no one's surprise is guilt.

'Since this beast refuses to die! I hereby sentence, HONDOR, for no living thing with a Gormon name, could be born into this realm with such horrific power, he is to be taken and bound deep within the wastes to the north, beyond the rims of the mountains! Where he will be buried deep within the ice and bound to the prisons under Mirym…!'

Rolom leaps to his feet. 'This is your decision?! That is foolishness! You will find no one willing to travel that great a distance with a being laced with the blood of genocide upon his lips!'

Many in the crowd cry out and agree.

'I say he be taken to the Vaults, for none have breached the Vaults before! They are impenetrable!' Rolom says.

'The Vaults were broken into…' Yuldurian exclaims. 'By Diin and Nilta, or did your oracles not see this? I know for I held their trial that imprisoned them, and if they wanted to, they could do it again, now that they have been freed and are on the run. We cannot keep Hondor so close to the city, it is far, far too risky.'

'I would not see Thylesian turned to ruin as Runegard was.' The Daughter replies.

'Well, what shall we do, what should be done? How can we deal with this threat to not just ourselves and all those in Thylesian, but across all of Aura? What fate can be placed upon a being that seems is impenetrable, a beast that cannot be undone…cannot be killed?!' Yuldurian poses the question, and looks over the stumped faces, a silent courtroom, for no one knows what should be done with this beast. And all eyes were in a stare, all minds were blank, except for they wanted to see this terror brought down, kill him where he stands, drain the black blood from his veins…but they could not answer his question…they did not know how, except for one, they knew of where all the other criminals were taken to be done away with, they knew what could slay, what could bring justice to all of Aura…though those were normal circumstances…this is something different. He silences the rising Oldgaur Clan, for he knows they would attack with their battle axes.

'Oldgaurs, be seated, for I know you would have at him with your axes and hammers, but they will not work!'

"…would it work?" They did not know. The deadliest of foes have been hacked away under their blades, but Hondor…he would be the deadliest they have faced, and it would be a challenge for them, nigh impossible…would they slay him…? No. Or would they simply stop in their tracks from exhaustion, of building fear, irk him to wake up and then they, every one of them, while the others fled, would feel the wrath of his power. But something had to be done, they could not wait much longer, for it was only a matter of time before the creature awakened…they could not afford to linger, action had to be taken.

The whole room is silent.

One of the Asyndians from the jury spoke up about the idea everyone else within Thylesian had in mind. '…what of the blades, what if we place him under the blades…let the teeth of the mountain take him! Let the incisors of Mt. Kar'durgra take him, chew him up…and spit his bones all over!' She exclaims.

One of the soldiers replies. 'I've seen what blades do…they do nothing! His flesh is not normal…it is folly, they will never pierce through him..!'

'The teeth of Mt. Kar'durgra are not made of mere steel and iron…they bear the essence of the Auroras within them…look upon his chest and his shoulder…' She points out to Hondor, motioning to the scar upon his right shoulder and the faint nick across his chest. 'If a sword did that…it proves he can be harmed, I know the blades will go through him, they will rip him to shreds…just as he has done to our own!' She replies, her voice in a steamroller of sureness of the plan.

Rolom snarls at the idea. 'The essence of the Auroras died with them, this plan will not work.' He looks to Yuldurian, who is in thought of the matter.

'…if this were normal matters of execution…I indeed would agree, that this plan would be…as you say, *"folly"*. However, the blades are strong…Agonan used one to cut open the stomach of the Dregor Ram and slice off its head many eons ago, the hide of this creature was said to be impenetrable…' Yuldurian is cut off by a gagging in his throat.

"Yes…continue, your plan will work! The Asyndian woman is right!"

'What was that?!' He cries, he heard someone speak…he swears he did.

Those in the courtroom all look upon him with awkward stares of confusion.

'Please…excuse me.' He takes a moment to rethink, he was just about to proceed with the plan, until…something cut him off, he was about to rethink the idea, but why? It's the only plan they have...the only option that is before them. It will work...he is...sure of it? Then, the Daughter speaks, her voice became louder as she spoke, turning an idea into an important speech, a decision, and the familiar power of her post, her title returned to her.

'I think we should do it!' She exclaims. 'My people, my land, everything has been brought to near eradication...I want to see this beast cut down, cut him down like he cut down my own! I'm in favor...if it does not kill him...I want to see him crawl...see his peeled flesh hit the ground and watch him have to scurry round and pick it up, collect himself, the way my people have to collect the pieces of their dead...!'

She feels the gag hit her throat as well, choking her severely.

"You speak truth my child...I admire your courage! You show more than that groveling Lord of Othetica down here!"

Something, she's not sure what, makes her look down at Rolom, she looks at him in an odd sort of way. What was that voice? *"So...strange, I felt so strange for a moment..."*

Yuldurian regains himself. 'What does the jury say?'

All hands raise, they are in favor.

'...and the judges?'

They nod in agreement. Rolom places his head to the ground, displeased, as he waits for the final judgment to be passed. Then, Rolom feels a choking sensation in the back of his throat, then he too hears the voice. *"Be careful tiny Civilian...your decisions and judgment are insignificant in these matters! I hope I make myself clear!"*

'Yes...yes master...' Rolom whispers to himself.

'Then it is settled…in one hour, this…Gormon will be taken to summits, the pinnacle of Mt. Kar'durgra…and there let him face the wrath of the mountain's jaws!'

"…excellent…a wise choice Master Asyndian…"

The sharp eyes of Yuldurian look around the room, searching out the one who has spoken out of turn.

'Who was that…speak up?! Do you have something to add?!' He looks to Rolom. 'I know it was you…you will speak only when I address you in this court… You will not mock the judgment of my jury or myself! I'll not have you speaking out of turn! Do I make myself clear?!'

Rolom replied, surprised and very insulted. 'I don't know what you're talking about…I said nothing, no one here spoke a word since your judgment of the Gormon has been issued…and I will not be insulted by you, I care not if you are a judge…I am the ruler of Othetica…and I will not tolerate your offense!'

Yuldurian tries to shake the nonsense from his mind. 'The sentence is execution…one hour…have the prisoner ready by then, and we will head by way of the pass.'

'You and yours will go…I for one, will not! I have seen enough of this city and of Asyndians and Gormons, and heard enough of their thoughts on matters!' A burning sensation churns in his guts. Rolom composes himself and motions for his guards and acolytes to follow as they leave the courtroom. Yuldurian watches in anger as they leave, wanting to say something more, but the Civilian is already leaving, just as he would have ordered, his duty as the judge of the high court.

'Gather what troops that are left and chain the beasts back up to the cart…I want Hondor out of here as quick as possible, but carefully…just as he was brought here, we get him out!' Yuldurian commands the nearby Asyndian guard, one of the guards that held back Rolom from reaching Hondor.

He looks to the Daughter who still stands by, unshaken by what has happened. Her Asyndian consort near her side.

'I will have word sent to my guards back at Runegard, that I will be accompanying you north to the execution...'

'Are you certain my lady...Mt. Kar`durgra sits upon the other side of a maze once used for execution by the ancient Asyndians. It has not been used for many a millennium, and many of the traps and creatures that dwelled within have long faded and decayed...but if, if *HE* wakes up....' Yuldurian cautions her, fearing for her safety, the last light of hope for the battered and divided Runegard Civilians. But he looks at her, he looks deep into those eyes, and he knows she is not the damsel many make her out to be, for she has been strong, in one of Runegard's darkest hours, and she has kept her people's spirits up, she has seen them through. He knows, she will not stand idly by, she will refuse the offer, she will not rest, until this foe, this monster is done away with.

She turns to her Asyndian guard that brought her here. 'Return and inform Roúgsver that I will be accompanying Yuldurian to the execution...but keep the counsel secret, I do not wish to get my subjects fearful or excited...they have been through enough.' He bows to her, then walks out the way they came in.

She turns her attention back to Yuldurian, she needn't say a word. Yuldurian knows the answer, just by her stern voice and the determined look she stares with the look of a focused woman, no longer the young lady she has always seemed. She means business, she means to see this through alongside her people.

'Very well, you are strong my lady, stronger than many Civilians of later years these...you show great tribute like the leadership of old, General Cezius Cabriel, King Edrin...these were brave men, but you are a brave woman...and I commend you...'

He gives a small bow in respect to her. She was amazed, never had an Asyndian bowed to a Civilian before...not since the Asyndians, Gormons, and all within Aura...bowed to the Hero of ancient times. He rises.

'We have a special transport you will take, you will stay near me and my Asyndian elite... we will take to the sky to guide the soldiers below while they pull Hondor through the valleys, and to the mountain.' He says to her, and she agrees with a nod to him.

'There is still some time...you have one hour. I will see that you are shown to a room that will be to your fitting, it was built to house Civilian visitors or guests I may have, with steps and doors for you to use and access.' He motions for the guard to come over. 'Escort the Daughter of Runegard to the east wing tower...'

'Yes my lord...' The Asyndian bows to comply with the orders.

'There are items there you can use as you need, clothing, a wash basin, at your disposal. From there, my guard will escort you to the northern courtyard in an hour's time, and then we will be ready to move out.'

She bows to him. The Asyndian walks past and she follows close behind by a few paces. The room she is taken to is of breathtaking architecture, with high white walls on four sides, all furnished with armoire, mirrors, a large separate room where several rows of Civilian clothes have neatly been folded away into marble cubbies, along with an assortment of shoes and boots, leggings, any outfit imaginable. Over in the far corner near the window is the wash basin, carved out of a large pearl, smooth and flawless in its shine, with a bright white cloth of marvelous cotton material, and the water as clear as the purest crystal. The size of the basin is nearly the size of a tub, but sits upon a metal table with decorative curved legs holding it up at the base. She walks over and places her dried, red hands into the warm water and splashes it to her face, the warmth seems to almost lift an impervious weight off of her body, she is for the first time in months, feeling secure...at peace, calm.

Her clothes, the tanned dress covered with soot, dark compared to the bright white of the room, the pale tunic is missing several buttons, torn away from crawling and making her way through and over rocky terrain, and knee high boots tarnished and worn, a large hole exists at the toe of the right boot.

She looks through the massive collection of clothing before her, the decisions within her mind is tremendous and nearly impossible to choose from. She likes the blue, but the green will suit her better, and feels more comfortable. Then, she sees herself, in the large mirror upon the far wall. She looks and sees...a woman covered in dirt, with a face washed clean by the purest water, now clouded by her own filth, no longer pure. The last she looked into a mirror, she saw a young woman...a girl, but these times, these long months have seemed to age her, for it feels as though eternity was passing by, and taking its time, slowing her down, but speeding up the aging, for now she sees an old woman...a hag with crow's feet and dark circles under her tired, pale blue eyes, so pale they almost resemble large moons that glow a dull blue aura, yet the aura was diminishing in them.

Her hair was once a fiery orange, but now seems almost brown like dirt, knotted from being unkempt and neglected.

She hated what she saw, hated what she looked like. She can't beleive she went to the trial looking the way she did, if she knew, she would have put on a new outfit, for she had plenty, but how could she...she has not seen a mirror in months, *HE* broke them all, *HE* shattered them, *HE* burned them....*HE* destroyed them, her palace, her clothing, her realm, her people....*HE* burned everything...took everything and destroyed it, leaving only ruins, leaving only ashes for her to scoop up into her hands and blow her kingdom away like dandelion spores...and watch them float away in the wind. She walks closer to the mirror, and looks in, looks deep into the eyes of that woman she sees, asking question after question...many beginning with *"WHY"* and having no answer.

She clutches both sides of the mirror with tight fists, turning white the harder she grasps the frame. She places her head forward upon the glass, and feels the cool touch of the mirror upon her hot skin. She leans upon the woman and the mirror and they cry...they cry together, wondering why. She then looks into the itchy red eyes, her vision blurred over by tears rushing like waterfalls down her face.

"What is your name...do you even know anymore? Who are you...do you even know anymore...will you always be Daughter...or are you in there...somewhere?"

A loud thump upon the door startles her out of her desperation, her plea for help. The guard calls to her from the other side of the door.

'My lady...I'm sorry to disrupt you, but it almost time to leave...we have to go soon!'

She does not call back...she feels she needs to take her own pace...but how can she think like that, there is an important task at hand! She cannot dally any longer, for it does not matter what her hair looks like, what color the dress is or if the boots match...she is a leader, she needs scars, she needs a dirty face, clothes covered in filth...she is not royalty, her people look to her as someone they can rely upon, someone they can follow, not someone who should rule them. She gets her gear together, for a leader wears gear, not pretty dresses, she is not a queen or princess, she is a leader, a commander, she is the face of her people and their struggle.

She is ready...she is ready to face this foe and see him be tried, punished, executed the way he executed her kingdom and her own. She is ready. Before she heads for the door, she can hear the commotion going on out the window, as the guards and soldiers chant along as they pull the Gormon prisoner and get him ready to leave. She looks out and sees them at work, the time has come, they were ready. She could see the Asyndians and Yuldurian nearby, overlooking the process as they worked in quick fashion and with great pace to prepare everything for the long road, the vast march to Kar`durgra, the faint white shape of a mountain that lays out past the city, along the horizon with the other mountains in the range, but Kar`durgra was the tallest peak among the others, it looms as a white sentinel over the area and surroundings.

The guard knocks again.

'My lady...are you ready?'

She rushes to the door. Her and the Asyndian rejoin the others as the final preparations are in order and they are ready to move out, to take the long voyage to Mt. Kar`durgra, where Glasgar's fate...will be decided.

If only Glasgar knew...what was going on, what fate was about to befall him...if he only knew, but he did not know, how could he, for he was being stalked, he was lost in that black realm, that dark nightmare as he passes through the mirror, but he is not alone, for the shadow has followed him, is haunting him, seeking him out, hunting the Gormon like a hound. What awaited in this realm for Glasgar...he would soon find out, for there is another passage that is worse than death.

Part V:

The Daughter of Runegard

~

The dreams came early to her that night, as she laid her head back, the wind taking her, the sound whistled through her ears, the breeze soothing upon her skin, it was a cool night, but the wind seemed unseasonable warm. She found herself slouching down and laying upon her side, drifting off...

***

She walks out to the end of the causeway, for ahead of her is where the true jewel lays, aside from the brandished opal soldered to an Aeridric chain.

Ah yes, the sacred metal, once unknown to many Civilians and others who have resided within Aura, an extremely rare mineral, once so rare, that its very existence, only lived and was told about in legends, but ever since the mountain, the Forge of Gonun, that was hidden away, deep under the southern seas, had been brought to the surface, it has been discovered by many others, mostly sea-faring traders, merchants, Asyndian scouts, any who passed, tried their hand at getting a chunk or two, for the cost they could sale it for...would be astronomical. And it was...and like anything that is said to be impossible, someone found a way, a Sasparian managed to find himself a loose piece of Aeridric deep under the sea, at the very base way, way down to the molten bottom. He used the piece, and had it crafted into a form of, pick axe, and used this pointed tool to mine the sacred metal, for only Aeridric had a hardness enough to break apart itself, it had been given the nickname, *"The Stone that Takes its Own Life."*

This Sasparian traded big, soon other regions were involved. The Asyndians and the Gormons were first, they tried to keep it a secret from the Civilians, for they did not trust the empire in its recent years. They knew there was some shady politics going on, and an even stronger effort to cover up what they did not want to leak out. Assassinations, hired bedlam among the aristocrats, suicides, shady deals going on between the aristocrats.

But then a younger Asyndian who was involved with the Aeridric ring, sold a very precious piece to one of these greedy aristocrats, the now leader...Rolom, who was purchasing it for one whom he loved the most, and he was to purchase this amulet for a hefty sum, and yet...the Asyndian was almost to pleased to hand it over to the Civilian, but every favor has its cost in some way...nothing is for free.

The Sasparian can't remember the Asyndian's name, but he would never forget those burning eyes as fiery as a burning inferno and feathers, as black as obsidian.

She walks out to the edge of the vast platform, to gaze down upon what will be her jewel...her kingdom to be, to rule over with her soon to be husband, Lord Rolom, who oversees the empire of Othetica. The man who placed the Aeridric chain around her slender neck, her mouth in awe at the tremendous weight and size of the opal at the center of the lavish, hypnotic piece, the jewel gave off a bright glow and was warm upon her chest, the heat soaking in through her blouse and warming her fair skin. She held the jewel up to look closer at it, it was comforting to the touch, it seemed to relax her, put her at ease. She could see her rosy face looking back at her, distorted a bit by the curve of the opal, which is shaped into a sphere. Her hair was fiery then, as red as the embers that glow within the jewel. She was his jewel...that was what he said to her, she is as warm and as beautiful as the eye at her breast...that was what he said to her...that was what he meant.

She pushed her way across country, she found herself running in the dark, the light of the moon was pale and indistinct, the pale eye did not watch over her. She collapsed by the roadside. She found the road, but she did not know how far she had come from Othetica, how long she has been running, she did not know whether she was heading east or west, north or south. It was not cold enough to be heading towards the desolate northern lands where the Mirym once resided, and the air was not so molten...she could not feel the bursts of heat upon her face from the blown gaskets and valves of the Greywaste, of the desolation, the scar left by Reignkiing eons ago, when even the race of Asyndians was still young, and Athilnovia...was the jewel of Aura, until that jewel was crumbled...tarnished and the metal that surrounded...corroded, just as her jewel was...tarnished and corroded, faded away, done away with...exiled by untried justice...exiled by his will, her failure...upon his whim...his orders.

She was his jewel...that was what he said to her, she is as warm and as beautiful as the eye at her breast...that was what he said to her...that was what he meant....before he grabbed her by the wrist...and held her over the edge, held her by the thread of her wrist, just let her go, and she will fade to her doom... *"You will become one with your jewel..."* That was what he said to her...that was what he meant...before he let her go.

She remembers why she felt sick when she looked into the mirror at her reflection...it was not her dirty red hair, browned and grayed with premature age and anxiety, it was not the ugly clothes she found herself wearing, nowhere near as beautiful as the ones in this closet...it was her, it was her and that scar upon her...not just the large incision across her chest, or the large hole in her right arm, where it was swelled with infection for weeks upon end...it was the scar branded upon her that she hated, the scar from Rolom, the scar from Tolm, the scar of being lied to, being chosen for mockery, a trick of the most malevolent sorts. And she fell for it, she was roped in, taken upon the wings of what she saw as an opportunity, for she was chosen from nothing, she had nothing, this was her way...of getting the life she felt she deserved...the life...she thought she wanted, though if only she had seen it coming, seen the darkside of this life raise its deformed head, laughing and swaying, mocking her, taunting her. She was the favorite, of all the women Lord Rolom had taken as his own, taken the wives of soldiers, stole them away...but to him, he was leading them away, drawing them out of their houses, out of the shadows of their sadness, like drawing medicine from an infected wound, and leaving the scar to swell and yellow with the passing days, not being treated, not being tended to in the proper way. But she had no house...she doesn't remember what happened, how long she has been crawling upon her hands and knees through these streets, until she found her way to the capital, where the palace of Lord Rolom stood, the palace built by the Asyndians many, many millenniums ago, built for the Aurora Othetian himself, yet has been rebuilt and reconstructed many times since.

She did not know how long she had been crawling, before she saw a group of women, women she would not beleive to be about her age, they were dressed exquisitely, laughing and giggling, not remembering, almost forgetting their husbands who have been away to battle, many they felt to be dead, never to return to them, to embrace them, and here was a true leader, a ruler that was willing to take them in, and give them whatever their little hearts desired. That which they were missing in their lives...the touch of their husbands, the touch of a man, to take them into their muscular arms and embrace them...or place priceless jewels and treasures at their feet, that works just as well. *(And, for the women who have gone to war...for Othetica, there are none, for Lord Rolom had forbidden women to go to war, only the men, he deemed, where of noble enough strength and valor to go to battle.)*

It was the last guard to spot her. He looked her up and down. It was as though it was meant to be...something...there was a reason she was chosen, but she did not understand why.

'You...you'll do just fine...one of these women got away from us, and I was ordered to bring Lord Rolom six for tonight...yes, we'll just say you fell in the mud and got that dress of yours dirty...!' He laughed at her. He pointed his sword at her, and the other guards came and escorted her into the group with the other women, who looked down at her with queer eyes and odd glances. They did not want to be near her, her smell was awful, the smell of a street urchin, one who has not graced a tub of water for some time. Her outfit was an eyesore to them, a tattered mesh of rags and linens with heavy black dirt stains upon the knees from where she was crawling, from where they found her, on the ground crawling through the streets. Compared to their violet and blues skirts, bright and colorful hues and the glittering makeup upon their faces finished off with a touch of lipstick, she was a mess and not presentable to Lord Rolom. Not even Tolm would want this creature the way she looks now. And this gave the soldier cold feet, made him nervous. He started to second guess his decision as he looked at her compared to the others, she was an outcast, the runt of the litter...this would not do, his plan would never work. He contemplated leaving her behind, but there was no time to go to the brothel across the other side of the city, no...he had to make do with this woman that he had found.

They got to the palace, and she was immediately taken aside, taken around through the servant quarters where she would not be seen, while the others were taken to a grand and luxurious lobby, to be seated and to be spoiled rotten, that is what Lord Rolom always did with *HIS* women, he treated them right.

She lay facing the dirt, this road that seems to go on and on, stretching endlessly in every-which way, and in the dirt, she can see that face, that wretched smile of Lord Rolom and The Steward, his brother Tolm. She tries to pound the dirt, but her arm locks up at the joint, and the pain is too much to bear and she cannot, she lays her arm back down to the cold soil, damp from the rain of the night before, keeping damp from this gray, depressing evening, gray in heart and in mind, reflecting upon the stale sky looming over her head. Her head was throbbing and she did not remember much of what just happened, how long she was knocked out, how far she fell, how many lies were cut upon Lord Rolom's tongue, a slash for every time he called her beautiful, every time he called her his jewel...every time...every time. The more she thought about it, the faster she tried to move, the harder she tried to run, run as far away as she could. She did not see the puddle of dirt water just before her, and her feet leapt and she lost her balance, the sound of the splash echoing in the stale air, the dirt was once again all over her.

The hand maidens to Lord Rolom had striped her down to nothing but her pale, naked skin, tossing her clothes to the large fire pit at the end of this room where they went from white soot to black ash. Her flesh shook, she covered her small breasts with her toned arms. She was quite toned for spending so much time on the streets, begging and surviving on hardly nothing, perhaps it was the strength of pulling herself along to get by. The red hair was dull like corroded copper. The women shoved her into a tub and proceeded to scrub her, almost taking the flesh off, making her skin as red as her hair, but she would be cleaned, she would be ready...she would be pristine, ravishing, only to be made filthy, not once more, but more than she'd like...more than she could handle...but she would turnout all the stronger for it, though if this were a lesson of some kind, she would have avoided it if she could.

The maidens heard the gruff, stern voice of the soldier in their heads *"Make her spotless...make her shine...or else your bodies will hang upside down nicely...with the blood flowing out nice and slowly!"* That laugh, they were terrified of that laugh...she had heard it too, she did not know what it meant, but she could tell by his tone, and the looks on their faces...he meant business, and he meant to kill them if they did not obey.

And she was presented, gift-wrapped in a stunning dress, perfumes that were insatiable and made her smell delicious, her make-up dazzled, and her eyes...her eyes were like jewels... She was his jewel...that was what he told her...he said he loved her, that was what he told her...while they were standing outside, under an autumn sky, where the gray clouds loomed, where those gray clouds forbade, to let the sun shine through.

She would have lifted her head out of the puddle...but she decided to let the water take her, let the murky water drown her...for she felt suffocated in life, so why not let death allow her to breathe, allow her to be in peace. That's what she told herself, that was what she planned to do, that is what she did. She held her head in that puddle of filth and dirt, and rightfully so, that is where she felt she belonged...with the filth that drowns and sinks to the bottom, she felt she could go no lower, this was it for her.

The last breath had long left her lungs, they were dry and felt they were about to collapse, her lungs were filling with water, the time was winding down, her reaction was to lift up her head, to expel this dirt-filled water from her lungs and take a breath of air, her chest was about to burst, her eyes were building, turning red and blood-shot, her face a pale blue. Painful, but drowning was not as painful, not like suffering in life, she would soon be dead, but to live, is like drowning only instead of just dying, she would slowly linger and linger on, keeping the feeling of suffocation upon her chest for the rest of her life, instead of another minute, only another minute, she holds her head down, just a little longer, don't purge this water you swallow, this water will heal your wounds and take you away...take you away from here...to a better realm...you will soon be in a better realm...all went black, the darkness had eclipsed her swollen eyes...and she drifted, limp as a doll lost by a girl in a pond, soon to be forgotten after just a short time passes by, after that little girl becomes an adult and doesn't remember... I don't want to...and a last bubble, the last pocket of air...leaves her throat now filled with water...wanting to choke...wanting to get out.

She walks out to the end of the causeway, for ahead of her is where the true jewel lays, the vast city of Othetica, the jewel of Aura, this pendant of Aura, given to her by Lord Rolom, she to be his bride, she to rule by his side...that was what he said to her...that was what he told her. She stood by the balcony to her room, and looks over the magnificent view, the many people walking through the streets, the vast depth and dimensions of this glorious civilization, how high the towers go, how they seem to touch the clouds above, getting lost within the ethereal mists crowning their heads like mighty lords, like her Lord and soon-to-be husband, a bond, an oath given to her by her Lord...a jewel of fantasy placed around her neck, she looks into it, she sees her reflection, she sees his reflection...a dark shadow passes overhead.

She turns around, startled...to see her man standing there behind her. She smiles, relieved that it was only him. She embraced him, wrapped her arms around his magnificent auburn and magenta robes of silk and velvet, his lavish diadem upon his brow, covering his dark hair.

And yet, there was something odd about the way he looked, his body was cold, the air around him was cold, his smile was gone. It seemed like a different Civilian was standing in front of her. It was a memory she had long suppressed about him, but she did not remember until now...he held his right arm behind his back, and grasped her with his left, he held the flesh of her arm in his hand tight. His grip was not loving, it was harsh and mean, this was not the man she...or was this the true man, the true Civilian she was meeting for the first time.

Yet, as fearful as she was at this new Lord Rolom standing in front of her, it was...it was those eyes that scared her, those two red eyes behind Rolom, the glare of a being standing high upon the ledge near one of the decorative windows of the palace, a fiend who seemed to float, a ghost she thought, some kind of spirit, for she could see right through his black shadow. He was looking down upon them, overseeing Rolom, to do what he has to do.

"I must spill your blood...I must kill you, so the lights will no longer exist...and that I may keep my rule...I would rule under darkened skies, than lose what is mine to the light of a new dawn...'

That is what he said, that is what he was going to do. He did not love her, that was what he said, but that is not what he meant. He meant to kill her, spill her blood where she stands. And that is what...he tried to do...he looked back to this master of his...he raised the knife, the sterling metal, jagged and bent out of a smooth shape, twisted and daemonic was the only way to describe it, except for the symbol upon the hilt, the jewel upon the hilt and the jewel upon her necklace was glowing. She did not understand what was going on, but she knew, by some instinct, that she was the one...but for what, she did not understand why. She broke free of Rolom's grasp and fell backwards, catching herself upon the railing before she could fall. Rolom did not hesitate, he lunged forward and struck her, carving a large scar across her chest. He spilled her blood, but she was not dead, only severely wounded, for the blood seemed to cover the smooth stone beneath their feet. He struck again, this time she moved to far and fell over the railing, grasping it, her feet dangling over the edge. She held on for her life, at least what was left of it. The blood was flowing down her gown, turning the white and sky-blue to a crimson red. The sight of the blood was making her dizzy, she looked down and the streets beneath her dangling legs, it seemed to be all the way down there, an endless fall. Her slipper left her toe, falling from these great heights and shattering upon a roof top, she could not see it, but she heard it. She tried to cry out for help, but her voice could not cry, it only crackled like a broken speaker, she grew weaker and weaker, the more she bled. Her body was cold and the velocity of the wind made her feel frozen and still. Her muscles were weakening, she did not know how much longer she could hang on...it would not be much longer before...

"You...will...fall!" Was the last words she heard, before she could feel the burning pain as he ran the knife across her fingers, and she let go...and the wind took her...and the fall, all went black, all was numb...all was no more to her...as she could see him, rising higher and higher up, as she fell, further and further, until there was nothing...

She doesn't remember how long she fell, how hard she hit the bottom, she forgot, she forgot....all went dark and she forgot. She was scurrying over the landscape, the towers and gates of Othetica was behind her. How did she escape, how did she survive, she doesn't remember, she forgot. Her body was broken, her bleeding dry, a large scar cursed her, marred her body and would be there forever. She got away, that's all she remembers, they would look, but they would not find a body, where there should be a shattered corpse, there was none, for that corpse had escaped...somehow has escaped. Maybe she was supposed to, but why, at that time, she did not understand how or why, she forgot, she doesn't remember what happened after the fall, except when someone had pulled her up, pulled her away from the puddle she was drowning in. She wanted to die, she did not want to continue living this way, the way she had been going. A hand had gripped her by the arm and heaved her up where she found herself laying upon her back, the faded vision of the sky coming into view. Someone had drained the water from her lungs, given her the kiss of life, returned her to this realm before she could fade away.

She then saw the face, the face of a man that had frightened her at first, but his voice was calm, anxious it was, worried, but she noticed a hint of care upon it, the breath was not foul but pleasant to her. She was gagging and coughing from the water, spitting up gallons from her lips like a fountain. Her vision began to clear, and the stars had been out, she must have been running all night. The man leaned her up, he was a Civilian like her, but he spoke in a different drawl, he was from the west. He held her limp, cold body in his arms, wrapping her in his cape to try and warm her. She was scattered, confused, he could see that look in her eyes like a lost animal, not realizing what she had just been through, but he would find out later. He would hear the whole story. The scar upon her chest, her infected arm, he would know soon enough.

He asked her what her name was, but she did not know...she could not remember, she simply shook her head with confusion. She could not remember, she had forgotten, she wasn't even sure if what happened to her was real or just a horrid dream, but the scar was there to remind her...that this was real, this was a nightmare brought to life.

He smiled at her, a warm smile, not the sinister smile of Rolom, not that smile...this smile was tender and comforting to her, but she had to be careful, for comfort could soon become terror in the beat of a heart, a loving heart that could turn black and a smile sinister.

He introduced himself as A`deon...Captain of Runegard, and that they were going to their encampment and that she would be taken care of.

'How you're still alive...I will never know...' That is what he said. But he would know soon enough, he would know later on why she was still alive, and how she was still walking. Another soldier came and they helped her along the road, placing her upon one of their mighty, gallant steeds, standing proud with a braided mane and polished armor, armor like their own, bearing the symbol of Runegard upon their breastplate. She rode with him, while the other soldiers followed him from behind as they galloped slowly off down the road. She only hoped, they were not taking her to meet their Lord...she did not know where she was going, she could barely keep her blurry vision upon the road. Her flesh was quivering from the chill in the air, from the fear of these people who had just picked her up as the others did. All she remembers before falling asleep was hearing the captain's words.

"You are shaking...do not be afraid of us...we will not harm you. You have been though enough, and we will make sure you rest easy tonight. Our soldiers are brave and we will look after you..."

That was what he said, that is what he had promised...and his promised he kept, an honorable man she thought, this Captain A`deon, a fine leader he makes...and that is when she found rest.

***

Lord Rolom is lifted into the air and thrown against the far wall of his palace.

'YOU...WERE SUPPOSED...TO KILL HER!!!' Duul`ak roars, his eyes a fiery blaze of fury and hostility.

'She's...she's dead...she fell from...' Rolom winces with pain and agony, grasping his sprained wrist. Duul`ak hovers over, grapples him and tosses him across the floor to the opposite side.

'SHE'S NOT DEAD! YOUR GUARDS COULD NOT FIND HER!'

'I don't know where she is...please master Naumokron...please...! AHHHH!'

Duul`ak grabs him by the throat and begins to crush Rolom's neck. 'Incompetent fool! Do not call me by that name!'

Rolom grasps for air. 'I'm sorry...I'm...'

'Let him go Naumokron!' Tolm demanded with anger. Duul`ak turns with rage and sees the Steward of Othetica with his blade drawn and several armed soldiers at his side.

'If you're so keen on destroying her, than you go do it!' Tolm yells at the mad Asyndian.

'I cannot reveal myself...not yet! There is Dregor presence hidden in the shadows of this realm...I will not allow myself to be alerted to them...I must find their source, where Maz Dregor has been hiding so I can unleash my ultimate weapon on him...'

'As for both of you...you will do as I have told you, you will find the last blood of the Aurora's and you will kill her! Do as I say!' Duul`ak cries.

'I will not!' Tolm replies.

'How dare you?!' Duul`ak retorts.

'No, don't brother...don't...'

'You cannot just walk in here and throw my brother around and command us like animals. We do not need your help nor power of wealth any more, do we brother?!' Tolm calls to Rolom, who winces with pain as he speaks.

'Don't Tolm...please don't...'

'Step off little Civilian, you don't know who you're dealing with!' Duul`ak threatens Tolm, clenching a red light glowing in his hand.

'We are done with the lady, and we are done with you and your *"monster"*, now I command you to leave this palace, or we will force you out...your influence will no longer shadow our eyes!' Tolm commands to Duul`ak.

Duul`ak spreads his black wings wide and hovers up into the air. The pulsing red light begins to hum as the power within Duul`ak's grasp increases ten-fold. 'Hmmm...killing you now, would be too easy...I will make you suffer, scar you, twist your mind and body into a shape that no eyes can bear to look upon!'

Tolm begins to shake, dropping his shield and sword to the ground. He falls to one knee, grasping his throat for air.

'You will be abhorrent...a living nightmare...you will be shunned and forced to live in the shadows of these dungeons! Lesions will boil upon your many limbs and appendages! Your eyes melted and blind to the light...only the cold, dark bowels of this world will give you any peace, as your mind slows with sloth , your bones crippled. You will never walk upon your legs again, but should you decide to move...you will crawl...crawl like a beast! And like a savage animal...you will hunger for the taste of flesh...sacrifices your brother will stuff your belly with!'

Before the eyes of all within witness, Rolom and their guards, they watch Tolm begin his horrific transformation into something terrible, something without words or definition to explain the metamorphosis he is going through.

'Wear your crown, Steward...prince of death!' Duul`ak mocks under his breath.

Part VI:

Within Darkness

~

And so the daemonic mirror…stares back at Glasgar, and within is a being he can barely recognize, his features are still familiar, a hint of him remains, yet there is something not quite right, his eyes seem hollowed, lifeless, a trance overcomes and dilates the pupils. The Gormon reaches out, curious yet a sense of fear is crawling up his spine, and he tries to fight it, hold it back, yet something unseen overcomes and attempts to take him over. He reaches for the smooth glass, as does his reflection, it to, holds up his hand to reach out as Glasgar reaches in. The mirror ripples as the tides of an ocean, and the tips of his fingers feel cool, yet not wet, a very ominous sensation that none of his senses can describe, or pinpoint a single word, not even his sense of touch can pronounce what it wants to say.

Glasgar passes through the glass, and finds himself within a chaotic realm. A land that waits before him covered in twisted faces and trees that howl and roar, their calls can be heard over the landscape, if that is what you can call such a hellish place. Fire shoots from the mountains and boils sand into glass valleys, carved by the sharp spines of nether-worms that burrow and dig through this tormented land.

Up over the furthest mountains, he feels his eyes deceive him, but it appears that the mountains…the mountain ranges are moving. These are not the mountains spewing lava, these are creatures, hundreds, maybe even thousands…the Terrax, the planet chewers, the swallowers, and the demolishers. These are huge, gigantic lumbering beasts with four thick legs suctioned to the base of the planet, and their body surrounded by a hard exterior, an exoskeleton around their abdominal area, that swerves and convex like a spiral, much like a shell with thorns surrounding and protruding from vast amounts of space and areas around the exterior.

Extended from the front of the shell, is a long, slimy neck, with nothing more than an eyeless, row of teeth and suckers upon the tip, these are the many mouths this thing uses to drain away and chew the life of planets and their systems. The lava that spurts from the pours in the body is a waste, and the slime drizzling from the mouths' is a deadly, corrosive acid used to break down rock, dirt, and forests into a pile of muck and bile to be devoured by these beasts.

The atmosphere above him is hot and the moisture is unbearable to breath. The skies are a sickly pink, not a bright pink, but a bloody, bile-colored pink, and there are no clouds, not even the sense of a sky, yet the atmosphere looks so strange and unnatural to a Gormon's eyes. But are these his eyes. He looks at his hands, and they are not his, they belong to this monster that's here, in this realm with him. Yet his brain, his thoughts still seem to be his, yet his actions are off, not coordinated to what he is doing or where he is going. But how much longer will this last, and his mind succumbs to this atrocity.

He does not know where this body is taking him, but he knows his instincts are not guiding him. The instincts of this beast tromps along over the screaming faces in the sand, he even takes the extra initiative to stop in his tracks, raise his large, massive boot, and trample down into one of the faces. The face cracks open with a ferocious scream of pain and terror, exposing a skull beneath and the blood splashes everywhere, covering Glasgar, no….Hondor's leg in hot, boiling blood. He feels no pain, for this monster does not know what mortal flesh wounds are and how they can cause pain to the one inflicted upon.

Hondor continues along his way. Over the ridge, he spots a beacon of light in the distance, Hondor, even what's left of Glasgar, seems to be enticed, and they seem to hear a voice that calls to them, beckoning them.

The beacon hovers high above a thick wall of black mist, a haze of putrid gases and fumes. The march across the dead ash plains is long and seems unending, no destination in sight, but the light still beckons, the light still calls, screaming from far away for them to hurry.

The mists begin to surround and consume them, as Hondor's enormous shape is lost in the haze. He can see nothing around for eternity, for this place seems more forsaken and barren than the ashen plains of skulls and lost remains. The only aspects to be found in these gloomy wisps of hysterical smoke, are the sounds of maddening laughter, the roars of something ferocious, and the hands with horned knuckles, decapitated bodies scampering about, and wingless Asyndians slamming into the ground, exploding into piles of guts and gore upon impact as their bones and spines shatter.

This does not faze Hondor one bit, he keeps to his path, lost in his own world, a world which may even be more altered than this world, a world lost in the stomach of chaos and darkness, being slowly eaten away by gigantic monstrosities.

They clear the black mist, and in front of them some hundred yards, stands a large structure, a tower and around the base is a construct of gears and wheels, at the left of the tower base is a fortress connected by what looks like veins that pumps a ghastly, horrendous liquid. At the right of the base, opposite of this fortress, is a huge hunk of muscle covered with the same pumps and veins, as the same black fluid pumps through, but this seems to be the heart, the contraption that filters the fluid through the tower and the fortress. There is silence around them, the only sound is the moans and howls of the fetid, living world in the background far off in the distance miles and miles away, screaming as the Terrax devour this world.

This is the palace of nightmares and the tower of empty empathy, the heart of chaos resides here. The heart is enormous, much larger than any structure to anything ever conceived by thought or mind. The beacon of light above spins in an elliptical orbit around a beam of power, and this power surrounds the pounding heart in a field of electrical pulses, keeping it beating, keeping the vile heart alive.

It is this sound that entrances Hondor, even Glasgar into a state of awe and wonder, this heart has a voice, it seems to talk to them, not in any tones or formed language or syllables, but pulses and beats. Glasgar can feel a tearing, which seems odd, for he had felt nothing until now, as though he were being separated, torn away from the flesh of this monster. The head turned and he could see two right arms, as one arm was pulling away, or is it being shoved, kicked out. Then Glasgar's torso began to peel back like a chunk of skin, and then his right leg stepped out. From behind the black mists closed around them, and the dark hands grabbed for Glasgar's wrist and body, arms and legs then rip him away from Hondor, unmade these two beings from one.

Glasgar is thrown to the ground upon his face, as the black soil expands outwards in a sharp gust from impact. He manages to get to his hands and knees, then struggles to get to his feet. He looks up, and up and stares into the burning red embers of Hondor's eyes.

The beast stands motionless, except for the expansion of his ribs when he inhales and exhales. The veins in his arms pump, and his fists are held together with a grip far superior to a vice. Hondor feels a scent, a strong smell of great and horrible power, looks over off to his right. Glasgar follows and sees he is looking at a glowing patch of red force trying to break through the black soot. The force is expanding outwards as though the ground were breathing, something is trying to break through. Hondor lurches over to the spot, looks down at the heaving glow for a moment, then shoves his hand down into the ground, piercing the crust as blood and bile and gore explodes and splatters everywhere. Molten bright liquid covers his arm.

Hondor rips open the ground, tearing away the crust in huge, thick pieces. Glasgar sees his chance and runs at the beast with full force, trying to drive him into the liquid. He hits the cold flesh of Hondor, it's as though he were running into a thick steel wall, not even budging or moving Hondor. The beast turns and looks upon this pathetic Gormon creature. A sharp puff of smoke emits from beneath the massive horned structure of Hondor's helmet, indicating the creatures breathing. The breathing is hollow and gruff much like a snorting predator before the prey is slaughtered. Hondor grasps Glasgar by the throat and slowly lifts him into the air, crunching the spine and bone with his clenched hand squeezing more and more, tightening like a noose around the thick iron neck of Glasgar.

He swings Glasgar around, and then, at that moment... Glasgar could see into the eyes of this bloodless, lifeless cold beast. There is nothing there to see, just two black voids that stretch far back into a darker time, darker memories, and a darker past of an unnatural existence. Yet, that was it, that was the answer, that is what resides within this creature, for he is nothing more than an empty golem, an automaton of pain and hurt.

Glasgar could feel the grip around his neck loosen, the fingers were unraveling. He glances down as he hovers over the boiling pool of rotting, bone decaying plasma. He wanted to scream, cry out, but his Gormon blood would not allow for this. The hand is open, Hondor lets Glasgar go, but the Gormon reaches out and latches onto the gauntlet with his right hand, while his body dangles. He can feel the heat of the smoke begin to blister his legs as it rises up and starts to consume him. He tries to grasp hold with the other hand, but he cannot.

Hondor observes the futile act, rears back his other arm, and strikes one fierce blow upon Glasgar's ribs, breaking open the mold of his skin, just as he broke open the ash-covered ground to reach this molten pit. Blood pours away from Glasgar's body as he begins to weaken, feel faint, death is closing in, yet he still will not give up. Glasgar tries to reach up one last time, one last pull with all his strength he has left to muster, but it is useless, his right arm gives away, and he falls, dipped into the boiling pit of bile as the liquid boils over his flesh and consumes him alive.

Hondor looks on as the juices cook and melt the flesh of Glasgar. The skin is baked red and the flesh has swelled. He grasps a rustic pole, an ancient spear from some long lost, forgotten civilization. He plunges it into the boiling pit, pierces it through Glasgar's body and with one arm, fishes the body out, as pieces of flesh just fall from the bones, the eyes are gone and the armor disintegrated.

Hondor tosses the body to the ground, grabs a large axe that lays upon a pile of skeletal beasts and beings that have decayed away, and then, in a crude, grotesque manner…begins to butcher the boiled corpse, chopping away the arms and legs, and piece by piece, tears away at the skin and muscle, eating the Gormon meat down to the bone, absorbing Glasgar's essence, taking his power, absorbing him in the foulest manner. Blood trickles down Hondor's chin, and flesh hangs from the corner of his mouth.

After the gruesome feast was over, and nothing more than a pile of mutilated bones remained of Glasgar. Hondor casts aside the axe and the last bone he just cleared of meat down to the last piece of gristle. He turns his attention now to the heart, the heart that thunders…the heart that commands. The pulses radiate across the putrid atmosphere and the fevered air.

He wipes his face with a quick sweep across his mouth, the crusted hair upon his arm already covered in dry splatters of blood and from the vile boiling pits from whence he pulled out the boiled flesh of Glasgar. Now, he sets his sights, his blood-red vision upon the black pumping muscle, the heart that pumps, and the heart that thuds with earthquakes and sonic waves that pulsates across the dome of this thick, sweaty atmosphere.

He hears the voice once more, the voice calling to his mind, his instincts…the voice that calls himself master. But, if Hondor had a voice, he would say, *"Hondor has no master…"*

"Come…come to the tower…!" This voice says.

Hondor turns upwards, watching the shadows pass across from window to window of the opaque citadel, the shadow of spread wings engulfs the spire as the master watches from above with crystal-red eyes piercing into Hondor's mind.

"Come to the tower…I command you…I, who created you, you are but the creation and I…I am the creator, the master…!" The voice demands with a sterner, threatening tone.

And Hondor complies. He walks to the entrance of the tower, faced with a mighty door surrounded by a convex hexagonal cage, and within are two double doors with the crest of a knotted serpent wrapped tightly around the slice down the middle where the doors will open once this bothersome snake is torn and ripped away from the roots of steel where it is encased and wrapped around.

Hondor reaches his hands out to grasp the cage, to tear apart the metal like a thin net of lace, and after that, to grab the neck of that serpent and rip it out, tear off the head, and devour the corpse. But the gates open up to him, and as he approaches the serpents upon the locked door, they come to life, hiss at the massive being closing in towards them, ready to kill, and the serpents unwind and crawl away into large black slots that have been drilled into opposite sides of the walls where the doors were riveted on eons ago.

"There will be no need for such brutality now…in time, you will once again get your hands upon flesh and metal, you will kill, you will feast…for that, is your purpose. Now, ascend the stairs and we will communicate further…" The voice says, ending with a low heckle of laughter.

The double doors open inward, and Hondor enters into the dark abyss before him, catching his massive boot upon the first obsidian stair and starts to ascend upwards into the hellish domain of his master's lair.

"…Hondor…has no master…for no one controls Hondor…!"

Part VII:

The Maze Left Behind

~

Mt. Kar'durgra rests at the very northern tip of Thylesian, rising far above, a white mountain of impressive stature in comparison to the low-lying royal tundra's that line the boarders of Aura's many regions where ancient Asyndian maps were used to separate the lands sections. The road through the mountains leading to the base of Kar'durgra is a winding maze of valleys, with shallow rivers flowing through, forking towards the center, at the heart where the valleys meet and intersect.

The valleys pose as a maze where Asyndians would send their prisoners within and let loose some form of creature as a way of punishment for them, but a game for the Asyndians. This was done for many eons until Yuldurian put a stop to this and ordered for all prisoners to be locked away inside the dungeons far beneath the Vaults under Thylesian. The passage is impossible, for Asyndians must watch from above and guide them along on the right path to take.

If they were to become cornered within the reaches of the furthest valley…and if *He* were to awaken…the hood of the executed would be placed upon the other heads.

It will be about a day's journey by the right path, as long as the Asyndians maintain the coordinates and watch them below, and they maintain an even speed, it may take them less time to reach the base of Kar'durgra, the tower of peaks that rises several thousand feet above them straight ahead. They could fly, but to prep the hofts and the flying prison for transport will take several days, and this is time they cannot afford.

It has been some time since the maze has been used as punishment, the creatures that once ran through these valleys and preyed upon these helpless prisoners that they tracked, trapped in the corner, then torn to pieces, have, like the prisoners, long been deceased, nothing more than dust upon Thylesian's winds and the ashes left from bones have spread through the valley.

(...that...is what they thought...)

The road ahead of them would be long and arduous, filled with the danger they keep with them, this Gormon monster they keep strapped to this cart they pull at the center of the army, ahead of the twenty or so battleaxes and shields at the rear, along with a handful of the best bowmen and archers they could assemble, at the head in the front are rows of foot soldiers bearing pikes and just behind the war-hammers and broadswords.

Yuldurian flies over head with his two Asyndian guards, and The Daughter is kept nearby, she sits upon a carrier being lifted by two stout Asyndians supporting her fragile weight, barely reaching the hundred pound mark. She looks over to Yuldurian, who looks back at her, each giving a look saying the same thing, *"...I hope this works..."* She turns her attention below and watches the army travel along, pulling the cart at what feels like a snail's pace, she grows more and more anxious by the minutes that pass, wanting this to be over and done with, salt thrown over her shoulder, in the past, what's done is done, and will never return. Her legs rock back and forth, shaking the carrier.

'Please be careful, my lady…it is a long fall and we don't want to drop you.' One of the Asyndian guards warns her, bracing the handle tighter in his grasp.

'Is this really necessary…I'd prefer to be walking along the trail with my people!' She says.

'Yuldurian insists…' The Asyndian replies.

She sighs…and watches below as the armies trudge on. Her Asyndian carriers circle around, several more Asyndians drift upon the winds in a perimeter above, keeping an eye on the paths. Some move further ahead to look over the area, those Asyndians are led by Yuldurian who travels with them, he is the one who traces the road, leads the armies along. The scouts at the lead of the soldiers on foot follows the instructions of the Asyndians above, and travels along after their path. She rides upon a hoft with a lush, silver mane, keeping her eye to the skies, as well as on the road, watching the silent valleys, hollow and empty. Nothing stirs, nothing remains of the mazes past, except for the skeletal remains of the prisoners and beasts that have been lost before, and either died trying to find their way out or were hunted down by the predators that tracked them for game, to satisfy their blood-thirsty hunger.

The maze was meant to keep in…and not let out, from above, the Daughter can see the various traps and pits, turns and twists, the grand design, the ingenuity of the layout is before her. Off over to the north, Mount Kar`durgra stood a white colossus overlooking the maze, a guardian and watcher over those who would struggle within. It had no compassion for them, it had no thought or mind, but it has seen many deaths, many slaughters, many who have suffered. It has watched since the beginning when the maze was first being built, to when the first prisoner was placed within these walls. It remembers, a mass of legs, the sects, the twitching, blood sucking pincers of the migs, closed in around him, and with their crab-like claws, tore him to pieces and devoured all remains leaving nothing left but a bloodstain on the cobbled path.

Back then the maze had roads built of new stone, but have long become broken and weathered, eroded over by dirt, debris and bones. The walls slanted at a twenty degree angle, slick marble, unable to be climbed, now filled with cracks and some holes. Every few turns there are placed false caverns, making one think they can hide, but it is only a trap. There are also false traps laid about here and there, laid with smooth spikes that kill in an instant, they were once covered up after every prisoner, but are now exposed, the spikes a dull orange and red, rusted and thick with ancient blood that has never been removed.

The leader upon her silver hoft keeps careful track of her directions received from Yuldurian, turning left, going straight a few paces sometimes miles, going right, and following the halts and stops, where Yuldurian decides to himself the best course of action to take, the best way to go onward. The Daughter watches and observes the communication between the two. Then, she sees a spark in the corner of her eye, a faint glint. She turns and there, at the crown of Mount Kar`durgra, the faint glint reflects off of the blades…the pinnacle of execution.

But she did not linger on the sight of the mountain top for long, for something from below, drew her attention to the valley, to the unsettling sight and sound of the disbanding ranks of soldiers from here to there. She heard the shouts emanating from the soldiers stark words. *"…there all around us!…"* Another soldier yells, *"…Where did they come from…."*

Someone shouts, *"....over there...more are coming!"* The Daughter traces the cliffs and canyons over to the northwest and northeast, where hordes of many foes were closing in around them, large black, stocky beasts, hulking upon huge muscular legs, clawing up dirt as they rush in with lightning speed, covered in rugged thorns and scales, slobbering jowls leave thick goop in heaps of puddles, and their razor teeth chatter and clamor for flesh and red meat, living, warm meat fresh off the bone. The Civilian of the group never had a chance, several of these beasts pounced upon her and the silver-mane hoft, and tore each of them to pieces in starved, excited furry, biting her head from her shoulders and tearing the hoft's struggling limbs away, it screamed and neighed until one of the beasts ripped into the jugular to silence the hoft.

Before one of the soldiers was attacked, he noticed these things had milk-white eyes, they were either nocturnal or blind, smelling the blood of their dead and wounded. But how would they have found out if no one was bleeding, how did they find the army...why are these things here, this place is supposed to be deserted. What if they....what if they wake up....what if they wake *HIM* up!

The beasts finished with the Civilian woman and her silver hoft, and chased the rest of the armies about. They leap upon them, scratch at their heavy armor and claw at their faces, biting and slashing about. The Asyndians draw their bows and take out dozens of the creatures and toss their spears, impaling them along the crumbled marble valley. A handful of the soldiers, mainly Civilian and Gormon have lost their lives to the ferocious claws and jaws, while piles of the black beasts rise higher and higher, scattered about the trenches.

The Daughter watches the entire battle in horror that this was happening. She watches as they drive the beasts away and finish rounding them up, slaying the remainder of them. She looks off to her right, she feels a cold air brush against her, a different wind than the Asyndians' wings that keep her aloft. She feels....eyes upon her, an icy glare feels her over with cold fingers. A presence is around her that makes her feels sick, makes her gag.

She looks around, and at first she sees nothing, but the sickness was getting worse, was she allergic to the flight, which seemed impossible, for she has soared through the skies before. But she knew, she knew something was there, intuition of some kind was warning her, telling her heart with each thud and beat, getting faster and faster, her nerves creeping up over her heart, trying to get the better of her, but her fears seem to be manipulated, as though she has lost control. She stirs about, shaking the vessel that carries her.

'My lady...please stop!' The Asyndian yells.

She feels the overwhelming power of anxiety grip her in a black hand of shadow, she is overtaken. The Asyndians watch as she thrashes around, not even speaking, but grunting, almost as a child would when not getting her way. She can see, but she cannot comprehend what she is doing, what is going on, what is causing her to act this way.

'My lady...STOP!' The other Asyndian reaches out to clutch her, but in an unforeseen, unsuspecting attack, she retaliates against them. They cannot keep hold of the clawing woman, as they lose grip of the carrier and she falls towards the maze below. Yuldurian turns his attention away from the battle and sees the Daughter's body, falling like a limp ragdoll. The Asyndians let go of the carrier, and the weight of the silver contraption falls with the Daughter. Yuldurian soars closer, watching as the Asyndian guards dive for her, and they vanish upon the other side of the marble walls several leagues away. He wants to rush over, but he hears someone call his name, he turns...

***

The Daughter stirs, she hears many voices, but no lips move, she sees nothing but darkness surrounding her. Her head is building with pressure, as though it is about to explode... *"or is something trying to get in, crawl within her skull and take over...the voice is here. The figure is trying to get through to her..."* Her eyes, soar and covered with a light film of dust, start to open. There is another voice near her.

'Look, she's alive! She's alright!'

She can barely see them from her blurred vision, but above them, the skies seem to be growing darker, the clouds swell over like a sickening tumor of dead flesh, corroded and black from decay. She can hear this horrible clicking noise in their throats, something is throttling their throats, crushing their lungs, as they clench at their throats with desperation, dying of some outside asphyxiation. The click is getting loader, the sound intensifying, their heads seem to almost be turning...around, to face what's behind them, but their bodies don't move...their heads, turning as though on a rusted axel, turning in a direction the head was not meant to. The clicking sound, stops for a moment, and then... *SNAP!*...*SNAP!*...both of their necks, one and then the other, is twisted the full one hundred and eighty degrees around, and they let out with their last gasp for life, this horrible gurgle, brief and cut short, only a second. The Daughter watches their bodies go limp and fall like their skeleton had been ripped out, and though the puppeteer reached behind, unzipped their latex skin and feathers, and pulled out the armature which supported their stance and structure.

She rolls over in the dirt and sees their bodies lying there, chest down upon the ground, necks twisted. The one is looking directly into her terrified face, the eyes bulged out and bloodshot, faded and lifeless, the tongue slung over the bottom part of the beak, a faint colorless pink, almost white, the tongue was dry of any saliva and moisture. Yet, it was the eyes that frightened her the most, the eyes seemed to scream at her, warn her... *"MY LADY! He...he is here...RUN! MY LADY....RUN AWAY...!"*

But she could not run, her body felt locked to the ground, bound by heavy chains. The wind began to pick up around her, and she heard more voices, where these voices were coming from...whose they were...she could not tell. They seemed to be all around her and closing in, she could almost taste the hot air upon her face as vile lips pressed against her skin and pours. The air is getting tighter, she feels her breath getting heavy. As she returns to her familiar state before the fall, confusion and terror is setting in at greater increments within her mind. *"...Why are the Asyndians dead? The carrier...is smashed to pieces upon the...ground...why am I on the ground...what has happened here...where am I? Where is...?"*

She could not finish her sentence, but she was thinking about where the others are...and most importantly, where was Hondor...is he still bound? Is he still asleep? Where was everyone?

She could not finish her thought, for fear of the shadow that is approaching her from the left, maybe two-three yards from where she lays. And from the right...another shadow is also drawing near. But the shadow, the silhouette of a tall, lithe man sent a tingling chill down her spine, the shadow of this figure on her right is aloft, gliding across the rustic marble, not walking like the other is...not like the figure to the right...he is floating, hovering with the winds. His loose clothing, flowing almost translucent like his pale flesh, his hair as black as his eyes, with grey sideburns covering his pointed ears, and thin gray eyebrows like starved caterpillars hovering over his wide glare. This man she has never seen, this wicked looking man that could have only existed within the realms of a nightmare *(or a realm of an even darker sort)*. But the other figure, his face shone through the winds, she knew him…it was Kale, the young captain of Runegard, only now he is wearing a suit of armor of blacker sorts, ebony as midnight, and giving off a fierce ruby aura that smells vile in the air and leaves a bad taste on the wind.

"I remember you child, I remember when you were just the seed in your mother's stomach…!"

This voice, this voice that speaks these words…these syllables, the tone in *"it's voice"*, for this sound, it was not the sound of a Civilian, nor any Gormon or Asyndian. What was this…this thing that spoke to her. The language, the language was so foreign, yet she could hear it clearly, almost right next to her, but it was inside her, inside the most dangerous, most vulnerable area…the mind. The closer Kale and the figure came to her, the louder the voice seemed to echo throughout her skull. The fear, the sweating, the nerves, the claustrophobia is becoming too much for her to handle. The words echoed in her brain… *"I remember you child…"* It spoke these words like an elder, an ancient, one who has existed for millenniums, even eons. She found herself speaking, but her lips were not moving, she is looking directly into the dark eyes of the figure floating aloft over the stale remains of the marble, her body still numb and unmovable, but he could do it, if he so chooses to, he could have used those eyes, the power within his mind to lift her up, lift her up forever like a parent lifts a newborn, with no effort, and in his case, without care for her safety. Her mouth would not open, yet the words were there.

"Who speaks to me…is it you Kale…?" She shifts her eyes to the other figure. *"…or, is it you, the one who gives me the most terror…do you speak of this terror, this language that would slaughter innocence with a jagged blade across the belly*

and throat, then leave it to gurgle on its own blood...is it you?!"

The two stand over her, looking down at her. Kale places his black helmet of some twisted soul upon his face, he draws the glowing blade from its scabbard. Kale speaks from under the helmet, the twisted flesh of the beast upon the surface glares upon her, then looks to the figure aloft.

"Now...the time is now...is it not?!" His tone is deep, much deeper than when he stood before the court at Thylesian.

The Daughter's eyes grow wide at the sound of her impending death, to be stuck like an animal upon the jagged blade held within Kale's hand. *"They do mean to stick my belly..."* She thinks back to what she said a moment ago. And the figure reads her thoughts.

"Yes...yes we mean too...I have felt your presence...you will not see the end of this nightmare to come...I will not allow it, and Hondor's time will come to...but I will let the Asyndian have his fun for a little while...just, a little while longer...but you, you are easy, you are timid, but to your people you are a beacon, a bright light to lead them...and all lights, when she has come...must be put out, like a flame to the ice, cold wind...now Kale...destroy her..."

At the signal, Kale raises the sword high above his head, and with a swift stroke, the sword falls. The Daughter braces herself to be slaughtered, she can feel the wind of the blade approaching her, she winces, then...a loud clang of metallic objects echoes in the howling wind, not bellowing into a storm.

She keeps her eyes closed, wondering what has happened, yet afraid...not sure what to expect, and anxious...why is she still breathing, she should be dead. She can hear a struggle over the wind, and her eyes open, covering them from the harsh wind, peeking in between her fingers to see the rough battle going on, Yuldurian has his staff raised against Kale's sword, pushing him back, away from her. The other figure watches in silence as the two duel, not an emotion upon his face, except for an empty smile, a sinister grin.

The two battled fiercely, until Yuldurian had knocked the blade away from Kale, and he was down upon his knees, beaten by the Asyndian. Then, that is when Yuldurian hears that sly voice from behind.

'Congratulations master Yuldurian...you have proved what I have known all along...that this once captain of Runegard, has weakness, a big weakness...he claims to be a stalwart swordsman, the best in the realm, and he can't even take down an Asyndian judge, an aristocrat no less!' He laughs to himself. 'He is nothing more than a big mouth, but I gave him a fair chance, and yet he still proves my point, that weakness can and will betray you, it will fail you! And it has failed him indeed...sorry to delay you, but you may kill him now!' The figure says with step in his words, trying to coax the Asyndian into getting along and killing the Civilian as fast as possible so he can move on with his agenda.

Yuldurian looks at the staff he holds to Kale's throat, then looks into the Civilian's eyes, and the weakness was showing through, he was terrified of what will happen to him now, not from Yuldurian, but from the figure in the flowing, pale clothing. Yuldurian thinks for a moment, then he hears faint words muttering from shaking lips, Kale is speaking under his breath, almost sobbing and trying to hold it back, trying not to show what is already obvious, he is indeed a coward hiding behind fancy armor and saber.

'...please....please...kill me, master Yuldurian...please kill me...if you don't...he will do terrible things to me, worse than anything imaginable in this realm...please...'

When Kale said *"this realm"*, something about that line stirred the Asyndian's guts and clouded his mind in a storm. He turned to the translucent, pale figure with black eyes and a smile as wide as a shark just before it tears apart the flesh of its prey. Yuldurian looks into those black beads and could almost see the mists forming in his mind and around his being, sucking the warmth from his blood.

"It...it's not possible...how could this be so...?" He thought to himself. And unknowing to him, the figure knew what he was thinking as well, and his brows furrowed into a sinister glare. He was waiting, waiting for Yuldurian to strike the final blow.

'Well...are you not going to kill him, this... nuisance, this feeble Civilian, useless and weak...did he not disturb your court...didn't he attack you now...does he not deserve judgment? Hmm...well from what I've observed, I feel that his judgment...is death! And if you will not execute him, then I will!'

The Daughter watches in horror, as the figure grasps the wind, and tosses Yuldurian away towards the wall with one arm, and with the other, he lifts Kale up into the air, Kale grasping at his throat, trying to force the invisible hand from his neck, but it is no use, he will never free himself from the death grip that is upon him. Then something happened that left the two in utter shock, and brought forth into this world, what Yuldurian had feared...behind Kale's uplifted, struggling body, a black vortex opened, a perfect, vertical rectangle that glistened like a mirror, and upon the inside was the reflection of some form of altered dimension, a world of abomination where horrible screams and cries of foreign entities and frightful species of deformed and decrepit monsters roamed aimlessly...and starved.

As the doorway opened, the sounds upon the inside, within the altered world, were coming closer, they could smell Kale's blood, they could smell his fear, and they were coming, they were pacing faster and faster towards the faint gray light that has opened within their realm, and they could see the worm struggling upon the line, and the jagged toothed creatures took to the bait, fighting one another, struggling to get there first, and be the first ones to sample the blood and take the bite. The amorphic shapes in the dark piled over top of one another and grappled their way through, and they clutched something, whatever this thing is, they had hold, and they were pulling in.

Kale could feel claws grasp around him, hands that were large and monstrous, grappling..fighting for his flesh, one hand is tearing at the shoulder nearly ripping his arm off, and the other clutching the ankle. He could feel his tendons tearing, and the pain was searing and hot like a torch. The other claws, hands, and amorphous tentacles were wrapping around his waist and clutching at the armor, trying to get a grip upon him to pull him in to begin the feast. The clawing continued and continued, they could not budge him, for it is the grinning man that is keeping him within this world, using him like a puppet, toying with him, torturing and playing with his fears. Kale is screaming at the top of his vocals, his voice growing more and more hoarse, and his crying becoming nothing more than a crackle like a busted speaker.

The Daughter is covering her eyes, she cannot bear to look upon the sight. Then, the creatures, they slid away, and disappeared back through the door. There was no sound for a brief moment. Did the creatures give up, just to leave their feast hanging there to rot away, a waste of meat...or is it something else, did something frighten them away, for when the smaller scavengers find the carcass, the prey...they attract the unwanted attention, of something even bigger. Kale could hear as the silence within the black world behind him, turned into something alive, as there is a low gurgle, and a gulping slush of throat, then a roar. Kale is dropped to the ground, landing upon his hands and knees. The roar is there, right near him. He stands to his feet, sweat pouring from his brow and glistening in his raven hair. He begins to cry, followed by a whimper.

'No...please no...'

"Go on Kale...cry! Cry like a child...! For crying stirs the blood...for blood runs thicker, in the mouth of the beast!" The figure's vocals roar deep and in long intervals, his eyes glowing with a piercing blue light, and the wind picks up more. The wind blows Kale closer to the doorway, the abysmal abyss before him yawns open, ready for the feast.

'I don't...I don't want to go in...' He cries.

"Oh, but there is no choice...!" The figure laughs back, but his voice reverberated with the sounds of many laughs, of many voices upon his slender, lashing tongue.

The portal roars, and then from the black, a large fanged hand reaches out, five massive fingers close around Kale, clutching his armor, and the bones can be heard snapping and popping as the fiend squeezes him tighter and tighter. Kale screaming uncontrollably from the pain, from the terror, from the fear and weakness. Kale's yelling and pleading echoes along as the hand pulls him through, and soon the screams fade out into the distance of that vast and endless darkness. And the moment he was gone, the doorway closes shut like jaws that have been opened to long, closing with a snap and a brief flash of bright cataclysmic light and the smell of burning in the air, as though a fire had just been smothered out, and the smoke was still lingering in the air, the smell still strong, not yet dulled by the air surrounding them.

Yuldurian holds his hand over his face and turns away. The Daughter catches looks with the fiend, the cause of Kale's demise. That...that smile still locked upon his face. She tries to move her arm, and to her surprise, she is able to move, her arms her legs, she is able to stand to her feet, yet her leg is limp and twisted, but the bones are not crunching and tearing with pain, they are not broken, for her Asyndian guardian was able to catch her in time before her head was splattered upon the marble road like a sacrifice, an offering to some idol of gore and bloodshed.

The figure holds his arms out and his robe spreads open, sleeves flail in the winds like the Asyndians' wings, ready to fly, but he is already flying, floating higher and higher upwards, commanding the storms, feet pointed down, his body in a crucifixion form. The Daughter can feel the noise in her mind, the high pitched sonic noise that is shaking the world around her, causing ripples in time and sound, avalanches, hurricanes building into typhoons and twisters attacking the land. She clutches her head, leaning forward, teetering upon the edge of a yawning abyss that seems to be opening before her. A little too far...and she will fall. *"You will...fall!"*

'AHHHH...please...stop this!' She screams, she cries.

"Your people see a figure of courage, a light of bravery, a leader...someone to DIE for! Your Nightmares shall bleed, infection will erupt from your womb, you will crawl upon your hands and knees, driveling...slobbering...pleading begging as you are now, begging for death, for me...for US to devour your weakness and spit you back out into a world of Chaos, where only strength rules!"

The wind almost takes her down, the struggle in her mind becomes too much to bear as she starts to collapse, and the abyss calls to her, welcomes her, as she lets herself go, gives herself away freely...just as she gave herself to Rolom, to

Tolm...she gives herself....to Chaos, she will do so, if it means the end to this travesty plaguing her mind, if it means the death of the Gormon, Glasgar! She gave herself for riches before being tossed away...now she will be willing to give herself to Chaos, if it makes the weakness, the pain go away.

"...I am the...call me The Daughter...that is not my..." And her body goes limp, but does not fall, for Yuldurian reaches out and catches her, lifting off into the air upon his great white wings. Yuldurian does not look back, but can hear the final words upon his lips, the lips of his mind, the roaring echo radiates inside Yuldurian's head. The Daughter can hear it too. It sounded as though all other sounds had muted, and all time slowed down to a crawl... *(She would crawl upon her hands and knees...she would beg, she would be easy...)*

"Take care...my Lady, for tainted are your visions, black your dreams will be, you shall see me, of many faces, of many terrors, we will be watching you...death and decay surrounds you. For I will be preying on your mind...and, in your waking world, your precious jewel, you will have to deal with the consequences you will soon unleash...for an even darker terror has been brewing for many years, many millenniums...many eons...your Runegard has only felt the taste of what you are about to unleash...what is about to occur, worse than the ages in grey...worse than the ages in black, a shadow will pour over every one of you, and will swallow all in its wake. WE were just the beginning, for the end is almost near...in fact, much nearer to you than you may think...you are about to awaken from its slumber...a power that should not exist, but does and will...and I will sit back from afar, and I will laugh, as he hunts all of you down, and one after the other, each of your races, your civilizations will crumble, and the bones will be tossed away...for when HE awakens...ah, that Asyndian was a clever one, and smart to hide this secret from us...only there will be nothing left of this world when HE is

through with it...and now darkness passes fast...and the end will come to pass..."

The voice laughs, then continues with one final line.

"HE can have this realm, once his food is gone, he shall starve...for we have another universe, and since we cannot have this one, then you shall join ours..."

And in a wisp of blue sparks and thunder, the figure vanishes.

Yuldurian returns to regroup with the others as soon as he can, gripping the Daughter tightly within his arms, coddling her like a child...for that is what has happened, that is what they do, those from the black void, for the taint of them, the Dregor...a name that Yuldurian has not thought of in ages, since the first Aura War, since the days of the...Hexagus Lords...but when he said *"WE"*, was it possible, could they still be existing...within one?! One entity! And the gray clouds within his thoughts, were growing black, the penumbra scale was sliding closer to the abysmal inevitability, of another universe, no question he was talking about the realm upon the other side, the one that has been long protected from by the Auroras, but the Auroras have long since departed this realm, passing over into the realms of Arla, the realms of light...except for one, the last Aurora that has been long lost in legend and existence, for he has not been seen since the final battle at the Second Grey Age, or what was supposed to be the last battle.

Could they have returned, from what Yuldurian was thinking and connecting the thoughts within his mind, it seemed more than possible, that all this time has been moving closer to Aura, and for over two hundred years, it would be close...too close, for there is no one to protect them now from what will happen, when the realm of Aura will be swallowed by total darkness...and in the middle of it all...a rift has been torn open, a link has been made, or has always been here and only laying dormant until recent events have awakened it...and...and this beast, this terror bearing the resemblance of the once imprisoned Gormon criminal called Glasgar, now his name whispers in dread upon every, trembling lip as Hondor, a name lost with the Auroras in legend, just as old, but more deadly, more terrible, more powerful. Who or what created this monster...is unknown and without answer, an answer that has probably long died and vanished with Agonan, the last Aurora when he went to Raukmar and was never heard of again.

Yet, this Hondor...this ancient terror has been brought back, for this was no ordinary Gormon, only the power held within a ancient evil could overcome and bring down an entire empire and its army...there was no other explanation for Glasgar's wicked strength and endurance that is not found in that great a number within his Gormon blood, for other blood has to be flowing within his veins to cause that much devastation and terror.

"And all bones will shatter! All flesh will melt away!

For when Hondor comes...there will be none,

to stand in his way,

to oppose him, for none...he obeys!"

Yuldurian looks back to the weeping, the hypnotized, entranced enticement upon The Daughter's face. He soars over the lowlands of the maze and can see the recuperating army just over the far ridge, gathering themselves together, reforming their ranks. Glasgar has not been phased, still locked away within his slumber.

"*... for when HE awakens...*" That voice of the Dregor fiend still echoes in his mind.

"I hope he never shall...I will see this execution be his end!" Yuldurian thinks to himself.

He lands and is approached by several soldiers that have been handling the forward guard alongside their lead who rode upon her silver hoft, yet now both are being collected their pieces to be placed into a makeshift ditch to be buried with the other dead.

'MY LORD! What were those creature?! These mazes are ancient, they're supposed to be deserted, long empty and no longer in use! Where did they come from?!' They cry among their group, prodding Yuldurian for answers as to what is going on. Then they look to the limp woman-like child in his arms, they see the Daughter, held there, her head next to his chest.

'Will she be alright! Where are the others...?!'

'She is in shock form the fall...she'll be fine!' Yuldurian replies. *(But will she...? And how will he explain what happened to the others when he was not there in time, to see their necks get twisted, he was not there in time to save them...but he saved her...or did he, can he?)*

'And what of the prisoner...I can't take it no more, I cannot bear to be in his shadow any longer, and the sky is growing darker and darker by the minute! I once heard tales of the mountains over in Runegard, that they have creatures there that burrow in the ground and will come out once the sky has been completely drained of light! Is that to happen?! Will this monster's shadow cause the rocks to open and swallow us whole! What is going on?!' Another soldier was becoming hysterical.

'Be silent! All of you! I have suspicions upon my mind, that is all I have right now, suspicions and guesses, but the more that is happening, the more these suspicions are closer to becoming truths! I just saw something...something over on the other sides of this maze that has proven something to me...but..'

The crowds begin to yell again. *"Tell us...tell us...what is it...what did you see...!"*

'BUT...I have no time to go into full detail! For now, we must get to the peaks of Kar`durgra so we can see this through, so we can deal with one situation , then and only then can we move on to the next! I will explain everything that I know in time, but that time is not now! For now, get these beasts moving and lets continue...these creatures will not bother us anymore...and this I know! The threat is not gone, but it has been dealt with, dealt with long enough to give us the brief moment we need to continue, we have to continue...'

'What are they?! If this place is abandoned, where did they come from...surely they didn't just appear!' One of the soldiers asks.

Should Yuldurian tell them? He thought to himself, for they have enough fear in the shadow of Glasgar...but if he told them that these beasts that attacked them, was nothing more than a diversion for something much larger at work...how could he explain the reasons for such chaotic, destructive forces such as the Dregor, and with little time to explain. Why must their frightened minds know now, right this minute? He said he would explain later, when there is more time...but was there, or would they only be cutting their time in half, or down to a fourth of what they started with. They were there, they are so close, the base of the mountain is just around the corner. Why could they not wait after they have dealt with this threat that stood right next to them, tormenting them, terrifying them, causing everyone to rest with one eye open and one hand on their weapons, ready to toss them aside and run...run screaming into the night, running in fear under a starless night sky. And they appear out of nowhere...he turns away from the soldier, and glances back...a look that verges between the answer of *"I'm not sure...maybe...that is the correct answer."*

Yuldurian's attention is drawn away from the gaping shock of the soldiers' faces, and is leering towards one of the cliffs overlooking the maze, where he sees a large black shape fly away towards the east, a large black bird, no it was larger... *"An Asyndian...could it have been...?"*

'A raven's look...curse us all!' One of the soldier's say as she gulps through her helmet, swallowing the cold stiff air.

'That...is no raven...' Yuldurian mumbles under his breath. 'Is the cart ready to be moved?!'

'We're ready...!' A voice replies.

'What of the dead...?' Another soldier asks.

Yuldurian looks over at the Asyndians who gather the Civilian's pieces as well as the silver hoft. He then sees the dead Gormons and Civilians tossed against the rocks and walls, blood covering their chewed up bodies, with pieces of armor laying within puddles of blood splattered about the marble road. The pile of dead beasts stands as a small hill to their backs.

'Leave them...if we don't get up there...' He points up to where the blades sit upon the crown of the mountain, 'Then we will join the rest of our brethren down here...and we too, will sleep upon the cold marble...where many have rested before...'

Part VIII:

Mt. Kar`durgra

~

The gray, slate mountain stands before them, the road ahead of them seems to point at an angle going vertical straight up, rising higher and higher as though the mountain were shifting and stretching its boundaries, and at the very top…is where they would find their final destination, there salvation to end this reign of terror, to bring down the beast, to slay the tyrant whose horror hangs upon the shoulders of every soldier, every Civilian, every Gormon and Asyndian, every presence that resides within the realm of Aura, for his danger will spread if the execution is not administered, every village and del, every city, town, empire, all the realm will crumble and burn, every living thing will be slaughtered and devoured if he is not executed. They must hurry, they must reach the top before he reawakens, for those chains and bonds will not hold him back, they will not be able to hold this monster back, he will tear through them like parchment, for none will stand in his way.

One of the soldiers swear they saw a twitch, this has placed fear and panic upon them all. Whether he did or not, they were not going to take the risk, they would rather face a hundred more of those minions instead of dealing with this unstoppable titan once more. And still in the back of their

147

minds lingered that one thought other than Hondor's awakening…is the thought of the manner of execution…they were not even sure if this will work, it was not in any way a fool-proof plan, would this work, would it stop him? They didn't know, but they did not know what else they could do. Their hands are bound, in chains thicker than the ones around Hondor's wrists and neck, they just needed to think about reaching the top, that is all they had to do, just reach the top and from that point, they would proceed with the next step, just take this road through the pass and up the cliff face and reach the top. Time has been darkening, the gray clouds brooding over them, taunting them, and mocking them, though not as threatening as the shadow, the aura that emanates from Hondor's black sleep and decayed visions in his mind. For if he awakens…if he awakens.

The day seems the longest ever, and the shades of night is not far off, though by how dark the sky has been of late, day and night, didn't even matter anymore, there is no more sense for its existence, for darkness is Hondor and the night was his dreams, his sick dreams of the realm he was lost in, for the more the shadows rearrange upon his face, the cold-blooded warrior shows through and the Gormon called Glasgar, is fading away after each and every passing hour that goes by unmonitored.

The Daughter is still unconscious, held still in Yuldurian's grasp, for he will watch her, he will protect her through this, and he will have to wake her, he will not let the punishment of her reckoning, her terror go unwitnessed. He will make sure she is awake to see Hondor's end come to pass, and maybe…then maybe, the realm can move on into a brighter age where the skies will not be so gray. The armies rally forth, the beasts pull their load…for they have a mountain to climb.

Yuldurian sticks to the ground and walks alongside the other troops, he will not risk having the Daughter fall again, he will not see it come to pass once more. Whether by ground or by air, to assume any safe passage would be foolish, for if these creatures still lingered about the maze, if they were given access into this realm by Dregor means, then what awaited them through these cliffs and high passes, they did not want to find out, they did not want to know, they only want to be finished. The men and women are restless, they have had enough lingering in the shadow of this creature they pull with them, more of a beast than the ones that pull him along. They want to return home to be with their loved ones, though their homes and their city, their empire has been destroyed by him…they were sick of all of this, they want the peaceful times to return. The frustration could been seen in their worn, tired eyes…they were through, and climbing this mountain towards their hope and final solution, is still no favor in the grand scheme of things. They just want to be done.

They see a faint gleam upon the crown of the mountain, not a gleam of light, but of some essence of power. The air was light, not thick with the stench of death or stale blood in the air. Unlike the maze, which has been run-down and forsaken, covered with the stench of justice and sweat from fear, the land up here upon these peaks seemed untouched by the presence of time and the litter of imprints from the living, a cleansed ghost land. They reached the higher planes, the cart wheels cry to a halt in the silence that looms over them, and the tall and mighty contraption stands before them. Held upon sturdy metal beams, at the center, is a massive pendulum, sitting idly by, waiting for the feast to be brought forth.

The blades gave off a brooding, foul display, lingering under the storm clouds, a sentinel watching, a guardian standing watch at the gates of death's twilight, gazing on with lifeless eyes as the cart draws nearer. Yuldurian stays behind a ways as the rest of the soldiers guide the beasts ahead, pulling the cart to their destination. They stop short of this sacrificial juggernaut, a symbol of Asyndian execution. The history for this death contraption, is very young, a brief puff of flame in the vast, burning inferno of Aura's lifespan. For Yuldurian remembers the first, and only execution to occur here, two hundred years ago...he can still hear the chain being pulled back, as the jagged pendulum is being pulled, hoisted back by two guardians pulling thick, chrome chains upon each side, hoisting the blade, the reversed sickle, the jagged smile of its many teeth, rearing back, the creaking pull of metal against metal, the sound of the axles and pulley turning. He could still see the blade held skywards at an angle pointed outwards, ready and waiting patiently. Yuldurian gave the signal, and they pulled the switch, the blade slung forward...and that's when the rivers of red flooded his mind, and placed his memory under a cloak of gushing blood...the sight was terrible to behold...a terrible fate...for a terrible essence bound within a Sasparian marauder who deserved what happened to him, for what he did.

This setup seemed very similar, the sky, the weather, the circumstances, it seemed as though history were replaying before his very eyes. He is silent, thinking to himself, momentarily lost in this flashback, this time trap within his mind. He is caught off-guard by one of the soldiers approaching him just off to the side in front of him.

'Your honor...shall we prepare the Teeth...shall we make ready to commence?'

Yuldurian nods. 'Let's get this over with.'

Yuldurian sets her upon the ground, he calls to her ear, trying to wake her. Her eyes flutter, as she stirs with movement, awakening to the dark skies, the lifeless gray cluster of doom above her.

'My lady…my lady…we are here…my lady…'

She can hear Yuldurian's voice calling to her, yet she can still see…*HIS* face in her mind…that pale, lithe face…and those deep, red eyes…sunk within the shadows that surrounded him. She awakens to feel relieved at seeing the Asyndian judge kneeling above her. She sits up, keeping herself steady so she does not become dizzy. Her hands cup around her face and rubbing the sweat of fear from her cheeks, her mind lost in confusion, as she awakens from this trance. The sound is muffled to her ears, but she can hear it as well as Yuldurian and all the other soldiers. She turns her head to follow the sound, the ticking of the gears, and the whine of the mechanism in operation. The sound brought a shutter to her heart, she looks over and watches as the crescent shaped blade is being hoisted high into the air, being prepared, placed into striking position. The machine stops, and there the blade sits, lingering in the air, a metallic moon of bad omen, a sign of the terror to come. Terror for Glasgar…for Hondor. Even though the blade is being used to destroy this foul Gormon monster…there was something about the words in the darkness of her memories that still lingered within.

(…for when HE awakens…ah, that Asyndian was a clever one, and smart to hide this secret from us…only there will be nothing left of this world when HE is through with it…and now darkness passes fast…and the end will come to pass…)

'Is it time?' She asks, rubbing the sorrow and the fatigue from her thoughts and from her eyes.

'We are almost ready, the blade has been pulled back and is in place, the teeth have been maintained and polished, to be ready for this time…for I had a suspicion, a haunting suspicion that this time would come…and now maybe, just maybe, we can put this all to rest, though the blood has stained...and the scent will never wash away.'

Yuldurian helps her to her feet, and escorts her over to where she will stand at the base of this executioner's device, as Yuldurian, as judge, will pass the final judgment, though she wishes they would just pull the lever already...maybe, maybe she will, she wants to, she's thinking about it...because what if he wakes up during the speech, and all this effort, was for nothing.

'Yuldurian...that man, I remember seeing a Civilian with dark eyes, who seemed to pierce my mind, he looked...he looked so familiar to me as though I had seen him before, in a dream or nightmare...who was he? He...he had to be a ghost, for I could not see none but his eyes, for my eyes glanced straight through him, white robes and a clean tunic that was aloft, floated in the wind.'

Her voice is still confused, she still seems lost, but Yuldurian senses her familiar, woman strength is returning fast, and there is much she doesn't understand, not the way the Asyndian's do, for they were around when it happened, when the Grey Age had occurred, many of his kind had seen both the chaos of Reignkiing and the Final War...there is much he must tell her, but there is no time now, yet he must let her know what's at stake, what true meaning this Gormon prisoner has in the fate of Aura...what his intentions are being used for, because his ferocity is deadly, when you add the deadly minds of two Dregor spawns who know how to use that ferocity and command it to their will. The ultimate weapon...for Hondor has been brought back as some sort of ancient weapon from an ancient time, yet the Dregor said that Hondor was not here yet, and the Asyndian was behind this...and the only Asyndian vile enough was the ancient Naumokron...but he has been deceased now for thousands of years, since he was last seen in Aura.

'When this is all over with, when the deed is done...then I will tell you what is transpiring, and what that Civilian is...for it is more complex than the way this appears upon the surface...' He replies.

A voice calls from over by the pendulum. They are moving Glasgar into position, preparing the final stages of the execution. One of the Gormon soldiers is guiding the handlers as they steer and control the beasts, leading them where to go.

'To the left...left...LEFT I SAID! Now, a little to the right...a little more...'

The beasts pull the cart across the rocks and stone laden crown of these cold peaks, for night is upon their backs, creeping with the sleek movements of an ancient Raumkat, primitive and feral, unlike the elite Raumkat warriors that patrol the far southwest badlands of Aura. And that dead eye lingers, full of craters yet its soft nightlight glow cannot penetrate through the black abysmal wall of clouds. Torches have been lit and placed about the area upon stands that have remained here for the past hundreds of years, ancient braziers upon polished brass polls holding the flickering waves of red and orange, with yellow and sparks of highlights as the flames crackle with the night and dance in the wind. They light the way to the end of the execution upon the last remnants of this darkened day, and may the light shine through the black clouds when the morning sun rises at dawn.

The Daughter watches as the cart is drawn forward...slowly, slowly, the anxiousness is becoming too much, *"Just be over with...just die...why can't he just die...!"* The beasts grunt and snort, for they too have had enough, they have been pulling this cart for the last few days, and have pulled enough. By the toss of their reins and rattle of their harnesses and leashes that hold them to their chore, she can sympathize, for this creature has in some way, affected everyone...is a burden to everyone. Just want him to die, just want to see him gone...done away with. Just kill him already! *"Why can't they just kill him already!"*She grasps and folds her arms, the breeze claws at her thin clothes and dress, nipping through and biting at her fair skin. The wind moves her hair to the other shoulder with its many fingers. She rubs her arm to warm herself, she rubs her arms anxiously, *"...just kill him already...and be done with it!"*

'RIGHT THERE...STOP!' The soldier yells. In her thoughts, she didn't realize that the cart is ,lined up, the cart has been stopped, the beasts have done their job and now they release them from their chains. And now...it is time for them, to do their job and pass the final judgment.

'Your Honor...Yuldurian, we are ready, the prisoner is in position and the blade is ready when you give the signal.' One of the Asyndian soldiers calls.

Yuldurian looks to her, and she back at him. He nods to her, they are ready, she is ready to get this over with. Finally, she will see this monster come to justice.

'Get to you positions...I will read the last rights!' He calls, and like clockwork, they gather round and get to where they need to go, they find a place to get a good sight of the massacre that is to occur.

Part IX:

Unleashed

~

And all are ready, ready to hear the final words, the soldiers stand by, waiting...and as soon as those final words are read, they will pull the leaver, they will all watch on as the blade slices through the Gormon, as they kill the Gormon criminal, Glasgar will be slain...and the legend, the terror of Hondor will be laid to rest.

Or will he, will they be able to destroy him, will this plan work? And if it doesn't work, if this will awaken him...they could not think about that anymore, the same thought they've been pondering in their minds over and over since this terror attacked, just charged across the farmlands outside of Runegard, tearing apart homes, devouring livestock and leaving the bones. Blood stains upon his face and drenched and tangled within his beard, as well as leftover chunks of flesh and skin, wool and leather hides. Upon sight of the aftermath, it appeared like a tornado, a voracious vortex of razor storms tore across the country to decimate the grasslands and fields.

But now, enough was enough, Yuldurian reads the last words of Asyndian court tradition, and then the prisoner is executed. It was a simple matter...this will be very simple.

"This has been easy...far too easy..."

And Yuldurian wondered to himself...*"if this Gormon were being controlled by his overlord, then why not unleash him now, why is the puppeteer waiting to put on his show, bring out the fire and desolation...we were all there in the courtroom, all leaders of each realm, why not then, why is this creature asleep, lost in somber and dark twisted corridors of the mind...for what purpose does this serve, only to allow him...to allow Glasgar to be brought so close to his demise...the legend, the reign of terror is about to end...isn't it?"*

There is enough to think about, there will be no consequences, they will succeed, and if the master of this creature is waiting, he will be too late, he already is. Yuldurian speaks to the sky, to the wind and across the world. He doesn't need his book of laws to remember the rights from the passage, he remembers them, the ancient code that was once used as the final rights of Athilnovia.

Yuldurian's words recall back to that day all those many years ago, when he read the words of execution against the Sasparian marauder...and then the lever was pulled. Words and blade brought justice on that day, as it would today.

'Today...we bring to this place, for crimes against all of Aura, and the desolation of Runegard...for the death of thousands...I call to this place, Hondor...for today your crimes, your reign shall be...'

Before the final rights can be finished...the pressure becomes too much, and the Daughter rushes forward. The guards cannot act quickly enough, she clutches the switch, pulls the lever away, and the chain falls from grace. The blade, the many teeth of the pendulum blade lets go, swings through the air with a swish, slicing away the air and sky in between it and its target, the sleeping, unsuspecting Gormon, chained and bound, his fate is coming in the wisp of the breath of the wind.

And all seems to slow, time slows to a crawl, as everything moves in slow motion, millions of light-years backwards in time, for the Daughter can see everything, every moment pass across her eyes, she can see what she has done. The guards grasp her trying to pull her back, trying to get her away before the blades of Kar`durgra make their mark and tear into Glasgar's flesh.

(...Glasgar could feel a tearing, which seemed odd, for he had felt nothing until now, as though he were being separated, torn away from the flesh of this monster...)

And the flesh of Glasgar is sliced away, the shell of Hondor has been severed, spliced open wide. And the blood showers, pouring down upon those within the area. The guts and innards, bones and bowels of the Gormon splatter across the rocky surface, painting the ground crimson. Splinters of the remaining chains lay scattered about to each side left and right. All around cover their eyes from the shower of gore, faces are covered and drip blood. They open their eyes to see, and raise their heads to overlook the scene of this ghastly execution.

"What happened...is it over? Is the terror finally over?"

When they opened their eyes, they want him to be gone, they want him to be dead...they want this all to be forgotten, left in the dark voids of the past...but it never will, the memory, the gruesome scene will always be there, lingering in their minds to forever haunt them until their final days come to claim them.

And what is it they see...nothing more than a sliced mountain of flesh splayed down the middle, with the arms twitching and the nerves convulsing abound. Many of the soldiers near the blade move around to get a closer look, and by their faces, through their eyes, Glasgar is dead.

Amidst the chaotic mesh of blood and pile of flesh and splintered armor, the remains cease for a time. The ranks move closer, one draws forward his spear, and pokes the grotesque scene, and picks up one of the massive pauldrons upon the end. Its weight is tremendous by the shock upon his eyes, not expecting to need help from two other soldiers to help him swing it over so they could examine it closer. One of the soldiers jumps away, a burly woman who screams in a deep shriek with curses that follow. She points furiously to the pile of Glasgar's remains.

'There…it moves…the bastard still moves!'

She is not crazy, they all look…they all gasp in awe, Yuldurian, all of them. There is a loud scream, it is coming from the Daughter of Runegard…she is screaming, crying her eyes into floods.

'NO, this can't be…this cannot be…why won't you die…JUST DIE!'

She rushes over blindly, not away with fear, but out of anger and rage, filled with the retribution of all her slain people, all those she lost, Civilians…as well as Asyndians and Gormons who followed her, looked to her for leadership, not to a queen or princess, but an honest to goodness leader. And she would pull through, she would not play the part but be the part. She will tear the rest of Glasgar apart, she will cease this half-life and splatter the rest of his remains everywhere, more than they already are. She'll grapple and fight with them and then jump over a cliff if she must, she will do it…because she's a leader, a protector, she is the defender of her people and she will persevere. She has taken a fall before, then another…and she will take a third if she must, she will by all of the dead Auroras, by all her living survivors…she will.

She charges, her clothes flutter behind her from the wind of her force, her clothes splattered by the impact of the teeth upon the bound corpus of Glasgar, giving them the tint of pink and a light maroon from the drying blood, but she will get bloodier, she will jump into that pile of guts and finish off what's left. She lunges forward, her fists in claws, ready to grasp until a force grasps her right arm as she raises it above her head. She turns ready to fight them off, she doesn't care who they are, and no one will stop her from slaying the rest of this beast. She sees the glimpse of white, feels the rough feathers of the Asyndian. Her fiery eyes meet the glaring opals within Yuldurian's face and can see the reflection of a monster in the making within them, a savage force that has all but lost her senses.

She's taken aback and must recollect herself, trying to calm herself but she cannot, the anxiety and blood has boiled over. Even Yuldurian's glare cannot subdue this new beast that has grown inside of her, built up from the heart below. She could have struck him, she could have lunged, *"Get away from me…let me go you winged abomination…"* She wanted to, she would take care of the Asyndian, as well as anyone else who would dare get in her way…then she would go for the pile of flesh that moves, the pile of pierced and slashed flesh that…grows. Something is growing, something rattles and clanks as it rises from its sarco ashes, its flesh tomb.

Yuldurian looks over her shoulder. She can see the terror building within his eyes as a dark force, a shape is rising. She can hear the brittle friction of bone rubbing together, the creek and whine of joints, her neck and spine revolving. Is it the sound of her neck turning, holding back, refusing to see, to look upon the dread that lurks behind her…or is it the figure she sees in Yuldurian's eyes, the figure of bone and darkness, the hanging innards arising from Glasgar's mutilated carcass?

A voice cries from the back of the ranks.

'IT'S HIM, IT'S HIM! Hondor has awakened! Hondor has returned!'

The foul yawn of the titanic skeletal being roars across the mountain top. The teeth of Kar`durgra rattle. Wasting no time, a call to arms is made, but they all try to run, they all try to flee. The massive hands of the charred, ash-colored bones lunge outward and grasp the metallic structure of the Teeth of Kar`durgra, he pulls himself out from this pile of flesh, the wall of a Gormon body that has kept the monstrosity a prisoner, held back the true ferocity of a creature bred for the purpose, for mass death and slaying. They were only gazing upon these bones, these dark bones that would lay the foundation of what's to come next, with just a slight hint of the guts, spleen, lungs and some veins wrapped around the ribs and spine. But it is the eyes, the hollow eyes which pierce through as black, lifeless pits, two yawning realms followed through these wormholes of black mass.

It did not speak, there are no vocals emitting from the rotten jaw, there is only a roar, a roar that turns their blood cold, a chilled wind that pierces worse than a storm of icy rain and sleet, and leaving a scar worse than the black, burning touch of frostbite. A scar that would linger on a dead corpse… *"For Hondor has come…and none shall stand in his way."*

And the Daughter stands without words, for not even a scream could be called from her dry, crackled throat, nor could the tears of a thousand fears release from her eyes, for they too, were terrified in presence of this monstrous figure of bone and dominion before them all.

Hondor grasps the bars of the structure tighter and rips it away from the ground it has been bolted into. The bolts and screws and metal goes array as the Teeth of Kar`durgra lands off to the side. The skeleton of Hondor stands a towering fifteen feet high, far above the brawn, mountainous Oldgaur Clan, the brothers who stand some eight to nine feet tall.

'We're not afraid!' The eldest of the brothers cries at the top of his lungs so that the mountain shakes, and the others grunted back in agreement, but…they should stand down, they should back away.

They charge all at once, their hefty maces, hammers, and battle axes drawn for war, drawn for blood and to break those black bones of this fiend.

With one massive swipe of his arm, he clears them away, a swat, and they scatter round and are flung through the air. Hondor steps out of the flesh and takes his first steps in this realm, for the time has been eons, millennia's, epochs since the horror, the legend of Hondor has been told, a tale of blood and slaughter, a once legendary figure of death and demise, a warrior with no empathy, no emotion, only the drive to kill, the drive to destroy *"The one who claims title as the new Destroyer…the true Destroyer…"*

One of the brothers scurries to his feet, reels back his hammer and charges forth alone, but before he can make the strike, the black hand of bleached bone grips him. The Gormon struggles to break free and drops the hammer as it's tossed to the side of the crown of this peak. The Gormon screams and curses the bestial skeleton, Hondor pulls back and with a strong whip, releases and sends the Gormon brother screaming through the sky and over the mountain as he careens out of sight, spiraling down and down and down, the speed of his raggeled body twisting and turning, and the only sound that resonates from below, is the sound of shattered metal, the splash of blood, and the crunch of splintered bones snapping upon impact, and before that, the horrible scream that echoes through the valley. The brothers rush again, a battle cry rushes from the shaking of their adrenaline-filled bodies as the brothers charge with vengeance and retribution for their fallen sibling. *"We'll scatter the bastard, break his limbs apart and toss 'em over the ledge!"* Is what they thought.

The next brother, his head down like a ram, charges, and Hondor reaches for the Teeth, the massive crescent-shaped blade, his legs wobble off balance but he is able to maintain his monstrous stance over the futile attempt to stop him. Hondor brings the blade around…first the upper torso of the Gormon falls, then the legs collapse, separated with the swiftest speed. The other brothers hold back their line, the soldiers surround the area, and many have fled, dropped their weapons and shields, and fled, their hoft's with them. The remaining that stay, those who were foolish enough to linger, cower back, trembling with fear.

But there is no time to be afraid, for Hondor wastes no time, for there are many and Hondor has his prey lined up…and the slaughter begins. The voice ticks in his head, echoing in his ear.

"You will kill them…slaughter them all! "Hondor…your prey approaches…you will slaughter them, you will devour them!" The voice of Naumokron commands.

Hondor obeys himself, Hondor obeys only his own instincts. And if it's his instincts that tell him to kill, if it's his appetite that hungers for the flesh, and his throat is quenched by the consumption of blood down his throat, then he will kill, he will feast, he will strip the meat, and raise the chalice filled with the blood of all, and toast in victory.

But there is no time to stand idly by, for Hondor can almost taste the flesh and leaps against the ranks of soldiers. There is no defense, Hondor hacks and slashes away, tearing apart the armor and skin, blood splatters across the rocks and dirt, the gravel is painted a crimson-maroon tint, shadowed by all the guts and gore. Screams and pain break the sky as more darkness flows through the gray clouds and the black sky of night fills the pours, fills the empty spaces where shadows lay darkest, are now darker.

And after the slaughter is done, there are only two that stand last...The Daughter, and by her side, Yuldurian.

Hondor stares down upon them, the permanent grin from his dark skull, grinds back and forth, the teeth screech, cry and whine. He stares at them not just as food, as the feast, but through another set of eyes, they are the barrier, the enemies in his way.

The Daughter is locked in fear, looking up into his hollow eye sockets, her body paralyzed, but something catches Yuldurian's eye, a tiny, bright flash of red. Yuldurian looks down to the rib cage, something is crawling among the stomach and liver, and coiling around the large arteries and then hangs from the bottom rib, looking back at the Asyndian, and the many, tiny red eyes flash again. It is a mig, yet the wind across its eight legs and the smell it leaves in the air, amongst the putrid rancid odor of death and a million cadavers from Hondor, is a smell not from this realm, the presence is all wrong, the same presence that surrounded the Civilian in white, surrounds these two atrocities.

"Hondor...is here...summoned back from the lost artifices planned long ago by Dregor worship. On that day, many, many eons ago...I stood next to the Asyndian with black feathers...and I smelled this same foul odor all over the room in

his presence...the choking, the thick air amongst us all, as though a powerful trance was being placed over us all..."

'So, this is how the Ancient One returns?!' Yuldurian says aloud.

The creature hisses and leaps into the air, as a spiraling trail of smoking shadow follows, and the tiny mig creature, begins to change its form, the many legs turn to two arms, two legs, and the black wings spread outwards, and the leftovers fall to the ground beneath his feet. And after just the blink of an eye, the Ancient One...Naumokron, the bringer of Reignkiing, stands before them. An aura of dark flames surrounds him. Hondor stands behind and looks on curiously, for the master has appeared into the realm of flesh, and flesh can be cut. All their flesh can be cut and hacked...flesh can be devoured.

'Yes...it is I. You were always clever since you were a young Asyndian, but a coward as well, fleeing from Reignkiing, from the collapse of Athilnovia...and now I can feel it in your wings and bones, they tremble, you wish to grasp your darling Civilian here and flee from Hondor's presence, for Hondor is me, I who brought him back, I who control him...for none of you, shall remain! For the time of HôՌdoR is upon all of you!'

Yuldurian smirks at Naumokron, then looks behind him, at Hondor, his bones ready to charge. He roars. Naumokron looks back to Hondor and sees the charging hulk of bone and loose guts heading straight for them. He then turns back to face Yuldurian.

'You will never be able to control that monster! He will destroy as he wills, as he was meant to...Hondor is the perfect killing machine, and we are all doomed...even you, the so-called master!'

Yuldurian turns his attention to the Daughter. 'RUN! Get away from here, back down the mountain...now!'

She looks on as Hondor passes straight through Naumokron, as he disappears once more into his smoke of darkness within a moment, Hondor slashing away with the Teeth of Kar`durgra held in both hands, swinging wildly, striking everywhere, at anything moving.

'RUN...!' Yuldurian shouts again, persisting that the Daughter leave now, or else she too will join the many that lay dead upon this mountain top. Hondor is getting closer.

'I...I can't...' She feels the urge of sobbing, the tears begin.

'There is no time for this....RUN NOW!' He shouts even louder, in a more stern tone, the tone he would only give to her when she was out of line, endangering those around her. The same glare when she pulled the switch, and freed this monster from his flesh prison, from inside Glasgar. Hondor was built upon the structure of the Gormon, while his essence lingered in Glasgar's worst nightmares.

'But I...how will I get pass the maze...I can't do it without you!'

But he would never answer that question. Yuldurian hovers into the air, ready to defend himself, as the Teeth come down. She cannot look, the Daughter turns away and runs, runs as fast as she can, back down the mountain pass, heading back to the maze where the first touch of darkness by the Dregor, had been felt, had her memory scarred...and after this, the memories would never heal. She could not watch what happened next, she could only hear that last-minute *"Ugh...!"* Before all was silent except for the swish of the blade cleaving the air, cleaving Yuldurian in two, as his white feathers turned to crimson, as his insides bled. She...she thought she heard...chewing...biting and pulling apart of bones and the sloshing of guts being scattered about, but she did not want to look, she did not want to imagine that thought for a single moment, for there is enough blood dripping in her mind, covering her thoughts and drowning her in nightmares.

Hondor never saw her leave, never saw her scamper away. He is far too busy with the feast that lays before him, and he has a hunger as old as eons, to satisfy. There are many bodies, much meat here to eat, much blood to drink...and he starts, by picking up the first half of Yuldurian.

The Daughter has been wandering for hours. She has seen the maze from above, but would never have been able to remember the different turns, corridors, and pathways. She has no hunger, no thirst, she was too appalled by all the dead soldiers, the beasts that pulled the cart, and even...even...Yuldurian. *"NO!"* She did not want to think that, his fate would come to such a horrid end, a judge of the highest honor, a judge of the High Court of Thylesian...would rest in the stomach of a giant, walking skeleton, a skeleton of black bones, black as the empty voids beneath The Great Divide, the stomach of a an ancient terror, a legend eons old but not forgotten by those who are old enough to remember. They remember the tales...of Hondor...and the chaos he would bring. For that's what everything comes down to, bring chaos to cleanse this realm of the weak, then everything would return to order, and upon the wasteland that Hondor would bring, a new empire...upon bone and bodies, would be built. The skies will go dark...and all the other races would fade. It was stopped once, but without the Aurora's...without the Hero of Ages...could it be done so again? Would this ancient terror of endless age, the final resting place of Yuldurian, would Hondor bring about the end of all Aura?

The Daughter grasps at the marble walls, dragging herself along, looking over her shoulder every moment, always watching to see if *HE* is coming after her...to devour her like he has all the others. She looks up to the crown of the tallest mountain, so white to her...so pure...she could see now, whether it is her imagination, she was seeing things...or her eyes were seeing what others could not...she could see the blood, the red streams and drops cascade down the mountain, spewing from the crown like lava from a volcano. Blood is erupting from Kar'durgra...and Hondor is the explosion.

She stumbles to the ground, she can no longer keep to her feet, but she must, she must get away, far away from *HIM*, even if she is to die in this maze, a lost batch of bones wearing this lady-adventurer's dress...at least this maze will have her, her picked clean by time, and not by the incisors of that monster.

She does not remember much of what happened after she blacked out, only a shadow that hovered overhead, a gust of wind against her chest, and a voice that cried... *"I found her!"*

She twists and turns all night, all through the twilight, plagued by nightmares, the eyes of that Civilian...his pale eyes looking into her...into her mind and her very essence. The wings of the one Yuldurian called Naumokron, the bastard who has brought Hondor into this world...Hondor...the name, the very knowledge of his existence, trembling under his shadow, a colossus of walking bone and death with bodies left in his wake, his feast...his power...power, *"Through Chaos is the Cleansing...to eliminate the weak...and upon their bones build the old empire, an empire of Power driven by Chaos...THE DESTOYER...!"*

She could feel the words leave her lips, but she was never aware of her speaking them. She awakens in a cold sweat within a familiar room. She is back at the palace, in the room given to her by Yuldurian.

"Yuldurian..." She whispers to herself, as she clasps her hands around her face and cries.

A sudden knock at the door startles her, then a voice.

'My Lady, are you alright?!' One of the guards on the other side asks, hearing the startling voices she makes in her sleep, and the sudden scream as she awakens.

She takes a minute to compose herself, too long, as the guard repeats his question.

'My Lady...?'

'I...I'm fine...!' She calls back to the concerned guardian at her door.

"But...am I really?"

Part X:

The Feast

~

Hondor cannot help himself, he feels the urge to kill, he cannot hold back this force that over powers him, this force he cannot disobey. He feels the stomach within him gurgle, and a hunger, an insatiable hunger comes over him. The voice echoes in the back of his mind. Is it the voice of hunger, or the voice of the master? But Hondor cannot get rid of it, cannot tear it from his mind.

"...feast...for they are but the cattle, and you...the butcher...! You can feel it, the hunger is insatiable, to feast upon life, to eat away existence of all that moves...you are the ultimate being...and this is survival! Clear the way of all those who are weak, and claim your title, claim your victory..."

Hondor tears apart and rips through the skin and swallows the meat and innards of all the leftover dead. There remains nothing of Yuldurian except for the pile of bloody feathers and bones, the robe of the judge to Thylesian tossed aside stained with what once remained of a distinguished Asyndian. Even the flesh along the wing blade had been picked clean. And after the feast...he could see clearly his surroundings, the power that was within Yuldurian has given him eyes. Two bulging blood-shot bulbs, red and itchy, soar and throbbing with pain from their growth within Hondor's skull.

He moved on down the line, mainly from largest to the smallest, the Asyndians were last. The hulking beast stomps over to the slayed beasts that pulled his cart, and after a time, after tearing through the thick hide and layers after layer of fat and muscle, biting and chewing, making a horrible groaning noise catching his breath, his mouth too full and pieces fall from his mouth all over the place, like wood-chips leftover from a saw.

He can feel the wind and cold, rocky soil beneath his feet, the tissue and muscle is starting to develop and envelop around his black skeleton, meat of a retched beast caged within these ribs of darkness.

Hondor tears his way through the Gormons, blood and armor are scattered across the Kar'durgra's peaks. More muscle begins to develop, more organs develop from the tissue, cells are multiplying every single moment at an alarming rate, before long, Hondor will have his full form...but his true strength, the terrifying truth of legends that has been lingering in fear for so long, has not even begun to reveal itself, shown its true face of chaos and destruction that is yet to spread far and wide, across the continents, across the realms, across Aura...everywhere and everyone will not be safe, when Hondor unleashes his true form, the truth to how destructive his brutality and warfare can be.

He tears...and that is the keyword, *"TEARS"*, *"TEARING"*, for this derelict scene of butchery and horror is a slaughter, an absorption, for Hondor is not eating per say, he is not programmed to enjoy the taste of food, to enjoy his meals, for these are not meals, this is hunger...a hunger for power, the ultimate power over many and all, he is the destroyer, the

"NEW DESTROYER", he is to take from others and gain for himself , for that is what it means to have power, he is tearing through the smorgasbord for strength, to absorb the flesh and blood of others to strengthen himself, a forced sacrifice...murder...to gain immortality.

The Asyndians have very little meat upon them, they are all skin and feathers, and Hondor is aggravated by the constant clump of feathers getting lodged in his throat, for there is no essence in them, there is no power to gain from a feather, unless one as these races can do, and that is fly, but Hondor needs no flight, for he can jump beyond the clouds, and if he could reach up and grab the sun, he would crush the orb of light and heat, puncture the eye of Lota, bleeding the lava and molten blood into tears of pain, and extinguish all that guides the denizens along upon their pathways.

"I thought there would be more to have here...not enough...not enough..." He thinks to himself.

The burning from the ground touching his feet muscles is subsiding, he looks down as scales and skin is developing around the toes and reaching up to his ankles. Not quite the armor of a warrior...yet.

He is through with the Asyndian meat, so he moves to the Civilian's, and by the end of the feast, a pile of bones, mountains and hills of skeletons and skulls, leftover armor and torn clothing has been built all over the place, the heads that were ripped away to drink the elixir of life from all their necks like a fountain, were tossed over towards the edge of the cliff's edge, some even rolled away, too far and have fallen over the side, to hit the bottom below shattering the cranium and brains everywhere, littering the roads with decapitated remains.

Hondor wipes away the blood, and looks down to see the blood smear across his arm, where there is now flesh upon his fingers and forearms. He clutches his fists, opening then and closing them, reaches over and grasps a skull, crushes it to dust, he can feel the satisfaction of bone splinters cutting his palm. He is not finished yet, he still is not the whole, parts still need to be filled. He walks over and looks over to the edge of the mountain top, still getting used to the sensation of the flesh upon the bottoms of his feet, with toes of jagged nails like claws and shags of hair beginning their growth. The stubble is thick, and it will not be long until his foot is covered.

While gazing off into the far distance, he can see the far, distant city of Thylesian, and knows where his destination is, where his path must lead, by instincts, of wrath and ruin, suffering and hunger, this insatiable hunger he must follow, he must heed. Hondor turns to walk away, when he looks down, and catches his reflection in a pool of blood. His face...his face has skin and lips, a tongue.

"So...this is why the meat has a iron, salty sweaty taste to it..."

He lets out the long, slobbering tongue to look upon it, he grits his teeth, a red, swelled cluster of gums is encompassing his teeth. And his face, he takes his massive hand, and runs them down the right side of his face, he has cheeks, skin covers the muscle over his face, he can see an identity of himself. There is an eyelid when he blinks, some eyebrows and eye lashes are beginning to grow. His face looks pale, a highlight of blue around his gaunt cheeks, for the blood has not yet circulated...no circulation. He looks down at his chest, and there is no heart, his body is pale and lacks the circulation of oxygen and blood through the empty veins.

He must feast again, he must feast to reach the final stages of his form, for if he goes on to long, the muscles and the flesh will die, and he will be nothing more than bones once more, until he starts again, and this realm can only provide so much food to satisfy this terrible hunger.

The left side of his face is still muscle and eye, his midsection is still exposed, as is his upper legs and biceps of his arms. He looks around the area, searching for something, something to cover his exposed form. The armor is too small for his titanic form. A large Gormon cape is stuck upon the remains of the scaffolding to the Teeth of Kar`durgra, he wraps it around his face and shoulders, and covers some of his upper body. But it will have to do, for there is more important matters to attend to in Thylesian on this day.

Behind the gray wall of clouds overhead, the atmosphere and the scenery over the land can be seen better, as the morning is awakening, for the next day has come, he has feasted all night and the dawn is upon him, his first morning into this new life. He cannot recall the scent of fear, of so much blood upon the wind. The Gormon, Glasgar, was but a shell, a window into this realm, but now...he is free, and this will be the beginning, for Hondor to unleash his true wrath. Runegard was only a taste, for there are more grand, bloodier conflicts to come.

Part XI:

Awakening & Recovery

~

A`deon feels his body being dragged across the ground. The ground and rubble of rocks and dirt is cold and harsh as it brushes against his back. He can barely open his eyes, but the right opal breaks a crack in the flesh and his right eye is open, yet the scenery around him is blurred and disoriented. He can barely tell what is what. The left eye will not move, it will not open for it has been swollen shut by bruising and the burst of blood vessels. The cool brisk wind, with a shrill draft and burns, sending the skin into shock, freezing over A`deon's flesh into the core and runs a finger down his spine.

The attack of Hondor has left him virtually crippled and limp. The eyes steadily open to the gray dawn that lingers out the window, a sun that resides beyond a vale of clouds as thick as smoke left from the smoldering embers. The land is too quiet, where is he? What is this place he has awakened to?

A`deon's head falls backwards, with a severe crack of his spine, he feels that something in his back has been severed and uprooted from its place in his anatomy. He cannot lift his head up, however he notices the shadows that pull him along his course. It's hard for him to tell, but there appears to be two

174

of them, two figures in front of him. He can feel the grasp of the one tug heavily under his arms and grip him tensely. The other leads them along, walking ahead in a stride, a small stride the silhouette keeps, not to far apart, yet just enough span to keep going at a steady pace. He notices the figure clutches some object in his ride hand, a walking staff of sorts used to guide the figure's brisk steps along.

A`deon falls back out of consciousness, this time for a long while, until he is once more awakened, as he feels the dragging stop, all movement has ceased, and his body is dropped to the ground, he is far too gone and out of the moment, for the pain has been delayed, but soon, all will come full-circle, and the aches and crunching of his bones will catch up to him in time, yet faster than he would wish.

He tries to sit up from the sting of the cold upon his back, for he can feel the bone in his back that is protruding outwards, but he can barely move, as he feels his bones crunch and grind, sending pain across his entire body. It did not take long, for now the pain has caught up to him. He cries out, and at that moment, one of the figures, the one who does not bear the walking staff in their grasp, rushes to his side and holds him down, trying to keep him still. He feels the cold hands upon him, griping his arms tightly to try and subdue him, but this makes him panic, and he tries to ignore the harsh pain, he tries to fight back, he wants to be free of this grasp that holds him down.

A`deon looks up to the figure, for the shape looks...different to him, it's as though he is seeing them now in a different light, for now it seems and feels as though the hulking figure of the intruder is grasping him, Hondor has found him, and is ready to break him once more, he has located A`deon and will finish him off for good this time, the general will not be allowed to escape again. The brooding shadow of Hondor clouds his thoughts and overbears this awakened nightmare. A drop of sweat, the pool of fear drips from his brow. He can't bear the panic weighing down upon his chest, he must move, he has to cry out!

He hears a man's voice, as the other figure hobbles over to his side as well, while the haunting shape of Hondor becomes clearer and the body begins to slim down and shrink, the shadow contorts within his eye and a different figure begins to take shape before him. Judging by the faint looks of the figure, and from what his blurred vision can see, "he", looks very feminine, a "she"...a woman has him in the harsh grasp, and she is very powerful by the handle she has upon A'deon. He once more can hear the other voice, the man's voice. By his tone, he is very calm and soothing, he tries to calm down A'deon, tries to ease his fright.

The woman says nothing, she only keeps him held down and subdued, yet A'deon does not know who these Civilians are or their motives for capturing him and dragging him across the harsh landscape, yet he can tell they are like him, they are not giants of the north-western lands of Fausengard, and they have no feathers and no wings, so they are not Asyndians.

'Please, try not to excite yourself, she will not harm you, she is trying to help you!' The man says.

But A'deon is not listening, he only struggles more to free himself from her grasp. The woman who holds him down raises her hand and strikes him across the face with a clenched fist to try and calm him, yet her blow hits too hard and he, once more, goes unconscious.

'Well that was a harsh way of doing it….but at least he's stopped.' The man replies to the actions of the woman.

Several more hours go by, and A'deon awakens again, this time, the sun does not shine, for the sky grows bruised and purple, similar to his eye and body, and the fiery horizon is sinking lower and lower into the backlight clouds that become swallowed up by the darkness.

It takes A`deon some time to get his thoughts together and to be able to think, as well as make a complete thought, a complete sentence within his head. He struggles to figure out his first words, for the last word he uttered, was a dark word, a hateful word one can shutter upon the tip of the tongue, the name of his attacker, his decimator, the terror and monstrosity that can only be called by one name, one word...*Hondor.*

"How much more punishment...can one take...can one Civilian handle...?" It's not much, but this is the thought on his mind, at least until he can get his senses together, and compose himself, and ask the right questions, and not receive the wrong answers. He looks up at the tiny flickers and clusters of stars, he can feel a warmth off to his left side. He tries to move his arm, but it has been fastened and will not budge. He slowly, carefully raises his head, yet he feels he cannot hold it for long, for his head shakes and his neck convulses from the weight and strain, not to mention the pain that is escalating. He sees his arm has been bandaged and put into a cloth sling made of some kind of animal hide, for it is protecting the broken bone from the cold night air.

He hears a voice over his shoulder, it is the man's voice.

'It appears he stirs...he is not dead after all. He truly must be strong to have endured so much...' The voice says. A`deon hears some shuffling.

'Please sister...do not disturb him. Stay here and let him move on his own, you have done enough helping for one day.' The man continued, A`deon can sense a hint of sarcasm in the man's voice when he says *"help"*.

A`deon shuffles about in his twilight, not asleep...yet not fully awake, not oriented to his surroundings or exactly what's going on around him. He has visions and nightmares, and floats and flutters in and out of consciousness. He twists and turns and twists and turns, his bones aching and cracking. He winces from the pain, and shakes from the cold chill of the early morning dew that settles over his flesh and shattered armor. He tries to cover himself with his cape and shuffles closer to the dying embers of the fire's remains to gather what warmth he is able to and conserve what body heat he is able to.

As his thoughts clear some more, he begins to ponder the notion of these Civilians as he eves drops on their conversations, picking up what words he can as he falls in and out of an unrestful sleep, they do not sound or seem as though they are a threat, for if they were, he feels they would have tried to kill or do away with him whilst he slumbered. Yet...he did not pick up anything on their location at this point or, the most important question of all, their reasons as to why they decided to rescue him from certain death and drag him away from the battlefield during Runegard's bleakest hour.

He needs to awaken, he needs to tough it up and move, pull himself around and face these two, ask his questions, get his answers that he needs, A`deon must act, yet his body has been through more than most Civilians can handle without dying in the process or from his wounds and injuries, but that's just it, he still can't quite move, he still can't quite get himself together, because his body, his bones, and his ligaments all still feel separated. Literally, he's still not quite all together, yet his mind is tortured, his mind is coming around, his mind is still functioning and wants to know what is going on, curiosity is making him anxious and the curiosity is killing him, almost making him stubborn and ignorant of his severe wounds.

The morning comes into full bloom, and the sun has long shown itself over the furthest peaks. A`deon has been asleep most of the morning, and he can feel himself being lifted up and slung over someone's shoulders. It is the woman, she is heaving him along, he can hear her heavy breathing as they tread along their route. He still feels soar, yet the pain day after day, seems to be fading...fading in small increments mind you, yet it still seems to be exhausting itself, just as the restless nights have been exhausting A`deon and keeping his strength crippled.

'Careful with him Nilta...he is still not fully healed...' The man says.

And finally, A`deon has a name, the woman's name is Nilta, and he also knows they are brother and sister, yet he does not know what the man's name is, and he has also noticed that the woman doesn't have much to say, actually he has noticed that she has not spoken a single word, at least he hasn't noticed or heard her speak while he was awake for those brief moments. She must not have much to say for herself.

After what feels like hours and hours of walking, but judging by the turn of day to night, it must have been a full day of travel. Nilta and her brother stop near the corner of a lonesome valley, which will provide them good shelter from the night air, which seems to be getting colder and colder, so as far as A`deon figures, they are heading in a northern direction, yet he still does not know why.

Nilta carries him into a crevasse of the valley near their camp, she sets him down just inside their cave and tries to adjust him accordingly and make sure he is comfortable and his limbs are straightened. She leaves him there to continue his long rest, briefly checking in on him every so often to make sure he is well off, at least as well off as he'll be.

There is some movement in his quivering fingers, as A`deon reaches out and tries to grasp for something, something to give him a lift up, for he feels ready, as ready as he'll ever be, for he needs to move, he needs to lift himself up, and beat the pain that holds him down, he tries to overcome it, and, at first...he fails, and slips...losing his grasp on the wall, and slouches back to the ground, but that isn't stopping him, and he tries again, and again, and again...until, finally, after days and days of twisting and turning, unable to move himself around, barely alive, he feels his old strength returning to his hands, and he manages to grasp the wall of the cave and hold on.

The fingers slip into a small crack, and he uses this as leverage and pulls up, sliding across the smooth floor and pulls harder and, after what feels like a struggle, he conquers the immediate pain and shrugs it off for a moment, and manages to sit up, and hold himself up against the wall, his back supported by the cold, damp rock. Yet, he can't escape the pain that floods through his limbs and tendons. But, it's not so bad, he feels accomplished, his pride outweighs the pain, and like a stubborn fool, he shakes off the pain, shrugs it off. The first step is complete, now, he just has to try and bring movement into other parts of his body.

He rubs his legs, there is still feeling, which is good, he is not crippled, yet his right leg feels strained and worn. Slowly, he tries to bring motion into his left leg, he concentrates with all his thought and all his effort, first the toes wiggle within his boot, the calf and knee begin to raise up, but not without the torturing aches. He covers his mouth, trying not to yell out, for he doesn't want Nilta to try and subdue him again.

The armor is heavy and weighs him down, so he uses his good arm to undo the latches around the back of his leg, and removes the plated steel from his calf and knee. Now, his leg has better locomotion and moves more freely and smoothly. There is a grinding in his knee, but is nothing major. He moves the leg back and forth, up and down as best he can. With that, he places the armor back onto his leg in its proper spots, and begins to latch up the straps.

He rests for a moment, exhausted from all the movement he just put himself through. He's not going to be right as rain for a good while, but he is damn sure going to work three times harder at his rehabilitation than what most would attempt.

There's a pressure on his head, its felt that way for a while, yet he has never been able to do anything about it before to figure out what exactly this pressure is. He reaches up and feels his scalp, it itches and feels something across his head. It seems either Nilta or her brother, have placed a bandage all around his scalp. He reaches around to the back of his head and unties the well placed knot, he unwinds the material, which has been wrapped around several times, and was placed with great care and skill, as to protect the deep gash that has been carved into his forehead, a deep cut a good four or five inches in length and has been scabbed over. How deep the cut was, A`deon could only guess, but it feels severe and stings when he rubs his hands across his head. This blow is what has been causing those headaches.

Even though he advises himself against the idea, he begins to pick at the scar, flaking and chipping away at the scab. He feels the coagulation and blockage has been disturbed, the warm blood begins to flow and trickle down his brow, he rubs it away with his fingertips, removes his hand and looks at the blood that stains the tip of his hand. He brushes his hair away from the now opened wound, and stains his palm with his blood.

The scent is strong and carries on the breeze that enters from the outside. A`deon smells the scent of his blood as it carries on the wind. As does something else, for there is something else with A`deon in these caves, something that lurks in the dark. The thing growls, and the jaws slather and crunch the air, drooling at the scent of fresh blood.

The sounds of the creature, or maybe creatures, moves closer, he can hear their scuffling in the black abyss, and the pale, white eyes gaze out to him, several sets to be exact, like a dazzling array of glowing moons in the abyss of space, or a cluster of pearls sitting far upon the floor of the oceans, sitting in the maw of a large clam waiting to claim its meal. But these creatures do not lure, they hunt, they track, they catch the scent of their prey and pounce. The pale moons get closer, and from the darkness, a long snout and rows of razor white teeth, stained with dried blood show themselves, and then a beast with a long, slender, lithe shape steps out of the darkness walking on all fours.

A`deon tries to summon a cry for help, a cry as loud as the screams when the shear pain strikes his broken body, but his body goes numb in a cold sweat of fear. Those eyes seem to hypnotize him, and then more of them crawl forward, several more in fact, a pack of them begin to surround and close in on A`deon, who is helpless, stranded and frozen like a wounded deer that can't defend itself.

What seems to be the leader of the pack, a malicious looking beast, with one pale eye, and a scar slashed over the other, leaps forward and crunches down upon A`deon's arm, the arm he raises to protect himself from the beast, his good arm, the arm covered in the blood which streams from his forehead. The pain is even worse, more severe than the crunching and grinding of his broken bones. Another from the pack lunges, and then another, A`deon cries in terror, terror for his life, the very fear and threat he felt with his confrontation of Hondor. He has nowhere to run, he grips the cold, stone walls, as they slip from the blood that splatters across and runs down like red rapids of a high waterfall.

A`deon's vision begins to blur once more, as he feels the familiar grasp of death tighten its grasp around his slaughtered, scrapped body, covered in deep gashes and gushing blood everywhere, free for the beasts in the shadows to lick their lips and feast upon. Out of the corner of his ear...he hears a high pitched whistle scream by his head, and feels a brush of cool air, as some projectile strikes deep into one of the creatures, sending him flying away from A`deon, releasing the latch of jaws that hold tight upon his flesh, and with a stark yelp, the creature is slung to the ground dead, laying lifeless like a curled up black cape, just a lifeless clump with a large spear sticking out of its rib cage.

Then Nilta leaps over the flock of black jackals, brandishing another long pike, tipped with a jagged spear-head, and a lock of hair tied around an object sacred to Nilta. She slashes and stabs at the voracious creatures and drives them back, they pounce, yet she fights back harder.

The single-eyed pack leader raises upon his haunches and jumps at Nilta, she falls back onto the cavern floor, tripping over a cluster of rocks just behind her, she raises the spear, and drives it through the leaders chest and out his back, ripping through his spine. He dangles for a moment, howling into the darkness, and then falls limp, its tongue dangles, hanging lifeless from the jaws of its corpse. Slobber oozes down to the ground in thick drops as he exhales his final gasp of air. Nilta tosses the spear aside to the cavern floor. Gaining composure on her feet, she proceeds to the dead beast's corpse, grips the shaft of the spear, and with a furious tug, wrenches the weapon loose from the beast's ribs.

Nilta rushes over and kneels by A`deon's bloodied figure. His armor protected him from most of the brutal slashes and bites, but his arm is bleeding severely, and his face has deep gashes that have been dug out by the creatures' long, sharp claws.

He looks, for the first time, into the eyes of Nilta. He sees her face for the first time, for he can see more clearly than before. She is no longer that wandering silhouette that drags and carries him across harsh, cold terrain. She is heavily protected by a stout, yet flexible suit of light, copper armor, that has appeared to been dyed in a dark maroon color, yet this could be the blood spilled when she was fighting the creatures of darkness, and slaughtering them one after the other. Two things struck him immediately however, her eyes were very wide and powerful, visually striking yet intimidating at the same time, the opals she gazed from are a deep green, like a lush emerald forest just days after the first spring rain showers over the landscape. And the other thing he noticed, is that across her mouth, was bound a sheet of metal, which seemed riveted to a piece of plate metal upon each side of her face, and wrapped around the top of her head, and she wore this contraption like a helmet, yet the front of her head and face is not covered, and this device was connected around the back of her head, just above where her hair hangs down over her shoulders, gathered back with a thin leather strap. Her bangs hung over her eyes, and are parted to one side. With a strong slam, she jams the staff into the dirt, for the ground to hold it while she tends to A`deon's wounds.

A`deon was fearful, and untrusting of her and her harsh ways at first, yet now that he sees her, now that he looks into her eyes, he can tell she is only doing what she can to help, how she knows best to.

He just sort of looks at her as he shakes from the loss of blood, for his body is very cold and drained, and in pain from the brutal onslaught.

'Thank you...for saving me...' He says to her. Her eyes look up sternly from what she was doing, and she says nothing, yet her eyes brighten, and though he can't see her mouth, he can tell by her dimples swelling, that she is smiling. She continues wrapping a piece of thin cloth around his arm to stop the bleeding.

'I...I guess I owe you two now, don't I?' A`deon continues, trying just some minor chatting, trying to get to know her more. She doesn't move her head, yet her eyes shift up for a moment, and her face begins to turn red, and her dimples swell more from blushing. She finishes up the dressing on his arm, then overviews him, seeing what else she can do. She sees the gash on his forehead, and begins to address it promptly.

'Are you...Nilta?'

She looks back up at him with a sharp jerk in her reflexes, her reaction to hearing her name seems to shock her, and A`deon himself looks at her bewildered thinking he may have insulted her.

'I'm sorry to have alarmed you, I heard your brother mention it while I was stirring in and out of conscious...that man is your brother right? Am I wrong?'

She simply stares at hin with shock and wide-eyes. Her breathing is heavy.

'You don't say too much do you...? Why don't you answer my questions?' A`deon asks sternly, yet not in a harsh tone, just in wonder why she refuses to speak.

'Well...my sister Nilta won't speak to you, because she doesn't speak...she is unable to communicate through speech.'
The voice of the man speaks over from the entrance of the cave.

A`deon turns to see a man standing idly, with a casual grip upon his walking staff, his cape flutters in the winds, while he has a hood pulled over his head, his face is enclosed in the shadows.

'It is good your finally awake, and returning to your senses. You've been in and out of sleep now for the past week or so. Ever since we pulled you from the battlements a broken and bloodied mesh of armor and flesh.'

'You already know and have met my sister Nilta...my name is Diin.'

Diin begins to sniff the air that lingers about the cavern.

'This cave reeks...I did not notice this until now, but it seems the slath have made their home here.' Diin says.

A`deon looks at him, then at Nilta with a confused look. 'What is a slath? Was that what just attacked me?! The damn things mangled me, am I infected or cursed by the bites?!'

'The slaths are an ancient creature who reside in the dark depths and reaches of Aura...they have a deadly bit, but do not procure any poisons or diseases like the migs do, for the slaths eat their prey as soon as they kill it, and leave nothing left for the scavengers that come across the remains of the corpse, say for the splinter of cracked and gnawed bones...'

Diin walks closer to them, to take a look at A`deon's wounds.

'...yet, the presence of slaths begs the question of an even greater danger that is close by, and we must be more cautious of our surroundings.' Diin continues his words as he gazes over A'deon's cuts and gashes. He puts out his hand and places it upon the top of A`deon's head.

Unlike Nilta, A`deon can't quite see Diin, his face is well hidden by the shadows in the caves. He removes his hand from A`deon's head.

'What danger...?' A`deon asks.

'Are you able to get to your feet and walk general?' Diin seems to ignore his question.

A`deon looks at him once more with the curious eyes, his attention shifts back and forth between both Diin and Nilta. 'Yes...but, where are we going...and you know me? How did you find me, and why did you rescue me?' A`deon asks.

Diin finishes his inspection of A`deon's wounds, and turns away back to the cave entrance.

'Good...very good, I sense that you have suffered much, more than most would be able to tell just by inspection of your battered exterior, yet your ailments will not take too much longer to heal, and by what you've been through, you have shown great resilience to your wounds and injuries...I see why you were chosen to be a general...'

'I..." A`deon tries to speak, but Diin cuts him off.

'I will listen to your side of the story in time...for I sense your need to speak, and well you should, but if your able to move, we must continue on, for we still have a few days left of travel ahead of us.'

Nilta raises a concerned muffle and removes a dagger from a sheath concealed within her armband, she furiously makes a sequence of tapping sounds upon the rocky ground of the cave.

'I understand your concern Nilta, but don't worry...he will be fine.' Diin replies.

She repeats another series of taps, this time even faster and differentiated in their sequence.

'...I...I understand that, and you will not have to carry him or drag him anymore, I have an extra walking staff for him to use.'

He shifts his voice to A`deon.

'Sorry general, she tends to worry...but you'll be fine to travel, you may be hobbling for a while yet, but in time you'll have your strength back.'

He pauses for a moment when he reaches the entrance of the cave, a faint speckle of light streams through the gray skies above and shines upon the maw of the cave.

'You see general...injuries have their privileges, though we all tend to not see it, well most of them do. In your case, you are lucky, for you will recover...'

He removes his hood to reveal a man of middle age, not old, yet has not felt youth in a good ten to fifteen years passing of time. The winters are adding up. Speckles of grey appear in his stubble, and his thinning hair is all but gone. And, a dark olive-colored band is tied around his eyes where lifeless pupils now remain as a lost civilization that once seen many lands and many experiences, yet now only can be viewed by thoughts and memories of days gone by.

'...unlike Nilta and myself, you will heal. As for Nilta, she was born mute, yet she has a very powerful way of communicating and showing her feelings...it's amazing how the other senses of our bodies strengthen, for her hearing is ten-fold, her sight...impeccable, better than any Gormon or Asyndians! And her feelings, I don't have to see her to know exactly what she is feeling.

'I was not always blind, my accident came as a punishment for a crime, but I deserved what I received, because I believed strongly in what I was getting into, in my actions...and though I lost something special, I gained something more...

'Are these curses upon us General A`deon? Maybe so, maybe some would feel that way, yet I do not for it helps us gain a better appreciation of things around us, for I now see in a different shade of light, in hues instead of tints.'

A`deon turns to Nilta, who lowers her head somberly, and looks aimlessly to the floor.

'So...you are both criminals...and is this why you have captured me? Are you really so cursed as to pretend for your own benefit of making me feel sorry for both of you!'

A`deon feels betrayed and with anger, struggles to get to his feet. He shakes intensely trying to maintain his balance and slowly crawls across the wall. Nilta tries to help, but A`deon pushes her away.

'Keep your hands away! I will not be the prisoner of charlatans and liars who only seek pity for a pardon to their crimes, I will now be your ransom!'

'You can barely move, you will not get far without us *"liars"*, as you so boldly and ignorantly accuse me and my sister of being...'

A`deon shoves Diin away.

'Stand down, I want no more of your lies or your help, I will crawl back to Runegard on my hands and knees, even if it kills me!' He roars with anger.

A`deon stumbles from the cave and fumbles along on the ground, ripping the bandage from his head, and removing the sling around his arm. He tosses them away, and continues to struggle along, slowly making his way past their encampment and towards the hill that lays further ahead of him, and judging by the direction the wind, west is off to his right, and begins his struggle towards the direction of Runegard.

Nilta rushes from the cave, but Diin stops her in her pace.

'Let him go for now sister, but before sundown, which is almost upon us, for I can feel the night air on my face, and the winds are blowing in from the east. I want you to follow behind and watch him, see what he does. Keep him just within your sights. If he gets in trouble again, you know what to do, we can't let any more danger come to him. We need to reach Arctalus-Hon by daylight on the third day. Understand?'

Diin places his hand on her shoulder, and he feels her body tensing up.

'Don't worry about me here, I'll be fine, the air no longer smells as foul, yet I smell something on the wind. I want you to be careful my sister, for the presence of those slaths means that there is a Dregor presence nearby...there hasn't been a Dregor presence for at least two hundred years, since...since the second Grey Age!'

Nilta looks upon her brother with heavy eyes, wishing she could say something of comfort to him, yet she would not know how to use those words to explain her concern.

'I know you feel it to Nilta, for something else is coming, I'm not sure what this all means, but once we reach Arctalus, he will be able to put this all together, but our general is a major key in all of this...and I have a feeling that our being set free, is a sign.

He rubs his hand over her forehead and feels a cold sweat come over her brow.

'Yes I know, I felt it too that day, I felt it upon my flesh, I smelled it in the air, for the presence of that black Asyndian reeked of the same, foul odor as the slaths. There is a connection, but what? I'm not sure. And what that Asyndian wanted with that rowdy Gormon...I don't know. But, I will tell you this Nilta...there was a familiar presence surrounding Runegard on that day...something was in the air, black clouds loomed over the Civilians of Runegard that day...and then, and then *HE* appeared...!'

Diin wanders forward towards the center of the camp, with Nilta following close behind him. He sits down upon a fallen stump of a long tree, and ponders quietly to himself.

'Go after him Nilta...we should not wait any longer, because the more I think about all these events and these questions, the more this worries me, and familiar signs appear before my blind eyes, I see black banners in my dreams...and I can see the visage of a mirror, and the swirling smoke and scourge of something dark, something sinister...something that watches over our shoulders while we sleep...while we dream...'

Nilta retrieves the staff from the cave, and makes her way past her brother, and moves towards the hills. She takes one look back to Diin, who sits there quietly, still thinking, still wondering about these questions that plague his thoughts. Before she leaves, she can hear him mutter in a whisper, she picks up these words with her sharp hearing.

"Could there be...could there be another? Or could this be..."

And he returns once more to his solemn state of mind.

She must move quickly towards the hills, yet in A`deon's state, he should not have gone too far. With stealthy speed and agility, she makes her climb over the rocky dunes of faded green grass, and rocky terrain, and at the top of the hill, she is surprised to see that the general has gained substantial ground for the condition he is in.

She does as Diin instructed her to do, and keeps her distance. She wonders why she can't just go over and grasp him and carry him back to their camp, but knowing her brother, he is very wise and often knows more than he leads on, and even keeps some things secret from her. There is something, she feels in her heart and intuition, that there is something he wants A`deon to either see or experience for himself. But again, she sometimes does not understand her brothers curious ways.

Part XII:

Visitor

~

A`deon continues to crawl across the shifting tundra. He feels the daylight coming to a close, as the wind continues into a downward spiral as it gets colder and colder, the more the skies go from a pleasant shade of gray, to a fiery burning blaze of orange and molten bronze. Funny, how the more the sky resembles a fiery cataclysm, the more frigid the air seems to be, yet we can't forget, that as the fall of daylight dims, the purple and opaque blue night slowly creeps over the mountains, and swallows the flames, for as the sun goes down, there will always be a tomorrow, yet the more and more this manifestation of day to night occurs, the greater the chances there will one day…be no tomorrow.

This cold wind seems to almost sip away at all of A`deon's strength like a vampire as it's time is about nigh to leave its coffin deep from within the undercroft, and creep across the land. He moves along at a snail's pace, his body throbbing more and more with each step, with each crawl. Behind his back he feels a sudden gust of wind trickle up his spine like a cold steel rain, and a massive shadow passes over head. He looks above to the sky, yet sees nothing around him. Was it a hallucination, was he imagining things, imaging the huge shadow that passed over. He would think so, except for the eyes he feels, he senses a cold stare, and can't help but feel that someone or something…is watching, keeping a close eye on him.

Nilta keeps back a ways, keeping to the loose clusters of trees that grow about the area, but this is no forest by any means. For a brief moment, all seems repetitive, A`deon stumbles and crawls a few paces, and then she'll keep behind and follow up as she needs to, yet for a moment, out of the corner of her eyes, she thought, no…swore she saw something, a large, massive shadow, a great wing span some ten to fifteen feet in diameter pass overhead, yet she is not sure.

A`deon notices a large tree ahead, yet the tree did not match the others in the area. The other trees consisted of Cedar and had a strong, sweet smell that flourished in the breeze. This tree, is contorted and twisted, gnarled by the creatures that once inhabited its trunk, yet now the corpses of tiny sects litter the grounds, some fresh, some as rotten as the tree itself. Its dark insides peer outwards, as though something spied out into the air from its retched lair within. Yet, it's not what could have been hiding on the inside that brought a chill of fear to him…he looks up, and there is a lone branch jutting outwards from the trunk. He is hypnotized by this singular spot upon this loathsome tree.

Then, a horrible squawk shrieks out into the open tundra air. This breaks A`deon's concentration, and he quickens his pace, which drives him closer to the direction of the hideous tree. A`deon doesn't see it yet, but Nilta sees, she sees clearly with her emerald eyes, as it appears a huge bird is descending from the sky, and it looks as though it's about to grab the general and carry him away to some terrible location and devour his bones. But, the creature does not, it descends and lands upon the twisted lone arm of the tree.

She wants to lunge in and get between A`deon and the creature, to protect him, but she remembers her brother's words, and waits, she stays back and observes to see what happens between the shape and A`deon. Though, she does not like the thick smell of something sinister which lingers in the stale, cold air. A`deon hears as the long, sharp talons scrape and scratch against the ancient wood, and that's when, he looks up, and he too now sees clearly, this hideous bird-like shadow, and stares into those icy cold eyes that have been watching him.

This figure…this Asyndian with feathers blacker than night, speaks to A`deon in a language that is foreign to him, a speech he has never heard in his speck of a lifetime, for this language is older than the time of Aura itself. A language that has not been used for the last two hundred years. Not since the last Grey Age, has such a dialect been uttered. Yet, even though he could not understand the tongue of this shadowed figure, within his mind, the faint whispers…are all too clear, the voice is very soft spoken, and seems almost distant with a faint echo, as though he spoke within a cave or maybe…another realm beyond the world of Aura, from a place where only darkness stays sleepless, with lidless eyes and a hunger that is immortal.

"Good evening…general." Whispers the voice within A`deon's mind.

A`deon stares, his eye lids flutter and blink to protect from the strong gust of wind beginning to pick up, and kick up the rocky soil and dry grass into the vortex of the wind. He puts his head down against the cold soil, the winds seem to blow stronger, trying to lift his head up.

"Do not turn your eyes from me general…I can speak into your mind, but how do I know I'm getting through, I need you to pay attention, or shall I pull at your heartstrings, bend

195

your spine, cripple you...shall I burn you from within, incinerate you? Hmmm? Shall I, for I can do so."

A`deon refuses to bow to the entities threats, and does not look up.

The faint whisper of the voice now seems very close, and the roar in his tone scratches across A`deon's ears.

"I Said Look!"

And a strong gust of wind chokes the air away from A`deon's lungs, as he gags upon soot and rocky soil. A`deon complies, and slowly raises his dirt-covered bloodied face up to look upon this creature. As he looks up, a faint flicker of the dying sunlight in the west catches the Asyndian's face, and A`deon recognizes him, he does not know his name, but he has seen this Asyndian before.

'I...I know you...though I know not whether through my eyes or from ancient tales, but I know you!'

The Asyndian's laugh is faint and hollow. *"Many know me, I have the name that is unspoken, for only those who walk with the shadows can say it...I have the face of many shades of night, though only the darkest eyes can see it, and those who fear all things empty and crumbled...will never forget my eyes. So...how close do you walk with the shadows...for cowards not only embrace what is hidden in the dark, they depend on it, welcome the embrace to be kept locked away, sheltered...!"*

'How dare you call me coward, who do you think you are to tell me when it's right and when I feel I should protect myself!' A`deon growls.

'I watched you fall away as the power of Hondor shook you, made you cower...made you fearful. I do not judge you,

196

general A`deon, for you were right to flee from Hondor's razor, for none survive his axe, and none ever will!'

The darkness shifts and stirs around in a thick cloud of smoke beneath A`deon's feet as the Asyndian laughs.

Nilta shifts herself around the tree, reorienting herself as the darkness thickens. She looks over to the far left, and standing upon a small dune, is another figure. Aumon is now here.

The Asyndian shifts his attention from A`deon to Aumon.

'Ah...the hour is late, and he finally reveals himself! I sense that all of you are here, the Dregor, Hexagus, as well as Kandarius! You escaped Hondor, you will not escape again!' The Asyndian cries.

'The scent of Naumokron is strong with you...Duul`ak! You have taken a weak ally under your *"Wing".'* Aumon chuckles at the pun he uses.

A`deon looks sternly at the black feathers of the Asyndian. 'Duul`ak...you're the one who broke into the fortress, you released all the prisoners and scum onto the land!'

Duul`ak's head snaps around and his voice changes again, this time a deep roar sweeps through his vocals. He looks down upon the groveling general.

'You will be silent, for now I speak! Listen, all you who rot within the bowels of this creature who calls himself Aumon. The true emancipator is free upon this world, he will cleanse the land for my return, the one true lord of Aura! But...I will take this play a step further...for this realm is not enough! I will establish my throne, then I will search and hunt down that black mass, that tumor of my very being, the entity

197

that keeps me suppressed by giving birth to your wretched spawn!' Duul`ak points furiously to Aumon. '...I will grab the throat of Wom, and make her regurgitate the realms which belong to me!'

Aumon's eyes glow a bright, ghostly blue. 'Well, then I hope you are ready...for the tumor that infects you, our mother...is coming, she will be here soon! It has taken her nigh light-years to cross the Galakaos, to reach this realm, and she closes in, for soon we will all be children in her womb! She will finish what she has always done, she will engulf the rest of us, she will swallow all of Aura and her realms away, and all will become one! Till all are one, in unity with the one, true order!'

Aumon opens his palm, and a blue fire ignites from his hand at Duul`ak. The Asyndian raises his defenses and forces back the attack of bright, blinding light. While the two entities attack one another, Nilta rushes in and grasps A`deon, trying to pull him away from the battle. She momentarily looks, her eyes catch the light and blinds her. Duul`ak forces the flames back, and Aumon reverts back for a moment, and is stunned briefly, for Naumokron's essence within this Asyndian, is extremely powerful. Duul`ak sees the Civilian woman and unleashes a powerful blast of feverish lightning, crippling her and bringing her down to the ground, where she collapses in the dirt and lays sprawled out on her side in pain and cold, her body goes into spasms and she can feel her nerves break down and fail. She goes into shock and all goes dark in her eyes.

A`deon crawls over to her side and holds her in his grasp, shielding her from Duul`ak's and Aumon's warfare.

Aumon stands again to his feet and releases a ferocious blast of power unto Duul`ak. 'You think your puppet soldier will give you the universe...he is only as powerful as his creator, and you are weak, Master Naumokron! Nothing but a parasite taking on an empty shell! Hondor is nothing more than an ancient, blood-stain in the pages of torn away parchment! Meaningless!' As Aumon speaks, he strengthens his force upon Duul`ak.

Duul`ak retaliates, and fires a beam of energy against Aumon's bolt of power. The two over-power one another and cause them to force each other into a rip, and blasting them each across the realm of Aura. The blast clears away the foliage and flora in the area. The grass, the trees, even the twisted dead tree Duul`ak was perched upon, has incinerated into nothing more than a wasteland of ashes and soot.

A`deon shields Nilta from the blast. She remains tightly held in his arms, or at least as tight as he can grip her. The blast clears, then dims down back to the pale gray it once was before. He looks at her, her eyes are closed, unconscious from the force that struck her, immobilized her.

There is nothing more to be had here, nowhere could he go. He stands up upon his two, trembling legs. His strength is weak and his limbs feel brittle, yet he has strength enough for this. He grips Nilta by her arms and pulls her up, then he tightly wraps his good arm around her waist and tries to put her over his shoulder, he feels he can do it, but he falls to his knees, and drops her back down to the dirt and her body hits the dirt with a thud, and she rolls away down a hill for a stint.

A`deon feels the pain in his back, riding up his spine much like the flow of water, only instead of a cooling, soothing sensation, he feels the crack of his back and the radiating waves of pain.

He attempts to straighten himself up, and he shifts his way down the hill to reach her. The fall didn't even disturb her, she still lays with her eyes in the dark, and her mind lost in the realm of shadows. This time he grabs her by the wrist and drags her along. A few paces, and then he stops, his body hurts to bad, he's bound to give up...and then he thinks back.

He thinks back...when he fled away from what should have been a sacrifice, a true general's death...but he could not go through with his actions, he simply could not...simply may be the wrong word, for his choice at the time seemed simple, but it becomes more complex the more he analyzes what he had done. But was it so wrong? Is it so wrong, to not want to die? But that was what he was expected to do, he showed his actions, he showed a momentary act that was to be one of the most heroic deeds in Runegard's history...yet at that last moment, turned him into a coward in the eyes of his soldiers he led...he was in charge of. At that last moment, he decided that their lives, were not worth the sacrifice.

If he is to learn from mistakes, if he is to become the general that Aura looks upon him to be, in the eyes of Civilians, Gormons, as well as Asyndians...he must find that something within him. And to start, he needs to get Nilta back to Diin, back to their camp. Even though, in his eyes they are escaped criminals, yet in his heart, they saved him once, and Nilta attempted to save him again, so he will not leave her here to die.

A`deon once more, wraps his arm around Nilta's waist, heaves her up into the grasp of his strong arm, ignores the pain, ignores the tempting voice of can't and quite, to lay her back down...he throws these thoughts out of his mind, and lumbers over the hills, for a time, his bones screaming, his joints agitated, but he presses on, he continues for her sake.

Finally, over the hill, and not far in the distance, as the pale moonlight shines through with a dim glow, he notices the fire Diin has made, and A`deon, hoists her and shifts about, adjusts her in his arm, and carries her for a stretch until he is within the area of the camp.

Diin can hear the footsteps approaching. They sound heavy to him, as though they are struggling.

'Nilta...? Have you returned, is our general with you?' He asks.

'No...it is I, the general, who returns with your sister.' Out of breath and staggering, he reaches the fire, falls to his knees, and sets her down. He then collapses back, leans upon a hefty sized rock jutting from the ground, and looks up at the empty sky, now fully cloaked in the shawl of night.

Diin hears where Nilta touched the dirt as A`deon laid her down. He tosses the walking staff aside, and falls to the ground upon his hands and knees. He feels his way around the fire, guided by the heat, reaches out his hand, and feels Nilta's long, brown hair sprawled across the ground. He runs his hand down her eyes, feels for a pulse in her neck, he feels the faint beat of life...relieved that his sister still lives. A`deon, his eyes blur from exhaustion, watches Diin tend to his sister as she lays unconscious. He takes a closer look, and notices the bandage around Diin's eyes is becoming damp. From Diin's lifeless, dead eyes...a tear of sadness, filled with all the sorry that cannot be seen in his stare...is visible within the one drop, the tiny pool of water and sadness that drips to the ground, lingers for a moment, then dissipates.

Diin says nothing, not one word, he simply scoops Nilta up into his arms...and holds her within his love, close to his heart. She listens to his heart beat, a sort of lullaby that soothes her, connects to her. Her eyes flutter, then close...after a slow, drowning moment, she gathers what strength she can, and opens them. Diin feels her heart beat pick up, it beats faster as she returns to life, back from the darkness that hid the world away behind her closed eyes.

'I'm here sister...I'm here with you, you know that don't you...I know you do, a brother's intuition can see better than any two eyes.' He replies in a soft demeanor to her.

Nilta is left to sleep soundly, to recover he strength by her brother's side. Diin sits by the fire, gazing past the flames in the direction of A`deon who has been in and out of dreams and nightmares for the past hour, as the night is now in full loom over their heads.

'Once she has regained her strength...we will move on towards the citadel. From here it will be about four days trek. The cold air is growing thick, and the snow caps along Mirym's borders can be seen just to the northwest.' Diin says.

Yet, A`deon doesn't bother to look. He is too preoccupied with trying to sleep, than to listen to Diin's words. The sounds start to drown out, as A`deon's eyes fade and his surroundings blur.

....through a nightmare, and the outlying worlds of darkness, from the land beyond, and the worlds were hope is swallowed away by fear...the shadow of Wom, will soon appear...A`deon holds his head up to the sky, a sky that covers a barren wasteland of charred ashes and incinerated bones, castles fallen, and the land carved into it, scored by a blade of despair. Within the gathering night, neither clouds, nor smoke, an ominous black shade blankets Aura in shadows...and then, he hears the chilling roar, of something sinister in his wake...

A`deon is awakened when he feels the clutch of a hand upon his shoulder, and a voice that calls his name. His eyes burst open, panting and sweating form the fear of the darkness and what has happened, but when he opens his eyes he sees the familiar gray landscape, and the dying campfire before him. He still remains in the same place, he must have slept through the rest of the night into the late afternoon. He sees the hand upon his shoulder, for it is Nilta, she has awakened and seems to be in a better state than what she was. She has a rugged blanket wrapped around her shoulders like a cape.

'Good, you are finally awake!' Diin says.

'I haven't had a long nights rest in some time.' A`deon replies, he rubs his groggy eyes and tries to stand upon his feet, yet can only make it half way and he seats himself upon the log he fell asleep in front of.

'You have been asleep for two days! I had to pull Nilta into the cave to protect her.'

A`deon looks at Diin.

'I sense you are confused...but so am I. I can't explain what happened, or what was going on with you. But the more you struggled in your sleep, the more the winds changed, and the weather patterns became more and more erratic, until finally you calmed down and Nilta came out to wake you up. It was the clash of thunder and storms that brought her through.' Diin replied.

A`deon clutched his face in the cup of his palms. 'I don't know what is going on. I've been having trouble staying awake, and these nightmares are getting worse. I don't know...I just don't know...' He stands up and limps passed them, not saying a word, just looking around the area, thinking, keeping to his thoughts.

'Arctalus will know...' Diin says to himself.

'Who is he? A`deon asks.

'Arctalus-Hon, he was once the master of the Asyndians in the far North. After the Grey Age, many of his clan gave themselves to the Great Divide, others were persecuted during the Cleansing. He is the only one left of his clan. Arctalus is one of the wisest Asyndians in Aura, and he will know how to deal with such threats of the mind and essence.'

'And this is why we are going to him? Is this why you carried me away from the battlefield unconscious?'

'There is something larger at work...many thought the second Grey Age would be the end...but it isn't...not for two hundred years, not until now. The Hero of Ages has faded into legend, and as the days grow darker, there are none to protect Aura, not even the Asyndians, not master Arctalus, not the Asyndians of Thylesian. All that I can comprehend...is that the nightmares have been realized...' Diin replies.

'I don't understand...I'm not sure if I want to. There is nothing I can do...what do you expect from me, to pull a magical sword from the stone...is that it?' A`deon retorts.

'It's more complex than that...and I can tell by your tone, your young mind will need some time to grasp hold of these delicate ideas...and it is time we run short on, because the days grow darker, and the nights longer.' Diin says.

He is quiet for a second, and though he cannot see A`deon, he seems to watch him, observe the general's actions. '...if...if I may ask you, why were you chosen to be the General of Runegard? Why were you given the task to be in charge of the mightiest army in Aura, and to be the protector of Aura's foremost up and coming leader in our diplomacy? Didn't you say you did not want the task...why did you not simply step down, instead of getting into such a mess?'

A`deon raises his head, and seems to ponder for a moment, these questions Diin has just asked him, though he knows exactly how he is going to answer the blind man.

'I fought alongside General Gabriel II, I wasn't a vain, and neither brash soldier. I wasn't fearless, I was cautious, more withdrawn from wanting to encounter the enemies head on. I always tried to find ways around, than through where the battle was deadliest. I was ridiculed and seen as a coward, shooed away from the other warriors...but I could not change, that was how I was...how I still am I guess.

Then, that fateful day came, our soldiers were split into two groups to stop an attacking hoard that was spotted amassing upon Runegard's boarders. General Gabriel maintained the main army at the walls, and we were sent ahead to spy out the land, see what they were up to, and if possible, to drive them back, and if we couldn't do that, we were going to sure as hell try!'

Diin could hear a faint tone of a general in A`deon's exclamation, but he did not say anything, he simply let the A`deon continue his story.

'Another soldier among our army, a highly respected one at that, was sent with a large force to the south-east, while I was sent to the north-east. We were to observe the forces from the cover of the trees, then circle around and attack them in the middle.

That...was supposed to be the plan...until I saw the force with my own eyes...I, I have never dealt with a force that large, not since the ancient days has there been such large numbers from the opposition. I could not understand where such a force had been lurking within Aura, surely the Asyndians who scout back and forth over the land would have seen them and reported to us. It was like they were summoned out of the shadows, they just appeared out of thin air...but that would be impossible, I thought!

Yet, it was not just the large numbers...but there was something else about those soldiers that grasped my courage with the black, left hand of fear. There was something cold, something unnatural about them, almost machine-like, not of Aura. Their dark army, and moving gears and leavers troubled me...I knew, when we made that charge, we would not return.

Too much, far too much was filling my mind like a growing cancer! The obligation to lead these soldiers, who were ready, ready to fight, ready to die for our land, our home. All of them, but one...their own leader. That was also the plague in my thoughts...the fear of death, of dying. I...I was not ready to die...'

A`deon begins to break down. Diin can feel the moisture of tears on the wind, for the breeze upon A`deon's shoulders is cold. He tries to maintain his composure, but he struggles, his voice shakes as he tries to utter his next words. He soaks up the tears and dries his eyes.

'The southern armies charged, I could see their torches and banners held in clusters and waves as they charged down the forested hills. The troops behind me were restless, the hofts and lines of men and women pushed up against me, irking me one, yelling...barking like animals.

"Charge...!" They cried. "We must go...what are we waiting for...!" They yelled. I could not say anything I froze...so they took the charge themselves...one of the soldiers cried the battle roar, and they all charged, they simply went around me, I could not move...all I knew was that I failed.'

The tears flowed harder, as A`deon closed his eyes.

'They...they were all slaughtered, cut down into pieces. I could not watch anymore, so I fled...I turned and fled upon the back of my hoft, back to Runegard to warn Gabriel to warn him of what he was up against. It was like fate...along the way, I found a young woman...she too was trying to flee. So I put her on my horse and we fled together. You know her as the

Daughter of Runegard. We were both terrified...there was no such leadership in either of us. Not in the shape we were in.'

A`deon wipes his eyes. Nilta tries to comfort him, but he politely shoves her away with the swipe of his arm.

'No, I need no comfort. There is no comfort in letting your fellow comrades get slaughtered and not be by their side.' He says to Diin and Nilta.

'Is there comfort in getting hacked to pieces? After all, you saved her...the Daughter of Runegard, one of the most respected and revered Civilians within Aura!' Diin replies.

'No, no their isn't...but I should have! I should have died bravely at that moment on the battlefield. Because those Civilians and Gormons were brave, and I just stood there shaking like a coward. And then running, running through the trees as even their branches point and taunt me! At us...we were both cowards both running from death! I'm, I'm just glad at least one of us pulled through it all and became something...'

'And what happened when you returned?' Diin asks.

'Something happened that I never would have expected...at first they were all shocked to see me, confused, and wondering what happened. Then they saw the terrified woman with me. I explained to General Gabriel what had happened, what we're dealing with. I reported how these beings fought and their movements and strategies. He mourned for the loss of all those Civilians and Gormons under his command, yet was very grateful with what I have informed him of, and would use this information to drive back these invaders. He thanked me for rescuing this woman and bringing her to safety. But that was just one...I let thousands of others die...I...I can't explain what happened...it was all in a blur.

I could see in his eyes, that when I described the army and how they fought, a haunting look came over his face, his eyes glistened, they were worried, as they should have been. He sent me on my way and got the woman to shelter with the others in hiding. I wandered the streets and made my way to my quarters where I passed out.

I woke up the next morning, to the sounds of cheering and applause through the streets. I went to find out what was going on...and they had done it, General Gabriel II had decimated the army of darkness, driving them from the borders of Runegard.

There was celebration and merriment throughout the rest of the day, and into the night. They celebrated the general's victory, they celebrated and mourned those that had passed. Everyone but me, I would not be a part of this. I watched from the furthest tower of Runegard, looking at the sky, looking at the vast space of Aura, over fields and rivers...my thoughts were as barren as the Greywaste to the south. Everything, every thought, every feeling, has been shriveled up and burned away into nothing more than fragments of smoke and dust. I wish the winds would blow it all away, but the fragments are still buried and left behind in my mind.

The festivities settled, and I watched every light, every torch burn out. Later on, there was a knock upon my door. It was General Gabriel II and two of his guard. I thought for sure they have heard that I had run, that I had deserted, they knew...though all who witnessed my cowardice were dead...somehow they knew.'

"Sorry to disturb you at this hour...might I come in? I want to thank you for showing your courage and brining me this information...without it, we would have been defeated, and the land of Runegard would have fallen. But, I must ask, what

happened on the battlefield...how was it you were able to escape unscathed, while the others had fallen in battle...?"

'...it's a hard thing to lie, it's harder to lie than to tell the truth...but that's what I did. I showed the general a wound I had received when I approached the gates. I fell from the horse only to have a sharp stick drive through my leg, the wound was still fresh for there was an infection surrounding the wound. I had the bandage undone. The general looked down and noticed the scarred tissue. So I lied, I told him I was struck by an arrow in the charge, and was unable to fight. He examined the wound, and it looked precisely where an arrow was lodged into my leg. All I could do, was ride back and warn him.

And that was when the moment came...he crossed his arms behind his back and walked slowly about the room. You could never imagine the guilt that pressed against my chest.'

"A'deon...I have observed you, and the way you strategize...you think like a leader, calm, collected, and you know when and when not to strike. The others are to hurried to rush in and get themselves killed. That is why you are still alive and returned. I mourn those soldiers, they were brave, and I wish they were still alive, I wished they would have studied the enemy closer, that is what you did, and when wounded, you knew to return with this information to help your fellow soldiers here."

'I said nothing, I only thanked him. But the sickness in my stomach was horrible, it felt as though he was insulting those who were truly brave, and praising the coward. He told me he was stepping down...and was looking for one to take his place as Grand General over Runegard's armies.'

"...I put out my hand, to you General A`deon, and if you accept, I place my sword and my honor to you. Now, what say you?!"

'So I accepted. I did not want it, but I could not say no to him, for all the better successors have been slain, I was all that was left to lead the newer troops coming into the services of Runegard.

The ceremony was bitter sweet and created a weight upon my shoulders I did not want. I did not smile, I did not feel any pride at that moment, and the applause I received was few, for many questioned this decision, as well as my appearance alive and well after my return. And they were right to, I could feel the looks, the stares, they knew just as much as I did. They knew the truth that I was a coward. I held the blade in my hands, not with the strength of a brave leader, but as though I had just seen a sword for the first time. A scared child looking at an adult's weapon...'

Diin replies. 'Perhaps he saw a patient man in you...one who thinks first, then acts. Your instincts told you the battle would go sour, you knew...and if you had not observed the fighting and did not bring warning to General Gabriel, then more Civilians, Gormons, and even Asyndians would have fallen to the dark armies. And you gave Runegard a strong leader in a woman no one would have ever known...who would have been left for dead to those of the dark.'

He snides, 'I think your mind is as blind as your eyes.' Nilta steps in and slaps A`deon across the face, sending him back to the ground.

'No Nilta, maybe he is right...maybe I'm not seeing this coward for what he is, maybe I should look passed what is good and refuse to help remove the weakness beneath his bones, beneath the thin skin.' Diin replies.

A`deon stands back up, wiping the trickle of blood from the corner of his mouth.

'Is that accurate enough for you general...' Diin says, losing his patience.

A`deon says nothing at first, only spits to the ground.

'You have a weakness A`deon...and if that weakness was turned into strength, then your tactical thinking along with having the strength to swing your sword in battle...you would be unstoppable. You were pulled from the battlefield for a second chance, to return to Runegard, to return to battle as the general Gabriel saw when he chose you.'

'And just how does he, this Arctalus, plan to do this? Unless he takes out my heart to replace it with another...what can possibly be done?' A`deon questions this agenda that sounds ridiculous to him.

'It's all about the essence within you, not the only the physical, but the mental as well. In order for your tactics to work, you must have the strength within your gut to back your plans up and pass this bravery onto your soldiers. Because when you are afraid, they will be too, though many will refuse to show this the way you do. They will be impatient, anxious, not striking with meaning but without finesse and aim.'

'Where is he?' A`deon asks.

'His citadel resides in the far reaches of the mountains, across the Glorial Tundra and mile after mile of ice and snow-covered wastelands where the sleet and hail blasts and tears through the winds at your face...and if you lose your way in the thick walls of mist, you will become one with the ice, when you are frozen in the deadly ice storms that wisp across Mirym day after day, without warning or pattern.'

'Can you promise we will make it?' A`deon asks.

'You...no, but Nilta and I, have been fortunate enough so far. If you know where to go, then you will be able to avoid the ice storms.'

'Then we're still traveling together I assume?' A unpleased look comes over A`deon's face. Diin can hear the disappointment in his voice and smiles.

'Yes, I'm afraid so...unless you want to suffer the fate of the ancient Aura of Othetica, then you have no other choice.'

A`deon rubs his sore arm. Nilta approaches him.

'Do you wish to hit me again?' He says with a smart tone.

She shakes her head no, and hands him a sword, the sword of General Gabriel II, the one he received when he became the general. The ruby upon the base of the hilt was covered in dry mud and scratches, and the blade was dull.

'She was able to retrieve it near your body when we found you. We held onto it until you were well enough to grasp it.' Diin says. 'I think it is time, don't you?'

Nilta holds out the sword, grasping it barely by the blade, careful not to slice her palm. A`deon hesitates for a moment.

'I did not want this sword the first time... I do not want it now.' He refuses. He will not take the sword.

'The fifth step to take...is acceptance in your duties...but this is not the case. You are not ready for this step it seems, though you cannot escape the inevitable conclusion. You are not leading the world with this blade, you are simply taking back the object that belongs to you...'

A`deon, still not sure, stands and his eyes stare deep into the ruby. He sees his reflection, the reflection of a bent and crooked man, a Civilian lost in helplessness and thought. He grabs the orb to cover the reflection, not wanting to see, not wanting to look upon himself. He feels the cold steel of the hilt in his grasp, and opens his eyes. Nilta has let go, and he now holds the sword of General Gabriel II in his hand. His arm is sore holding up the heavy blade, but he clutches it, not with strength, but with a questioning thoughts, if he will truly be worthy to take on what was left to him.

'You have completed the first step...and now, onto the second...' Diin says.

He keeps his focus upon the sword as he speaks. 'To Mirym...?'

'To Mirym...and the citadel of Master Arctalus Hon.' Diin replies.

Part XIII:

Troubled Vistas

~

And over beyond the rim, pass the ancient mountain peaks, across a swift, burning cold, the desert of ice and blue fire, the frozen wastes of Mirym lay before them. The forgotten tribes of Mirym have long departed these lands for the warmer climate south, of what was once called Greenhaven, now has been renamed and located on all maps and topography as Greenrym.

The winds are cold, burning upon each of their faces, turning their cheeks to a fiery red, and lips…bruised and blue, as the ice and frozen streams of the far eastern boarders along Stonehaven. The sun is going down, setting upon their departure from the west, as refugees from the ruins and debris of Runegard, for far behind them, they can see the smoke still rising at their backs, being absorbed into the atmosphere, into the black clouds above, as though something were…absorbing the black mist.

A'deon, still soar and bruised, his left arm still fractured and bandaged in a sling around his neck and shoulder, a scar dragged down his right eye, looks outwards ahead with his two scouting eyes, Diin walks just behind A'deon with his hand on the Civilian's shoulder, as a guide, and Nilta walks just ahead of them, as they traverse down the slope of the icy hill, where a rocky, stone road lays out before them, fractured, and most of the path is buried, but they are able to follow.

Ancient skeletal bones from lost herds and tribesmen, along with their women and children, are scattered to their left and right.

'These winds burn my eyes…I see nothing but white…what is it we're searching for? Where is this place you're taking me to?' A'deon realizes what he says about seeing nothing and quickly apologizes to Diin. 'Diin…I am sorry…'

Diin taps him upon the shoulder and motions for him to not worry about the comment.

'This is where the ancient Mirym tribes used to migrate across the snow and ice, and a miserable cold march it was…miles and miles of desolate, frozen bitterness…and then…that's when they thought their hope came, that's when they were the most vulnerable, with their women and children, their people dying around them, more and more each day, the black tongue of Kandarius Lockmore came in the night…turning their bitterness and suffering, their rage and anger, against our ancestors of Othetica, fueling their hatred against all Aura, turning them to the side of darkness with empty lies made as promises to them by the minions of the Destroyer himself…Maz Dregor. They waged flame and steel against blood across Civilian and Gormon lands.'

There was nothing around them, the only movement, was the racing of the winds, and the only sounds, were the screams and howls of the icy throat the banshees cry from, into the darkening sky. The cries of the fallen ancestors can still be heard if one listens carefully, one can hear the pain they suffered at the hands of their slow, icy death, as they were buried under in their tombs of frost, and covered in snow and sleet, frozen by ice rain. The cold touch claws at A'deon, Diin, and Nilta, burning their skin to a cool purple, the beginnings of frost's deadly, painful bite. The temperature is with each passing minute, becoming more and more unbearable, and is slowing down their trek significantly. Diin speaks once more to A'deon, his voice fragile and weak in the wind, the howling is overcoming his tone, forcing him to speak at a higher volume as they cross over the plains.

'A'deon...you now see, what it is I see...as you said...nothing. You can hear what I hear...'

A'deon listens, but he only hears the wind.

'...that, is the sound of bitterness. You can feel what I feel upon your flesh...'

'What's that? I'm so cold, I feel nothing, and my flesh is becoming numb and bruised!'

'It's vulnerability! Your flesh and life is vulnerable to this cold, I am a man without his sight, my flesh and life is vulnerable all the time...unless I'm careful.'

And Diin is correct, for he can feel, understand what A'deon is thinking and feeling.

'You see, an old Gormon once said, *"It takes more than just sight...to be a great warrior..."* for all senses need to be utilized in combat as well as wisdom. That Gormon was Roaur Greatbeard, master of Stonehaven, inherited from his father after he was killed at the hands of Dregor worshippers many, many years ago.'

Diin stands silent for a moment, they stop, and Nilta turns to see what is holding them up. She pulls out her dagger from her hilt, and taps twice upon her gauntlet.

'Yes Nilta, I know I know, we need to continue...' He turns his focus back to speaking to A'deon. 'I'll say this to you A'deon, when we reach Arctalus-Hon, you will learn to harness all of your senses, for this is no simple trainer Nilta and I take you to. With my blindness, I've learned to master my other senses and harness my greatest weapon of all...instinct. I sense feelings, emotions, and thoughts, most others cannot. You see, we all give off waves, we pulsate with energy, and when you take the time...to listen, and to harness the energy around you...and from within, your mind and your heart, you can see things and do what others will never be able to.'

A'deon ponders this notion as they travel along, for this thought helps to keep his mind off the cold bite of the coming death that seems to loom all around them.

Diin's empty eyes gaze off into nothing, but this is really the vast epitome of cold emptiness, as cold as the storm approaching, as cold as Aura's dead bones. Nilta falls back and taps A'deon on the shoulder, awakening him from his thoughts. She points off towards the northwest, a ferocious storm, a wall of ice and dark clouds will be upon them within the next hour.

'The ice is coming...we need to reach the tower by nightfall, or else we will become one with the ancients who are frozen beneath the tundra.' Diin exclaims. Nilta wraps her arm around her brother's arm, and using his guiding staff, they proceed along down the frozen pathway. A'deon wraps his cape around his body, and tightens the string, and covers his face with his hood, and follows up from the rear, as they quicken their pace.

This bleak road is a long, low-lying trek into an icy chasm, followed by a snowy trail that heads upwards through a valley of icicles, and onto the main bulk of the plateau of the Glorial Tundra.

Along this barren wasteland they travel, they come across faces, faces in the deep ice, many faces, blue and icy, twisted and miserable, dead faces with lifeless doll-eyes that either roll back or stare up at them from the cold hell beneath their feet. Eons of frozen overcast and snow has buried these ancient beings deep in this tundra. Limbs with frost-bitten fingers, reach upwards, long have they been icicled over. How many of these lost souls have been swallowed within the Glorial Tundra? It's impossible to tell, could be thousands, could be millions, could it have been genocide? Nearly an entire race of Mirym dispersed of, the ancestors of the north, have become extinct, for their southern brethren have long abandoned their old tribal ways, and live more like the Civilians of Othetica.

Those were the unfortunate ones to never migrate south to the Greenrym territories, maybe they tried, they were trying to escape their fate, they were on their way, traveling to better, warmer lands, but the ice, the hurricanes and cyclones of the tundra, caught up to them, they walked right into the horrible fate they were trying to avoid, and they never made it to their new life to be one with their Greenrym brethren.

Nilta points, farther to the North East, hidden upon the summit of the furthest mountains. The crags and towers of Arctalus-Hon, a vast and intimidating structure, is a castle-fortress built into the thick ice, and the lumbering northern mountains of the Glorial Tundra. Upon its furthest point, a vast and mighty tower, stretches far into the summit, past the ethereal mist, and disappears into the clouds above.

Far above them and off over beyond the furthest, highest peaks of the northern mountains, through the cluster of mists and snow that swirls abound, as thick as clouds, a tall spire peers through, then as the winds blow, the more the mighty spire reveals itself, for this is the mighty citadel of the Asyndian, Arctalus Hon.

'It takes some days to get to the nearest entry way, over there…to your left.' Diin motions for A`deon to look towards the front of the fortress all the way to the far left hand side where there is a dull golden doorway off to the side of the tower.

'Is there no front door?' A`deon asks.

'Asyndian towers have no doors, for they fly to their entrances, which are built all the way up, at the very top.' Diin replies.

'And what of the storm approaching, it will be only a few hours until we are buried under the ice and sleet!' A`deon shouts at a louder volume, for the winds have been picking up for the last hour.

'There is a hidden valley pass just through here, we can pass through the mountains safely away from the deadly ice. It takes longer than the direct way, but it is our only way of reaching the citadel alive!' Diin replies.

Nilta looks on as the two discuss the plan, she looks off to the oncoming sheets of ice and wind, and the storm will be on them in less than an hour. She grabs A`deon's arm intently and points to the northwest, the blizzard is swallowing up, engulfing the mountains as it approaches them.

Nilta grabs Diin around the arm and she leads him along, A`deon follows behind. They go around the base of the mountains for a pace, away from the main stairway carved into the rocks that head straight up to the main citadel, they round a corner and ahead of them, is a slight downward trench that has been carved into the frozen ground, the passage is much like a slope, with no stairs but it leads downwards into a dismal cave. Nilta holds onto her brother and they both slide down the trench and disappear into the darkness. A`deon steps onto the slick ice, his leg kicks forward, as his body falls back and slams upon the ice hard. The rush of cold takes him as he slides away to join the other two who wait beyond the cave.

He feels he is sliding on and on, not coming to any end. The daylight has long faded behind him, and only the darkness lays ahead in wait. Breaking icicles and choking on the cold air that hammers against his face, blowing up from some unknown source far beneath these mountains. He hears what sounds like running water, but this would be impossible, for any and all water that once ran through here would have frozen over. There is a faint flicker of a dancing flame just beyond, and then, out of nowhere, he falls off the edge of this harrowing, dark ride.

Diin and Nilta are standing off to his right awaiting him so they can continue.

'This way general...' Diin says.

'Don't call me general anymore...just call me by my own name...but not even that's worth much anymore.' He replies, remaining on the ground where he fell, taking heavy breaths.

'Unless your superiors say otherwise...you are a general.' Diin replies. Nilta holds out her hand to help A`deon up. He looks at her for a moment, then accepts the help and she lifts him up.

'I say otherwise...I didn't want to be general, I was chosen. There is no more Runegard, all those who fled to the caves are probably long dead, including the Daughter. I turn my sword in, I take off my cape.' A`deon unsheathes his sword and unbuttons the two metal pins upon his armor, he grips the cape tightly before the subterranean gust of wind can carry it away. He wraps the cape around the sword and walks over to the edge of what looks like some form of wind stream. He looks down into vortex that swirls around and about.

'What is this current?' A`deon asks.

'That is a current powered by the source of these caves. Those vortexes lead to eternity. What slips in, never comes back.'

A`deon takes a step closer to the edge. 'Then let this vortex take these items...I know longer need them...' He holds the wrapped blade over the yawning chasm.

'I know what it is you would do...but I beg you do not do it...there are still dangers left to be faced within these caves!' Diin warns A`deon.

'I care not...let them take me...only a coward holds onto weapons.' With that, he releases the items, and the winds swallow them away.

'Then...you have made your decision...' In Diin's voice however, there is no sigh, nor any sign of him showing regret towards what A`deon has done.

'If I make it to the end of what may come, if I reach the citadel alive...then maybe I'll be worthy of something.' He replies.

They make their way through the icy passages and tunnels. The tunnels are dank, dark and cold, the smell of moisture is thick in the air, and if these walls were to melt...the three of them would be drowned in an underground ocean of freezing liquid. But that has not been so for eons, even epochs, these lands have always known ice, warmth for these barren wastes is but a far-off dream, a glint of light in the distance that has been clouded and smoldered by thick gray clouds. Many walls still have ancient scripture and hieroglyphics of the old tribes, who have departed these lands years ago and migrated south to inhabit Greenrym.

Diin can feel the tingle of the sun's rays upon his flesh.

'A`deon…look ahead…do you see the daylight? We are coming into a vast opening that separates the mountains of the northern and southern ranges. You could say this would be the courtyard.'

'Won't we exit into the storm outside?!' A`deon exclaims.

'No…nothing touches this side of the mountain, this was a pasture…a keeping ground for the Mirym beasts, the tribes herded and there was a small settlement nearby. Now there is nothing here but leftover skeletons and crumbled, thatched buildings.' Diin explains as they traverse along their current path, heading for the end of this tunnel.

'That would mean there are predators in this area?' A`deon asks.

'Were…they would have long left this area with nothing left to hunt or prey on.' Diin replies.

Nilta nods her head in agreement.

'It has been a long time since we came this way though…who knows what has evolved within the bowels of these mountains…keep your ears open.' Diin comments.

Once outside the cavern, they look up above them, the mountains seem to stretch almost in an endless spiral into the sky, within the clouds, the crackle of lighting laughs and the tiny fingers of electrical bolts strike the mountain peaks, turning unkempt snow into spots of cinders. The goliath of mist and fog swirls round into higher, abysmal dizzying heights.

Nilta turns back to A`deon and points to these clouds of lightning.

`Why does she point to the sky?' A`deon asks.

'She's showing you that there is a current that flows round these mountains, it protects these inner lands from the outside ice storms that ravage the landscape. Whether magical or natural, no one knows.' Diin replies. This, Diin explained, was the reasons for the storms and lighting upon the clouds.

'Does this energy come from this source you spoke of?' A`deon asks.

'It does…the energy you see, the energy that clashes above us, and all around us, these streams are all connected to this source.' Diin replies.

'Where is it located?' A`deon asks.

'At the heart of these mountains…some say after the cleansing took place, the heart of Tundrok, the Aura of storms and the winds, was placed within the mountains, and that his heart was revived to keep the balance of all the winds and storms. Whether or not that is true…I don't know, for our path leads further away from the heart. I have never laid eyes upon these legends to see if they were, indeed true. I may not be able to see anymore, and what the heart looks like I will never know, but I still feel the essence and sense the power it has over this place. The Mirym felt this power as well, they felt protected by it, and this area was a sanctuary to them, away from the storms on the outer rim.'

'A paradise which included predators that hunted them?' A`deon replies.

Diin laughs. 'Man can defend himself against beast, but put him up against a wall of ice and razor winds, and he is doomed.'

They walk across the fields and pastures of powdered snow that has been lightly sprinkled across the ground, some small patches of field grass protrude above the snow. The crumbled homes that once stood upon these grounds are dotted here and there and about the area, yet keeping to a cluster.

'This is odd, I always thought the Mirym tribes where nomadic in their ways and lifestyle. These homes and settlements look like they were permanent.' And then he found out why, for just about maybe a quarter mile away, there lay the main area of the abandoned Mirym settlement, and at the center, a massive lake that has long froze over, and off to the eastern shore, a mechanism had been built, it had a large wheel with odd coiled and wired connectors that led to a large device of many levers and switches, and from there, the wires stretched further out, and then into the ground.

'What is that machine over there beyond the frozen lake?' A`deon asks.

'That is a contraption the Asyndians of the north had built long ago for the Mirym who dwelt here, it harnesses the power of the mountain's essence, and created friction pumped in waves of heat, and that heat, was just hot enough to keep the ice melted, yet not hot enough to boil, the water was pure, drinkable…the machine allowed for these Mirym to live here. The machine's source helped water their crops, and keep their fields growing for allowing their herds to feed and thus producing a surplus of food and water, so they did not have to wander, hunt or gather.' Diin replies.

'Why was the settlement abandoned?' A`deon asks.

'Predators…predators from the outside, started living in these caves to hide away as the ice storms became more and more frequent. They started preying on the herds, and soon the Mirym which resided here. They lived all their known years in peace and excess, they were dependent on these machines, they spent their entire lives making sure they were in repair. They spent all their attention towards these contraptions that they never bothered to raise an army or have soldiers, because they never had to defend this land, the ice storms kept enemies out, until one day…those storms, kept the enemy in, and there was nowhere else for them to go but here.

Just as this area was a paradise for these Mirym, it became a paradise, a hunting ground for the creatures that invaded. The Mirym were either eaten, slaughtered, or they fled, only to be the victims of those ice storms beyond the protective fields of these mountains. The machines fell into disrepair, and the cold froze over these lands.' Diin explains.

They continue their trek over cold ground and dead fields, as they walk through the bones of ruined structures. Nilta stops in her tracks. Diin feels her tense up.

'What's the matter? A`deon…what is she looking at?' Diin asks.

A`deon's not sure, but he thinks he's heard something as well.

'She's looking off to the northeast, something caught her eye. And I'm not sure, but I thought I heard steps scamper across the ground.' He replies.

Diin pulls Nilta along on their way. 'Come sister…let's continue.'

'Was it safe to come this way?!' A`deon asks sternly.

Diin doesn't say anything at first. 'These grounds should be abandoned. Nothing could survive here now.'

A chill goes down his spine, he senses something, smells a terror that he did not notice before, for now it's closer to them than it was before.

'There's something here with us…'

'We will be better off than with the ice storms…just keep your pace…' Diin replies. 'Let's go Nilta…we need to reach the other side of the valley…'

'Whatever is after us…even if it is just our fears…they will not strike till nightfall that is the hour of when the predator strikes…that is when the warm blood tastes the best within these beasts' mouths!' He exclaims…a small amount of alarm struggles in his voice.

They quicken their pace…Diin holds his staff out straight, tapping the ground for objects in his way, Nilta holds his arm and pulls him along to keep her brother's speed up with her pace, while A`deon marches on to see what is ahead of them. Thus far, there has been nothing more than the aforementioned crumbled homes, long-houses, and bleached bones scattered across barren fields.

She draws her spear that's strapped upon her back, to prepare herself.

'We will do what we can to aid you…but without your weapons…how will you defend yourself general?' Diin asks, huffing as they run along, looking over his shoulder, trying not to fall as Nilta leads him on.

'I told you not to call me general…and I will handle myself where I may…after all I've been through, I'm not dead yet…' A`deon replies.

The swirling sky above them darkens as the shroud of night is pulled over further, as the darkness is upon them, it will be night soon, yet with how gray the atmosphere is, it will be night at a faster pace. They take a sharp left, and are almost to the far edge of the settlement from where they started. Then, from behind their backs, they hear something, a sound that sends the hair on their neck standing on edge, as a blood curdling roar echoes through the air.

They pick up the pace and move a little faster. They hear the roars and snarling, slobbering maws of something horrific infecting their air…yet there is no sound of footsteps, or the patter of claws, or the crunching of snow as the hooves move and gallop over the winter wasteland. There is nothing else to be heard.

'Where are they…there's nothing there!' A`deon yells.

He turns and looks at Diin and Nilta…and is horrified. Nilta, it appears, is kneeled over Diin, who lies on the ground dead, and is covered in blood, as Nilta eats away at his insides, tossing bones and blood all over the snow. She scratches away at her flesh as she gurgles her brother's blood. She scrapes away flakes of skin, to reveal crusts of scales and twisted veins that wrap and contort around some form of exoskeleton. Her fingers separate, and five Civilian fingers, turn to a trio of large knife-like claws upon each hand.

A`deon calls to her, yet she does not respond, she keeps eating away all the guts and fat within her brother's rib cage that has been splayed open. He walks closer, his footsteps catches her ears. She turns and looks at him, piercing his horrified eyes with her blood-shot stare, the stare of a frenzied animal. Her long pincers jutting from half a jaw torn away, drip blood, and within her mouth, is a throat lined with rows of teeth that pull and twist away at the flesh. Her gurgle, a malignant roar screams, and she now places all her blood-lust attention upon the prey in front of her.

A`deon slowly paces backwards in steady, quick steps. The bones in Nilta's ankles, grow and snap, bending backwards like the hind legs of some horrific insect, much like a locust. The mutated Nilta, the despicable shell of what was once her being, now this hideous beast, crawls on hands and hind legs towards him, sizing up her mark. She leans back, stays motionless for a brief moment, her breathing is heavy, heaving in and out, inhale, exhale…then, she pounces.

A`deon leaps away, falling upon his injured arm, feeling it wrench and tear once more. The force of Nilta's leap tosses her into one of the ruined buildings, tearing down the rest of the crumbled structure. She crawls back, this time her familiar shell is gone, and her armor decayed away from her transformation. Her mutation is complete. The creature lowers its head, and charges with two large prongs jutting from its forehead pointed at A`deon, ready to impale him. Its pincers snap and clip, ready to devour him, tear away the armor, and feast on the warm flesh and blood beneath.

A`deon turns and starts running away, then he thinks to himself…is he really a coward? Or is he willing to turn around and raise a defense against this beast…even if it means his death. Diin has been slain, and Nilta has become the concubine of some horrific beast, A`deon figures, he will make his own way to the citadel, he will find the way.

Nilta just barely grazes A`deon's flesh as he moves aside, and grasps the beast by the horn, the creature kicks her head and whips him into the air, onto her back. She bucks and shakes, trying to reach A`deon, she raises upon her hind legs and with a strong head thrust forward, sends A`deon flying into a pile of rubble and snow, injuring his back upon impact as he hits the pile. Still conscious, he stirs around, looking for something, gripping any piece of something to use as a weapon.

There, off to the side, laying in the snow, he sees Nilta's spear stabbed into the ground. He stirs around and gets upon his feet, his bones cracking as he moves, yet with all the pain he perseveres over the splinters of wood and charred mud brick that crumbles into a chalky substance as he walks over the bars. He makes it to the spear...then just falls short of grabbing for the shaft, a sharp tightening grips at the tendon in his ankle. A`deon looks back, and the beast has its crushing vice-like pincers biting down and grinding upon the bone in his leg, tighter and tighter she rips and gnaws and bites his leg, tasting of the blood, and a mouthful of flesh.

He flips around and kicks at the grotesque, scale face of the creature, puncturing a vessel just below the eye, as a thick black substance gushes forth from her eye. She winces and cries a sharp scream that echoes through the mountains. He kicks again, this time much harder, and with more vindication. The puss-filled, gelatin eye is sent hurtling through the air and lands upon the ground with a splatter, as distorted juices color the snow, a mixture of eye-bile and black blood drizzle across the ice, and flow with the direction of the wind.

As the creature pulls away, she takes A`deon's leg, and the pain sends him into shock, for it's so great, that the feeling is numb, there is no feeling, there is no more leg. A`deon clutches in vain for his limb, but to only grasp at a blood-squirting nub.

She tosses the leg away, rears up once again on her hind legs, and charges full force. The beast is upon A`deon, he can feel the hot wind, he is crippled and helpless...and at that moment, he feels a metallic force, bludgeon him across the face, the force feels strong enough that his bottom chaw detaches itself from the muscle.

'General...! General A`deon...!' A voice cries over and over. The light in his eyes becomes too bright for him to look, and then, he sees a great set of wings unfold before him.

Part XIV:

Arctalus Hon

~

"You see general...we can give you the power and the courage to face any obstacle...". A soft voice whispers in his ear...the voice sounds as though the figure is standing to his right, speaking into his ear. As the voice speaks, it multiplies, and the echo of many lingers in his mind.

A`deon awakens, surrounded by shadows, his arms and legs bound by chains against the cold, brick wall, of a dim room. The shapes spin and blur as they move around him. One of them calls, yells to him, does this twisted shape call his name? He cannot tell, he cannot see direction or faces. Another voice cries out, but not of his language or in the tone as the previous voice, this is a chant, a bright blue fire ignites the area, and a wave of energy pounds against his body and pulsates through his veins and bones. He receives a heated shock as his body feels as though it ignites with the blue fire. He hears a horrible sound, his throat vibrates and his vocals roar, a terrible sound, the sound is emitting from his lungs and belching into the air like vomit, then...he blacks out.

An eternity seems to drag by on chains, and his weighed-down eyes are forced open. A large, animalistic eye gazes into his, examining him, studying. The being utters words, words A`deon cannot understand, for they sound like mutters and syllables jumbled together through his ears. The being lets A`deon's head slouch back down, for the general is too weak to hold his head up.

He enters in and out of consciousness, and with the passing hands of time, his head is less muddled, and his vision is becoming clearer. He looks up, and out to the window on the far side of a large space blanketed in darkness, the braziers have been smoldered out for the evening, the smoke is still fresh in the air, yet A`deon can't help but feel something looms nearby, something is watching him, keeping an eye on him.

A`deon cannot get back to sleep, he watches the window the rest of the night, he sees the sky outside light the fires, as the sky turns purple and orange, and morphs into a somber, gray ominous wall. The light has been filtered out by a depressing gel of doom which blankets over.

'The skies are growing darker...with each hour that passes...' An ominous voice speaks from some shadowed part of the room.

'Where am I?' A`deon asks.

'You are in a safe place for the time being.' The voice replies.

'...why...what, what happened to me?' A`deon mumbles.

'That would take a thousand years of history to explain...but in short, the energy of the mountains has been touched by the finger of corruption, and the influence was driving your brain to madness, disintegrating your sanity and this would have continued had I, Arctalus Hon, not intervened, you would have killed both Diin and Nilta, and after a time…you too would have been destroyed, for that is the way the Dregor maneuver their attacks, they strike from the shadows and invade from within.'

The voice who claims to be the Asyndian master of the northern wastes named Arctalus Hon, the one whom Diin had spoken of, their master, the one who they report to.

'What is it you did to me?' He asks.

Arctalus enters further into the room, catching the faint light that still remains and lingers around with the darkened day. A`deon can now see the Asyndian, his feathers are slate gray tipped black, with a section of white on his chest, his eyes are a deep brown with stained pupils of coal. The left eye has traces of pale blue film glistening upon the surface.

'The source of these mountains has been infected…as were you. I was able to reach in and pull the blackness from your heart…but these mountains is another story. We built the source many ages ago to help these nomads find a stable structure, to reach their promised land, but the shadowy fingertips of the Dregor are sneaky…they always find a way.'

Arctalus seems to stop in mid-sentence.

'…a way to what?' A`deon asks, urging the Asyndian to continue.

'It was thought that two hundred years ago…these monsters were destroyed for good by the Hero of Light…but like any disease or virus…if just a piece of it is left, it will reform…it will come back. A piece was missed somewhere…These beings feast off of essence, their darkness can warp and bend any light to its power. Once this power infects…it spreads.

It infected the source of these Mirym and led them to madness, thus their eventual demise...there was nothing we could do...the poison was too deep and we had to put them down. Their warriors killed the old, their women, as well as their children, and their herds of livestock they kept to the fields.'

A`deon keeps his eyes upon the Asyndian, wondering what he was getting at.

'And...do you plan to kill me as well...have I know hope as to be kept locked within these chains?' A`deon replies.

Arctalus leaps through the air with a mighty gust of his wings and lands in front of A`deon. He once again forces the general's eye open and examines him closely, staring deep within him. He turns and walks away just a few feet, and with his raising hand, the lights slowly begin to dim inside the room.

The space is more enormous than A`deon could even comprehend, even larger and more grand than the Daughter's throne room in Runegard, with a ceiling several miles up, and smoothed round like a dome, the dome is made of thick stained glass and the room from wall to floor to wall, is built and laid with solid, adimantium marble which runs in a rhythmic pattern of faint glowing light that is powered by the energy in the torches.

However, for as grand as the room was, there were no statues, no tapestry, except for the violet floor runner across the hall and drapes down the windows. The braziers burn faint hues of pale blue and warm orange tones burning within a basin of sacred oil only the Asyndians know the secrets to creating.

Arctalus waves his hand, and the chains release A`deon from his bounds. He falls to the ground and rubs his sore wrists.

'You have a strong will General A`deon, if you didn't, you would have died. You have an essence as powerful as an Aura's, though you lack this understanding. You keep it buried deep within you, and it can't be free.' Arctalus says.

'I am not a general anymore, I've denounced the title...I don't know what I am anymore...' A`deon replies.

'Titles mean nothing...they are only a standing within civilizations, all of us use them to keep order...Asyndians, Gormons, Civilians...even the barbaric Skahljah used these titles. It's what is in you that is of interest. I know why you are troubled, you coward away from Hondor, and you feel that as the general of your armies...your death would have shown true bravery, is that right?'

A`deon shifts his eyes around the room.

'You don't have to say a word...because it isn't, you were truly afraid, and you wanted to save your life to fight another day, and you were right to do so, because you were not ready...and your other day is coming, you are needed for what is to come...and I will help you.'

'To harness my essence...?' A`deon replies.

'...and instincts. You will spend some time here and learn from Diin and Nilta, for they have been my best students, for their handicaps made them weak, but once they learned to harness all their power...'

A`deon stands upon his feet, still nursing his wrists. 'Where are they now?' He asks.

'Safe...but you must watch out...you have been marked and the eyes watch you...your very essence is still in danger.' Arctalus replies.

'I'm...tired of hearing about essence and darkness...what I need is a domineering voice and a good sword arm, I need power and the ability to rule.' He replies.

He watches the Asyndian speak, but the words that come out don't match...his voice has changed, it sounds like the voice her heard earlier.

"...you will have it...you will have it all! We can give you what you seek! You will not get power from this Asyndian, he will make you weak, he will break you down!"

Arctalus's voice returns to normal. He speaks in his tone as though nothing has happened, then he sees the peculiar look upon A`deon's face.

'A`deon...what is the matter?' He walks over and places his hand upon the general's shoulder. 'Something...something's still not right...' He touches A`deon, and his hand catches fire as something horrific with razor teeth and black winds, and shadowed hands reaches out to slay the Asyndian. Arctalus leaps back and forces more pale blue energy upon A`deon's flesh.

A`deon grasps his head and squeezes tightly, screaming at the top of his lungs, feeling his body engulf in flames. He lashes out at Arctalus.

'ENOUGH...!' He cries. Arctalus ceases his attack.

A`deon shouts curses at the Asyndian, but his voice is...changed, the tone is lower, and the attitude is much worse.

'You...damn...Asyndian!' He recover's himself from the blast. 'You strike me again, I'll rip your wings off!' He reacts with a hateful fervor.

'Listen to yourself! The taint is still with you! They have grown stronger indeed...but, what if...what if your growing strength...together?!'

A`deon glares at Arctalus.

'You must listen to me...you are allowing them to infiltrate you! You must not let this happen!' Arctalus cries.

'I...I don't want your help.' A`deon replies gritting his teeth. 'I can help myself...I can make my own way.'

'You have been touched by the nightmares...it's your choice, but think carefully...you walk out from these walls, I will not help you...neither will Diin or Nilta. The two are still shaken up from the attack earlier. If you leave these walls...you will have no safety from the ice storms, and if the winds don't get to you first, the visions will be back, they will be waiting!' Arctalus retorts back.

'I have strength...' A`deon replies.

'I said you are strong...but you're still not strong enough...' Arctalus says.

'Look at my arms, my face...my body, my legs broken, and my pride gone...these nightmares have nothing left to take from me!' A`deon replies.

'They seemed to have taken your ears, because you don't listen, these beings don't want your items of your physical flesh, they want what's inside...your essence, your mind, to get inside...' Arctalus says.

A`deon limps passed him, then turns. 'They can have it...because I don't.' He replies. He heads in the direction of a huge stairway that descends to a lower level where Diin and Nilta are.

Arctalus turns to gaze upon a shrine, the shrine where A`deon was bound, to help release the chaos within him. He walks to it, and gazes wide-eyed to the shrine dedicated in Airical's image.

'Airical...if you can hear me, help us if you can, may you and Y`nahlia bestow unto us, some of Arla's light, so that we may once more banish this foe away!'

There is a disturbance that catches his attention downstairs.

'...help us all!' Arctalus whispers to himself. Then, he hears a cry...the muffled cry of Nilta and her brother pleads to A`deon to be merciful.

Part XV:

Voice of Darkness

~

Diin and Nilta hear the footsteps coming down the vast stairwell. Nilta gets to her feet, Diin stays seated, still feeling the sharp pains in his ribs, and feeling like something had dug into him and scooped his insides out. He doesn't quite remember what happened, and by Nilta's confused, sorrowful looks, neither does she. She stays on her guard though, still not forgetting nearly being run through by A`deon, that raged, red-eyed look in his glare. She knows not the reason for A`deon's attack, but she will never forget.

Through the doorway, the shadowed figure of A`deon limps into the candlelight, where Nilta can see his scars and bruises and the limp upon his leg, slowing his progress, his storm towards them. Diin hears the feet of the Civilian general stamper closer towards them. Nilta no longer sees that red fire in his eyes, but she can sense something emanating from him, something that reeks up from underneath his flesh, she stirs with uneasiness.

'I feel it too Nilta…at ease, let's not try to rouse him.' Diin says to her with a whisper, for he too can sense it as well.

A'deon stops just in front of them, for the door lays beyond further across the mass-expanse of the entryway.

'Master A'deon...how are you feeling?' Diin asks.

He's silent at first, making only minimal eye contact with them, he looks curiously at Nilta who is eyeing him up as a threat, for he doesn't remember what happened to him, the rage, the outburst, but he can feel it lingering upon him, like a taste upon the tip of the tongue, and whether that taste of anger, that sudden burst of power, whether its taste is good or bad, bitter or sweet, he still is unsure, but he feels it inside of him, he feels something stirring inside of him, a storm, the calm of the waters rising, boiling higher and higher as the veins pump and the blood cooks inside his mind. The waves of the mind gushing out, and the tide taking them back again, taking the memories, and these nightmares, back out to sea again.

Nilta leans in a little closer, but A'deon knows what she's up to, and calls her out on it.

'Looking for something my dear? You may not say a word, but your body language is so loud I can almost hear the shouting loud and clear!' He turns to Diin. 'Well...why not tell me what your sister is looking for? You're the master of the senses...so, out with it!'

"His voice, A'deon's voice is all wrong." Diin thinks to himself. He gathers his composure and speaks. 'Nothing...she is simply making sure you're alright, both of us were worried. Did you learn of anything from Master Arctalus? Why this...happened to you?' He replies in a cool, calm voice.

Nilta looks on in horror, as she can see that...that look coming back, a look she recognizes all too well. A'deon turns back to face her.

'So…what is it? What do you see woman! Are you piercing my flesh, gazing into my very body to find the parasite?! The source of the nightmares…*these, these headaches…!*'

There it is again, the voice is of A`deon again… *"There is…is there something in there with him?"* Diin's thoughts are running rampant, trying to figure out what is going on, for there was something, something back at the source of that mountain, something had tainted it, and its affects seemed to have a heavy influence upon A`deon's mind.

"Power…power and tyranny will wipe away the weak…!"

There is the echo of a voice, Diin can't quite place where it came from, but he heard something. *"Who…who was that, it has the voice of a Civilian…but has the taste and the gurgle of something…darker…"*

'Are you feeling alright?' Diin inquires.

He snaps. 'I'll be wonderful…when you tell your damn sister…to quit staring at me like some…villain!' And he lashes out at Nilta, Diin gets up to intervene, but a force holds them back and stops A`deon in his tracks.

'Enough!' Arctalus' voice cries out behind them, his roar shaking the entire fortress. 'I can do no more! If you chose this…to let this taint of chaos infect you, then I will no longer try to help…but, you cannot leave this place. If the Dregor have you…then I must do what I have to! I am sorry, I wish there was more hope…' Arctalus raises his hand, and a powerful wave of energy surrounds him.

"Weak…he is…weak…you are strong!" The voice calls forth within A`deon's mind. He can feel his arms fill with the energy and power of twenty thousand soldiers.

"Get out of my head..." The last glimpse of what is left of A`deon, tries to defend himself, tries...with one last push, to fight back against this voice, this corruptor of his body.

"KNEEL!" The voice roars, and all time seems to stop, all around him freezes in this moment.

With eyes filled with tears, A`deon falls to the ground on his hands and knees.

"You are at a disadvantage...here you kneel, about to be betrayed...about to be destroyed by those who sought to help you...now wishing to spill your blood...and you would not raise a finger to defend yourself?" The voice says.

"You twist words...you're the one doing this to me..." A`deon retorts.

The voice laughs, the echo runs deep into his conscious. *"No...I only offer you the choice, for power is the true strength...power will last, survive...they are weak, and if they were strong, they would have helped you, but no...they have given up on you, turn their backs on you like everyone else...but I am still here, I have stayed with you, helped give you the strength to persevere this far...they cannot fathom the power you and I both have, for together nothing will be able to stop our forces.*

These Asyndians are old, they linger like unburned history books and scripture that needs done away with. As for these Civilians...they are but a speck, a parasite that feeds off of everything that has come before...they have no identity nor strength. They are weak.

But you...you are different from them. Your mind, your skills, your tactics...you run on instincts to survive...you're a survivor, I can see it in you, smell it on your flesh..."

"I have failed at every turn...let them take me..."
A`deon replies.

"HA! You say that, but deep down you don't believe
it...for I know you have a burning desire to kill them, kill all of
them...come now...?!"

"I...I want to see the Asyndian dead...see those who
refused to follow me...I wanted to achieve victory, but they..."

"You feel they held you back...held back your true
skills...your true power!"

"...Yes."

"And...what of the giant...what of the menace
called...Hondor?" The voice snickers in a sinister tone.

"He did this to me...he broke me, shattered my
body...shattered my sword arm...he is the one who took
everything away...what pride I kept for myself...as well as my
drive..." A`deon felt his rage burning inside at the thought of
Hondor.

"And you lived...you're the only one to survive his
attack...you faced him and lived..."

"I lived so he will die!"

"And he will...they all will...?" The voice dissipates
away like a faint layer of morning mist laid across the land.
The fog clears from his mind, shaking the voids away like a
brief daydream.

"Arise! Eliminate them, and when you leave...make
your way north to the border at the tip of Mirym...I will await
you there..." Is the last faint sound of his mind before all fades
out, and time...returns to him.

And in a quick flash of power, A`deon turns, slaps away Nilta to the floor, grasps her spear from her back, uses the handle and bashes Diin across the face. He feels alive, this power, this rush within him, it's unbelievable, he's never felt anything like it before. He only had a small taste, but now, now his strength is one thousand fold, his speed undetecting, his body and reflexes impeccable. The bruises and scars were gone, he has been healed, reformed…reconstructed.

He looks above towards the ceiling, as the Asyndian Arctalus has taken flight, his great gray wings spread wide on the wind, for the windows and doorways burst open from the wave of energy still slowly collecting within his grasp. Diin and Nilta hit the floor, and A`deon leaps into the air, with a mighty jump, the spear is held forward like a harpoon. The tip of the spear glistens and reflects the source of power radiating from the mountains across the entire area around him. Smoke from extinguished torches flees, scatters like lost souls.

Diin and Nilta come to, as they listen to the dripping of hot blood upon the marble floor. They look up and see Nilta's spear driven deep, and far out the other side of Arctalus' chest, the old Asyndian limped over dead, and at the other end, the hands that clench the spear, are A`deon's.

A`deon tosses the Asyndian away, as the old, gray body of feathers hits the floor with a thud. Diin and Nilta rush to their master's side, tears of disbelief rush from their eyes as they crawl to him, and then they hear the voice, the voice of darkness above them.

'Yes…crawl…crawl to your master's side…weep for him, gobble up your sorrows as quickly as you can like depraved animals! For both of you are next!' A`deon roars, his body holding aloft, floating in the air by some powerful force, an aura surrounding him.

'What have you done A`deon…what have you done?!'
Diin cries, feeling the life-force of his master fail. Nilta lets out
a wail of sorrow, muffled behind her facemask.

With no last words to them, A`deon simply laughs and
soars through the vast open doorway to the outside of the
fortress. He lands upon a cliff at the foot of the palace, facing
towards the massive tower and embankment. He summons to
his fingertips, a binding power, slamming the doors and
windows closed and locking them down, sealing them shut.

'The only way to kill insects…is to smash them!' He
focuses his concentration upon the base of Arctalus' fortress,
and all around the miles of perimeter, where the walls and the
tower above rises upwards towards the sky, past the crown of
the mountain it had been built upon, now is where it will be
buried.

He makes a crunching motion with his hands, and with
just a fraction of his power, the bricks begin to crumble,
breaking down into nothing more than powder and rubble, and
then, the tower, the mighty tower high up, the steeple of Mirym
that looks out over the Glorial Tundra, cracks into shambles,
withers and breaks away, down to join the rest of the rubble as
the pieces overflow one another and fall down the cliffs and
rolls down the mountain upon the tundra below, hammering
cracks into the thick, frozen lakes and seas below.

A`deon looks on with eyes blazing as the heavy mortar
and bricks and stones pile upon and crush down upon Diin and
Nilta within.

'Suffer my little insects…suffer…freeze…may this be
your tomb!' A`deon cries above the winds and howling vocals
of the furies that whoosh about franticly and in panic, for the
source of the mountains has been tainted…now destroyed, and
the guardian, the watcher of these lands, Arctalus Hon, has

been slain and his body lays crushed within the rubble of his tower and fortress above these mountains over the plains of snow.

And so it is north that A`deon goes, to traverse over the uncharted paths and seas of mountains of snow that line Mirym's borders around from the southern tip of Runegard, to the east on the line Fausengard and the Gormon territory, and out to the icy seas west. For it is he who waits for him up north by the boundaries of the Great Divide, where the Hammer of Gonun abolished the joining of Raukmar and Aura many eons ago, leaving only a vast and endless abyss in between.

The tower of Arctalus Hon lays dormant for some time, before the rubble is disturbed and pieces of stone rolls away from a center pile, as something shuffles around underneath, someone is moving, and a hand reaches up to touch the cool air, feeling around, trying to break free.

Part XVI:

The Barren City

~

And the ground shakes beneath her feet. Has a mountain exploded, has the very throat of Abhor to the furthest southern seas vomited up revulsion in the form of flesh-burning lava...no, for his footsteps are the thunder, and the vile tongue lightning, that lashed out with hunger and destroys all in his path. His footprints are coated with the bile of the dead, the baptism upon his new-found flesh and bone, feeling them tremble with fear, smelling their cowardice, for the first time in eons.

She smells it, she smells the scent on the hot breeze through the open northern window. In the distance the mountain tipped with a fresh layer of blood stands gulping and gurgling for more. She smells that familiar scent on the wind, the smell of death is approaching, and he follows...He's coming.

The roar cries out like a thunder, the thunder travels with the storm approaching Thylesian, the once mighty, protected elysian field for the Asyndians, now stands defenseless, for the guards and soldiers lay scattered in pieces across the mountain top, and their flesh in the stomach of Hondor, for she can smell their decay, his breath on the wind.

"No...No..." She says in a faint whisper to herself. As she gazes across out to the furthest reaches of the city, there is only silence upon the still wind, the streets stand vacant and silent. Were they warned? Did they smell the scent as well? Do they even know what's approaching as they sleep under still towers and rooftops?

That's when the first of the many screams to be heard...rings out in the still gray air.

'He's here...' She trembles.

The thick, marble walls in the north begin to crumble, the watch towers shatter to pieces as bodies of the fleeing Civilians and Gormons upon the ground try to flee. The surrounding populace hears the terror and commotion, as a grand exodus of bodies and horrified faces flee through the streets, making their way towards the mighty ship that had brought Hondor here, hoping they can escape, hoping to get away.

Smoke and fire begin to rise in the north, spreading east and west, as the terror stomps towards the southern outskirts of the city. The mighty titan of abomination towers above roves and buildings, bringing down crossbow towers with his mighty fists, cutting down upon the fleeing bodies with the diamond tip of the blade, cutting and slicing them to pieces, their bodies flying through the air like ragdolls and chunks of meat, their blood splattering over the homes and palisades around the towers.

The many who flee, dare not turn back, for they will either be trampled to death by the hordes of Civilians and Gormons, or be devoured by this monstrosity, who picks up one, sometimes two bodies at a time and chews away at their bodies, tearing away everything down to the bone, then tossing the remains away.

The Daughter looks on speechless in horror. He is bigger, nearly double the size than before. He is growing, getting larger the more he feasts, and this is a buffet to him, and his hunger endless, insatiable.

"He may be as big as a mountain before he's through here!" She exclaims to herself realizing this horrifying revelation.

Her door is forced open, she whips her head away from the window to see her Asyndian guard standing there, weapon drawn for battle, and his eyes are bulging with terror.

'My lady! I have to get you out of here!' He exclaims with insistence.

She says nothing.

'We have to leave immediately, I have to get you to the vessel now!'

She takes one more look out the window, then turns and crosses the room, storms past the Asyndian, then walks in the opposite direction from where her guardian was planning to take her.

'Where are you...?'

'We're not going to the ship! It is too late for those people...the ship is a death-trap! I wish there were time to explain, but you need to get what soldiers you can get together...' She interrupts to tell him.

'Where are we going?' The Asyndian asks.

'We're going north...we need to find General A`deon...don't ask me why...but I have a hunch we'll find him somewhere north.'

'I have a few men stationed by the vessel but...' He stammers, but she turns and gives him a cold look to obey her orders.

"It's too late for them..." She said, her voice echoes in his mind.

He bows his head. 'Very well, I will go and collect them.' He replies.

'Have one go to Runegard and relay the news of what has happened here...warn them, and tell them to escape. Have half escort them east towards Greenrym. The other half will meet us at the northern meeting point just at the boarders of Mirym, I have a few things to get, meet me back here as soon as you can, we will head north from here...now go...flee!' She cries, and the guard whisks away down the hall and out the far window.

Hondor continues his rampage through the streets and more desolation is left behind in his warpath. The remains of the bodies pile higher and higher, tossed asunder, as the red rivers of blood cascade and slosh through and across the pristine ivory marble roads, as the red crimson splashes everywhere as Hondor trudges along.

He can feel, he can see, he can destroy...he has become, whole.

The Civilian troops toss their spears screaming through the air with swift speed upon their footwork and maneuvering, but the spears crack and snap, bouncing off of Hondor's flesh, as tough and thick as armor. The Gormons blindly charge in, but a Gormon centurion's rage just isn't enough this time, as their kin had failed to show earlier, for Hondor had devoured them, and now he will devour these beings foolish enough to challenge him, for they will not win…they will never win, and they only have once, and in that one instant, they will fall to Hondor's crushing blows, and they will feel his shards of teeth as he crunches down upon their skin and muscle, ignoring their screams, their pleads to let them go, and he will not, he will swallow them, as he has all the others.

The Asyndians swoop down firing their arrows tipped with fire and poisons, but they will never break the skin of this monster, like throwing rocks at a vast mountain titan, they have no effect. Hondor swings the mighty guillotine blade around with devastating blows, as blood, feathers and armor splatter and fly every which direction, raining down upon the streets upon the bodies and puddles of entrails and blood. A lone helmet, a golden winged contraption worn by one of the slain Asyndian soldiers, sits sullen at the end of the furthest street near the southern walls, at the entrance to the city, and then…the large foot of Hondor slams down, as he stands face to face with the obstacle in front of him, and beyond is the end of the line, for there will be no escape for those who flee, they may have been able to escape briefly, but Hondor has awakened…

Clumps of many after and upon the others, cram and strangle themselves, crushing over the meek and weak, clawing their way desperately to get inside the war galleon, the mighty golden hofts are frantic and terrified, smelling the devastation of Hondor's flesh on the wind. The soldiers have lost all control of the screaming crowds, and now it's everyone for themselves to try and get to safety, even if they have to push someone back, push them out of their way to get in, to get themselves to safety. Leave them to the invader, let him keep busy while they can get away.

Those who are last in the crowds, hear the slam and the crumble, as the walls begin to give way and crumble down by Hondor's fists, slamming and pounding, driving his way through the thick stone like an indestructible augur against diamond, no matter how hard the matter, he will break through. The cries intensify, as many look back now, watching as the time is running out, the sand dripping, spiraling downwards right before their eyes.

And the last of the wall, with an explosion, some twenty feet or more, a huge chunk of marble and splinters of the mortar, scatter through the air and many of the larger pieces slam down from the sky and smash large clumps of the crowds, squashing them with a crunch like the steel boot down upon the exoskeleton of an insect fleeing from its destroyer.

The doors to the vessel begin to close shut, many fall from the dizzying height of the massive draw bridge as it raises up higher and higher, falling to the harsh marble road, many breaking their necks and cracking the bones in their legs and arms upon impact. The golden hofts begin their ascent, pulling away from the ports of Thylesian where they had landed earlier days before. As the vessel pulls away, more and more bodies lose their grasp and fall down below, kilometers down to the harsh Aura soil below at the base of the mountains beneath where the vast expanse of the city had been built. Their corpses will join the remains of the ancient ruins of Athilnovia that existed hundreds of years before, before it crumbled under the dark hand of Kandarius Lockmore and the black will of Maz Dregor. They will join their ancestors…of skulls and bones.

Hondor pummels away the last of the wall and bellows through like a cyclone across flat, desolate plains, destroying all in his wake. He lunges forward into a brisk run, charging like an angry prowl with deft-like, swift speed. His eyes roll over red with rage and hunger, aggression and fervor, his prey in sight, first for the hofts, he pounces down upon them with a mighty jump, and with the vice of his hand, grapples the chains and rips them away from the vessel. With a great spin, around and around, he slings the frightened hofts around in circles above his head, and then tosses them, like a bullet from the cannon, throws them over the edge of the city, as they tangle themselves in the chains from panic, trying to get away, and cripple themselves from being able to fly, unable to free themselves, and then they fade out of sight, as they will soon be smashed against the rocks below.

Hondor turns his attention to the prison vessel they brought him…Glasgar…to Thylesian for judgment, death for Glasgar, but freedom for this monstrosity, for he has been freed, she freed him without even realizing what she was about to do, what was about to be done…and the consequences it would cause, the chain reaction…

He grasps a large chunk of the ship with each hand, sinks his massive fingers in deep, and the Civilians and Gormons within, feel the ship begin to rise up, they think they are leaving and…in a way, they are right, but they will be taking a trip they will never return from.

Then, a voice screams at a volume above the others. 'He's lifting us…he's taking us…' And the panic explodes tenfold. Hondor lifts the prison ship over his head, the vast expanse of a mile long haul is taken up as though it were weightless. More bodies fall away like debris and trash. Hondor leans back, brings back his arms…then throws, putting little effort into such as massive chore, but to his magnitude of strength, effortless. The vessel goes sailing out for miles, then begins to take a dive down, down, down…down…and the echo is heard far and wide as the ship explodes and scatters everywhere, boards and wood, metal, bones and blood liter the mountains…and the screams of the dying, fall silent with a sudden mute upon the winds, for the breeze across the mountain tops, only carries the silence of their eradication.

And the city is left empty, silent, not even the dead speak, for the barren wasteland of genocide has nothing to say, for the prequel of the dying screams, only leads up to the eventual decimation of all. Except for one, who still stirs, for one looks on over the disaster, one will rise up, and one...will always escape under death's eye and pull through.

The Daughter emerges from the armory, neither sword nor axe, but armed with a mace by her side, a mace, for if she gets the chance...the opportunity...if courage does not fail her at that last moment as it failed the general...she will strike with the mace, she will bring it down with crushing fury with all her strength, into his skull, into the skull of Hondor.

Through the armored helm of mighty wings and glistening silver, she looks out upon the wasteland, the now empty city of Thylesian, drained of all life, the blood of the people and of her majesty of her power and awe over the other civilizations. The winds creep through the streets as silent ears of the Daughter listens, hoping to hear the sound of one whisper, one voice...there was nothing left, he claimed everything. The cup of Thylesian was once overflowing with Asyndians and Civilians, Gormons and visitors from other lands, other planes, trade and commerce...but now....he drank it all, swallowed every last drop.

A single tear fell to the stone floor, and a gust of wind blows across her face. Her guardian has returned, and there are several more Asyndian elite with him.

'Are you ready my lady?'

'The people of Runegard have been warned then?' She replies.

He bows his head. 'They have...'

'Very good...we will proceed towards the north as planned...and I was thinking, maybe we can find the ancient Asyndian fortress that was spoken of...'

'Arctalus Hon my lady?! I thought they were practitioners of Dregor worship?' The guardian panics.

She shakes her head. 'I don't believe a word...you Asyndians have been long enemies of the Dregor...I only ever heard tale of one...one who delved into Dregor worship...'

The other Asyndians stand silent.

'I am young in life, but to your many lifetimes...I am but a speck of dust...I don't know everything of Aura's history or past, I admit ignorance of this...but I have this intuition, this sense that there are things happening that have happened before. In that maze I had strange visions, nightmares I am beginning to believe are real, and a threat to us all. Hondor is a catalyst for something...he is being used, something is...controlling him, at least that is if he is still under control. I feel a division...a divide like the rift between Aura and Raukmar, not by lands and empires...but something darker. Darkness is splintered and eating itself to become the ultimate dominion.

I feel we need to go north and find this Asyndian of the Mirym wastes, that is the only lead we have for finding General A`deon...and that man...that man I saw is after him as well, for what purpose I don't know...but we must find him first...'

'What of...him...' They could hear his noise on the wind, chewing and spiting, cleaning up what mess of bodies there are around Thylesian, growing stronger and stronger. Their faces twist and cringe with disgust at the horrible grumbling, gnawing and chewing.

And she says the next few words, with the vilest looks of hatred upon her furrowed brow. '...We'll just have to let him have his feast today...' Her stomach cringes as she says these words.

'She points to one of the Asyndians. 'You...I need you to go to Othetica...you must warn the Civilians...they need to get out as fast as possible, speak with the advisors to Lord Rolom, they are still sensible in these pressing matters.

They looked at her curiously, as to why she would not tell Lord Rolom. She retorts, '...we have a history together...let's just say...he can have his limbs torn from his body...' And none of them asked any further questions.

She tells another Asyndian to go and warn the Gormons of Otoni` and Fausengard, and he nods in understanding.

'Those Gormons are stubborn, they will not run...and if anything, once Lord Oldgaur hears about the death of his sons...he will personally lead his entire armies against Hondor...but he must not! Yet...' She sighs. '...I know he will not listen to reason...who would...what reason is left, I ask...?'

They all fall silent, as the destruction in the background grows.

The Daughter breaks the silence. 'You two...off with you, we will rendezvous at the northern position, be no longer than a day if you can help it, and I know it's not much time, but we have none left.'

She climbs upon the guardian's back and they fly off with several of the other Asyndian's behind them. The other two travel east side by side for a time, until they see the rising city of the towers of Othetica off in the distance. One verges off and heads beyond the walls, while the other goes onwards, first to Otoni`, the battle capital of the lands, and then his objective is onwards to Fausengard, to a worried and enraged leader, Chief Oldgaur of the Gormons.

Part XVII:

Escape

~

Those of Runegard are in an uproar, the panic and the horror, the same thing is said upon each and every lip...the gasp of terror...the Asyndians sent by the Daughter needed say anything, they knew deep down why they had to run, to flee once more from their homes, barely recuperated from the last attack upon them, but they knew Hondor was still alive, for they too could sense the dread in the Asyndian's voice, the quiver, the shaking of his hands.

"He...no...he can't be...we thought he would be dealt with, we thought he would be executed...how foolish we were to think...to think such a monster could be killed so easily...killed, ha...he cannot be killed..."

That...is what they all thought...and how foolish they were indeed.

The Asyndians tried to keep them calm, but there is no reassurance.

'I thought you were to destroy the bastard!' Roúgsver yells.

'We need everyone to keep themselves together...the Daughter is handling things in the best way she knows how at this time...please bear with us...' The Asyndian replies to the fearful crowds. He looks upon them from the ruined tower he stands upon, looking over the broken men, terrified women and children, in tears...crying, and they know that no matter what they say, these Civilian and Gormon peasants and denizens will never rest, never sleep again knowing that Hondor still draws breath.

'Where is she, where is the Daughter of Runegard...my lady reassured us that the beast would perish?!' Roúgsver inquires.

Why does she desert us here, her people?! Why does she not bring us this news herself?' A brawn Gormon woman cries, holding her large child within her arms.

'Our Lady has not abandoned anyone...' The other Asyndian steps forward and cries back. 'She has pressing matters in the north to handle, she is trying to not only protect all of us, but also the Civilians of Othetica, the Gormons of Runegard, and anyone else that can be warned, now we must ask, no force all of you to get whatever you are able to carry, for she has asked that you be escorted...'

'We don't give a damn about Gormons or their cities...as for the others...the Dregor wiped most of them out two hundred years ago!' One of the Civilian soldier's yells, while one of the Gormon soldiers storms towards him in rage.

'You damn ignorant filth! How dare you! My people have fought hard to keep Fausengard safe, and we will continue to do so, we will die for our land, not run like the rest of you!' Other Gormon soldiers raise their arms in agreement and join by the soldier's side, some fifteen Gormon troops are rallied to his call. 'Go on Asyndian, lead them...run away...as me and my Gormon brothers we will face against this Hondor and do what you have failed to! Let a Gormon show you how situations get handled…' He calls to the others. 'Come my brothers!'

'I was there…Thylesian has fallen, master Gormon! I watched as Hondor broke through walls like parchment…he slaughtered everyone, every Gormon, Civilian, as well as my own, for few of us now remain, even the women and the children, the commoners, peasants…everyone, my home now lies silent and in ruins, a fate worse than Runegard…he killed and…ate, all at Kar'durgra…only our lady escaped! If you and your followers chose to face him head on, you will get no help from me or anyone, for there is no one left…if you choose to do this and leave the company when we need you here…you will end up like those butchered skeletons that lay mutilated at the top of that mountain…so, what do you say…'

The Gormon soldier eyes up the Asyndian and spits at the ground.

'My ancestors have faced worse, you do not scare me Asyndian, I watched that bastard fight, he will not defeat us…he's no bigger than one of my own!'

The Asyndian flies down to the grounds with the Gormon. 'This is not the same beast as before…when the blade sliced open the Gormon prisoner…something else…was born, this is a new creature, more vast in scale than even you master Gormon…' The Asyndian replies.

The Gormon laughs with a mocking gesture. 'Good for us, the bigger he is…the harder he will fall! When I watch his head rolling across the dirt, I will be sure to think back to all of you, and laugh at how terrified you all were…cowards, that's all you Asyndians and Civilians are…always leave the dirty work for us!'

And with that said, the troop of Gormons march off, heading north in the direction of Thylesian. The others of Runegard look on as the band of Gormons fade over the horizon of the long road ahead.

'Are we just going to let them go?' The Asyndian asks the other under his breath.

'There is nothing else to be said or done...they have chosen death, all we can do now is take care of the rest of them...' The Asyndian guardian replies. He then turns to the others that look on, all eyes are upon them.

'And what of us? What shall become of us?' One of the Civilian soldier's asks. His arm has been severed and the entire left side of his body has been bandaged up, the rags across his body and forehead have been leaking blood, but has coagulated up only a few days before.

'We are to take you on the road, away from here, away from the direction of Thylesian, we are to protect you as best we can...this is to be a silent run, off the main roads, through the forests, keeping out of eyesight, furthest beyond the trees.'

'We're not going back to those caves...I won't...I refuse to be cooped up with those damned monsters underground...those things there...Hondor up here! Where will we go I ask...where will my family feel safe?! I lost my arm after that bastard's last attack! How will you assure me we can still trust the royalty which graces us all within these crumbled walls?!'

'We do not talk down to any of you...the Daughter never has, we have always kept ours and all of you informed, and the truth is, there is little we can do, there is little hope...but as long as some of us still breath, that should be something, and we need to do what we are able to, each of us, in our own way with what ounce of strength we keep...you

261

know as well as us or anyone else within what is left of Runegard…is that we are in trouble, doom engulfs us all in light and our nightmares, and the darkness is darkening, even more than the sky above our heads.'

He falls silent for a moment.

'We're but a flicker of a small ember…in what light still exists within Aura.'

The rest of the crowds begin to settle, they know the truth, they know the Asyndian guardians as well as their Daughter, knows it as well, all too well and more so than the others. They are doing what they can, with what power they have, but what can be done…against a threat that revels in death, yet refuses to die himself?

'There is a place that my Lady has given orders for me to guide you…and that for now, is the only plan we have. We will deal with any threats as they show themselves…and with hope…the lady will meet us there.'

'And…what of Hondor?' A Civilian woman asks.

The Asyndian says nothing and stays silent.

'Soldiers…prepare everyone to move out! We must leave as soon as we can, we must be out of Runegard before dawn…' Was all he replied.

At dawn, upon the bleakest, darkest of twilight mornings, the Daughter and her guardians land upon a peak some miles away from Aura.

'Will they be safe? Can they get to…some safe haven?' She asks.

'There is no guarantee any longer my lady…there is a change, a catastrophe…once it was in our mists, now I fear the mists have cleared away…and this doom, this death and destruction has reached its hand through, to grab us all, this world as well…by the throat to squeeze what life is left away…'

The Daughter says nothing, only carries herself away, over to sit by a lone rock, lone…lone as she is this rock, she wraps her arms around its cold touch and consoles herself upon it, laying her head upon the flat top of the crag, laying her weapon aside, for she does not need such things, in this moment to just take a breath and forget about all the pain and this destruction.

'I've…I've spent so long cringing and biting, fighting like a mongrel against the politics of this land, beating my chest like the crazed man who wears the crown of a ruler to intimidate and try to keep his people in check…that…that I almost forgot what it feels like to just cry…to emote…I need to remember that I am still a woman and not some brute…I still have an innate daintiness still within my heart and under this fair skin, I just cannot show it…especially in these times, when the people of Runegard need a leader, not a princess or damsel…'

She almost could not believe what she was saying, for it has been so long since she had the feelings of a woman, for the ruler, the responsible one has taken hold, the roots have grown deep within her, tearing at and eating away her feminism, her instincts to just be a woman…not the brutal, hardened form that the monsters of this land have shaped her into.

Her guardian walks over and kneels down to her. 'Begging your pardon my lady, but if I may, I beg to differ with you…only a little, for you may have been through much, more dark days than any man or woman should see, but…if I may, you are still a woman, and that doesn't mean you have to been dainty, nor feel weakness…for you show the strength of

263

what it means to be a true woman, a true leader to her people who would die for you...for they know you have sacrificed much and have made many difficult choices...they know you are willing to make the ultimate sacrifice for them...you have shown this time and time again...'

She dries her eyes as the Asyndian helps her to her feet, holding her up for a moment, reaching down for her weapon, and holds it up, the handle facing her.

'Here...I give this back to the Daughter of Runegard, for no man or woman, Asyndian, Civilian, or Gormon...could ever replace you, could ever be the leader you are...and me and my brethren...we will follow you to whatever end is in store, whatever fate awaits us...'

He kneels to one knee, and all the others around them follow, all kneel and bow to her, their leader, their ruler, the Daughter of this mighty realm they call their home. And her hand, shaking just ever so slightly...reaches out for the shaft of the weapon...and clutches it with the strength of a protector...the strength of a defender, for many depend upon her and her choices, for they not only affect her...but affect one and all, of not just Runegard she realizes this...but all of those within Aura.

She steps forward to speak.

'Please...everyone rise...we are not out of danger yet, we have to leave these lands...we go north...'

All of her Asyndian guardians arise.

'But...there is no further we can go than the ice lands or Mirym...' One says.

The Daughter says with all the sternness in her voice she can muster, 'It's not Mirym that is our destination...we must go there to locate this Asyndian who watches from the peaks of his citadel…find out what has become of General A`deon…but then…we go to Raukmar…!'

One of them lets out a baffling chuckle. 'I thought we kneeled to a leader…not some mad-woman! You give us two choices of death…there is no hope in those words! Raukmar is on the other side of the Great Divide, there is no way to cross it, and in those lands, the Rauks are nothing more than savage giants, fighting themselves and anyone that's not them! They would smash us under their heels like insects if they were to see us…if they could for we are nothing more than insects compared to their size!'

'And we keep to the shadows like insects…until, until maybe, just maybe we can find ones who will listen to us…' She replies.

And another Asyndian steps forward. 'Listen…listen to who? To us?! They'll kill us!'

'Don't you remember the old legends and tales, there are a few who have helped us before!' She retorts.

'…My lady, I hate to side with those who speak ill now to you and those who dare question your authority, but they are right…for you yourself said you have little understanding of the histories and tales…because that was one Rauk, and he helped the Gormons…not Asyndians…not Civilians…if this is your plan…'

'It still is…'

'IT IS FOLLY!' The Asyndian guard screams to her, hoping to break through to her.

'Then…I want to learn something…of you or any of you…what was this one Rauk's name?' The Daughter asks. They look around at one another, a baffled look upon them.

'I…I don't remember, that story has been nearly lost to the ages in its relevance…the Rauks are a near mystery, none ever took the time to truly get to know exactly what they are and why they are at constant war with themselves and all others. They are a mystery as much as why one of them chose to help the Gormon…' He replies.

'Maybe…maybe their neighbor took the time to understand them…maybe he knows something others don't…because it appears I am not the only one who is…less than knowledgeable about these things…' A slight smirk comes over her face.

'And you think the gray Asyndian of Mirym…Arctalus Hon, knows of these things?' The Asyndian guard asks.

'If he's as ancient from what I've heard…then I'll wager he knows more than any of you…and I'll bet he has quite the collection of volumes and books, ancient scrolls of knowledge to give us the answers we seek…'

They all look to one another, and once again their lady surprises them once again with her tact and ideas.

'Very well…when do we leave?'

The Daughter looks over the cliffs and off towards the direction of where Runegard's walls once stood high. 'How many are protecting the convoy of citizens along their path?' She asks her guardian.

'I've placed in charge twelve of my best soldiers to guide them along, six soldiers for battle, and six scouts for coverage and to keep them hidden, they also know these back country areas better than anyone else...they will be well protected, except if...well...except if the worst should happen...' He replies.

"...Hondor..." She whispers under her breath.

Then, from behind them, one of the scouts from their own group is approaching in a hurry from the northwestern direction of their road ahead.

'My lady! One of the scouts has returned!' An Asyndian soldier cries from among the lookout.

The scout lands, rushing past the other soldiers and kneeling before the Daughter. 'My Lady!' He cries, then he arises to his feet.

'What is it...what have you spotted on the road?' She asks.

'There are two figures approaching from the north, heading in our direction!'

'Is there a threat?!' The Asyndian guardian asks.

'I don't know for certain...but they were moving slowly, one was injured badly...and the other was helping them along...they could be refugees of some kind.' The scout replies.

The Asyndian guardian storms by. 'There is nothing out here for there to be refugees...' He roars.

The Daughter calls to him as she rushes to catch up with him. 'Only the fortress of the gray Asyndian is all the way out here...what if they come from there...?' She asks.

The Asyndian turns. 'Then that would mean...' He quickens his pace.

'Something…something has happened!' The Daughter says aloud. They reach the western cliffs and look off towards the direction the scout reported the two figures were approaching from. And there, off in the distance, a young Civilian man and woman were struggling along the road, it appeared the woman had the man braced firmly holding him up as he held a large bloodied pool of clothing upon his side. The man's eyes were wrapped in a green bandage and the woman's mouth was muffled over by some vice.

The Daughter proceeds down the cliff and heads towards them. 'My lady! It could be dangerous...' The Asyndian cries to her.

She watches as the woman slinks down upon her knees and the man falls next to her, his arm still around her. She reels him round and carefully lays him down upon the ground gently. The Daughter reaches the bottom of the rock-face and breaks into a sprint towards them. She calls to them and the woman looks up, seeing the Daughter heading towards her.

The woman begins to pat down upon the man's shoulder fiercely, who then cries out in pain. 'Ah…damn it! Don't do that Nilta, the pain! I can't bear it anymore!'

Nilta recluses back at her brother Diin's command. 'What?! What is it…is there someone coming?!' She taps franticly upon her shoulder pauldron fiercely, and Diin listens to the tink upon the metal intently as he can, trying to ignore the pain within his bones and the fierce burn across his flesh.

'Someone's coming?' He asks.

She taps once upon the pauldron.

'One…there is one?!'

She taps once again.

'Is…is it the general?'

She taps twice.

'No? Then…who is it?' Diin then hears the voice call out to them, the voice of a woman, and the voice is getting closer almost upon them. He can then hear the sound of a blade being drawn, as Nilta takes the dagger from the sheath, then he can hear her faint growl beneath her mask.

'Nilta…Nilta don't…I don't think she's…' But it's too late, Nilta never heard the faint quiver of his voice. She charges forward in rage at the approaching woman out of fear and hostility with the knife high above her head.

The Daughter sees the brandished weapon as the woman leaves the side of the injured man, and charges full force at her. The Daughter stops in her tracks, removes the mace from her holster and readies it for an attack, then from the skies, several Asyndian soldiers cut off the woman from the Daughter as they land before her, spears and bows drawn, ready to slay the crazed, hostile woman in her tracks.

'Drop it…or you drown in your blood!' The Asyndian guardian cries with a spear to her neck, but Nilta only looks on in fighting stance, ready for their challenge, blood pumping and ready to die to protect her brother.

'No! Don't hurt her! She means you no harm…sister, do as they say…lower your dagger. Diin tries to stagger to his feet, Nilta looks back and rushes to his side to try and hold him up.

'Get back here at once!' The Asyndian cries, but she pays no heed and grapples upon her fallen brother. She holds him close as the Asyndians close in around them, holding weapons to them.

'Please…we mean no harm…' Diin pleads to them.

'This woman dares to attack the Daughter of Runegard, which calls for her blood to be spilled!'

'No…please…we did not know…I know of the Daughter of Runegard, but I have never seen her, for I am a blind man, and my sister here…she does not…'

The Asyndian raises his weapon to attack. 'Spare me this you murderers!' But before he can plunge the spear down, the voice of the Daughter calls from behind.

'Don't…you dare touch them!' She pushes her way through her guards to look down on the blind man and his frightened, angered sister.

'I will handle this…all of you get back…now!' And the Asyndians lower their weapons and back away behind the Daughter. She steps forward.

'Please…forgive my men…they are loyal to me, and are only doing their duty…as I see your…sister is towards you…' She speaks in a much calmer voice and holds out her hand. Nilta leans forward in a growl, but Diin holds her back. Diin holds up his hand. 'Please…take my hand I can't see yours.' And the Daughter grips onto Diin's arm and helps him up. He leans away from Nilta and grips upon the Daughter's shoulder and keeps hold upon her hand.

'What are your names?' The Daughter asks.

'My name is Diin…and this is my sister Nilta…you'll have to excuse her for she cannot speak…'

'If you are blind and she a mute…how is it you communicate?' The Asyndian guardian asks.

'Please...my dear lady...Daughter of Runegard, we come from the remains of the gray citadel in the north...we have traveled for days...if we may have but some of your food and drink, whatever you are able to share...' Diin says, but is interrupted.

'The gray citadel...in ruins? Has something happened? What of Arctalus Hon and our General, A'deon?' She asks in quick bursts.

'Please...food and rest...then I can tell you everything, and if my sister may have access to any healing you can provide, for my side has been split open, and I have lost much blood...'

'Of course, we have very little, but we'll provide you with what we can.' She turns to her Asyndians. 'Fly them back up to the cliffs...' Then she speaks to Diin. 'My Asyndian's will take you now back up to our temporary encampment...' She motions for one of them to step forward. 'Grab him upon the shoulders and hang on.' She instructs him.

'I have never been on the back of an Asyndian before, even though I...well, we'll discuss that later. I only wish I were able to see the view from above.' He winces in pain as the Asyndian hoists him up, and carries him on the wind. Nilta is hesitant at first, but after seeing her brother has been taken in good hands, and that they are willing to help, she takes upon one of the other Asyndians and follows behind her brother. The Daughter is carried up as well, and they fly back to the cliffs they have retreated to.

The days have become so dark, they no longer can tell whether this is night, twilight, dawn or dusk. The air is moist as an early fall morning, but the chill of night runs down their spines. It matters not anymore, for darkness seems to consume them all, internal and external, and the shadows to come linger around upon the horizons, beyond the mountains is where it still lays darkest.

Several Asyndians pass overhead in a circle, patrolling about the area, while others stay closer towards the encampment near the Daughter and these two Civilians. They prepare a make-shift fire within a circle of rustic stones and rocks gathered from the hillside. The Daughter walks over to them bearing small tin bowls filled with fresh water from a nearby stream, Nilta is hesitant at first, but reaches for both of them, and helps Diin gain a handle upon the one she hands over to him. He takes large, slopping gulps as water splashes over the ground, wipes his mouth of the dribble, and proceeds to speak.

'I appreciate you taking us in, but I will ask one question before I answer yours…'

'Very well…ask…'

'Why is the Daughter all the way out in these forsaken lands?' He asks.

'As I've said…we look for our General, Master A`deon…and now I ask you, where is he? Last I heard, he was seen leaving with two Civilian strangers…strangers that I've heard bear your resemblance, strangers…that I heard are criminals, thieves…murderers in service to a darker power in these lands…'

Diin smiles. 'You are correct, but wrong, my lady…if I may…my sister and I are thieves, but were not murderers…we broke into the Vaults of Thylesian for a special purpose many years ago, before I acquired this injury that blinds me…an injury these Asyndians gave me…and yes, we did abduct General A`deon from his near death…and you are wrong in our motives…'

'And what were these motives?'

He takes another drink from the bowl. 'We were trying to protect our future, as well as everyone's future in these lands...me and my sister were sent to acquire General A`deon, for he was to lead an army, an army of might and astonishing power, against the fiend we all call...Hondor...'

'And where is he...where is the general, why is he not with you?!' She exclaims in her question.

Diin's voice goes grim. 'I'm afraid your general...is no longer on our side...our master Arctalus Hon was to train him, prepare him, as he had trained us. General A`deon would find this sacred army our master spoke of and return to Aura to purge Hondor from this realm...but he has fallen to the taint of the renewed incarnation of the Destroyer...and he will lead a new force of Dregor to conquer our realm...sneaky...those bastards are.' He smells the air. 'They can be deceptive...'

One of the Asyndians cries from among the group. 'I knew that bastard was a coward! Traitorous bastard!'

Diin smiles to himself, the stench in the air is getting worse to his sensitive nose.

'That's why A`deon has fallen to this darkness! Maz Dregor twisted his mind to think this very thought! That he was nothing among all of you, and that with the power of the Hexagus coursing inside of him...he would find his true inner strength...strength the rest of you failed to see!' Diin shouts back.

The Daughter falls silent. 'I...I remember my father...he, he had assurance in General A`deon, admittedly more than anyone else...I remember him...I'll never forget what he did for me...' The Daughter speaks in a whisper.

'What did he do, my lady?'

She goes into a flashback...to opening her eyes and seeing him there...hearing his voice. And unknowing to her, Diin listened to everything, she doesn't have to say a word...he just knows by her feelings.

'Well...it does not matter now...our master was the last one who had any chance to combat this taint within the general...and he failed, resulting in his demise...'

Nilta gets up and walks away from them, tears streaming from her eyes. The other Asyndians proceed to follow her. The stench is getting worse.

'No...leave her alone, she will be fine, just leave her in peace...!' Diin calls to them, and they return to their previous positions with reluctance in their steps.

'How...how did your master die?' The Daughter asks.

Diin turns in her direction, following her voice. 'He killed our master...General A`deon, drove a blade right through him, instead of us...A`deon attempted to kill my sister, then our master intervened and...and that was the last I remember before we were on the road...his tower crumbled to the ground around us...if Nilta did not break through, we'd both would have frozen to death...' And he drifts off in his memory of what happened.

The Daughter rises to her feet, and walks away from the fire, leaving Diin seated and to his thoughts. Her guardian then walks over to her side.

'Now what...how are we to cross the Divide now?! The Asyndian is dead, and his records lost...' He looks at the sorrow upon the Daughter, she's trying to hold back with a tight lip drawn across her face, feeling her knees ready to bend

274

and break, feeling everything more and more, crumbling around her. But, as though a faint light pierced through the dark skies above them, an idea hits her, a chance has been fated to meet them head on. She looks back at Diin, still groveling by the fire, now taking slow sips of water.

She rushes back over and seats herself.

'By the rush of wind upon your clothes my lady, I'd say you had an important idea upon your mind...' Diin says.

'We need to know how...' She is interrupted.

'...to cross the Great Divide?' Diin finishes her sentence.

'How...are you telepathic?' The Asyndian asks.

Diin laughs.

'Ha...I just heard you whispering, that's all! My blindness has heightened my other senses tenfold. Time is short, so I'll make this brief...I know how to get across, and my sister knows the way...' He replies.

'Then that is a yes, there is a way to get into Raukmar?' She replies in excitement.

He nods. 'I will speak to my sister, she will guide you along, all I ask, is that when we get there...you let me do the talking.'

Everyone looks upon him in confusion, but she agrees.

'Is there something that blocks the way...a guardian, a monster of some kind?' The Asyndian asks.

He laughs. 'Much more dangerous...there is one who protects the way, but he has long since disappeared from the sight of all, keeping way up north along the Great Divide, keeping the Rauks in check, making sure none try to toss rocks across to smash up our cities.'

'What is he?!'

'An Aurora...' Diin replies.

All fall silent. 'That is nonsense, all of them were killed over two hundred years ago during the Second Grey Age! I don't believe a word! Nor do I believe there is a way to cross the Divide!' The Asyndian shouts.

"You reek of darkness my friend..." Diin thinks to himself.

'There was one...who did survive...but, so be it. If you don't believe me, we won't take you...' Diin replies.

The Daughter steps in. 'No! No we believe you, we need to go there, and we leave...' She looks up at the lifeless black clouds and no light shines through them. '...we leave when I deem fit.' And she goes away to her tent, but turns back again commanding her guard to lead Diin to his tent.

The Asyndian guardian walks forward. 'Let me know when you're ready, and I will guide you to your tent...'

Diin holds up his arm. 'I am ready, you can take me now.' And the guardian leads him along. 'Please make sure my sister is able to find me...'

Later that evening, Diin and Nilta are awakened by a sound, and Nilta watches as the sheet to their tent is pulled back and the Daughter walks in.

'Who is it?' Diin asks.

'I'm sorry to bother the both of you...but I had further questions.'

'Then please, enter my lady...are you alone?' Diin asks.

'I am, all my guards are asleep. Why?'

Diin thinks for a moment about it, but decides it's better not to alarm her at the moment.

'Good, because they may not like the things they hear, Asyndians are very sensitive beings...full of pride and stubborn. I actually find it amazing they bow to one of our own...but anyway...what do you want to ask?'

'Well, I heard many things earlier I did not understand, about the Destroyer and this Maz Dregor...I've heard of the Auroras and that they all were killed. Then you say that one of them guards the way to Raukmar. With all that has transpired, I do not have a full understanding on history. Before I never bothered, but it sounds now like history is repeating itself...and that I am at a loss and misunderstanding of what to do.'

'Why do you speak different in front of us...me and my sister?'

'What do you mean?'

'When around your Asyndians, you spoke in a...I dare say...a lie. There was a trembling I could hear upon your tongue like a loud rattle...and now, it is gone...'

'I guess, being a leader changes you, or tries. You have to put on the courage in front of others, be a leader to them...'

'...be a leader, my lady...not a lie...' Diin replies.

"Which is more than I can say for these "guards" of yours!"

'I...your getting away from my questions, who is this Maz Dregor, and this Aurora?!' She stammers with a temper.

'Very well, but did you ever come to realize that maybe your subjects...'

'My people...they are my people!' The Daughter interrupts.

'Of course, forgive me...your people see and feel the humanity and the Civilian within you...they see one that is like them, and not one who would try to subdue and bring them down? I've spent most of my days living under an Asyndian, my master Arctalus...they are intimidating, they have always looked down upon Civilians...as have Gormons...and yet you rule over both? This has nothing to do with your position...it is you and who you are. You hide your fear, bury it deep within so the others will not sense it, but I do and if the situation worsens, then everyone will find out about your fear.'

'I guess you want me to confess to you why I'm afraid then?' The Daughter asks.

'No...because I know why you're afraid...but as good a reason you have to be...there is more to the darkness afoot, because Hondor is a means to an end...Duul`ak and Aumon know this, Naumokron has returned, taking on the form of Duul`ak, one of his disciples to help bring his essence back into Aura's realm...and Glasgar...Glasgar was a way to bring a horrible legend, a legend that should have been left dead...back to life...'

'How does this involve this Destroyer and an Aurora?'

The Daughter asks.

'Naumokron was once in service to the Destroyer, Maz Dregor, one of the Hexagus Lords deep within their realm of Wom...Naumokron, the ancient one, had bestowed upon him unspeakable power as well as his knowledge as an Asyndian, knowing a vast wealth of history and ancient knowledge, allowing for him to summon Reignkiing to destroy Aura and the Asyndians and Gormons...after Reignkiing's fall, he vanished from the world, hidden away for thousands of years...and no one knows why or what his reasons were...but now it seems too clear, that this...Hondor, has arisen from legends to be brought into this realm for one malicious reason, to destroy all of Aura, a cleansing that the Hexagus and the Dregor had hoped for, only Naumokron would be in control, not his Lords and Masters...'

'And...the Aurora?'

'They were the protectors and guardians over this realm, during the Second Grey Age, they were hunted down and killed, all but one...Agonan, the brother of Tundrok and Gonun. He stood with the last defense against the Hexagus Lords, he stood side by side with The Hero of Ages!' Diin declared in a loud tone.

'The... the what? What Hero?' The Daughter inquires.

'The fabled hero of Aura...' A voice growls behind them, 'all the nonsense tales of Hammer Wielder and Drog Slayer...the Civilian who rose up to become immortal!' It was the voice of the Daughter's Asyndian protector. 'The Hero of Ages does not exist...he is only a legend!'

'I never heard of him?' The Daughter says confused.

'You wouldn't have...one as ignorant as yourself and your ways to not know your history, and then to go behind our back and ask one such as this...nothing but a weak blind man and his pathetic sister!' Nilta leaps up to attack but two of the larger guards pounce upon her, and over power her. They attack her savagely, leaving her bloodied upon the ground, then the guardian grasps Diin by the throat, lift him up as he's kicking and gagging, then toss him aside to land upon his sister's broken body.

Diin grasps his bruised neck, 'Just as I suspected! I could smell you bastards a mile away! Quite the company you keep my lady!'

The Daughter pounces to her feet in anger, her arms tremble with anxiety as to what will happen next. 'What do you think you're doing?!'

The guardian laughs. 'I'll keep this short...my master has promised me quite a bit for you...power...immortality...so I will oblige his wishes...'

'Master what master?!'

'The Destroyer you imbecile...for Maz Dregor returns and he is more powerful than ever...the Mother has heard his call, and *SHE* is coming!' He motions to the other Asyndians.

'Seize her and take her away! Get her to Aumon as soon as possible!' The two then grab her by the arms tightly as she struggles like a child, unable to break their grasp. They rush her from the tent and make for the clouds, the guardian leers out and watches as she fades off into the clouds and far north over the snow-capped mountains.

The guardian walks back into the tent, he and a few other Asyndians look down upon the broken and beaten brother and sister.

'What are we gonna` do with them?'

'General A`deon has ordered to kill them, and their still alive...so the decision seems simple, we kill them...toss them over the mountain, and if the fall doesn't kill them then the cold will freeze them nice and slowly…' He laughs with a low rumble.

One of the Asyndians grabs Nilta by the ankle and drags her over to the edge, then another grabs Diin by the cape of his robe and drags him along close behind.

'Throw them over!' The guardian commands, and Diin and Nilta are cast over the cliffs and sent to fall, spiraling towards the bottom of the mountain, their broken limbs raggle in the harsh, swift wind like rag dolls, as they pass out of sight beyond a veil of mist below.

The Asyndians watch them pass beyond the veils of mist and haze, they turn and spread their wings, and in less than a moment, they take to the skies. It won't be long until they catch up to the others that carry the Daughter to their master, at the furthest peak, due north far over the Glorial Tundra and over the mountains that are close by to the southern edge of the Great Divide. There he waits…the Destroyer awaits their return.

Part XVIII:

Destroyer

~

High above the tundra's of Mirym, the cold desolation that is settled in far below, a bright, terrifying light rises up above all suns and shadows, above all towering spires and ethereal clouds of misty mountain tops, A`deon rises higher and higher, ascending past the summit and there at the pinnacle at the end of Aura's landscape, stares into the lifeless eye of the ice-ridden crag, a hole in the diadem, the lair of where Aumon has dwelled throughout this conflict of Hondor's blight upon the land.

And the voice within his mind, leads him, beckons him to enter.

"Come...there is much to discuss...much to do...my general, my...champion...please enter so that we may meet face to face..."

The icy winds swirl round and engulf A`deon's blighted aura, the intense heat of the rays melts the hail and haze down to nothing more than frozen slush and rain drops. He proceeds forward, over the cliffs and enters into the cave where the hollow voice calls from.

'I will…my master!' He calls out as he descends into the darkest recesses of the mountain's corrupt diadem.

Further down and down, into the corrupt throat at the end of the world he goes, no stairs, no tunnels along the way, just a long, wide drop down, and the essence of the candle-aura surrounds him with nerve-shattering power, to all mere Civilians would cause a painful, slow death if engulfed within. But to A`deon…it is the feeling, of ecstasy, a pleasure to feel a power unlike any he has ever felt within him before. And the further down he flies, the more powerful he feels himself becoming, all the anger, all the rage, all the malice and pain from scars and broken bones, he feels are fueling his power more and more. The source is near, he feels the whisper of darkness echo abound the cave, many voices, and many a presence lingers here, ghostly but within this physical realm, a place where the essence is power. The voices speak in tongues, his ears do not recognize, but his mind can make sense of everything, all the gasps and whispers, the screams and cries of agony, beaten liars, demolished cowards. He has seen it all before, he has experienced it all before.

Something lingers here, hidden here, something ancient…the darkness is hot against his face as the black tapestry of tentacles and flowing shreds of bile and tails adorns the sidewalls and smooth gray stone. And on he goes.

"Do you know where you are?" The voice whispers to him.

'I…I am in a wonderful place…a powerful place, a sacred dwelling, a prized possession the futile and the weak wish they bore…'

The voice laughs. *"You are almost home my chosen…close, so much closer you are…we will speak again very soon...you will bask in the glory that is everything...as it should be, as it once was so long ago..."*

At the very edge of the throat, there lays in chaos and disarray, a murky, black ocean within a chasm at the very bottom. He plummets through, the iqour of fluids never dampen nor touch his skin, the seas part ways as he emerges, from, an ocean that has been turned around, now hovering overhead, endless from boarder to boarder, except for the peaks of black obsidian dots in the distance, faded black upside-down mountains, of islands where nameless, unnamable tortures and creatures await the putrid and disgusting. The seas boil black, sludge-orbs down into a bottomless sky of pale blue and fiery serpents of damned light with scales dripping blood and fins of rusted flesh, churning through the endless chaos and discord of this tormented realm.

He soars across the pallid skies, and ahead of him a harsh red light dims the pale blue sea of skies to a ruby inferno, molten and fierce, yet there were no flames, only the hot red light. Within the light, burns a figure draped in solid white robes, his skin bears the image and flesh of Aumon, yet his looks differed drastically. Across his elongated forehead and pointed brows, crowning the snarling demonic face are rows of jagged horns, the two upon each side of his head are longer than the others. The eyes are black as jet stone, and his jaw is stretched away and the chin pointed. His arms outstretched several feet tipped with claws of razors, as are the legs with clawed toes like massive talons. His jaws grin with delight, for the Destroyer's champion has arrived.

A`deon need not say a word, for their thoughts communicated to one another.

"I...I am here...to serve...for the power and for the glory I deserve!"

The Destroyer laughs. He raises one of his long arms and closes his hand into a fist, pointing his finger, from his hand, erupts a powerful force, a blast of the blackest of essence. A`deon feels even more power rush through him, his veins pulsate with uncontrolled shakes and spasms overtaking him.

"The weakness you kill, the more power you gain...you will feed on the blood of those you slaughter...smile as they fall dead at your feet, for they are now yours, they will feed your reign, they will perish so you will rise..." And then a surge, a burst of electrical energy explodes in front of them. Hovering in front of A`deon, is a massive claymore, the blade twisted, wrapped around the hilt with breathing serpents and upon the blade, are pulsating veins filled with the black sludge, the blood from a source more foul than any A`deon has ever felt.

"Behold...the Blade of the Destroyer...the ultimate bane of Aura..." The Destroyer's voice echoes across the realm.

"The...that power...I've never felt anything like it..." A`deon tries to keep his eyes upon the sword, though the force upon his body and chest is extremely potent and immeasurable.

"That...my champion...it is the blood of Wom, taken from the very heart of our dearest mother...it is her power that charges this blade, it is her will that keeps it's sting sharp, it is her love...a gift from her to you...go on and claim it! Wrap your fingers and palms around and embrace your destiny!"

A`deon reaches forward towards the Blade of the Destroyer, and as though it were magnetic, sensing A`deon's new found thirst for blood...the blade soars into the palm of his left hand and the veins and tendrils of the serpents and creatures burrow into his hand and through his entire arm, traveling up and across his shoulders, over his face, his entire body is soon encased within a black cocoon of foul malevolence. The shell hardens over the quivering dark flesh and scales that binds him within. Then, after a long moment, his mind and body seem to pass beyond all space and time, to a place of forgotten wastes and deserted ruins, of crumbled spires and cities brought under a black tide of oceans consisting of ashes and waves. All time stands motionless as A`deon hovers above all, gazing at his surroundings, and then upon his reflection, his body bound by thick, stalwart armor of shaded black-gray steel, bolted down and pieced together by hands that were tortured and enslaved, from forges beyond forgotten shadows where none there can speak of the ferociousness, all the sickness and decay.

"In the name of the Destroyer,

the blessing of our mother Wom,

I shall lead these armies, conquer all,

for I am the general I was always meant to become…"

A force returns him, as red lightning cracks and erupts through the black shell, from among the debris and broken pieces, a warrior of chaos and power arises.

The Destroyer smiles. *"Tell me…what did you see?"*

"I saw…a wasted land, left in ruin taken under waves of black, down into the darkest depths, a massive wave has taken everyone and all, and those who were left…they were run through by the blade, slashed and burned, executed…the weak…they were destroyed…they were faded from existence by…by true power…"

A`deon clenches his fist, and the armor upon his body glow with a red aura, as does the blade within his other hand.

"The waves of blood and dirt are rising, the war is coming and you will bring it...you will bring the Age of Darkness...it was never the waters of Reignkiing, nor the Cleansing of the Auroras...no, they were simply the beginning, for the Gray Age was nothing more than preparing...for the Age of the Black...the rule of the Dregor...of the fallen Hexagus...has come...the tides of shadows, or rule and reign, it is you my champion...you will clear the rest of these miserable, weak wretches away..."

A`deon holds the blade in front of the Destroyer. *"I will...and my will is your will...our will is the darkest secrets of Wom...and it shall be done!"* He roars.

"And Hondor?" The Destroyer grins.

"...by my hand, he will be nothing more than an aborted legend!"

"Then go...the armies of my shadow await you upon the borders of Othetica and Fausengard...if Naumokron's worthless pustule Duul`ak or Hondor should cross you...take them out, make that monster of his bleed across Aura, chop off his limbs and rain his blood from the skies! It's time we rub that pathetic legend of his in his face, then drive Naumokron into the dirt, crush his skull, slice off his wings, do what you will as long as he feels pain...make it excruciating!"

"None may stand against Hondor...but Hondor stands no chance against me!" A`deon replies in a growl beneath his thorned helmet.

"Then return...and raise the waves of war...bring the tides of chaos and death to those intruders upon what was once a land we held in order...a land in me and my brethren's rule!"

A bright flash of red and thunder clasps around A`deon as he finds himself kneeling, head down…his red, popping eyes of flames gazing upon Aura's brown soil and yellow grass, for the hours of less daylight and summer warmth are upon Aura this season, gray and worn…this land that has seen many seasons come to pass and die away in the shadows of yesterdays.

As for Aura's fate…A`deon rises and gazes out over the land, the Destroyer bound to his left hand, he raises the sword into the air, then plunges it deep into the flesh of the ground, past rocks and dirt, and from the crust, boils over a pool of thick, iron-smelling liquid…the blood of Aura will be spilled…a sign…a warning for the reign and warpath of A`deon that lays planned ahead within the general's sickened thoughts.

Part XIX:

Shadows of His Past

~

A dark shadow, the watcher Duul`ak, passes over high above Hondor, his talons gripping upon the ruins of a crumbled steeple. Hondor hears the scratching of the nails across ruined stone and turns up to see the fiery eyes looking down upon him. Hondor catches eyes with Duul'ak, no longer the minion lingering just above his spine, but now takes on the form of the Asyndian in the shadows. Within the dark skies, the two red orbs of Duul'ak looks over the carnage and ruin, a mile across his beak, yet in the night, no one would ever see it. Then, the smile rearranges and he frowns in anger upon Hondor.

"Beast will not listen...will not obey...I have returned to this world and you will obey me...I gave you life, I your father...your mother that had suckled you on poison and malevolence...I who spawned you from the legends that kept your physical form dead! You will atone for this insolence...you have destroyed, just as you were created to...but you are out of control and will regain your harness...!"

'I hope you've had your fill! Now, I command you to do as I say...you will head south...track the essence of Kandarius and the Dregor to the remains of Daskar! There you

289

will find it, your final piece to the puzzle of your existence…you sow the seeds of your destruction…'

Hondor looks upon him, a razor-toothed boar ready to charge with rage. And then, an idea comes to his mind.

'…ah, very well…I can't believe I have been so lack-luster, so foolish in my thoughts…the mighty Hondor obeys none, no words, it is the destruction and death, the master of the sickle is what you heed, what you obey…very well…I cannot control your mind or your form…but maybe…I can hold the tantalizing smell of blood in front of your nose…'

He soars down to the battlements, the remains of Thylesian's rubble and grabs the severed head of a dead Civilian soldier, with the crested helm still upon it. He holds it in front of Hondor, who stands some twenty feet away, covered in the blood of many, his large cloak wrapped around him soaked in blood and dirt, tattered and torn asunder by the battle and slaying.

'Is it…this…yes! You understand this…well then, I shall give you more of what you want, I will spoil you, I will indulge you, for this realm is still ripe with the flesh and blood of many living things…and you shall have it all! And once it's all done…then can dominion be rebuilt, a kingdom anew!'

"Just what to do about you when it's all over…hmmm…I know you will attack me, you already have…but you cannot fly…hmmm….I wonder…" Duul'ak whispers under his breath.

'Very well…' Duul`ak soars up high with the head in his hand, flying over Hondor, heading south in the direction of the Greywaste. 'Follow me…for your slaughter has only been tasted…soon the rest of Aura will know your hunger…'

He whisks away on the blackened wind and Hondor charges in pursuit, tossing the massive blade of Kar'durgra aside. Hondor reaches the edge of where he tossed the mighty prison vessel below. Duul`ak hovers about a hundred yards away, mocking him on, taunting Hondor with the promise of death and destruction. Hondor takes a few steps back and then charges out into the nothing, leaping outwards into the air. He shifts his body and takes a dive, a cannon shot gaining speed and falling fast, falling down...down to Aura's soil. The force of the winds tears the shroud from his body, and he is left more than a bare, naked monstrosity crashing into the rocky soil, flames consume his entire form. Off many miles and kilometers away, he would appear to be a meteor, a falling chunk of space, on a crash-course towards ruin, only...it will be Aura's ruin.

Across desolation and forgotten lands of gray ash and barren wastes, the vast expanse of the abandoned Greywaste lays far beneath Duul`ak in flight, and not too far behind him, the soot and dust kicks up, as Hondor charges at a furious pace, his stride wide as the titan of death closes in under Duul`ak's shadow, his vast black wing span stretching far across some fifteen feet in width as he glides at several machs per minute. And Hondor's thick legs of muscle and solid armored hide is increasing, his lungs pumping, the vile heart churning, veins pumping, expanding and contracting.

Duul`ak looks back towards the charging fiend. 'Come...we are almost there! My wide eyes can see the buried steeples, the mighty towers of black buried long ago. Kandarius had built himself quite a fortress I now see, I see the sinister reputation that betrayer had made for himself, such a deceiver...I guess he learned from the best...' Duul`ak laughs to himself, but it was not his laugh nor was this his voice, for the long forgotten vocals of the black chime of Naumokron is seeping through. Long has it been since the voice of the old dark one has been heard, though none but Duul`ak was around to hear or recognize it.

Just ahead, the ancient remains of Kandarius's long lost fortress shows through the gray sands, darker than the mountains in the distance that line the backdrop of a horizon, mountains blinded, misted and flooded over by the sharp, razor winds of the storms that blight the Greywaste. Yet, no darkness of these final days can overshadow and imbue upon the obsidian stone of Daskar, welded and fused together by the enflamed blood of races, pumped out by Kandarius's campaign of shadows years ago, blood pumped out to be concocted and blended into these walls and towers…and the ancient gate, the passage way of the Dregor where the Hexagus had stepped forward from there vile pits of sludge and decay, and walked upon the dirt of Aura once again.

The gateways, the points and teeth of the gateway to annihilation were jutting upwards from their tombs under layers of thick ash for dirt, and around the far perimeter lay the remains and rubble of the black walls and gates, dead in form, but their essence, something still lingers here, keeps them warm, keeps them living, icy to the touch for none would go near them, none would dare to move them and clean this land away of its filth and desecration. There are many stains, much history of blood and horrors tainted upon these lands furthest south of all territories and realms, but there is something, a presence that still haunts this plane of oblivion, a world that may as well be its own.

Something…deep beneath, keeping to the roots beneath of these battered and twisted ruins, pulsating with a damndable fiery glow.

"I can feel it…it's still here…it's been in my thoughts, my sleep has been dedicated to its image, the double blade, a single shaft of the pythons severed tail, the boiling blood and

bowels dripping from its forked mouth…it's here…give me a sign…where are you?"

And then…only a moment later, Duul`ak looks off towards the west, and over near the main altar, where the vast and many stairs led upwards towards the portal once stood, there is a beating, a heartbeat thudding, echoing in his mind, in his ears, and in the direction of the source of this sound, there is a pulsating mound of ground surging upwards and then down again, engulfed by a fiery glow of faint light from somewhere beneath.

Duul`ak heads to this source, and Hondor trudges along behind, now waiting patiently, waiting for this Asyndian to descend to the ground.

Duul`ak hovers there for a moment, he looks down upon the beating ground, the surging spot of fire and light. He then looks to the wild-eyed Hondor.

'I cannot make you dig you stubborn monster…so I will let your thirst, your will to silence the beating heart, take control of your insubordinate mind…'

Duul`ak tosses the head down from the dizzying heights upon the ground, as the head rolls away from the helmet some distance away, and Hondor lunges forward, Duul`ak only looks on and observes. Hondor ignores the head, as well as the Asyndian prey above him, and instead is mesmerized by the soft warm spot beneath him, hypnotized by the luring call, to silence that heart, that beating that calls to him, slams within the haunted shadows of his thoughts and mind.

The heart beat…the sound of the heartbeat…something about that sound awakens something within his thoughts…a…a memory to us, though he doesn't know, he knows not the meaning. Like a scroll unraveling, a book opening…a…an infant child crying…something shatters the

293

long still in his mind, that has haunted what was a thousand years sleep, eons it has seemed, a memory of the legend is just the beginning…

***

From the darkness, steps the leering figure, watching the massive body swinging upon the chain to and fro. His large black wings are folded in, the tips to the black obsidian floor, dragging across as his talons make a scraping sound as he steps across the shrouded room, the atmosphere thick with poisons to the mind, the horrors of the crude experiments within that have taken place over however many thousands of years, even eons passed.

Behind the limp body on the swinging chain, are several tube-like coffins, broken and damaged from the failures, all the failures that came before…but now, now he has been perfected, Naumokron knows he has succeeded. The body is perfect, the muscles and tone are immaculate, there is only one final test left, one final step…and that is the step of life.

A smile raises across Naumokron's beak, and the shadows underneath his ruby eyes tighten around the red ovals. The ancient cracks upon his aged face show, his feathers dusty and his skin underneath, chalky and old, his once robe of darkness frayed and torn, the energy he drinks from his prisoners can last only so long, he is tiring, but he has strength enough for this, enough to see this through! Reignkiing has fallen, nearly the entire western realm of Aura is underwater; he has been in seclusion for hundreds of years, perfecting what he calls his *"master creation!"* He plans not to fail this time, he is aware of what Maz Dregor is planning, he knows the Destroyer will use his new puppet, Kandarius, to bring about his downfall.

'You…you will be my instrument of destruction, you will be their downfall my son, my child…my creation…you will cast the ultimate darkness upon Aura…the Hexagus will fear you, and all these pathetic Asyndians and Gormons will flee from the sight of you…you will feast upon the flesh and bones of everything that moves, and it will turn this old skin into armor, your bones to the strongest and hardest steel! For none you fear, none you obey…except my voice. Hundreds of failures, but you…! Oh yes, you have been perfected!'

His voice radiates through the dark halls of his mighty citadel in the far northern mountains of Raukmar, Gargoth and the citadels, the dome of Na`bata, the blackest of steeples and spires rises to the thick clouds of smoke-gray, the eerie eternal shadow that looms over the gloom that is the home of the titans of the realm, the Rauks.

Naumokron holds up his hands, the crude laboratory around him quakes, as vials of bloods, poisons, and other vile samples of plasma and liquids crash and break upon the ground, creating foul-smelling pools of acids and giving off choking fumes and deadly burning steam. Dissected, hollowed out bodies of Raumkats, Prowls, gigantic beasts, and other cruelties fall from their hooks and shelving upon the floor. Tables turn over and collapse. Caged souls howl as their eyes alight with the fires of fear, for they feel it, cries echo down below from the dungeons, for the tormented can smell it, taste it upon their dried shriveled tongues…that chaos and domination was about to be born. Mangled, twisted bodies curl round themselves and others within their lost cells and cages, clamped down within the iron maidens. Life…at his birth will die, while death will suffer, death will be his association, death and destruction will be his name.

And the power, escalates and rises, flows through his hands, as Naumokron places his black hands upon the hanging body, and electrical, thermal waves blast and radiate across the corpse, causing the muscles to contract back and brings the veins and cells within alive, stirring the life within and seeping into the deepest recesses of the darkest places of his mind.

'You were but a legend, a darkness nobody wanted to cast light upon...you have a story, but no body, no form...ethereal within the ancient scrolls and writings of history. Blood and warfare is what you are, what you were born to be...may this Gray Age take the Auroras, may it take what life there is upon this world, but I fear the Hexagus will underestimate there is another power, one carried within the one they will call, this...Forgemaster, the pupil of Gormons and child among the Civilians...but let us see what happened of things to come, for I do not fear them, none of them...for I will give you a form, I will give you a face, a name....yes...for when Hondor comes...no one will live...to see another light of day.'

Naumokron cackles with rowdy laughter at the thought of all his masters perishing, falling to his will, bound to his dominion, his new found power in this one lone warrior, this warrior of death and destruction, once but a legend, a shadow of the past, now will soon be a reality, a tragedy and blight, he will be here, he is almost here...he is...the world will be rendered to nothing more than shattered spines and broken nerves, the most gallant and brave of heroes will cower before his might and power, his axe will splay, his hammers will crush all in his way, castles, towers, fortresses and enclaves of guardians will fall...

"...all...will...fall..."

And the flames of lightning cease, and the earthquakes settle. The room and all time seems to come to a halt, as Naumokron's two eyes watch on with anticipation, waiting...waiting for that moment, waiting...

296

All is still, all is silent, by the mighty power of Naumokron's force that radiates at his fingertips, even the silence outside the walls of Na`bata engulfs the land, for all wind and life ceases to be for the moment, *"For I must hear...I must see...I can bring the power of nature to a halt, I can...I can create life...this must work...I know it will succeed...there is no room for failure, no room for weakness..."*

There was nothing.

Naumokron's rage becomes one thousand fold, and with a jarring burst of energy the power at his fingertips, storms across the surface of Hondor's flesh with fury. Bright lights and storms burst from the empty eyes of the windows, filling the tower with violet and blue lights of static, sounds of sonic bursts echo forth through the gray skies.

'You will obey me, you will live! I command you to live...!'

Then the chaos ceases, and deathly silence once more falls over the barren lands, and the tower, in all the aftermath, still stands.

Naumokron turns away for a moment, then his sensitive Asyndian hearing picks up a sound, the sound of a creaking bending joint. He turns and looks at the body, and at first he sees no movement, but the sound, the sound of creaking bone rings in his ears like thunder. Then, he looks up at the hands tied above Hondor's head, and the index finger...it is moving, bending, folding in and out back and forth, over and over again and again.

'He...he lives...he's alive!' Naumokron's voice roars in an excited tone, for he knows his conquest is that much closer. He pulls the chains of the mechanism towards him, and the body of Hondor is pulled backwards to a thirteenth coffin of glass and metal, twelve have been broken, but there is another, for Naumokron had built a new one just for this purpose.

The chains come to a halt, and Naumokron walks over to the body, he caresses the face, looks at the eyes, turns the head, looking at the features and perplexities of the skin and features of the face and upper body, testing the joints of the arms and legs. He can feel a tear almost begin to trickle from his eye.

'Perfect...he is perfect...'

Naumokron goes over to the far switch and crank upon the wall just behind the row of coffins, and turns the lever and lowers Hondor down into the coffin.

'Sleep now...this sanctum will give you the energy you will need for later, we will perfect you, your movements, your sight, your hearing...there is so much work to do, so much that we need to do...'

And thousands of years later...they would discover the empty coffin, the shattered glass and remains of the destroyed lab.

Part XX:

The Axe of Blodaur Ror

~

The black thorns arise from the ground, the barren battlements that surround the ruins of Daskar. Upon each side are the remains of the ancient gate, the Arc of Daskar, where the Hexagus entered into Aura. The overcast above looms like a crown of shadow upon each neck of the twin pillars some hundreds of feet high. And there standing within Daskar's shadow, stands the monstrous beast Hondor.

He sniffs the ground, smells the air, his prize is nearby, and it lays in wait for him. He walks several paces ahead, and goes round in a circle, brushing away dirt, pushing aside ash and debris. The ground beneath is cold, the soil harsh, the massive heart thumps....thumps, something is alive, something lays dormant but alive, waiting to be awakened. The ground quivers, terrified of what it keeps, wanting to be rid of this object, this entity.

Hondor kneels upon the frozen, rocky dirt, and with one huge clump, one huge handful after the other, starts to dig, not even fazed by the cuts and bloodied knuckles from rocks and hard clay mantle the further down he goes.

Hondor peels the dirt back, rips open the clay earth like the flesh, the skin cells of the planet Aura. The air around him swelters, beads of fever and sickness pour off the sour flesh, the flesh that neither bleeds nor breaks, at least not of feeling. Around him, the walls rise higher and higher, the pit is getting deeper, and the ground, the ground at the center begins to glow, pulsate with wicked hot energy, causing the clay to swelter and melt down, boiling like a thick consistency of oil and the smell of blood, millenniums old.

A power still rests here, for two hundred years it has been here, buried over after the collapse of Daskar and the Hexagus powers of old. Now, it has been resurfaced, it will be brought back into this world, a weapon of horror, a weapon created by the dying screams of billions and billions, over millenniums and millenniums of passed time epochs old.

And after he clears away the rest of the molten earth, beneath his feet, a tunnel opens inwards, spiraling down to a molten area, the heat reeking forth is a bad smell of charred flesh and skin. The stairway is crumbled, an ancient pillar of steps that once led downwards, down to the base of the Daskar altar beneath his feet. Hondor heaves past the heat as though it were nothing more than a cold dampness upon his back, not even phasing him, and leaps to the bottom, hitting upon the altar stairs with force, creating a large crater into the black obsidian architecture found beneath.

Surrounding him is what remains of the fortress at Daskar, now melted and in ruin, long buried beneath sand, rock, dirt, debris, piled over by time, covered since the fall of Athilnovia, and buried by the Eleventh Dust Storm that has raged throughout the last one hundred years, blowing hot wind and obsidian, long crumbled to ashes and dust. In the recent decade this storm as settled, now nothing more than brief showers of acid rain and sludge-storms, polluting the decayed carcasses and bones of those who dared to pass this way, those who fed themselves to the dissolve of this rain, of this plagued land littered by melted skulls and bones.

Hondor paces back and forth, no thought nor plan, just searching, hunting, and looking for the next destination, the next step to conquer before him. The voice speaks, whispers to him, tells him where to go, what the next step is, where to go after entering the bowels within, beneath the ruins of Daskar.

"...take the tunnel that lays ahead of you..." Hondor pretends not to hear, seeks out the voice in his mind to try to destroy it, yet he cannot, *HE* is there...the master is there with him guiding him. Yet he cannot find it, the source from which these commands seep, like a sticky sap, leaving a trail, a taint that's hard to wash away. Yet...it sounds close, closer than he may realize now. The flicker of tiny red eyes glistens behind his ear, within his helmet.

"...take the tunnel that lays ahead of you..." The voice repeats. Enraged, he grasps his head furiously, for Hondor does not like to be told twice, don't repeat your futile commands to Hondor. He bashes his head against the obsidian wall, hand clutched tight so he can drive his skull harder, trying to shake the voice out of his head, to break the jaw, the source of this unseen whisperer in the dark, the whisperer that talks down to him, repeats this command like a parent repeats to their child when they refuse to listen *(For none, Hondor obeys! He is strong...he will find his own way! Damn it! He will...make his own way, he will carve through the rock if he has to! He will cleave through their flesh...he will drink all the blood...he will burn all the land...the death of Aura...and what he shall do to it...rests in Hondor's hands.)*

He removes his head from the beaten wall, taking more punishment and beaten away more than he is, he who is unharmed, unbeaten.

"You can beat your head against the wall all you want...you cannot get rid of me...for I am near you, I am away from you, you cannot fight my voice Hondor...I created you, I made you...you will, in time, understand this. Too long have you slept, too long have you been locked away within your mind, lost in your slumber, for you never had the chance to walk in your own flesh, awakened a skeleton, no flesh, no essence, for the form of a Gormon I had to give you, so you could rebuild yourself anew, and become the warrior I made...it is I who created you...and you WILL obey me! Now...take the tunnel, reach that which lays at the end...this I command you! Now, GO!" The voice spoke to Hondor as though he were that child, as though this unseen figure is the parent overseeing to him and what he does, keeping a tight leash around his neck. *(...for none Hondor obeys)*

Hondor could see it ahead, the light beamed through the tunnels, but it was the scent, the scent led him down this tunnel, it is the scent of metal, its screams echoed from the forge of atrocities from whence it was born, it smelled of sweat, the horrid, wretched smell of Blodaur Ror's salty discharge from his flesh, as he hacked away and slaughtered millions of lives eon upon eon, the bodies piled upon bodies, a pile that would rise higher than any mountain, cover the most vast plane in distance. But, it is the smell of blood that lingered in the air...the scent of crimson waves in the endless ocean within the pit of its stomach, the shaft, the blade, covered in layer upon layer of ferocity, slaughter, torture, malice, animosity, with a thick skin of metal fused with blood, the blade dripped with so much blood, that a swirling pool, a vortex rest beneath it, and the axe is the uncalm eye at the center.

Around this pit of blood, lay the remains of leftover, long forgotten bones, the bones of the ancient ones themselves, namely, curved about the subterranean dome, miles high and vast in its length and thickness, is the spine of Maz Dregor, the remains of the destroyer still remain, as they have gathered ash and soot, molten heat emanates from the source of these bones, for they still remain preserved, yet slightly weathered. The three heads disconjointed and scattered about, two of the massive skulls lay across on the other side, while at the center, on display among the altar where the axe is hovering above the boiling pool of blood, is the middle skull, the third head of Maz Dregor, the fangs sinister, and a mirage of those luminescent, ancient yellow bestial eyes, could still be seen, for preserved within these bleached bones, a small faint hint of Maz Dregor, still remains, his foul stench could still be smelled swept up into the choking atmosphere of this underground grove, forgotten by the years, forbidden by the fearful…for those who, are deemed weak among the eyes of the Dregor and the Hexagus Lords, for none would dare venture this way, yet the voice, deems it's part of Hondor's path, the road Naumokron had laid out long before, all part of the scheme, the divine plan of a crazed Asyndian who has kept to his shadows during his existence in life…and keeps behind the scenes and once more to the shadows…in his death.

"…for none Hondor obeys…" But Hondor would obey him, for he created this monstrosity, this abomination, this killing machine, to do his will, his bidding, to bring about the Cleansing that was supposed to be…Hondor will obey him…for only he can control Hondor…he will…he shall.

Hondor stands face to face with this instrument of destruction, he looks at the blade, the twisted maw that rises up from the pool of blood, wraps its serpentine neck around the shaft and swallows the half crescent metal that concaves forward. He ponders the meaning, what wonders could this blade bring…he was the method to annihilation, not some symbol, the weapon of a bygone warlord, for *HE* is the warrior, the eater of worlds, the devourer of flesh, the terror, the turmoil to spread, this weapon could do no more damage than he is capable of. He grunts, sneering through jagged teeth, laughing to himself the ridiculousness at such a need for this tool, for that is all it was…nothing more than a tool, a means to an end that he would bring, for nothing would take Hondor's place to do that. He knows what is to be done and how he will go about to bring a reign of terror.

Hondor would show this piece of fetid weapon, the spawn of a dead Hexagus, but like the spine and bones of Maz Dregor, within the axe, a small amount of Blodaur Ror still exists…still lives. Hondor plunges into the whirling pool of boiling blood, unharmed, the strength of the heat blistering his flesh, but he trudges through unscathed through the knee-deep whirlpool that spins counterclockwise. He reaches the center and grasps for the shaft, clenches the serpentine tail with a harsh grasp of his rough fists, the hair upon his knuckles like spines. The tighter he squeezes, the more the veins rise through his arms and across his chest, his neck swells, he grinds his teeth, chipping the incisors and with a strong yank, tears the axe away from the force that keeps it rooted to this pool of blood. He raises the axe into the air, grasps the other side, the blade side with his other hand and prepares to break the weapon across his knee. Then he feels a force pulling back, trying to get the axe back, but the force no matter how powerful, would never break the death grip that Hondor had upon the handle.

A thick pale cloud of smoke hissed from the blades maw as it glows and pulsates a bright red, a large drop of slick sweat with a viscosity of sludge and oil, falls from Hondor's brow, lands upon the blade and singes into puffs of steam. A voice echoed throughout the cavern dome, which roared like thunder, the black speech of Dregor upon the tongue of Blodaur Ror himself.

"ITAK`KHAN`DO! TULBADOR`LRAOT!"

The thick air of smog takes form, the silhouette of Blodaur's hideous, and fowl shadow has been summoned into this world. The colossal shape rises high to the ceiling of the crust above the surface, the air of the room thickens, it would suffocate the average denizen upon Aura, but Hondor would not be intimidated by Blodaur's wrath.

He leaps through the air, raises the axe over his head and swings, swings to the right, to the left, he stabs forward, thrusts, attacks again and again, but he cannot harm or even scratch this eclipsing monster that is nothing more than a conjoined union of disgusting air and wretched winds. His fists like cyclones attack back, driving Hondor against the far wall, but Hondor pounces back to his feet, shakes his head to clear the blow and returns to the foray of the battle, slashing and attacking over and over, but Blodaur simply looks down upon this futile creature and laughs...bellows a festered hark of satisfaction, seeing this creature fail...but Hondor will not fail, he will keep coming and coming, he will fight back, he will not stop, he will not fail...for he is the bringer of destruction, he is the new Destroyer, he will see this puff of hot air fall, this being that no longer walks among this world in a physical form, only a puff of ferocious gas.

And then...Hondor thought to himself...for no voice would tell him what to do, he will persevere, he will win this battle on his own. For he is the devourer, he gains the strength and domination through battle, then feasting upon his victims. Blood he drinks, flesh he chews, air he...inhales. Hondor raises his arms up to his sides, the axe clenched in his right hand, he leans forward, and prepares himself. Blodaur Ror looks on with curiosity, wondering what this creature is trying now, what trick is it planning, for it will never work against the might of a Hexagus Lord...for his essence will never die!

Hondor reels his head and body back, his mouth takes a gulping inhale, taking in all the air around him, his face enlarged, his eyes bulging, the veins in his neck were pulsating, and that's when the look came over Blodaur's face, as he could feel the pull upon his body. Hondor, this insignificant thing, was absorbing the Hexagus Lord, he is drawing him in with a swallowing inhale. Twisting like a cyclone, trying to escape trying to get away, it was futile, he could not escape, for Hondor would swallow him whole. Hondor draws in the Hexagus warlord, as Blodaur Ror tries to break free, trying to get away from the suction, but it is no use, there is nowhere for him to go, no way for Blodaur to run away, for it was unheard of, for a Hexagus Lord…a titan of the black gaping birth canal of Wom, to be terrified of a spawn of Aura…what is this creature, this monster…what had Naumokron created, for in his thought, he knew the Asyndian…the once chosen of Maz Dregor, he was behind this scheme, for Maz Dregor knew Naumokron would betray them…but this, the warlord would have never expected anything like this, as the last of him is being drawn in, and the mouth of Hondor closes to swallow the last of Blodaur Ror.

(…for none stand in Hondor's way…)

And the last of the Hexagus Lord is absorbed, to become one with he who deems himself the new Destroyer, he who is the last to stand, still clutching the axe of Blodaur Ror in his grasp. Hondor looks at the axe, he's not sure if it is the sudden presence of Blodaur Ror within him, but the curvature of the blade gleams in his eye, the axe takes to him, and he to it…for this will be his pet, his henchman, his slayer to do his will, and with his hand, he shall command this axe to kill, to destroy, to mutilate, to conquer, to rule, to command dominion over all, just as Naumokron had planned…yet Hondor will change that, for there will be a new master…for none Hondor obeys, and no one…no one shall stand in his way.

Part XXI:

Who She Once Was

~

The Daughter is led over the furthest mountains and hills, beyond the rims of the decaying northern lands, beyond Mirym, from where any trees grow, nor is there any lush grass or twinkle of snow fall; no birds sing, nor is the fauna pattering about the ground, or howling and whining up to the skies, where the essence of the moon and sun once held dominion, now only a lifeless pit of black lingers above all Aura and across the vast southern borders of Raukmar. As is the endless abyss above vacant and hollow reaching up to the nether-reaches of the beyond, so too does this fact reside deep within the Great Divide, the eternal pit to the below.

Bound by chains and led as a slave, a prisoner, she has been taken betrayed by her most trusted guardians who swore to her protection. Far below, along this path through the valleys and the twisted canyons and fissures she is taken, there before her is the vast crowd of her people, herded up and gathered like livestock, the survivors she had gathered and rescued from the wrath of Hondor's attack upon Runegard. She sees none from the east, no Gormons of Fausengard, nor those of Othetica, and by the betrayal of her guardians and their deceit, it is most certain, that the situation for them, has or will...become a slaughter.

Her people of Runegard, Civilians, Gormons, and Asyndians have been shoved and crammed into cages and barred shut by massive locking mechanisms. More groups have been separated off to the other side of the compound and separated by massive posts and fencing covered in razors and rusted nails to prevent escape, one corpse hand, limp and rotten upon the side, showing the futility of escape.

And that's when she sees them, patrolling about the compound, keeping a deathly sentinels watch upon the prisoners and cells, warriors assembled together of crude gears and machines built into their dark armor, their flesh as black and as greasy as sludge and tar, and their sweat drips with anger and rage.

They are brought into the encampment, where she is shoved and dragged along, through the dirt and mud, shamed in front of her people as their widened eyes catch sight of her; they call to her for help, reaching from the cages to her, like vines to the rays of the sunlight that gives them growth, light, and energy...and hope.

'My lady...it...could it be her?! My lady...she is here!' Roúgsver's head rears up from its slump to see what is going on, and catches sight of her. The others stir about.

'My lady, help us...what are we to do?!' They call aloud, and the many join in chanting for her.

'My lady, they torture us! They beat us! My lady...my lady...'

But in her mind, through her ears...all she hears is...

"My lady...you lie to us!"

"My lady...you said we would be safe!"

"My lady...why have you abandoned us?!"

The Daughter reaches out with her shackled hand to grasp's the wrist of one of her people, trying to consul them. She can feel his flesh profusely shake with terror and fear. One of the Asyndian centurions, with feathers as dark as midnight, grabs her by the arm and pulls her away, back to her place in line. She whispers to herself, her voice quivering under her breath.

'What is this place...I feel...weak, this is horrible, the smell, the creeping sensation of the skeletal hand leaching on the back of my neck...this place is wrong, the sensations I feel...'

'Shut it, ignorant woman! These are the Dregor, the rightful civilians of this realm...not *"YOUR"* weak sort! This realm belongs to the Hexagus!' The Asyndian soldier roars, shoving the Daughter to the ground. She tries to fight back but she is back-handed by the soldier.

'That means...Asyndians too! As well as us Civilians and Gormons, will be cast out...slaughtered by these monsters, these spawns of chaos pumped out by Wom's loins!' The Daughter retorts, and the rage in the Asyndian's eyes went frenzied, and he bashed several shots at Aura.

'You're wrong there...we are loyal to the Dregor and the Hexagus, to be one with the echelon of true power! The pioneers, the founders, the redeemers of a new world, when we return to our mother, and she will embrace us with open arms...as her children!'

'And what is to become of us? What is the meaning of...not just killing us out-right and getting the deed over with?!' The Daughter cries.

'Mind yourself Civilian woman! You will find out soon enough, for this is a happy day…a day for rejoicing!'

A group of the more burley, dark-feathered Asyndians, ones who once swore to protect the Daughter of Runegard, they swore fealty to protect her with their lives, now encircle her, and tear at her clothing, trip her and kick her around, they jab and pierce at her flesh, with their spears and weapons, and their fury, humiliating her, mocking her, desecrating the one last idol of hope, that those of Runegard once had.

All eyes were on her, as the Asyndian centurions wail and throw everything at her, weapons and fists, each blow, each strike more severe than the last. All the timid and scared to death looks of the Civilians, Gormons, and Asyndians of Runegard, their men, women, and children, all look down upon her, a messiah lost, a leader beaten and broken, the last of their hopes and salvation, dashed away and spilled in cut flesh and dripping blood.

The memories…the nightmares come back, the images flash before her eyes…the fall…the deception…the lies…the, the name…

A voice shrieks under heavy breath and out from beaten lips, lost among the battering and beating from the Asyndian centurions.

'She's still speaking, hit her harder…harder than that!' They cry aloud.

She grasps her broken ribs, struggling to get to one knee.

'I…I am…' She whines. And they beat her down more and more.

She stands once more, holding the palm of her hand tight against her slashed cheek; she gets to one knee, wobbling from side to side and stirring and shaking.

'I am…I am…' She cries even louder. The people from their cells and prisons cry and plead, beg them to stop, crying for these brutes to leave the Daughter alone.

'I…am… A…' She spits blood to the ground.

'Arise…O lady! O Daughter of all Runegard! We know you can!' The prisoners cry.

And then she staggers to her feet, her clothing in shreds, armor torn away, except for a thin chain gauntlet upon her right hand, covered in dirt and her blood. She balances herself, she raises her fist, covered by the chain, into the air, tightens her fist with anger and declaration…with an intent for retribution.

'I am…I was once hidden…a secret kept forbidden, but now I am here in front of all of you! I was twice beaten and broken…I have fallen…but I have risen up again and again! My lineage…is my blood and my flesh…'

She sways a little, but maintains composure; her body and bruises swell and ache.

'I am the union of a separated land…the mourner of the fallen, bearer of their names and keeper of their legacy…protector of the defenseless, I carry…in these veins the blood of saviors and legends…bane to these,' She spits upon the ground at her feet, 'these Dregor!'

She shuffles forward lowers her arm and grasps the large cut upon the side as the sting radiates through her muscles from the wrist to the shoulder. She grits her teeth enraged.

'I…am…Aura!'

The pain overtakes her and she drops back down to her knees, as all falls silent among the wide-eyed, gaped mouths of the crowds and the lifeless eyes of the Dregor, and the dark Asyndian eyes too open with shock. Then, the voice of ice and chilled, shadow-winds, crept over and licked her ears with its black speech.

Flashes and distant memories dash through the forests of her mind like wild fawns and fleeing animals in chaos. She hears the voices at her birth, *"She is to be kept hidden...she is the key, you must listen and make sure she stays away from the eyes of the darkness that look into our realm through broken gateways!"* She feels the grasp of a loving, yet nervous embrace of a young, childless couple established beyond city walls upon distant farmlands, *"She has descended from the legendary one, her and her brother! They must be kept secret! The Dregor will be looking for her, and they will do everything to get to her if they found out, even use the brother!"* She sees the trees above her head, it is night, and she feels the grass and crumpled leaves beneath her feet, it is fall and the hours of the sun have long died away. She sees the child in front of her, a child like her, but he is a Civilian boy, he smiles at her and puts out his hand, but his eyes are dark and sinister. She wants to trust him, she knows this boy, she feels love and comfort for him, but he is not himself, there is something else which resides behind those eyes, she feels the cool touch of the wind, the nip in the air and the rush of frigid air, a winter breeze in the earliest hours of the fall. She shuffles back upon her tiny, naked toes and filthy heels, her reddish brown hair blowing in the breeze.

"Take my hand...I won't hurt you...I want to play..." He whispers to her in the dark, she remembers keeping one hand behind his back. This dark-eyed child was hiding something. And there was the voice telling her to go on...and the shadow behind him, keeping to the trees, that beast with the black wings and eyes of fiery rubies glistening in the dead light

312

of the moon's glow on that night. She remembers the sting of the metal tooth, and the blood left upon the fang lying upon the ground by her body, she looked up to the sky and gaze beyond the windows of death…before all went dark and she woke up back at her home…she had forgotten all about that time so long ago, and that child with the dark eyes…and, and that shape of an all-encompassing abyss hovering over that child, the thing with the black wings and ruby eyes. She had forgotten…until she saw that being…as he hovered behind Lord Rolom…the same one…as Lord Rolom held out his hand, embraced her docile body, placed beautiful jewels and kisses upon her neck, as he slashed at her with the dagger, just as that dark child had done, and then she fell…and all went black…her life she thought, fell into complete darkness permanently, until she found herself wandering through the woods, along the roads and trails outside of Othetica's rundown walls, a jewel brought down by corruption and ruin, just as she.

"Aura…" The voice seeped into her soul, planting a blackened seed deep within her thoughts as it spoke. *"So, there was another…the sister of that worthless Kandarius…so it seems is true. I have followed you for some time, and kept an eye upon you…and as it seems to be, the Auroras, the protectors of Aura, they fought, and they died to keep you a secret! That bastard Naumokron was more clever than I gave him credit for and he knew for so long, seems his agenda to slay you didn't work to his favor, because you are different, for you are correct, because the blood of an old foe of mine flows within you, as it did with your brother…and now that you are here…nothing will stop me now! Your brother has been dealt with and that bastard the Hero of Ages has his hands full, as my dear mother's legions of Dregor hordes siege Arla as we speak!"*

She turns and sees that familiar image, that floating being in white, only now; his face is more monstrous and daemonic, with rows of horns and elongated teeth arms and hands. The jointed legs of this beast floats above a swirling pool of darkness and mists beneath.

The being floats forward towards her. She backs up, then two of the Asyndians grasp her tightly around the arms in a forceful vice grip. The Destroyer curls his hand and runs his finger across the bottom of her chin.

"You are such a strong, brave woman...able to keep yourself together the way you have, it is very impressive. So, to answer your question why not just slice your throat with this razor upon my finger," he motions to the claw of a nail upon his hand, *"Because this is a celebration, for you are the main entertainment in celebration of my new general, the one who will lead my armies across these lands in war..."*

'There will be nothing left once Hondor has finished slaying everything!' Aura retorts with a bleeding grin.

"That beast will be dealt with...I will feed his master to him, and then..." He took a moment to think about the situation, *"maybe he could be useful...or he might just have to be taken care of, either way, I will not have you ruin such a joyous moment for my Dzjurger, the highest honor a general of the Hexagus may reach!"*

'And just who exactly is this general of yours!'

"You know him...for the same hand that saved you...shall slay all of you!" He watches the horror tear up in her eyes.

He looks back to the black peaks of a jagged hill that rises behind his back, and there standing at the top in a suit of armor crafted by broken, bloodied hands, the metal a razor to the touch as sharp as the jagged weapon within the sheath at his belt, and the helm two pointed thorns curved and slanted back in curves wrapped about like ivy, and there was no face to be seen, for the rage and anger in the eyes could not be seen, but the emotions of this twisted psychopath could be felt in the air, for it lingered over all the prisoners and over Aura's head, for she too, can feel the deadly nature of this being as it radiates pain and torment from his darkened heart.

Upon his left arm, is a massive shield covered in decrepit faces and twisted limbs and rods of spikes and metal, the weight to any living creature, would break the limb away from the shoulder, snapping the bone from the muscles and nerves. And grasped in the right hand, the being holds a flag bearing the twisted star form of the Hexagus symbol, the symbol which had been only last witnessed upon the necklace that once hung around the neck of Kandarius Lockmore. The black banner waved upon the winds that howled through these rotten valleys of rock that have been decayed not by the hand of time but by the finger of the Destroyer himself, for his power and influence upon the land has been growing, decaying the land in secret for many moons and many days that have long passed by, until the day was right for him to crawl out from beneath the ruins of the ground and rocks, to take upon a more powerful form and walk upon the lands among the Civilians, Gormons, Asyndians and all the other races which still linger within this realm, watching, waiting, spying, manipulating and deteriorating.

And now...his time is nigh, the time of the Destroyer, Maz Dregor...has come once again.

The being Maz Dregor has called Dzjurger, slams the banner of the Hexagus into the heap of black ash of the hill, and leaps from the high cliffs to the ground below and walks through the ranks and battalions of Dregor minions. They take rank and line up in precise rows as their general walks past. They jam their spears to the dirt and raise their blades to his honor, and the closer he came to Aura, she could feel the bones freezing up by the essence which reeked from his flesh, a cold, sinister wind coursed across his shoulders, and he stands at attention next to Maz Dregor, facing Aura and she catches glance at the eyes glaring out behind the twisted helmet, for they seem so familiar to her.

'A`deon...A`deon is that you?! Please, if that is you...you must help us...help our people, help us fight! You must fight this possession that has come over you! You saved me...now I want to save you!'

When she says the name A`deon, the prisoners gasp in shock, some yell aloud in a growl, *"I knew it! I knew he was a damn traitor!"*, some are horrified and refused to believe, *"No, it can't be!"*

There is no voice, for he only speaks in huffs of anger and bestial roars, as he eyes her up with animosity. He draws his blade to threaten and intimidate them all. He looks behind Aura and the lines of Dregor, and walks down the line, glaring down upon them all, as their captors hold them down.

"TUUTH SOK RA..." (I thought all of you had perished...) *"SO MAGGT..."* (No matter...) *"DOOG MOKT DUHGRAHK..."* (Your death will come soon enough.)

He roars and huffs steam at their faces in threat. A`deon walks back up the ranks and faces Aura once more. To her, his speech reverts to the native tongue of the Civilians.

'Please...my lady...won't you stand and have conference with me.' He raises his hand to instruct her to stand up, but her legs are so soar and disjointed, she can barely move. A`deon grows impatient, and growls to his guardian Asyndians.

'STAND HER UP!' And the Asyndians wrench her tight by the arms and hoist her up to her feet, the shackles around her wrists dangle and clang in the still silence.

He walks closer to her, his eyes beam and blazing beneath the helmet of razors and thorns, he holds the jagged blade up to her throat.

'How did you enjoy the way my soldiers...handle weakness...how we treat those who cannot defend themselves, for in this realm, there is only room for the strong, for one cannot gain without shoving, to push away those who are stationary, afraid to move, they get shoved into the abyss of nothing, and then the strong survive and live on, and with strength...comes...'

Before A`deon can finish his speech, Aura spits into his face, a wad of blood and dirt, saliva full of bitterness and hatred for this beast, this monster, this traitor A`deon has become.

'Go crawl back into the hole these monsters drug you from you bastard! You were once a brilliant strategist, cautious and patient...now your brain is twisted and your flesh stained with darkness as these other monsters! Your no different!'

He laughs. 'I should have let you drown...' as he back-hands her across the face with a powerful blow.

'No, there is no difference from me and my brethren...for we are strong, but you and I, lady Aura, you and I are different, for I am strong and you...you are weak...and we will exploit your weakness, your fears here this evening, in my honor, in my choosing...for you will face the Crucible, and you will be exposed to your worst most terrifying fears...' A`deon laughs.

'Why not just get it over with...if your strong, just brood your muscles with your sword in hand and kill me! Why not get it over with, for I am beaten and battered, there is nothing left of me!' Aura cries back.

The Dzjurger grabs hold of her chained arms and tears the chain away, then gripping her tightly by the bruised and cut right arm, he drags her staggering body over to the edge of a massive gaping pit.

'Because...I want to hear you scream...feel the pain and humiliation that I felt...' The Dzjurger roars with laughter in her bruised face, filled with gashes and bloody beads of sweat.

Part XXII:

Reflection in Blood

~

There is no more room for pleads, for she has none, and none would be worth to give. The Dregor chant and holler into the blackness, and Aura looms over the pit, the Crucible, head spinning and dizzy, a trickle of blood flows down her swollen lips, and she feels the drop let fall from her chin, and she looks over the edge and down into a steep, smooth edge, elliptical upon all walls, no edges no place to grapple onto, and at the bottom, a shallow pool of thick, red richness, a bountiful of blood, added over time by all who have fallen victim to such execution, of the ancient times for prisoners, eons of mutilation of a slow, painful death by the Hexagus Lords of old.

Aura looks over her left shoulder, to the hovering shape of the Destroyer. A smile of razor teeth is drawn across his face.

"I have fond memories of the Crucible, where me and my brethren gathered around this place, for it is sacred to us..."

'And what…may I ask, will I find within? Shall I drown? Shall I be bled and become one with the victims of those before?' Aura retorts, spitting into the placid, stone hole.

The Destroyer says nothing, and looks to his General. *"Dzjurger…KUTHRA`NO`TUTH…Throw her in!"*

A`deon, the Dzjurger of the Dregor, jabs the sword into her back, and all gasp, as she plummets down, limbs tossing and swaying, trying to grasp hold of the edge, though there is nowhere to go, nowhere to grab hold, there is only one way to go, and that is to the bottom.

She hits the floor dampened of the vile blood of the victims' eons past, and her face and hair lay down in the pool, her body flat and broken. There she lays motionless for a time, and the Dregor surround the circumference at the top, looking down upon the weak and pathetic, the broken and battered Civilian woman who claimed herself Aura. They snort and laugh aloud, taunting and mocking, throwing down old scraps of bones and scraps of skin and fleshed, peeled away from their feast upon many of the prisoners.

One of the large femurs strikes her upon the back of the head, as she begins to stir. She holds upon one arm, and slams it underneath her body, splashing the blood, then she plants the other palm firmly down, holds her head up as much she can, the hair hangs before her, in front of her eyes, clotted with the putrid stench and bile of the liquid covering her and surrounding her. She peers up above, and only sees, the flicker of lights across the sky. Around her, lay the dead faces of many, faces she recognizes, faces of her people, of soldiers, Asyndians, Civilians, and Gormons alike, bound in their armor, battered and broken, peasants stripped of their torn clothes, the faces of the dead and their eyes gaze upon her in a lifeless stare. She smells the flames, the fire of the charred brick, the kiss of flame upon flesh, burning brick and metal, she hears the cries of the fleeing, of the dying, of the slain, of those who pleaded…called her name, called for their lives, needed her to be there for them.

She staggers to her feet, above her, across the skies, scenes of the past, scenes of many images and lights fly by, soaring with the winds at the speed of many seconds, eons, years, hours and days, all pass her by. She can see then, upon the horizons of her mind, a future…a future that has not yet come to be, as the skies run red and the atmosphere a sickened green, the smell…an odor of illness, and there, amidst a black throne, upon the crest a faraway mountainside, seated there is the burning figure, the fiery eyes of a being, the Destroyer maybe? But she cannot quite make out the image of all that surrounds this deity of many limbs and heads, many tongues and speeches, many faces and many slaves that surround at its feet beneath the mountains, at the base of the throne. The slaves they linger about in unison and construct many citadels and raise the banners high up, held against the sickness that fills the atmosphere and the reddish skies, upon the banner is that symbol, the symbol of Order and Dominion, the crest of Maz Dregor and all the Hexagus Lords. These slaves, they rush to and fro, bringing vile dinners and drink, to a large table constructed over the ground, a table of black obsidian and beyond it, the main citadel where these beasts will rest, and at this table, several horrifying shapes and figures indulge and glutton upon the vile dinners and drinks, served by the slaves, upon pristine obsidian platters and jet-black goblets and chalices. They raise their many arms and limbs, tentacles and legs, to a cheer, a celebration of their victory over all…Dominion over all. And, at the last glimpse, the figures drink, and the eyes shift and turn to her, as all rejoice…as all has come to true order…for all has been won, and all will be one.

Then, she hears the whisper within her head.

"And all will be one...come, my lady, and share with us this moment...raise the chalice and embrace forever more...this most wonderful of times...when all has come to order, and with all this passing chaos...we now have peace!"

She grips her head and shakes back and forth violently, trying to rid her mind and consciousness of these images that plague her, and among the commotion, she looks down and sees her reflection staring back up at her, a pitiful state of a being, she sees clearly, all the scars and the bruises, her severed shoulder, the faces of all those that surround her, she gazes into those eyes, and sees...a figure she's not sure she even recognizes anymore, looking for the person she once used to be...before she fell, as Aura fell, so did she...but was she once before, but a forgotten woman on the wayside of the dusty streets of Othetica, taken in to be tossed away. What was all this for? All these moments of pain and suffering, of sacrifice for her and her people...what has all this lingering, holding onto been for? In the end...what will all this mean?

A tear falls into the blood. 'Times have changed...and so have I...so have we all. Oh my dear Civilians, my Gormons and Asyndians...all those within the realm of Aura...a name given to a fallen land and a fallen woman, I am no Daughter of Runegard...no Lady of Aura...what weight could my name possibly carry that isn't already upon my shoulders and my mind. We're clinging to broken limbs upon an overflowing river is all...'

The pools of blood beneath her begin to swirl and shift, as her image becomes distorted and twisted. 'And...and a familiar fear is coming back to me...'

And the reflection begins to settle, and the clenching fist of terror strikes at her heart, as she can see clearly, the vast image of *He*...Hondor is embraced within the blood and his eyes of unfeeling rage are fixed upon her. She begins to step back, until his gigantic hand reaches out and grips her around the waist, the fingers close around her in a vice, as this massive lumbering arm holds her above the blood, clutching tighter and tighter, she can feel her bones breaking and snapping her in half, and then she begins to rise up higher and higher over the blood, over the pit, and the red seas begin to part ways, rising higher, the bodies of all the dead sink under the tides of slaughter, and from the slaughter…Hondor arises, in full armor bolted upon his bulk, hulking form. The titan raises her up, and she looks down and finds herself far above the Crucible, nearly touching the clouds of darkness and overcast above.

Her eyes open from wincing and screaming in pain and agony, looking up to nothing but darkness, for despair is the limit, and below…only *He*…only Hondor, for his reign has covered over all, as darkness is above, so run the seas of blood below…

"…for Hondor has come…and none shall be saved…let the oceans of bile and sickness…of death and suffering…wash them all away…"

The massive hand of Hondor tilts her about, watching the puny Civilian scream in agony. He turns her around, her body upside down, the blood coated hair dangling in the frigid wind, she is left there, feeling the blood rushing to her head, dizziness and sickness overtaking her as the world spins round and round, and then as disorientation takes her, Hondor throws her, slams her down into the realm, and she hits the bottom of the crucible, the bones in her snapping and tendons ripping.

And then, the present once more begins to reemerge, the Dregor chant and cry in blood-lusting roars of satisfaction, to see the Civilian get pummeled and beaten more and more. The Destroyer looks over to A`deon, who looks down upon her with wide eyes of satisfaction.

'Now...she has felt the pain I have felt...for I have been cast aside to the battlefields, to face Hondor, only to be beaten and have my body and pride destroyed, and she ran, she ran like a coward while I stood and faced that monster, that beast, for it I who has courage and strength, not her...and now, the rest of this realm will feel my wrath...'

The Destroyer hovers over her, peering deep within, deep within her inner essence.

One of the Asyndians speaks from behind the ranks of encircled soldiers of Dregor. 'Why is she not dead?' Noticing her frail chest heaving in and out with choking gasps.

'Death...' He says with a snigh grin of his razor teeth. 'This one...it seems is not meant to die...but to suffer, to linger, for death is what gives the martyr strength, and to leave her as a beaten, broken thing in front of the eyes of all her caged animals...breaks them, keeps them oppressed...hopeless, that every time virtue and hope rises, it will always fall in despair.'

He removes his hand and laughs. 'I wanted her to see the future of all, what everything will become...she will drag on to see it, in shame and failure, a reminder of her weakness, a symbol that the strength of all has failed, to be slaves for us...my brothers and sisters, my family, and to our mother we serve, for her time is almost upon us...' He motions to the black abyss above. 'See for yourselves, as all the realm darkens around these weak and pathetic denizens!'

And the Dregor and black Asyndians raise their arms in chant and praise to the Destroyer.

Aura, holding up a withered arm places it upon her heart in despair, before all goes black. She listen on as the Destroyer, the ancient spawn of Wom speaks.

A Civilian within this prison, he and his family sit across from the brutality they witness. He holds his wife and child snug within his arms, feeling their tears damp upon his chest, listening to them, he raises his head to speak.

'Look at her...she's barely able to move, she can't stand, can't turn her head, can't speak, can't fight back...how can she do anything? My dear, you heard that beast...she is to linger, as we suffer enslaved or killed by these monstrosities...how can we still believe in our last hope, there is none, no one who can help us?! Some leader she is!'

Roύgsver overhears this and replies, 'Have courage...the fact that she still lives and breathes gives me hope...she lives and breathes because of us, she has not given up on us, not you nor any within these cells...'

'It's because of her that me and my family are here in the first place...' The Civilian retorts.

'All of you would have been killed, slaughtered by Hondor! The beast risen by the hand of Naumokron! These are dark days, but thus far, we have had some small luck, as slender as it is...we are still alive!' Roύgsver says.

'But for how long...I've seen these bastards rip us from our cages to feast on us, and use our blood to light that horrible red flame piercing my heavy eyes that cannot sleep...we escaped the fire, and ended up on the ignited coals, we're only dying slower...you may see hope...but hope's not good enough for me, for I see a fallen idol, a statue long crumbled turning to dust...and then taken on the savage winds to be scattered and never rebuilt.'

'Like the old Othetian tale...and all the other Auroras, just like the legends of old...' A Gormon interrupts.

'And from those turbulent days…came the hero of light, the Hero of Ages and saved the land!' A Civilian woman cries.

'Then where is this Hero of Ages? Where is our Daughter? All I see is a beaten woman…there is no Hero of Ages, and there is no mystic legend to Aura, if that even is her real name…I do know for sure…that we're not leaving these cages alive, if at all.' The man ends his argument and goes back to being silent, watching the Dregor picking up the limp body, broken and shattered, being carried over to a nearby cage. He keeps his family closer.

Roúgsver stands up and looks out the cage, over to where they carried Aura, his grip tightens around the bars with frustration and anger, wanting to break down this cage and attack all these Dregor, take them all on one by one. As he watched A`deon, those cold, bloodless eyes shifted their glance from Aura, over to him, and he looks away, sitting back down next to the others, putting his hands up to his face, rubbing his soar and tired eyes, wanting to sleep, to wake up from this nightmare.

The Civilian woman creeps over towards Roúgsver, and takes him by the hands, startling him and waking him up.

'I listened to every word you spoke…do you really believe that lady Aura will prevail…is there any hope for us?' She pleads to him.

'She cannot give up, dear woman…and we must not let her.'

'What can we do?' She asks.

'Stay as strong as you can…this is the only asset we have now…' Roúgsver replies.

They approach Roúgsver's cell and toss her in. They stand over her body, kneel down and lift her, carry her over to one of the make-shift, filthy mats tossed out upon the ground. They hold a moment of silence over her broken, beaten body, weeping in sadness, hoping for her to awaken…thinking the worst. Roúgsver keeps watch, grasping her hand, staying with her, looking out for her as he has always done.

The night slowly moves on, though this precedence seems to matter not anymore, the days have become so bleak and shaded over by the blackened skies, the days seem to slink back into a faded legend, nothing more than a mere memory. Without the rays of the sun, the times may as well be considered a forever night.

The Dregor burn no flame, nor fire, instead they take pails of the slaughtered blood and pour the liquid into a series of placed braziers. The mixture of the blood and dormant oils ignite into reddish flames which shine across the dead, the lifeless, and the tortured prisoners' faces, who sit and weep themselves into a restless slumber, with the pangs of hunger wrenching at their empty stomachs, there dried lips chipping and cracking away like old paint from ancient artwork long in disrepair.

Throughout the night, Roúgsver keeps the exhausted watch over Aura, as she begins to stir from her bruised-eyed slumber. She tries to force her heavy eyes open, and all shapes contort and blur. The Gormon's distorted shape begins to conform and she looks up into sunken brown eyes, and he looks back to her, a wide grin forms across his lips beneath those jovial, gray whiskers of his.

'Tis good to see you awake, my lady…we feared the worst…' He says in a low voice, quiet and away from the ears of the guarding Dregor.

Aura, her face and lips cut away and bleeding, her cheeks shine with bruises, gives a weak return smile, though the best she has the strength to. 'Roúgsver...' She tries to say, greeting her old Gormon advisor. He helps, with gentle care, as she struggles to try and sit up.

'I'm not out of this yet...' She leans up a bit, bracing herself with her arm, holding for a moment, then makes it up the rest of the way, leaning her back up against the bars of the cage. Her head has been beaten in severely, her thoughts all muddled, memories clouded, but she can still see within her mind, the reflection, then...the blood rising....and becoming, *Him.*

'What...what has happened, I can't explain what those images, those...those old memories, and....it was there, all there in the reflection before me! Of all that blood...and then time, seemed to transcend and surround me, all those past lives and events, the rush of memories surged all around me, and then...that was when...I...I saw him! I saw him rising...rising from all....and there was all that blood, all the bodies! I can still hear their screams, there pleads...I saw his face so clear, he was right there in front of me...' Tears fell, and her voice trembles as she retells these visions of the Crucible to Roúgsver.

'I know who you saw...you, saw...you know who, don't you? You saw', his voice falls to a whisper, 'you saw Hondor.' Roúgsver spoke as though he were reading her thoughts and sensing her fears.

'Do you know what this all means then...what the visions and all...and the reason for his appearance?' Aura asks Roúgsver, still in a dazed bit of confusion.

'Hmmmm....' he rubs his beard in deep thought. 'I think, my lady that maybe...it sounds as though, that what you have experienced...is a form of, Gormon meditation, my people call it *"Drkter'Szkarghn"*. This occurs in Gormons for two reasons: one is during a state where one absorbs their purpose battle, they hone their skills, and focus on the ultimate victory. And the other...is a deep emptiness, a chasm broke open by a force of guilt, regret, that Gormon feels they have wronged or betrayed, and the guilt is eating away at them...though it is curious, for I never heard of this happening to any except us Gormons. It is, my lady, quite perplexing.' He tugs at his beard harder, then he looks into her eyes with sincerity. 'Even more alluring than this new paradox...is that you show both...I seen what you saw, though I can't see beyond sight and into thoughts...what do you think it means my lady? Are you guilty of some unknown deed in which you take cruel blame for...it seems Hondor is a haunter, a devourer of your thoughts, your being, your essence, he is not just an enemy, but a symbol, a catalyst...a means to an end, but what end? HôɲdoR, lady Aura...that is what we call it...the end. That could be it, I don't know...' He finishes and waits for her to speak.

'You were always the smartest Gormon in all the realm...I see why Lord Gabriel chose you. You have all the answers.' She smiles.

'Perhaps...perhaps not.' He shrugs. 'But I feel you have some answers that need to be said.' He looks at her now with all seriousness. 'Is there something you want to tell me my lady? What happened at Kar'durgra...at the execution?'

Her eyes start to turn into lenses of fear and despair. Just the very thought of that moment...

'I...I was there, I was the one who released that creature into this world Roúgsver! I did not protect Runegard when he attacked, I fled, I told everyone to flee, but I was terrified, scared of such a creature...and now not only is Runegard fallen, but so is Thylesian, and pretty soon...Othetica, and your home Fausengard...shall follow in step...and I led all of you into a trap, captured by traitors to our homeland of Runegard...'

A single tear falls. 'I have watched Runegard fall, I have watched Thylesian and all her own, devoured...and so it seems I'm to linger on, to see the rest of this realm, as named after me, decay away...Aura will fall, of flesh and of dirt and soil...' Her voice fades as she looks up into the Roúgsver's eyes.

The Roúgsver looks on her in pity. 'You have been through much, as have we all...' He takes her hand within his massive, yet gentle grasp. '...but I want you to remember, what's done has been done, and this blame you carry, is a burden you must drop before it overwhelms and eats away what is left that you hang onto, because it is not your doing for this nightmare we face, for we all face it together in our own way, not just on a battlefield or with weapon and shield, but in sadness and sorrow, some weep, some still hold out hope that the Auroras shall return.'

'And you...what is it that you believe Roúgsver.' She asks.

'As Master Roar told me before he passed... "Even when you feel surrounded...and the battle lost...if your still standing, capitalize against your foe, and show him he's wrong!" And I still believe in those words, my lady.' He replies

'I see...and what happened to your master? You never did tell me about this Master Roaur of yours.' Aura asks.

He shrugs. 'No one knows for certain, there are many myths and legends behind what happened, but none have ever been confirmed, but the tale always begins the same way, he went on a long journey one morning, many years ago...and never returned, never to be seen in these parts again. There have been rumors that there have been those who have seen him fighting wars against the heathens far to the southeast, remnants of the Skahljah, some say he spends his days teaching the Azimoths the lore of Aura further down ways south, and on their holidays, helps fight off intruders upon their borders. And there are some sailors that say he is spending his retirement riding upon the backs of sea serpents in the far seas beyond our borders. But...no one knows for certain where master Roaur is.

'I will also say this to you, our lady Aura...one who has been beaten down, able to stand again and again...you are the inspiration of not just me, but all of us who linger within this prison of ours. Ignore the bars that surround us, for it is this realm we are trapped within. The Dregor have returned, and they have us all under the confines of this regime, under the rule of him...the Destroyer.' Roúgsver says.

Aura looks at Roúgsver with doubt swept across her confused brow, not knowing truly what to think of this statement by him, for she feels she is to blame, a failure, she has lost their homeland, the homeland of the Asyndians fallen, and her people now waste away in cages... *"How then...how can* Roúgsver *feel I will save them from all of this...wake them from this nightmare?!"*

She notices Roúgsver looking over her shoulder at something. She turns around, and standing there near her is a young Asyndian child, he stands by her side and looks at her with wide eyes as deep as the endless space of the Galakaos beyond the darkness which hovers above their heads. The youngling looks upon her shadowed eyes and the cuts upon her battered face.

He's very timid and doesn't speak at first. He looks back at his mother who seats herself upon the ground behind him. He then focuses his attention upon Aura.

'Mother covered my eyes; she didn't want me to see the attack...' He gently places a finger upon the large mark across her forehead. 'They hurt you badly.'

Aura smiles at the child. 'Come here.' She lifts him up and seats him upon her leg and ruffles his head feathers a little. He sees her smile and the child laughs with her. She could feel the leather ties that binds the wings upon his back so he cannot fly away. All the Asyndian prisoners have had their wings bound.

'Yes they did hurt me...but these bruises and cuts are nothing. Do you know where they hurt me even more?' She asks the child and he shakes his head no. Aura holds her hand upon her heart. 'Here...they betrayed me, deceived and lied to me.' She looks at the wondrous sorrow over the boys face.

'What is your name child?'

'Hrend...my full name is Hrendrowäoln, after my father...' He replies.

When she hears the name, her skin begins to go cold. She notices the eyes of the child fall away, looking to the ground. She tries to hold her composure and keeps a smile to the child.

'That...that is a brave name your parents have bestowed upon you...where is your father now?' Though she already knows the answer and feels the eyes upon her.

The boy asks another question, changing the discussion, not wanting to speak about his father. 'My lady?'

She looks at him, awaiting him to ask what he will.

'I used to always hear passing travelers and odd folk, as big as that man there...' He points to Roúgsver. 'They used to talk about all sorts of stories and adventures...they would talk about the great heroes of the day and how they would fight, big epic monsters as they called them, many things with twisted heads, many limbs and elbows, monsters in the seas swimming the ocean depths, and soaring across clouds and over country, grand wars, the changing of the times and of the coming days...then, then my father told me that such tales were rubbish, made of legends that were not to be believed, even what he called, this B word I never understood what it meant, it was *"Blas Fe Mous"* and that...I would hear him whisper other things under his breath too...'

'Hrɛnd!' His mother snapped, so he would say no more. Aura looked to her, then back to Hrɛnd.

Hrɛnd asks Aura, 'Lady Aura...why are there no more monsters to be talked about? Where have all those heroes gone? Why will nobody come and save us?'

She looks around the encampment, feeling the chill of the cold black stare now fixated upon her, barely able to look at the child, feeling the pressure of what Roúgsver has said. She then looks to him, and the Gormon's face also falls into a troubled look.

'What is it?' Roúgsver asks in a whisper.

'We're being watched...' She replies, not saying a word, but mouthing the words with her lips. Roúgsver looks about them carefully, not seeing anything but the cold faces of the prisoners, and the statue-like demeanor of the Dregor soldiers, stationed into one place in a solid stance, and the Asyndian Dregor worshippers with their wings curled around them, their talons clenched up upon the cliff faces around the area, eyes in slumber. Roúgsver scans the area with his excellent vision, and notices all Asyndians and Dregor in an odd state of brief hibernation, all except one. Roúgsver sees two pale yellow eyes piercing through the dark, staring down upon their cage like a vulture watches its prey from a distance.

Aura notices the worried look upon Roύgsver's face. She then feels a tug at her ripped tunic.

'My lady...why are there no more monsters and all?' Hrɛnd asks.

'Because...because an even bigger, more terrifying monster, more horrible than all the others...ate them all.'

'What monster is that?!' The boy gasps, eyes widened like saucers.

She does not answer.

'Is it that monster there...is that it!' He points to one of the Dregor soldiers.

'No, it is not him, nor any of them...this monster's much larger, very mean, very ugly.' She replies, setting the boy down and trying to stand to her feet.

'Do you need help my lady?' Hrɛnd asks.

'I'll be alright, go back to your mother now, okay?' She says to Hrɛnd nicely, the boy watching the pain on her face as she struggles to get up off the ground.

Hrɛnd goes back over and settles into his mother's arms, Aura staggers over and stands next to Roύgsver. 'He's watching us...isn't he?'

Roύgsver nods and motions over to the far cliff, where a large shadow, the Asyndian as charcoal as the storm cloud, soars through the air and lands near their cage, his eyes seem to almost burn through the bars upon them.

'So...this beautiful child...is yours Hraʒon?' She looks back at Hrɛnd and his mother, the fear building within their eyes and trembling feathers. 'Stay close to your mother...we will not let him harm you.' She whispers to him.

Hrɛnd's embrace tightens around his mother's torso and she holds him closer to her, they back slowly to the end of the cage. Hraʒon calls to the boy in his native tongue. The prisoners and the Dregor guardians are stirred, the Destroyer has vanished and is nowhere to be found. This summons the presence of the Dzjurger who marches from the howling caves beneath the ruined cliffs, maddened by what was the meaning of this disturbance, and that blood of these worthless prisoners would be spilled.

Roúgsver stands by the lady Aura's side.

'HERIKDATH... Hrɛndrowäoln!'

Hrɛnd refuses to move, still clutching his mother, now even tighter, terrified of his father's harsh words and stern tone.

'HERIKDATH... Hrɛndrowäoln! HERIKDATH!' Hraʒon roars now even louder, at the top of his lungs. 'Let go of him woman! You coddle him too much...you taint our son's blood with weakness! I will show him how to be strong...the power of the Destroyer knows the key to finding a child's true inner strength!'

Then, The Dzjurger roars at his back. 'I command you end this idiocy at once Hraʒon! If you do not silence them both...I will silence you!' The general roars. 'And besides...my soldiers are due for a feast of flesh, before we set out for Fausengard! Kill your child and your wife, slaughter the Gormon too...the Destroyer has further plans for Aura, for we must use her as an example to the rest of the realm...'

'As the Destroyer wills...so it will be done!' Replies Hraƶon. He grasps the heavy lock upon the cage and rips the chain away with ease, the door flings open and he storms in. Aura stands between him, and Hrend and his mother. 'You will not touch that child, nor his mother...I will not allow you!'

Hraƶon raises his fist to the air, and strikes Aura to the ground with one mighty blow. She tries to stand her ground, but falters and sways. Roúgsver lunges forward, but Hraƶon grips the Gormon's fist and sends him slamming against the cage before he can land the strike.

Hraƶon stands above his wife and child, with those burning eyes. 'I said...come here, Hrendrowäoln!' She whispers into Hrend's ear, he leaves his mother's grasp reluctantly and stands next to her. She lets go, turns her attention towards Hraƶon, and in a split second, she lunges into him, hoisting him through the air as far as her bound wings could carry her, and the two go soaring out the cage. He lands upon his back, and kicks her away, hard in the chest and flies back landing upon the ground.

'You miserable bitch! You dare humiliate me! I will destroy you!' Hraƶon screams.

Roúgsver lumbers over, clenching his ribs and helps Aura to her feet. 'My lady?'

'I'll...I'll live...' She replies, grasping her face and wincing.

The Dregor and Asyndian's round themselves in flanks, surrounding the prisoners and the oppressing the commotion, forcing the other prisoners down to their knees, while Aura and Roúgsver tend to Hrend, who stands by and watches helplessly as Hraƶon and his mother destroy each other. Hraƶon gets her to the ground, as a pulsing energy convulses through her body, leaving her a limp and empty vessel, barely able to move.

'Stay here my lady, I'm going to help her!' And Roúgsver charges at Hraǥon with full speed, clobbering him back. Hrend cries out to his mother, trying to get to her, but Aura holds him back.

'No child...don't! Stay here with me, help me...help me get up...' And Hrend braces her under her arm as she walks out from the cage.

'No...mother! There killing her!' Hrend cries. Both watch on with hopeless eyes, Aura feeling terrible, pity towards the young Asyndian child, wishing she could muster the strength to march out and face the cruel one who has betrayed her and all of Runegard.

'Keep close to me... Roúgsver will do what he can...he will protect her.' Though deep inside, Aura knew, she could feel this would be their final fight, for Hraǥon and the legions of Dregor, were far too powerful for them to face, they had to do something, they have to flee, but how?

Then, the roar of A`deon, the Dzjurger, calls from behind. 'Hraǥon! Finish this at once, this has gone on long enough!'

Hraǥon unsheathes a smooth ebony sword, where upon the blade, is inscribed the words of the hollow speech, the black tongue of the Hexagus, the words *"After Death...comes Pain..."* And all time seems to expand motionless, drawn out and slow down. First, Hraǥon charges at Roúgsver, and the Gormon, even with his exceptional sight and eyes like a hawk, never saw the blade and the line of blood trickle to the ground as Hraǥon cuts across the stomach to the ribs, slicing the Gormon away. Roúgsver grasps the burning flesh with a gasp and desperation, the sting of the blade is almost numbing and struck with stealth under the cloak of darkness. Aura cries out, toppling to her knees in anger, watching as Roúgsver slinks down, the mighty Gormon shrinks down to one knee, then in motion, lays upon his back as the blood floods into the back of his throat then gushes from his mouth and lips.

Hraʒon eyes up his wife, she climbs to her feet, swaying upon the golden talons, her wings bound her body broken. She looks upon the blood lust within Hraʒon's fiery eyes, as he moves towards her. She crawls upon her hands and knees over to her crying child. Aura lets Hrend go to her, he grasps his mother weeping and trembling at the sight of his approaching father, the rage fiery and burning within his eyes, he means to finish this upheaval once and for all. Roúgsver has faded away, his breath has ceased, and Hrend knows, deep down…his mother is next.

'Hold me…one last time my son, before we must part.' And they grasp one another, Hrend feeling the strength fading from his mother's feeble body, weakened by Hraʒon.

'It's too late for me…but, there is still a chance for you my son, and you must promise me…when I say run…you run…ok?'

Hrend nods, not understanding what his mother is planning. He watches as she reaches around the band tied about her right calf. She searches and her face grows frantic. She then looks into her son's eyes with horror.

'Is this, what you're looking for?' Hraʒon laughs at her foil. 'Perhaps, you should take better care of your things! But don't worry, after I drive this blade into your heart, I'll make sure our son is…' Hraʒon is cut off by the sound of a loud bash from one of the far cages. Nilta has rushed the area, grabbed one of the Dregor soldiers, slammed his head against the bars, and she grasps the soldier's blade in hand. Diin is close behind her.

'My lady Aura…use this!' Diin cries, and Nilta tosses the blade through the air, and the black steel strikes the dirt. They hold off the many guards and soldiers while Aura stumbles over, grasping her arm in pain, but grips the blade with what strength she still bears in her hand, and clutches Hrend by the straps and bonds that hold his wings pinned to his back. She pulls the tassels back, and slices the holds down the center. The straps and sliced leather and iron bursts away, as Hrend's wings spread with wondrous length and majesty.

'Mother! Mother I'm free!' He turns to Aura. 'My lady, free my mother, hurry!' He cries.

'Hrend…you need to leave me, fly…run…flee! Get as far away from here as you can!' His mother cries.

Hraʒon lunges forward to strike his son down, but Aura grasps him and pulls him away. As Aura falls to the ground, Hrend takes to the skies, tears soaring down like rain. He turns, to see his mother looking up to him, and the proudest smile a mother could have, across her face, just before Hraʒon plunges the final strike, through her back, severing her spine, and through her stomach, and the puddle of blood and the shadow of death…overtakes her.

Hrend looks back to the sky, and turns back to the past no more. Hraʒon leaps into the air with rage, taking several more of the Dregor Asyndians in pursuit of Hrend. The last breath of life leaves her. *"Don't look back Hrend…always move…forward…and this…this darkness will fade away…focus…on the light that's ahead…"*

The General…The Dzjurger, hears the voice within his mind. *"Gather your troops, and move out towards Fausengard and the Gormon territories… Hraʒon will fall soon enough, he is no longer of concern. Focus all your efforts towards the Gormons, for Hondor storms upon Othetica as we speak…send a small force there to keep patrol over the ruins, but do not engage Hondor...take out the surrounding territories and wait...let's let Hondor will do the work for us, and once he's destroyed everything, we will conquer, we will rebuild, and when at full force, then we can deal with him once and for all! Leave Aura to the Slaths, and then return to take these prisoners to Othetica, they will start the rebuilding there..."*

"What! It is I who will conquer Aura! And now you want Hondor to do it?!" The Dzjurger roars. He then feels a jolting pain in his spine and nerves. He grips his head in agony.

"Do not dare question me...just do as I say...I have a new idea in mind, and that is all you need to know!"

The Dzjurger is released, catching his breath.

"I understand..." Dzjurger replies.

'Form ranks and prepare to move out...we march upon Fausengard by morning...let the prisoners watch lady Aura and the intruders, get torn to pieces by the Slaths...let the beasts from Hexagus devour their flesh and consume their bones in their acid-filled jowls!' The Dzjurger roars.

And the vast Dregor armies line up in ranks and files, leaving Diin and Nilta fallen from the fight. The prisoners watch on as the armies of darkness and twisting, screeching gears, trample away through the dirt and rough terrain of the northern lands just before the Great Divide upon the other side of these mountains and valleys. The armies head a ways southeast towards the terrains and rocky soil and mountainous plateaus of Fausengard, the lands of the Gormon.

One of the prisoners shouts from the cell. 'Hope you enjoy the motherland you bastards! Us Gormons will drive you back...they'll kill every one of yah down there! *Diudun Ayack*!'

Just as the last of the Dregor legions stomp away, the Dzjurger looms over the fallen Aura and looks down upon her broken body. He says nothing, he only draws the fanged blade from the sheath, and jams the tip into her breast, turns the blade right then left, and removes the blade, watching the crimson tides run like tears of blood, a storm of blood creating oceans of red across her chest and staining her tattered clothes. She can feel her life force weaken and the scent of her blood upon the wind, brings the Slaths from their caves on leashes of black chains and corroded collars, gurgling and slobbering as the sounds of their many victims that have suffered at the fate of their jaws. Their faces concaved like a skull and their flesh black and skeletal, with eyes of pale, faded white like two dead moons faded in the eclipse of the night. Their unhallowed maws howl and whine in the darkness of the still skies above, ready to break loose, break free off their rusted chains of corroded iron.

The Dzjurger grasps the dead body of Hrend's mother and tosses it to the Slaths as though it were a rag doll. The Slaths grapple and fight over the body, as flesh and feathers scatter across the ground and the blood stains and covers the walls of their burrow where they were kept away.

The Dzjurger looks over at Aura. 'Your next, my lady…' And he raises the blade and cuts the chains away from the collars of the savage beasts. The slobbering Slaths leap as they run, rushing at Aura with crunching jaws ready to feast upon flesh, not feathers. The Dzjurger roars with laughter, and leaps upon the mighty black Stryder beast and follows along behind the rest of the armies of Dregor who await his orders ahead, the orders bestowed upon him by the Destroyer, the first reign to begin this war, this campaign to reach total order through enslavement, breaking backs, and leaving the weak and the dead to rot where they fall, and their skeletons will help build the basis and the structure for the mighty colossus of jet black towers and obsidian fortresses that will smother the landscape of this realm. The armies in black fade into the bowels of the furthest valleys of shadow...and beyond that, they eclipse the dead grasslands as they pass the foliage and dead branches of fallen trees and crumbled structures, ancient towers and fallen civilizations. And all decays, as the Dregor march upon a land once covered with light and green, now fallen and decayed, devoured and raped by the slaughter and hostility...of the monstrosity of Hondor. Aura raises her arms in front of her, as the bestial Slaths clamp and bite down upon her arms, and the swelling of the mark engraved across her chest by Dzjurger, swells with the sting of the cold air, and the smell of blood is sweat in the air, before all goes dark before her eyes.

Aura's body twists and contorts ferociously within her mind, eyes bleed and mind gasps for air, suffocated and condensed by the swelling darkness encompassing her thoughts and feelings of wanting to cry, wanting to run away and flee, hide and become one with the shadows, so nobody can see her, nobody can find her...the pain is too much, the failure is too much to bear, for all has fallen away, swallowed between the maw of black skies and blistered seas. All drown...and all past and present...and any hope for a future...sinks and fades away, in the endless decay and rotation of time, as the hands start to decay, and the old man, the father has finally passed on, no longer keeping track of time and events, no longer does it all matter... *"What has all this been for, I ask? What has all this struggle and defense, all this fighting, all this living and dying been for? For what, are the reasons to all of this...this chaotic stream of events that gets tossed along upon raging seas?"*

And the black speech of the Destroyer, like a darkness piercing the brightest light, that familiar smell, that familiar anxiety and hatred fills her essence and body, she feels his presence all around her, near and far, inside and outside. All eyes look down upon her at the lowest of levels. He speaks down to her, an ordered man with the face of a monster to a child helpless and fearful, not knowing what to expect, afraid of what's to come next in this stage of events.

"This world was created from chaos, why bother in your attempts to stop what can never be undone. You take away chaos, and these things know nothing of the delicate nature of rule to order, chaos to build civilization, death...to create anew...the Hexagus had a tight grip and organization upon this world until the Auroras came with their rebellious nature to want of peace, but peace brought war, and war brought their death...and death to all my brothers and sisters. Before the Auroras...we were at peace...and we will have peace once more, when the unruly, the undeserving who crave power are destroyed, and those who deserve power...prove they are worthy to hold and keep their responsibilities in order. It's a never ending process my Lady Aura, for even if you bring about your peace...chaos will always arise once more...because your kind are weak, and you will lose until all of your kind have perished to dust..."

She tries to speak, but she feels her mouth, now covered with a blood-soaked cloth wrapped around her face, for she has bit her tongue so long, that she has bit her tongue away and can no longer cry out, can no longer speak against that which is wrong...the oppression against her and all of the realm of Aura.

The darkness swelters and surrounds, and the portals to all realms of shades and shadows, of all chaos and murky depths to drown within opens wide and takes her along with the floods of the nightmares.

And the lady Aura awakens once more, to the sounds of drums and roars, marching armies and bestial devastation surrounds the charred embers and the dead soil of the realm that still remains. Overcast of black clouds part ways, as burning meteors fall across blood-red skies, bled by the sickles and the sabers of the Dregor as they cut their way and conquer, the Dregor Juggernauts stomp the fauna and the dying trees into a pulp of blood and stains, and emperors of darkness ride across the landscape at the lead upon their roaring, slobbering beasts, both dawned head to foot in armor of darkness and flesh-shredding gears that crank and turn ferociously with rage and friction against their pale-scaled skin underneath.

And Aura looks around with eyes blurry, becoming more and more clear by the passing second, though the time seems to drag on further and further year after year, and Aura looks upon her hands, her wrists shackled down by obsidian chains and bonds. The flesh upon her hands is withering away, as she watches age course through her skin and blood before her very eyes, as she ages with each passing moment, the life-force within her is being sapped away. Her clothing has long rotted away and her body is left barren and naked, exposed to these bestial monsters that destroy and maim the land. She looks down to see she is placed upon a large cart being pulled along by two titanic monstrosities with massive horns, many red eyes, and several bullish limbs, trampling and crumbling the road and ground as they stomp along the way. She looks into the seas filled with black ash, and she can see her reflection within, an old woman, her face cracked and marred, hair gray and flesh withered away like old leather, useless and worthless, forgotten and on her own. She has failed all, and there are none left who can save her from her turmoil, a prisoner to forever be in pain and kept a symbol, a mascot of the day when Lady Aura, the Daughter of Runegard...had failed all who had hope in her. She has been bound upon this cart, to a large "X" it pulls along...and the wagon wheels begin to slow down, and upon the hill before her and the entire legions of Dregor and Hexagus, is a black mountain rising above the clouds, and the mountains and the fortress walls that surround begin to crack, and from the ruins and crumbling rubble, a piercing, bellowing roar strikes into the air and into the deepest fear within her heart. A large hand breaks from the dome of the mountain peaks, a large hand covered in thorns and metal, bearing the axe of Slaughter and Wrath...as all bow down to the shape of terror and genocide rising before their eyes. Aura cries out in terror, and the eyes of Hondor...his burning terror, is the last thing she sees...before the realm falls to darkness.

She returns back to life, and the gnawing upon her arm has dissipated. She looks up to see the bodies of Slaths piled high upon the other, as Nilta sticks the final blow in the last one moving, quivering, howling in pain. The people walk about, all Gormon and Civilians and Asyndians free from their cages and bounds.

A hand reaches down to her, 'Here, grab my hand...' And Diin helps her up to her feet. She feels the shaking and jerking of his bones, he winces as he pulls her up. She looks at the two in shock, as Nilta joins by Diin's side.

'How...how are you two still alive! I thought the Asyndians destroyed the two of you?!' She exclaims with surprise.

Diin smiles. 'I'm surprised at you...it'll take more than a fall off a cliff and a fortress crumbling on top of us to keep us down. Like you, we're pretty tough and can take a lot of punishment...wouldn't you agree?'

Aura winces a smile, holding her bloody wrist. 'Looks that way.' She replies. Nilta walks over and wraps a bandage around her arm, stopping most of the bleeding.

'What are we to do now?' Aura wonders, not knowing where they have been led or where to go from here.

'Just over this hill, me and Nilta know of a place to lay low for a little while, where everyone can get some rest...then I say we proceed with your plan, that is, if you still wish to go to Raukmar?' Diin replies.

Aura nods.

That night, they lay underneath an overhang of rocks and a few trees that still maintain their roots in this barren soil. The barks are dry and the leaves are shriveled and brown.

All have fallen asleep, but Diin, Nilta, and Aura still stir around the fire, watching the flames dance to the music of the crackle and pop of the embers in which it emanates from.

Nilta stares and thinks about everything, she still sees the fall of Roúgsver, of Hrɛnd's mother...wondering if that poor child escaped his father's wrath...she lays her head down upon the ground, falls into a trance, as the cool night air tends to her pain, cooling the burn of the cuts, drying the rivers of blood, and soon, she falls asleep, not blacking out or passing out, but feeling the slow, legitimate feeling of sleep coming over her and she drifts off.

Diin and Nilta watch as lady Aura takes to a long and overdue sleep she has not had for many days now.

'Dear sister...once when my eyes were full of sight and tranquil beauty, I saw with them...a realm so beautiful, so precious and dear to my heart, precious to you and to our master, precious to all these Asyndians, Gormons, and Civilians...and now it seems, that all of us, shall witness what I witness, with a gull pit deep within Wom's despair...and that my sister...is eternal night, with no hope for a coming dawn the next morning.'

He grabs Nilta's hand and they stare into the fire. 'You don't what such a fate...no one should bear a sight of nothing...no beauty, no pleasantries of a dawn, of the trees and vast oceans beyond our realm...we can't let this happen

Nilta…even if it kills me…something must be done. Aura must stay strong…she must pull through, and we must help her Nilta, she is the last hope this realm has.'

She turns her attention to her brother as he ponders into the skies, thinking...wondering. She lays her head down upon his lap, as he continues to ponder within those thoughts.

'Why do I believe in Aura, Nilta? You may be listening…I don't know, but I'll speak anyway…but it's what master always said to us, he always taught us about the essence, and how to read a being and what's on the inside, like the feelings of Pry and Lota, the sun and moon, all essences have a bond to specific destinies and meanings to a final destiny…I could never understand the words of master sometimes…but now, as I have experienced more, even without my sight…I feel I have a understanding now, it's not something that can be put into words, it's just…just a knowing, and I know you have it to Nilta, you know as well, perceive those hidden meanings written upon us that many never see or sense…how could I explain to her...what she truly means to us? I can't, but me and you know, that's there's a destiny within the blood of Aura…for she is born, descended of legends…and as we know, no matter the dead large or small, it's the magnitude of what is tried, and more often enough, accomplished…she is yet to be a legend, it is her birthright and her destiny…she is to be a legend during a time when legends are needed, when hero's that have tried stand back up, and try, try again…and that's why, I believe in Aura, for she is to be a hero…a legend….and legends, they never do truly die, and do you know why?'

Nilta stirs in her sleep.

'Because legends only die…if they stop trying…'

Part XXIII:

The Final Stand of Othetica and Fausengard

~

Upon the western watch, one of the Civilian soldiers on duty, his armor rusted with neglect and the Othetian Crest upon the breast of the armor has been removed and only a clean outline still remains in the shape of the symbolic crest of a "Ć". He lifts himself from the rickety chair he sits upon with feet propped up and looks over the cracked walls out upon the vast horizon out beyond the distance, where a once lush, green land surrounded this jewel of Aura, is now brown and ridden with jaggers in the woods and the vampiric roots of weeds has bled away the green in Othetica, the ground has decayed and faded away, it's over this faded landscape, that guard watches as a black shape, a large winged figure approaches…and darkness treads not far behind it.

The watchman lumbers himself over to the thick rope hanging down from the tower, he lays down his arms and shield upon an old wooden table, grips the serpent of intertwined threads tightly, and pulls down with all his strength as the massive bell within the highest tower of the bulwark rings out in a low thunder over the decayed and run down ruins of this ancient city, lost over time under the ruling palm of its careless leader, Lord Rolom.

Deep within his throne room, where once the mighty Aurora Othetian sat upon the mighty and marvelous throne, now lingers hunched the brooding enclosure of Lord Rolom and his perverse thoughts that drag on with his age. Scattered across the cracked floors thick with dirt, are old braziers tossed over and covered with webbing, the windows beam in the darkness of the air with the curtains tattered and ripped, pieces strewn across the floor. The high walls and ceilings of vast architecture chip and pieces and chunks fall away, Lord Rolom's guards lay about in a drunken stupor, with their helmets over their eyes, asleep with little care or regard for anything by their short attitude towards any orders. A sickness clutches Rolom's stomach at the fact that the Daughter of Runegard is still alive.

"I saw her fall...I watched her fall..."

He kept pondering in his mind as he runs his hand over his harsh face, eyes closed deep in thought and anxiety ticking in his chest like needles pricking at his heart and nerves. He feels the rattle across the floor, the mist of dust rises, and the echo of the bell from the western tower rings through the crumbled walls of the palace. He raises his head, steps from the throne and steps towards the window.

The main hall doors rattle, nearly breaking the hinges away, the loud cry of the squalling hinges alerts the guards in the throne room, awakening them from their slumber. A small troop of soldiers walk across the vast floor towards the window where Rolom stands. Rolom turns his attention to them.

'What is it? Another interruption?' Rolom scorns them.

'Lord Rolom, the western defenses have spotted a single Asyndian approaching and fast.' The guard replies.

'Another Asyndian? What do these damn creatures want with me?! More warnings of invasion! HA! We have nothing to fear here! If he gets too close just shot an arrow in him and we'll feed him to my brother...he enjoyed his last feast so much, we'll give him another...because he's my brother and I love him dearly!'

The guard's eyes look to the ground in fear and step back a bit.

'Well...why are you just standing there? I gave you an order to kill the Asyndian, now go and do so!'

There is a sinister itch upon Rolom's spine, as he feels his hair stands on end. A huge shadow eclipses him in darkness, he turns around and sees hovering out the window, the glaring red eyes of Duul`ak staring in upon him. Lord Rolom feels his blood go cold, even more so than the scheming, slimy reptile that he is. A sudden force of wind shatters the glass within the throne room as the window explodes. The guards and soldiers cover their faces, Rolom crouches down and covers his head and face from the blast and rain of glass. The daemonic being of Duul`ak soars over their heads, and he closes his wings as his talons land upon the top of the throne, using the top as a perch to close his claws around. Duul`ak watches as these pathetic beings choke upon the haze of dust and dirt that has been left upon the neglected floor.

The soldiers and guards take one look upon the burning eyes of the black Asyndian, and the fear in their carotid hearts sends them fleeing the room.

'Master Naumo…I mean master Duul`ak…its…I'm surprised to see you here.' Rolom mutters with a trembling lip, and eyes nearly in tears.

'You know damn well why I'm here Rolom…your trembling cowardice shakes these very walls, your fear stinks like the sewage pits beneath this sorry excuse of an empire…' Duul`ak roars.

'No…please…you promised he would not harm us…!'

'Sniveling Twit! I have no room for weakness within my legions! I promise nothing to weakness…and him, well…he promises nothing at all, only death….and if you listen closely…you can hear the dying screams of your pathetic wretches, as they run through the streets of this city!' Duul`ak laughs.

Rolom rushes to the door in sheer panic to try and get away, he forces the door open and rushes down the long hallway, hearing only the echo of the last sentence he will ever hear.

'*HE* is here…Lord Rolom…and when Hondor comes…no one escapes!' And then the echo of a stark laughter echoes throughout the palace.

'Now…to see to his brother…see how the young lad is…feeling after his….transformation.'

Duul`ak walks down the long and dank decay of the hallways, once smooth stone, now rotting away with ancient corrosion. Stair by stair, further and further, the smell of the rotting flesh, the piles of bodies, next to the throne of Lord Rolom's brother…reeks back.

Far below these ancient stones of Othetica, lingers in isolation the foul, putrid smell, a stench that has stained these walls and entire city from beneath this soil, up to the peaks and steeples of the highest towers.

Through the eyes of Duul`ak, Naumokron sees all amongst these halls of sickness and horror, his memory transpires back...back to the ancient twisting towers, the obsidian colossus that once stood in the Greywaste, back into those yawning catacombs of Raukmar...the flash of lightning, the roar of thunder and chaos, the gathering of the clouds above, the smell of putrid chemicals...the flesh...the creation...the first gasp of breath by the *Beast*, by *Him*...brought to life by horrors unimaginable to reign with terror...that none should witness and none are left alive to remember, only the loved ones carry the burden...only the lingering...bear the tortured images...of all the flesh eaten...and the world swallowed away.

Duul`ak enters into a large portal through which resides a room shrouded in shadows and the dim flicker of braziers, with the flame upon its last leg of existence, before the heavy, dry heaving of some abominable creature extinguishes them, with its massive winds of horrid air...and pieces of skin ejecting from its throat, landing back upon the floor covered in a grotesque clump of saliva...fresh after the feast.

"...eeeerrrrrrrrr....Roolllllloooommm....is that you..." The creature roars.

Duul`ak watches, as a massive hand, purple and chained, reaches out from the shadows with massive, thick yellowed nails, and grasps upon one of the many corpses upon the pile nearby.

"...eeeerrrrrrrrrr....the smell of must and feathers...blight and vengeance....so, our lord, the dark one Naumokron, graces my halls with his presence...so, I assume Rolom has been done away with...no, not that easily...is my

brother to suffer such as I...linger in a pit of his own gathering of feces and leftovers, drowning in bile and acid day after day, eon after eon...well...what say you Naumokron, why has the blighted one returned to Othetica?!...SPEAK!"

Duul`ak is silent for a moment, steps forward, the scratching of his talons echo across the wretched floor, built upon by eons of dust and rubble.

'He has come...son of filth...brother of Rolom...you and your brother...and all of Othetica and her Civilians...are going to fall, for the foundation underneath has been corroded and weakened, and now...the final smash of the hammer...and the wind will take all the dust and remains away...'

The horrid figure of Tolm the Steward, brother of Rolom, reaches from the darkness, a wretched claw of twisted fingers and purple-blue flesh from lack of oxygen, locked away for many years down within these dungeons, by his own brother, for his own protection, to be hidden away from the eyes of Othetica's Civilians, reaches forth from the darkness and grasps a corpse from among a pile of hundreds and hundreds of bodies piled into this massive room, clumped into the far corners like dust swept up and collected into a legion by a broom. The wretched Tolm pulls the body into the darkness and Duul`ak listens as the crunching and biting and gnawing of flesh and bone echoes throughout the hollow rafters and beams and rotten columns of this space, massive as it once was, is now closed in by the many bodies, piles of filth and remains, no longer cleaned up by the servants of Lord Rolom, for Tolm, in his decaying, wretched state, has lately taken to attacking all who come near his death throne, for his craving has turned from eating corpses to wanting and lusting for fresh blood and skin to satisfy his hunger.

"Naumokron! Wretched, black fiend! You...and that...that monster...are more fowl and more repulsive than this

353

horrible disease and curse you have brought upon me...transforming my body into an abomination...my flesh into a monster...bringing the shadows of storms and chaos over my brother's mind, bringing this...this civilization to its knees, the trembling legs of cowards and broken backs of angered ancestors! Betrayed and shamed by what we have done...what you and your black speeches and promises have done!"

He takes another body, and tosses it at Duul`ak.

'Now now, the tendencies and the animosity of scum has and always will exist within you and your brother...for I merely brought it to the surface...for my own personal gains...for I need this civilization, this world to be sick...to put it down, kill it...then, only then can rebirth take place, use what means I need...for the better, improvements to take place within this sick, pathetic realm you Civilians and Gormons claim to share with Asyndians, but this realm does not belong to you, nor to my once strong brethren, whose minds have been twisted by Maz Dregor! You will all be cleansed away, as will the Dregor and the remnants of the Hexagus...they have tasted death once, and the will so again, only this time I will put all down for good! And Hondor...Hondor, the ultimate tool, his hunger and insatiable appetite that I gave him, may have twisted his mind, but he is all but immortal...and he will cleanse this world, as it should have been all those eons before...and once I stand at the pinnacle of all, master without equal, the creator...the harvester, the judgment...the redeemer, the one and only, the highest of beings...I will bask in the new, dawn of the black sun, over the remains of all, and resurrect a new world in my own image! Free of weakness, full of devotion...to serve me, to kneel and to obey...only to ME!'

The surface above rattles the bones of the ceiling below, tearing apart some of the beams in the room. Duul`ak's voice echoes about the room in hysterical laughter, as he watches the ceiling above, begin to crumble away, and chunks of rubble begin to fall and hunks of corroded marble and stone fill the desolated room.

"You only come to mock us! To laugh in the face of our fall...only to gloat over...what you think is a conquest, a win in the books and scrolls...of Duul`ak, the foul and hated of all Civilians!"

Duul`ak smiles as he listens to the last words of Tolm spill from his rotten, disfigured lips, through jutted teeth and layered fangs.

"Lord Rolom and Tolm, the Steward of Othetica, may have fallen, helped bring a once great and mighty civilization to its knees...but once...once we had honor, once we held these lands within the casket of jewels, as the greatest and brightest gem of all, once...we had honor, but we lost it, we have lost everything...Rolom does not remember, but I still have my mind within this horrifying shape...I remember...I remember when I once commandeered the greatest armies and most noble of soldiers and generals, but no more, not for many years...then came the dark clouds and the sickness in the shape of power, greed, a lust to rule with a lack of concern to all the defilement, all the warning signs that were there...that we failed to see, and then...then the shadows clouded our minds, blinded our eyes...but I saw...I knew...but you, you made sure I was put away, never to let my brother see...see through the smoke as I did, and the veils shut over by you...the foul NAUMOKRON...!"

And a chunk of ceiling breaks away, knocking over one of the braziers of flames, and landing in the shadows, uncovering the roots and twisted limbs of Tolm's multiple, overgrown, and swollen legs, meshed together by years and years of metamorphosis. The fires strike across one of the many feet, and blazes across the sensitive, puss-filled skin, raging up his legs, across his body, and lighting up the shadows, exposing the mutated, horrid form that Tolm, the

Steward of Othetica, has become this day, a form of many eyes and teeth, several heads across shoulders , adorned with many diadems of power that hove long meant nothing and corroded away into useless tinsel and empty shells...nothing more, than meaningless.

The screams of the burning Nine-Headed Tolm, raves and cackles throughout the bowels of these catacombs and crypts under the palace and towers of Othetian.

'Honor? Nothing more than a vessel...a shell filled with cowardice, deceit to your people...lies...dishonor! And now, your civilization, falls and crumbles before you...the lives eaten away in front of you...time covered and bled around you...and now...let all of Othetica, and all the Civilians...and all the realm of Aura...die here now! Die I say...die now!' Duul`ak cries upwards to the skies that bellow in darkness and thunder, as a massive chunk of rubble falls through the ceiling and crushes the horrid figure of Tolm, and Duul`ak soars above and away to the top of the spires above, as the blood and puss from the massive body, washes across the floor in waves, covers the walls, and begins to fill the room.

***

High atop the mighty tower of Êchoŭm, the massive gears and leavers turn, the time is nigh, hovering upon the broad pauldrons placed upon Oldgaur's shoulders, a heavy weight, a burden upon him and the entire lands of Fausengard. The gongs and heavy chimes strike, the time for battle is nigh. He looks out to the horizons, across the vast lake and to the southern and western shores on the mainland, where miles away, the mists and vapors of darkness and shadow manifests, brooding with omens and the warnings of the armies of fate bearing the blood-soaked red flags upon their backs.

Oldgaur looks back into the quarters of his room, where his war-queen is seated, still and patient, as her attendants go about braiding her hair into the patterns and braids of a warrioress, while others place her armor upon her body. As the final braid is laced, and her gauntlets are shoved over her broad hands, a young Gormon retrieves from her private armory, a sturdy, mighty spear, with a tip made of solid Aeridric metal, a mythic mineral that she had hidden away, for Aeridric metal has not been seen in many years, since the last remaining deposits within the realm of Aura had been depleted. She clutches the spear in her right hand with a grip of rage and anger, of sadness and sorrow, mourning the loss of all her sons, fallen by some despicable creature the Civilians and Asyndians are calling *"Hondor"*...to her and her Gormons...this meant the end. Her sons went to represent the Oldgaur clan in the trial to execute one of their own, the Gormon named Glasgar Vor`, a voracious butcher who terrorized the entire region. He was locked away deep in the prison vaults, until he was freed. And then, at his execution, he broke free and slaughtered everyone present, including their sons.

She grips the shaft tighter, remembering the bastard Asyndian's eyes, he came on stale winds, the bearer of this news, his poisonous words and black tongue, threatening her and her husband to surrender...to bow before the rule of the Destroyer...Maz Dregor, or else they would suffer the same fate as their sons...as the monstrous being would slaughter them and all within Fausengard. It wasn't long into the Asyndian's speech then, that his head rolled across the stone floor, and with a swift kick from her boot, the head went flying out the window and into the canyons and valleys below Fauldsgrad. For several days, her and war-king Oldgaur, sat and mourned, silence in respect for their fallen sons, the bravest warriors all of Fausengard and Aura have ever seen. Fighting off mighty armies and hordes of foes and villains, mighty beasts and all the like, never afraid of any foe, never any fear. Her eyes began to tear, *"...for what monster...what kind of beast is this...this Hondor...to be able to slaughter armies, regions, devour civilizations...he slaughtered my children, the most powerful and best of any sons a mother could love! What kind of monster is this...?!"*

'There hasn't been any reports from Otoni...I fear something has happened to them over there...' She says.

'I fear they have felt the storm already...' Oldgaur replies.

Two days ago, a scout reported smoke upon the southwestern woods, he followed for a closer look, and saw over the hills...smoke and fire rising from Othetica.

'War-queen, War-king...the entire area...everything, everyone...dead, there was no sign of life...none except for *HIM*...the monster stood there over a crawling man, pleading for his life...begging to be spared. The man had been beaten and ripped apart severely, covered in filth and ashes from the fires and ruins, though I could tell by the robes and the crest upon his torn cape, it was indeed Lord Rolom...and what happened next, I dare not explain...' The scout trembled at the very thought in his mind, that image which will never go away from his memory.

'Tell us, what did you see!' Oldgaur exclaims.

'The beast...he...he took his axe in hand, an axe already covered with all the blood and bones of its butchered victims, dripping with their leftover clothes and flesh...he took that most foul of weapons, which gave off a foul wind, a breeze licked with the saliva of death, he took the axe in hand...and...and swung over and over, chopping Lord Rolom into large chunks and pieces...'

Oldgaur raised his hands to silence the scout. 'That's enough...that'll be all, we've heard enough, go now and spread the word to the soldiers and all able-bodied man and woman, prepare for an attack, if this monster has taken Othetica...he'll be coming for Fausengard next, we must take action and set up our defenses as soon as we can...'

'I'll stab this spear through his heart...the way my heart has been pierced!' She cries.

The war-queen squeezes the shaft tighter and tighter, until she feels a hand upon her own. Oldgaur looks her in the eyes and she looks back, he leans his forehead against hers, and they just take a moment to look at one another, reading the same thoughts and pondering the same feelings reflecting upon each other, of their sons, their fellow Gormons, all of Fausengard, and all the fallen of Aura.

Oldgaur places his arm around his wife, and she around him, with their weapons in their other hands.

'We will kill this bastard or die trying...for our sons and our people...' Oldgaur says.

'For our sons and our people...for the Oldgaur clan...' The war-queen replies.

'For our sons and for our people...we stand together!' They each say to the other, and they stand back, and clash weapons together. A small group of soldiers, armed head to toe, faces covered in helmets of thick bronze and shields of brawn steel, enter the room.

'We are ready to move out war-king and war-queen!' The head general exclaims, slamming the shaft of his mighty mace against his chest in salute.

***

Lord Rolom rushes through the falling streets and crumbling structures, the bodies of thousands being slung through the air and rushing away in mad panic, trying to escapes the beast's wrath, as he brings down the living axe of eyes and flesh, of jagged incisors that bite and devour away. He comes to a clearing at the center of Othetica where all goes quiet, the screams and cries of the many...have died, red flashes of lighting and the gurgle of thunder fills the skies of darkness above, for the storm is getting closer...Rolom feels it in his blood...*SHE* is almost here, the infection is nearly upon them, soon to engulf them all into a boiling pool of infinity.

The fires rise higher and higher, surrounding all of Othetica and all within. Lord Rolom is trapped, it is now he who watches across the other side, to the buildings beyond, as they fall away, and up from the rubble, is raised the massive axe of Blodaur Ror in one of the beast's hands, and then the other, and clutched within Hondor's grasp, a large mass of movement, and as the flames light the mass, Rolom sees that there are many Civilians clutched within the palm of Hondor's left hand, and Rolom stands by...for once in his miserable life, he now feels, the misery and the suffocation upon him, of helplessness, just as his subjects have felt under his rule, as he watches in terror as Hondor closes his fist tighter...and tighter...and the screaming turns to silence, and the remains of the Civilian's drip away, in a waterfall of blood, bones, and flesh, dripping through Hondor's grasp, and the rest that resides within his hand, Hondor raises to his mouth covered in shadow, and slurps them away.

Just as Rolom absorbed away all the beauty and tranquility of Othetica, just as Naumokron had taken away any self-respecting lordship of Rolom or his brother...Hondor...this monster will swallow all denizens away...and then she, when she comes...the Mother...Wom will swallow everything away, down into her abyss of the Hexagus realm, back to where all shall be reborn.

And Hondor raises his foot, and brings them down, buildings and towers crumble around him. And Hondor raises his axe, and brings them down, all life dies around him. And Hondor raises his other foot, then the other, and then the other, both eyes of red, eyes of hatred, eyes of hunger and rage, set upon the only thing left moving, the only thing left alive within the charred remains of Othetica, Rolom tries to run, he trips upon his robe, as a piece of it tears away and the cloth is left to tremble in the winds that travel across the fresh, barren ruins. Rolom tries to run faster and faster, over dirt, over rubble, each step like quicksand.

Is it exhaustion that slows his run down into nothing more than a baby's crawl, every muscle, every fiber of his body and around his bones, in pain and agony? Or is something else, some kind of unseen force or power holding him down, not letting him get away? Like the others...like all the others.

And step after step...thunder upon clasp of thunder, Hondor's footsteps pound beyond and are gaining, nearly upon him, as the rest of the city begins to crumble down around them. Lord Rolom reaches the base of one of the few, maybe even the last tower that still stands within Othetica. He looks back, and there above him, the eyes, the glowing red eyes of Hondor, the breathing of the Axe of Blodaur Ror, the heaving and crawling of his living armor, made from the bound flesh of living beings and creatures that have perished in the most nightmarish, horrible ways imaginable.

Above, upon the edge of the highest peak of the palace of the once Aurora Othetian, the shadow of Naumokron looms and the eyes of blood and fire watch over the desolation, the veils of ash lower, and the choking smog of fire and smoke arises. The grin of savagery overtakes Duul`ak, he watches the axe of Blodaur Ror rise up higher and higher, past the burning rooftops, nearing the pinnacle of the watchtower, Rolom raises his hands, helpless and struck with terror, cowering back more and more, until...the jaws strike down and the teeth bite into Rolom, as the lifeless body is raised up into the pitch-black sky, tossed into the air like a ragdoll, then down into the blade of the axe, as Rolom is swallowed away, absorbed into the living metal and blistered shaft of the despised weapons.

Hondor lowers the axe, as the forked-tongue licks its lips after the feast. He turns to see the presence of Duul`ak looming upon the steeple of the tower of Othetian's Palace, and the voice within his head speaks, of rage and anger, to charge...to attack.

"Bring down this palace...eliminate the last remnants of this pathetic culture...the last stronghold of these Civilians...!"

And Hondor charges, with rage and fury, bashing with his spiked shoulder into the mighty base of the tower, and then he punches with the left, hacks away at the stone with the axe, cutting through with little effort, the Hexagus blade tears away and eats at the stone like acid, corroding the surface and then burying its face deeper and deeper within. Hondor reaches up and sinks his hand into the stone, crunching away the surface like bone, then he sinks the axe in deeper and deeper, he rocks the tower back and forth, the mighty palace begins to sway, debris begins to fall. He grasp harder, and the tower leans and the tower sways, the fortress begins to crack, the throne room begins to cave in, the hallways and stairwells fall away, columns tilt and fall, and the palace begins to crumble, Hondor rips away chunk of stone after chunk of stone, trying to get to the Asyndian, seeking to destroy the master which gave him life, to destroy all things living, all that moves...to be ceased. The palace crumbles and the palace falls, stone by stone the palace leans forward and upon Hondor, the rest of the vast and endless streets across Othetica, the palace lands and its last remnants shatter and explode, a fume of dust arises and spreads across the roads and crashes down upon the remains of all the dead piled around.

Duul`ak soars round, across the sky, black wings of death spread and hovering over the destroyed fallen tower, Othetian's palace now crumbled down into nothing more than concrete and marble soil. The debris and rubble shifts around, and the massive clumps of rocks are tossed aside, as Hondor emerges up from the rubble that has fallen upon him. The eyes of rage beam forth from the thick cloud of smoke, and Hondor leaps into the air, and lands back upon the ground upon foot and knee, fist pounds into the ground, cracking the surface apart, leaving a massive crater beneath him. He watches as the black wings of his master...his prey...flies off towards the northeast, to the land of the mighty Gormons, the land of Fausengard, where Lord and Lady Oldgaur of war and battle, prepare themselves and await the terror that follows behind this shadow of Naumokron.

Hondor rushes his way through the ruins and rubble, chasing after the Asyndian master, as each step thunders away from these charred and forsaken grounds, where a once proud and mighty city...civilization once stood, long in decay after the failed reign of Lord Rolom and his brother, who brought about its downfall, and then the coming of Hondor spelled its doom, and it is Hondor, that rips away the heart, takes away the last breath of Othetica and all her Civilians, then tears away the roots, so no stone may stand and no creature may walk or crawl upon these grounds ever again, for the hollow winds and the scars of the Greywaste, have stretched far indeed, as the third Grey Age...an age of black has begun...and as the scales of shadow slide down further and further into the realms of the nether, the Age of Grey...turns to darkness.

Hondor bursts through the burning walls of Othetica, and the flame leaves no mark upon his immortal flesh nor living, breathing armor, and the steps of thunder fade east, under the wide-spread, eternal clouds of storms and shadows.

***

Hundreds of mighty steam ships of iron and steering gears and levers, set sail towards the mainland. All of them have come from every direction of Fausengard, for this was it, the final stand, the final battle of Fausengard...and all able-bodied men and women Gormon have answered the call, bearing sword, axe, spear, hammers in one hand, and mace in the other, some lugged along tower-shields more than half their size. They came for battle, for war, for the glory of death to defend their lands and realm. They were ready to die against this new terror they would soon face, the flesh-eater, as he marches across scorched dirt and fields sewn with skulls and belched-up bones, of livestock and denizens, for all are his food, all are here for his consumption, for his survival, for his immortality.

Rank upon rank, the Gormons lined the hauls of these mighty ships, the cool, brisk wind of the Fauldsgrad winds whisked through their mighty beards and extravagant locks. The war-paint and tattoos upon their faces cracked as they grit and ground their teeth, at the very thought of getting their hands upon this fiend that has caused so many atrocities, so much pain to Aura and all her lands, to all her people, all Gormons, Asyndians, and Civilians.

Waves rise up and metal grinds and crashes upon rock, as the ships hit the mainland of Fausengard. The chains rattle and creak, as the draw-bridges lower, and the Gormons see land and mountains over the horizons, and the quake of ground and thunder approaching in the distance and closing in fast towards them.

The brave Gormon soldiers take a deep breath and maintain their composure and their brave hearts from failing, and their minds focused on what awaits over on the horizons. In the back of their thoughts, they keep with them, the faces of their children, their sick and ill, their loved ones that had to stay behind, within the protected walls of Êchoŭm.

And they proceed, they march forward in file, their boots stamp through mud and water as they trudge up the banks and hills, and once they reach the top, the lines spread outwards over the plains before them, and the skies grow darker.

Oldgaur grapples onto a large rock protruding from the ground, climbs up and walks out to the edge, eyes focused outwards, watching the sky grow darker and darker, encompassing the grey and cloudy skies already above their heads. His warrior-bride and soldiers gaze up to him, marveling at his brilliant and magnificent armor clashing against the dreary skies upon them, for even within this gloom, the armor still shines, a flame of metallic golds and silvers, colt iron and steel. He unsheathes the mighty battle-axe and his shield, the unbreakable, impenetrable, tower-shield, the mythic Hiidraun, The Mountain-Fortress! Dipped many centuries ago into the undying springs far over the ridge, near the old caverns and falls of Iurnhall, once the fortress keep of the ancient Gormon warlord Urdaul` Fôf. The shield was named after the ancient Gormon warrior and descendant of the Oldgaurs, Hideron.

Oldgaur turns and faces his thousands of troops and armored soldiers, they hum in a low, resonating tone, an old, almost forgotten war-hymn. The last time it had been sung, was at the Battle of Rfh, when one of Oldgaur's grandfathers and his men made their final charge upon one of the warlords that terrorized the Gormons of Fausengard with their reign of terror and brutal tortures and hold over all the land. Oldgaur's grandfather was outnumbered, and they sang the blood hymn as one last and final hurrah before all were slaughtered under axes and flesh and armor was caked upon the spikes of maces and hammers.

Our blood may spill and splatter,

but the rain will clean our wounds with its shower!

our flesh broken, but our essence lives forever,

we may die in battle, but we die with honor!

We may perish this day, but our legend will live forever!

They stand at attention.

'Long ago, during the battle of the Second Grey Age...Hideron, my ancestor, our mighty father of all of Fausengard, fought the hosts of Dregor upon these very fields! The blood of many Gormon, was spilled beneath our feet! We walk upon a field of battle, upon an altar of sacrifice! Are you ready to give that sacrifice and join with your ancestors who have fallen upon these very fields, to join the glorious dead in the halls of our forefathers, and be one among the many eternal legends and heroes that fought to keep our name and our people strong?!'

Chants and cries burst forth, weapons clang and armor bashes together in compliance and support towards Oldgaur and his words. One of the Gormon off to the far right of the plains cries aloud, 'It will not be our blood, but the blood of that monstrous bastard that we'll water this grass with his blood! Let's meet him head on and we'll show him!'

'Yeah, march head on and show him that Fausengard will never fall! The realm, hard as rock, will continue to stand, sturdy and hearty, forever!' Another soldier calls aloud.

'That's what I want to hear! You do your ancestors proud! We fight together...we die for each other!' Oldgaur cries back. He raises the axe above his head in salute. 'Heroes and warriors of Fausengard...raise your arms and repeat after me:

'Our blood may spill and splatter...'

"Our blood may spill and splatter..."

'But the rain will clean our wounds with its shower...!'

"But the rain will clean our wounds with its shower...!"

'Our flesh broken...but our essence lives forever...!'

"Our flesh broken...but our essence lives forever...!"

'We may die in battle, but we die with honor...!'

"We may die in battle, but we die with honor...!"

'We may perish this day...' and the crowds fall silent, waiting for it, waiting for the final line, before all instinct of war and the fever of battle overtakes their mind, and the final charge...will commence.

'...but our legend will live...FOREVER!!!!!'

"OUR LEGEND WILL LIVE FOREVER!!!!"

And Oldgaur, turns and leaps from the large rock, hitting the ground and charging forward, wave after wave of Gormon soldiers, in lines for miles wide following behind, as they march across the fields, weapons and shields, and arms waving crazily and wild, ready to strike their mark upon the beast's flesh.

Oldgaur and his armies reach the boarders where black meets the last touch of grey, they have almost reached the shadows edge were the clouds of darkness swirl and gurgle above like some living, writhing thing. Then, Oldgaur sees a faint flicker of a shadow pass beneath his charging boots, as something has passed over his head, something going at an incredible speed, he stops in his tracks, as his soldiers charge passed. Oldgaur looks up and sees there, hovering in the sky, an Asyndian with eyes of fiery ruby and feathers blacker than the vortices of the unknown. The Asyndian glares upon the Gormon warrior-king, his warrior-queen, who leads the flanks upon the eastern side, sees her husband standing motionless, looking up, and she too sees this black Asyndian. She orders the soldiers to continue, as she makes her way over to him. Time seems to stand still, as she sees the Asyndian raise his hand up in front of him, and clenches his hand, slowly...with force, into a tight fist and squeezes. She looks back to her husband, her warrior-king, as he clenches his chest, as a sharp pain overtakes him, and he falls to his knees, his breathing weak, his body crippled by some dark, cancerous force that has seemed to overtake his entire body. She gets to his side, and crouches to help him.

'What is it?! What has happened?!'

But he cannot reply, he only trembles. She looks into his eyes, she sees something within him that she has never seen before. There is fear, terror in her king's eyes...as though he has just bared witness to something horrible, unspeakable. Her glare shoots up to the Asyndian, who does not move, doesn't flinch, he only looks down upon them and smiles, a horrid, blood-curdling essence within his stare.

She holds up her spear and draws it back, she aims...and with all her force and rage...she fires the projectile with all the strength she keeps stored in those massive arms of hers. She watches with intent, as the spear is about to make its mark, and as its about to rip through Duul`ak's chest...the spear stops, some force created by the Asyndian, an invisible force turns the spear around, and aims it back at her. She then hears a mumble. She looks back and sees Oldgaur looking up to her with intense, frightened eyes.

'Speak...what are you saying? What are you trying to tell me...?'

'The...the blood...the slaughter...I've...I can see into that fiends head...we are the last! We are to complete the final stage of...of this monsters transformation!' He cries in terror.

'We're the last? I don't under...'

And like a missile from above, the spear shoots through the air and strikes Oldgaur straight through the heart, leaving him there, lying on the ground choking on his own blood. He takes one last look in to the queen's eyes and then he is gone.

Tears flood her eyes, as raw emotion and sorrow shakes her entire figure, in disbelief and shock, in horror, in sorrow, for her husband is dead, her sons are dead...all that she held dear in this life, is no more.

She turns back to the Asyndian, and Duul`ak still stays hovering above the battleground, the same smile over his face.

'You! I'll butcher you for this! I'll...' Before she can finish, an eerie, horrific voice floods the through her head.

"Silence you pathetic animal! Turn, and witness the slaughter and butcher of your own cattle! For Hondor has come...and you're all going to die!"

And echoing over the hills and rivers, tainted with the blood of her people, she turns, and there over upon the far ridge ahead, she sees it...the hulking beast, the titanic stature of living armor and thatched pieces of living, breathing horrors that have been absorbed and become one within the form of this bastard Hondor, and now that she sees, she too feels that which she has never felt, that same look of fear, engulfed her entire being, her heart and essence gone, for she has never seen anything so cruel, a being with as much rage and hatred, a want to kill and feed, to destroy and bring all around him down to nothing but ruin to never exist again. An agent of genocide, for no evil nor wickedness within all of Aura or anywhere else in

369

all of the Galakaos...can equal the horrific nature of this killing machine.

'What can one do...against such...such a bestial thing?!' She says to herself as she drops to her knees, watching, petrified with horror, as the entire army of Fausengard is cut away, sliced and hacked up, swallowed and torn to pieces in handfuls, as Hondor tears open the flesh and spits the bones and armor away. The screams and whines of the soldiers as their skin and body's ripped open, becomes deafening upon the queen's ears.

She has never seen such a terrifying revelation before her very eyes, nor could she ever imagine such a thing within her mind, for none...none are left, only bones and bloodied scraps remain littered and splattered across the landscape. Only the silence of black can be heard over this field of silent screams, as all life, all at once, just vanished around her, and she is the only one left, and she takes one last look down at her king's body, as a huge, clawed hand wraps its fingers around the body, picks it up into the air, and she looks up to the opened, gaping maw of Hondor, as he engulfs Oldgaur, the warrior-king, whole. The sound of chomping jowls, slobbering lips, and that pinnacle, that final swallow as Oldgaur becomes one within the gut of this horrific monster.

The shadow of Hondor eclipses over her, as he lowers the axe closer to her. The Axe of Blodaur Ror sniffs the air, smelling the living, crawling flesh of blood and fear, and the living blade lashes out and snatches the queen within its jaws, and the warrior-queen sees and feels no more, as jagged teeth crunches her bones into splinters.

***

The tides and waves splash and splatter in a storm of rage and devastation, as Hondor trudges over the mighty lake to cross over into the lands of Êchoŭm, for the metal walls and defenses are only keeping his next meal warm, before he reaches the city, breaks down the walls and tears open the homes that shelter these, weak, defenseless Gormon that will not be able to put up a fight against such a crude, voracious monster.

And their bones will line the bottom of the lake, and covered over by the tides of a watery grave, for the last defense of Aura has fallen. Othetica has been brought down to a steaming pile of smoldered ash. Fausengard remains nothing more than a land of punctured metal, crumbled rock, and fields tainted with spoiled blood of defeat and genocide. Runegard was the first to suffer at the hands of this monster, soon the eastern shore, all the Baldushan will perish, a feast to the axe of the Hexagus lord. The southern denizens, the Azimoth will not last the night, for as quickly as the lightning strikes, their entire civilization has been crushed beneath Hondor's jagged boot. Greenrym has become ripped away, as all trees have been torn from their roots, and the soil corroded by Hondor's poisoned saliva, and nothing will ever grow their again.

And now, the shadows have nearly eclipsed all the realm, and the days and nights are getting darker and darker...for something is approaching, it has its sights upon Aura, the final realm, and now, the last light of the Galakaos is gone, and the Age of Darkness...the Age of Wom is nearly upon them.

Now Duul`ak knows the time is almost nigh, as he looks to the north, where Lady Aura and her people scurry away, fleeing to Raukmar where they think they will be safe, only...when Hondor arrives, there is nowhere that is safe.

"...and once the guardian of the Divide is taken care of..." Naumokron looks back to the rampaging Hondor chasing behind him as he soars through the skies towards Mirym and

the Great Divide, where he...Naumokron, was summoned back into this realm.

"...the Divide awaits...Hondor...!"

Part XXIV:

Bridge Over the Great Divide

~

Aura and her people trek across uncertain cliffs and rocks, she stops upon the steepest edge of the cliff face, walking nearer to the edge, distracted by the high columns of smoke rising from the south and east of the realm, for now, Greenrym, Othetica, Fausengard...all the last remaining lands and civilizations of the realm of Aura...now joins Runegard, in ruin and rubble, a mass graveyard of fallen cities and slaughtered bodies, burned and broken, eaten and annihilated, exterminated, wiped away from the face of the realm.

Aura, Nilta, Diin, and all the remaining Civilians, Gormons, and Asyndians, bow their heads in sadness, many tears, many sorrows, and much sadness that can never dissipate so easily, to taint, to stain the memories and fuel the night terrors.

Aura sits through the passing twilight, looking away and up into the abyss above them. Diin approaches and sits next to her.

'You're not sleeping?' He asks.

'There is no rest to be had...no sleep nor slumber. The only certain rest it seems, is the eternal slumber of death, to not awaken into this...this waking nightmare around us...I miss the days of the light, when no darkness covered these skies...the light was the one joy I still had, and all the high towers and buildings reaching up to her, and the golden rays blanket the cool stone in warmth at morning's dawn...it's been so long dwelling in this cold wasteland, that is hard to try and remember the touch, the feel of warmth.'

She turns to Diin. 'Will the light ever return...?'

'Before my eyes became dark...I too remember the beautiful sight that was Lota's eye, the mighty, splendid world above us, the ancient city renewed by the Asyndians after the second Grey Age brought all to ruin...this is not the first time we have lost the light...all things I always thought, renewed themselves, a rebirth I guess you could say...only now...' He stops and ponders.

'And now?'

'And now it seems...it seems that darkness may be permanent for us all. You ask me if there is any hope...'

'No, only if there will be light...hope is abstract, an illusion...the light is real, it once existed, it was here...I only want there to be so again...just to see the great eye in the sky, the blue sky, the mighty oceans and seas of trees, fields of green and the many faces of lives that once walked upon marble streets...' She replies.

'I don't know...when was the last time such a thing existed?' He says.

'It seems like it was so long ago...but not even that long...the days under this blanket of darkness seem endless, the night drags on and on...I just want to look over there, over those mountains and see the light, rising over the mountains again...' She says.

'Well...' He smiles grimly, 'I know I never will...but you may, my lady...just maybe...you and your people, you may see a beam of light break through all of this darkness.'

She looks off over her shoulder. 'Has Nilta returned yet?'

'Not yet, without her spear, the wild boar prowling around may prove a little more difficult for her.'

After the nights feast, the first they have had for some time...not since their families and friends and loved ones crowded round the laden tables for the evenings meal, now all those memories lay burned away in piles of ash and smoke beneath the ruins of Runegard.

'She should have not gone alone, I could have sent some of the Gormons along with her.' Aura says.

'Nilta can handle herself...she is far stronger, quicker, and...dare I say, smarter than any of those Gormon and Asyndians. I don't know what I would do without her...she is all I have left, our mother and father died when we were very young, and now our master...he is gone as well...it's only me and her now.' Diin replies.

'We are here as well...you two are not alone.' Says Aura, and Diin gives a smile.

'If...if I may ask...how is it you two are able to communicate? I asked you once and I can't remember if you answered. You are blind and she...she cannot speak. You seem to just "know", what the other is thinking.' Aura asks Diin as polite as she can.

'I guess it's just our bond, a connection between siblings I suppose...I can't explain it really, I just understand her movements, her body language, when she's excited, distressed, angered, sad...I can just feel it radiating off of her...like the warmth of light or the cold wind, an instinct in essence I suppose you could say, just as I can sense other behaviors and moods around me...I just know.'

'I see.' Aura replies, not really sure if she understands or not...for the fatigue in her legs, arms and body, makes thoughts all the more difficult to comprehend. Nilta returns from her hunt with a sizable wildebeest full of meat.

They continue on after a long rest and feast. They come to a tall ridge just beyond them, and one of the Gormon rushes ahead to the top and looks out over the brim of the dirt hill. He calls back to the rest of the group.

'Over there...beyond the hills and valleys! We've reached it, the bridge of the Divide!'

And the rest make haste and scramble up the hill as fast as they can muster their speed with the little strength they have left in them, and over the peak they see it, Aura lays her eyes upon the mighty bridge, a ancient marvel of a much older time long before, for the Bridge of the Great Divide stretches out beyond over the yawning abyss below for miles and miles, as up from the deep, sounds of pulsating energy and thunderous tremors shutter forth, and magnificent bright and colorful energy and beams of natural sparks and lights pulsate through the dark above them, like serpents and blades intertwining round the other, flashes glisten and blind as though many-limbed exotic dancers skip and leap about in super-sonic ballet across the sky. All of them look up and marvel at the magnificent show and cower at the thunderous burring and gurgles from the sounds emitting from the chasms beneath them.

'Alright everyone, stick together, down the hill now..watch your step...be careful all of you!' Aura calls to the group as they proceed downwards to the flat rocks below where the bridge begins upon its southern side of the Divide. The trek is a long ways ahead as they have many miles to go to cross over the Great Divide.

Aura stops for a moment, just before her descent, and looks back from where they came, for a cold runs down her neck, as she feels an evil omen grow over her. Her eyes dart around the landscape, out over the valley they came, across the plains, out to the mountains around them and over the horizons, but she can't see anything, nothing, all seems so lifeless were they are, for there are a few fauna lingering about, but they are very scarce to be concerned with. This however, is not about some predator that stalks the wildlife, this is about something larger, she feels a force getting closer.

"Can...can it be?" She thinks to herself.

Diin and Nilta stand nearby, looking towards what she looks at.

'I feel it too my lady...we need to move...faster. We need to get across this bridge and into Raukmar as soon as possible.

She nods, and they return to the rest of the group and take their first steps over the Great Divide.

The fantastic lights seem to be dissipating around them the further they move on, and soon, there is nothing left to look at, only the dismal abyss below and the black sky above them, for this bridge holds no symbolic reference or ancient markings of the sort, only a plain, marble causeway stretching out for miles and miles and miles and beyond, to the other side where the lands into Raukmar awaits.

As they approach the end of the vast bridge of all times, there upon their far left, Nilta sees a mighty structure, a tower nearly endless in height, and as far up as it stretches, at the edge a crumbled rim looks as a small crack at the tip, and the rest of the group point and gasp in wonder, for there, sitting upon the barren hills of running sands and stagnant boulders, at the crown of a mighty waterfall that flows from the Ckrynig River, the southernmost, and greatest basin of water that resides within all of Raukmar, even more vast than any lake or river within the boundaries of Aura, and the mighty falls empty into the Great Divide, seeming nothing more than the size of a faint trickle of water, and there, at the pinnacle of the falls, a silhouette in the dying sunlight that begins to fade in these lands, of a mighty figure, the shape of a virile male of great muscular power, whether his flesh be of stone or natural, they cannot tell, for the figure doesn't move nor sweep, even in the mighty blows of the heavy winds pounding against them high above the mighty Divide. Diin begins to feel a strong presence, a sense of protection come over all of them. Nilta taps upon her brother's shoulder and Diin nods his head in agreement.

'Yes Nilta...I know!'

Aura turns to Diin. 'Is...is that him?' She asks.

'Yes, my lady...he is Agonan, brother of Gonun and Tundrok, protector of the Gormons of Fausengard...he is the last of the Auroras and has sworn himself, dedicated protector over this bridge of the Great Divide, to monitor the Rauks and any Dregor doings...' Diin replies.

Aura looks on at the figure, as the faint sun begins to shine through, and remove his face from the shadows.

'The last days are upon these lands, and the last hope of this realm, enters into this forsaken place....her and the rest of her subjects...for what is it you hope to find here?!' The booming voice of the mighty Aurora growls, looking down upon the crossing company in disappointment.

'I seek to keep my people safe, I will find refuge within these lands of Raukmar...away from the death that has been brought to the southern lands...the realm of Aura!'

'My lady...I asked you let me speak!' Diin nudges her.

'You will find no shelter here...for the death that you run from has spread further than you think, for the red eyes of the black Asyndian are always watching....and the hands of the Destroyer...are clenching...squeezing tighter and tighter together. No, my lady Aura...there is no refuge to be found here...' Agonan replies.

'Guardian of this bridge, master of the portal over the Great Divide...I appreciate your concern, but I will take care of my people, I would put myself at any risk, to see that they are taken somewhere safe...now, will you let us pass?' Aura replies.

'You, Civilian...you speak brave...like one from before...I admire your dedication to your people, and the bravery you pledge to them. You are not my enemy, and may pass, but I must warn you...this is not our realm, this is Raukmar, and there are many dangers in these lands you must be extra careful...I must warn you that...'

Agonan is cut off by a pulsating quake that rumbles through the dirt, the thunder of heavy, armored boots drives through the ground, at a faster and faster pace...something massive is approaching...

'He is coming...' Diin whispers aloud to Aura.

Part XXV:

Agonan's Challenge

~

There is a tremble beneath their feet, as the entire bridge begins to quake and the flesh upon Aura's neck begins to prick with fear. She can smell it, the scent of blood is near, almost upon them, the smell of chewed bone lingers within the stale winds blowing due north towards them.

A shrill cry shatters the still, as the crowds look, turn to witness the rising shadow in the distance, and so the exodus of Civilians, Gormons, and Asyndians scramble to get across to the other side of the bridge as quick as they can.

'No...no...!' Shutters Aura under her breath.

And in the distance looms the empty silhouette upon the horizon, his stomach full with the flesh of thousands, of lifetimes, his razor jaws yawn with rage, a roar that shakes the cliffs of the Divide around them.

'He's...he's bigger...bigger than before!' Aura cries.

'Please my lady, we must get away...over the bridge before he brings it down!' Diin calls to her, and Nilta rushes forward trying to lead Aura away, gripping her by the arm and turning back to guide her brother along as well.

Agonan leaps from his throne upon the rocks to the bridge, behind the fleeing crowds, making sure none are left behind or injured in the stampede.

'Fly, all of you...I will deal with this monster!' Agonan yells back to them, then turns and faces towards Hondor, as the thwamping steps march forward and onto the mighty bridge.

Agonan grips to his sword at the ready and clenches down upon his shield, raised high into the air and at the ready.

'If I go...I'm taking you and this bridge with me! He yells. 'Go...go now! Take your people and go!'

Agonan begins the long trek out towards the center of the bridge, as the gargantuan giant proceeds from the other side. As Hondor stomps further, Agonan looks down and sees miniscule serpents of cracks forming, extending, growing outwards as a corruption of the beast spreads over into the lands of the north, Raukmar.

The crystallized stare of Agonan meets the blood-dripping maw and fiery eyes of Hondor, and then he sees within the grasp of the clawed gauntlets, the horrid axe, the bestial eyes and razor-teeth of Blodaur Ror's essence and malice within the Hexagus Lord's weapon. Agonan turns back and the crowds of Aura's denizens fade in the distance as Aura herself turns back once more, the hopeless look within her eyes.

Out of the corner of his eye, Agonan sees something, a shadow, soaring through the sky around them, he feels the cold icy glare of whatever is watching them, but he cannot pin-point where it is, as its speed wisps within the shadows of the darkness above. He catches the movement behind him and when he looks to his throne upon the high tower, there is perched the black Asyndian looking on. The presence of this creature is familiar to him, a darkness from past lives long ago.

"It...it cannot be!"

And Hondor charges forward, Agonan turns back and sees the monster almost upon him. He raises his shield as the blasting strike of Blodaur's axe slams down upon the shield, throwing Agonan back a great distance across the bridge, the shield fumes with an acrid, foul stench of melted, corroded metal as the strike of the axe has melted the shield away, leaving only a large, gaping wound within the ruined Aeridric steel wall, smoking and steaming, boiling into the Auroran's arm. Agonan tosses the shield away and grips the mighty claymore, forged by his lost brother Gonun, into both hands and retaliates back at Hondor, leaping into the air, ready to bring the blow down upon the terror of Hondor.

Hondor obliges and charges at Agonan, leaps to the Aurora's heights and with the axe, strikes away at Agonan, as Agonan strikes back upon the scales of the axe-face. And they land upon opposite sides of the bridge from their starting positions, Agonan takes the advantage while Hondor's back is turned, and charges at the beast, raises the sword and drives it down into the back of Hondor, twists the blade around and then tries to rip it free, using all his strength, but...the flesh of Hondor seems to have hold of it, as Agonan looks closer and sees the tiny clawed hands reach out from the skin upon Hondor's body, and grapple against Agonan, gaining the upper hand on the blade, and Agonan looses grip and falls backwards, as he watches the minuscule hundreds of hands, rip the blade away, and the flesh swallows the rest, except for the hilt, that falls upon the thick beams of the mighty bridge.

Agonan reaches and grasps what is left of his brother's sword. Hondor turns around and faces the Aurora, whose defeat is nearly eminent, but Agonan is not ready to give up yet, he looks at the sword and tosses the remains aside. He sees the stone and marble beneath his feet is giving way, the cracks are getting worse. He looks over the sides, and realizes there is only one way to win this battle and get rid of this monster...for the Great Divide...is an eternal fall into nothingness.

Duul'ak sees what is happening, he can see their thoughts, he knows what the Aurora is thinking and he watches with great intent as to what is going to happen.

"The darkness of the Great Divide is deep Hondor...far deeper and darker, than the darkness within your mind!"

Hondor raises the axe up high, and then within a moment...he strikes, Agonan steps away before the blow hits its mark upon his flesh, and the jagged blade of malice strikes through the thick marble walkway without resistance, piercing through, and a chunk of the bridge cracks and falls away.

Hondor strikes again and again. The bridge begins to rumble and shake, swaying and thrusting right then left, the cracks growing, the bridge is bowing inwards. And Hondor strikes again and again, with the final blow tasting immortal flesh, as the axe tears away Agonan's arm, and the Aurora cries of pain up to the black skies above and across the canyon's way to the other side, where Aura stands upon the high cliffs looking out over the gaping abyss, watching the battle, as Agonan is brought to his knees, and more and more, the bridge begins to break away.

'I accept my fate and take this fall...this fall for all of this realm to be free of your terror! When I fall, then so shall you...fall with me!' Agonan cries.

The crowds of Civilians, Gormons, and Asyndians, Diin and Nilta, all gather around Aura and all eyes are fixed upon the bridge.

Duul`ak's stare intensifies, as he too, watches on as the battle rages. *"And now, you will perish you foul spawn...I created you...to be your master, you were to be my ultimate creation, my weapon...after all those years spent...and now...? You have fulfilled your purpose, you have cleared this land for my reign to commence...I will find some other way to deal with the Destroyer...that fetcher Aumon thinks he has won this war! But I will persevere...I will inhabit the minds of those who will NOT disobey me, nor try to devour their master, their ruler! Fall into the abyss you foul creature! FALL!"*

And with that, Duul`ak disowns this monster he has created, to leave him to fall.

Hondor raises the axe....for one final blow against Agonan, who raises his last arm to shield himself, but the axe eats straight through the flesh of the last Aurora, and the final stone that has held this bridge together, falls away, and Aura and the others look on in awe and shock as the bridge crumbles away, stone by stone, the marble is absorbed down into the darkness to be swallowed away by the Divide, and with Agonan, the last of the Auroras, Hondor falls with him, and all watch as the bodies flail about as they plunge downwards, fading into the subterranean, eternal night as is above their heads, so is beneath their feet.

The quakes cease, and all that remains, are the roots of the bridge that hang upon the southern tip and the northern side. The bridge is gone...but...a sigh of unbelieving jubilation fills all their empty, starving guts...Hondor is gone too.

'Is...is he?' One of the Civilian women tries to speak, but her tongue and jaw is flabbergasted by what she has just witnessed.

'He's dead! That bastard! That Monster...he's finally dead!' A Gormon cries out, and a moment of celebration spreads through the small crowds with what strength they have to cheer and be merry. Diin approaches closer to Aura, who stands still, an inquisitive blank look enslaves her eyes, she cannot pry them away from the blackness beneath her.

'Lady Aura...the darkness has, it appears has overcome that which has destroyed all, all the families and loved ones of those who cheer and clap and dance with glee over the fall of this monster...yet I feel, and I know that you do...as long as Hondor falls, there is no guarantee of death, for a heart-beat still echoes from those depths...you know this my lady, you know it seems too good to be true...'

She turns to Diin. 'What are saying? I don't understand Diin...he's fallen, he's gone...that beast is not coming back!' She replies.

'Do you know this for certain? Or is this what you want to believe. My eyes may be dark, but if there is anything being blind has taught me, is that my mind and my heart see more than my eyes ever could, they allow me to feel what is real, not what an illusion shows me.'

She gets closer to Diin. 'You dare try to tell me that the beast is not dead, when all of us, except for you, the one who is blind, has witnessed his death...and you try to tell me otherwise?!'

'All I'm saying is that we need to keep moving...and keep cautious of our steps ahead, yet keep our ears open behind us...let's say hypothetically, that all you wish for is true, that Hondor has fallen, never to return...but there still remains Duul`ak, the Destroyer...the Dregor armies...' He now speaks louder outwards towards the whole group. 'Do you not see the darkness above you, the shadows that follow us, watch our every step?!' The celebrating halts abruptly, 'why are you so happy, so anxious to grasp for joy that isn't there?! Sometimes

I wonder if I am the only one who can see and it's the rest of you who are blind! The realm of Aura is gone, soon to be taken over by the forces of Dregor, and the Destroyer, Maz Dregor has finally won, all the land of the south now belongs to him, and we are stranded in a land foreign, unknown to all of us, and the keeper of the beast, Naumokron, he's all around us, above us, watching and waiting to strike us! We do not possess the means to return to our lands, but it will not be long before the Dregor find a way here and the black Asyndians can come for us at any moment they please!'

He looks back to Aura. 'You celebrate as though we had won, this is not a victory lady Aura, Hondor was only a pawn, a catalyst to these black spawns of chaos, spawns to their queen, their mother! For I feel her creeping across the Galakaos, and with each day she gets closer and closer! The skies around all of you are darkening, soon you shall all know...know what it's like...to see only night...'

He falls to his knees and weeps, Nilta carefully takes him by the arm and leads him over to a rock to sit down. Aura is speechless of Diin's outburst, it was not like him to despair so much, as wise as his words have been, his voice and mind has held back so much pain he has kept deep inside, it building up, and has been unleashed.

He whispers something into Nilta's ear and she gets up and walks over to Aura, who leads her over to her brother. Diin looks up to the sound of her steps, and Aura looks down to the dampened cloth tied around his eyes, tears drench where his dead eyes linger within his skull. He holds out his hand, and Aura, hesitant for a moment, reaches out and takes his hand gently, he closes his hand around hers tighter, but not grasping her to hard. She kneels down to him, a tear flowing down her cheek.

'So...is this it then...is this to be our fate...do you already know what is to become of us...you seem sure of it...' She says.

'I am no seer, I see no future...I can't...because, I never would have thought, nor could I have foreseen...we would have made it this far...a ragged band of refugees, beaten and bruised and battered, a leader who has lost everything, and yet...you still take us further. You have proved something to me my lady...'

'What is that? All I've done, is what I can do...to not let the rest of my people be fated to such a horrible death to that beast...and I will go to the ends of this realm to escape that fate if I must...I will not let it happen...I will not give up on any of them...I will give what life is left to be had to each and every one of us! I may have lost myself, I may have made mistakes and bad choices....maybe it was fated we were to all die to that monster or to the forces of Dregor...maybe...but nothing is definite...for as long as I am alive, my people will remain alive...as long as I'm alive Diin...the realm of Aura, you and your sister, my beloved Civilians, Gormons, and Asyndians will remain alive...Hondor has fallen, this is a small step maybe, but a step is better than standing idly by and doing nothing!' She looks around at Nilta, at all of her people looking back to her.

'I will not let the death of Agonan go in vain, we will keep going, we will find our place, we will get to where we need to go...I will see to it if all of you will...I will not abandon any of you...ever! Even if it was me on that bridge in the place of that Aurora...I would have fallen, for all of you! Do you hear...I would have fallen and taken that beast with me! All of you can call me strong or call me weak...but I will never give up!'

She feels the grasp upon her hand tighten.

'You still give us some hope.' Diin says to her.

She helps him up, and Nilta grips upon his arm. Aura lets go of him. 'Hope...hope is a fantasy...we will continue onwards into Raukmar, I don't know what will await us there...maybe hope...maybe despair...nothing is certain anymore except that we're still alive and moving onwards...and another thing is certain, these skies are not getting any brighter, the days grow darker.' She looks to Diin. 'No Diin...I don't give hope...guidance Diin, we are nothing anymore, and here I am...nothing more than some progeny of an extinct world, I'm just trying to guide us, maybe...just maybe to...to what I don't know...will you help me?' She asks Diin and all her people. Nilta taps Diin upon the shoulder.

'Nilta and I are still here...we will be by your side my lady.' He replies.

'We are with you Lady Aura...' All Asyndians, Gormons, and Civilian's reply.

And into the lands of desolate mountain ranges and vast deserted plains they tread. To Raukmar...they go.

Part XXVI:

Raukmar

~

With the gap between the lands of Raukmar and Aura fallen, there is no going back...there is nothing to go back to, for the final stand of the last remnants of Aura have been cleansed, eaten away by warfare waged by Hondor and the legions of Dregor under the banner of the Destroyer. And now, the Lady Aura, Diin, and his sister Nilta, and several of the surviving captives of Runegard, stand before foreign lands, filled with piles of crags, broken mountains, and fallen citadels to the mighty giants of these lands, the Rauks. They look out over the vast plains and rocky soot that looms in fogs and mists over the hills and landscape, kicked up by the howl of the ferocious gusts of winds and storms, thunder echoes and lightning strikes in the distance, though there is no rainfall here, there hasn't been a drop of rain in Raukmar for many, many eons, not since the long war of the Gormons and the Rauks that were fought among these peaks. Aura takes a step out closer to the edge of the steep cliff-face and looks off to the right, where a huge series of monolithic stone structures juts from the surface, stones and crumbled rocks which almost seem to look like massive appendages or fingers of some kind.

'So…this is Raukmar…this is our retreat?' A tear drops down her eyes in sorrow. 'This is where we are to start anew?' And Aura weeps. 'Is there to be any end to this nightmare…will this darkness ever subside, and the light be brought back to our realm?' She kneels down to the ground and takes a handful of gravel and dirt in her hand, then lets it go, as it is taken on the winds. 'Like the dirt that falls from my hand, as the sand runs down an hour glass…our time runs thin.' She stands up, holding the wound upon her arm where A`deon's blade was driven through. *"…though it was for what? I should have died; I should be dead…for I have escaped the clutches of my fate far too many times."*

Nilta leads Diin over to her, as he kneels next to her. 'Take heart dear lady, for I too feel it, when my sight was taken from me, when me and my sister lost our master, killed by General A`deon…we were left for dead and you have taken us in, to be among the good people of Runegard…we found a new family and someone to look up to, to get us through this. I will never see the light again, for I have seen darkness now for a long time, and will for the rest of my days…but you, my lady, you, my sister, and all these other folks, still have a chance, and I will stand by your side, so will Nilta, and we will do all we can to help you.' He puts his hand upon her shoulder, his words seem to bring some comfort to Aura, and she places her hand upon his. Nilta walks to her other side, and holds out her hand, Aura grasps it tightly and Nilta pulls her up to her feet.

'We will get through this my lady…somehow, we will make it through the darkened days…we will be here right by you.' Someone from the crowd spoke aloud behind her. 'You're not alone in this.' Another says.

'Let us continue my lady…I will help lead you, just follow myself and Nilta, for we have some knowledge of this place, though I will say, that there is little in the way of hospitality and civilization here, for Rauks…and Raukmar.

390

Aside from some citadels which are settled deep within the chasms far beneath the ground, accessed through fissures and broken plates of ground, there are no territories nor towns and empires. Let's just…take it slow. Agonan has taken Hondor down with him, whether he's dead or not, I cannot say, for the Divide falls endlessly into nothing, so we have a little time bid to us at last…if your people are ready, let us head onward.'

They find a narrow side trail around the large steppes of rock, and follow along down, heading into an opening at the bottom. After a time, Nilta halts in her tracks with Diin hooked to her arm.

'What's the matter?' Aura inquires to the wide, wondering eyes upon Nilta who looks about the area above and beyond her. She then taps upon Diin's shoulder.

'Raukmar was once a place of warfare and battle amongst the Rauks…and now…' Diin replies.

Aura waits for him to continue.

'…now, just listen.'

They go silent, and listen, only hearing the cries of the sirens upon the winds as the air whistles through the hollowed out caverns and crevices of Raukmar.

'All is silent…at one time you could hear their fighting all the way across the Divide, and now there is nothing.'

'What has happened?' Aura asks.

'There's no telling what went on here, the ways of the Rauks are still mysterious aside from their warring ways…'

They too have been walking forever, nothing to see for miles and miles but the sight of crumbled rocks and ruined citadels of massive width and height, once the dwellings of ancient Gormons from the wars long before the lands had split and both Gormons and Rauks once shared this land in bitter warfare.

They pass through a long and winding valley for some distance, and upon the other side, off to the right, fused into the rock side, is a large massive stone face, as though it had been carved into the piles of jagged boulders and crumbled debris that surround the area for miles and miles.

'Look there, an ancient statue! It must have been enormous!' A Civilian exclaims.

A stout Gormon walks forward and taps on the tip of the nose with a hammer. 'It's a Rauk...no doubt been here for some time.'

Nilta looks closely at the massive face, an uneasiness comes over her. She turns to her brother.

'I can feel it too Nilta. This Rauk has not been fallen for long...and all this, this fallen rubble and ruin around us, the silence this place casts off from it...a battle was fought, but there seems to be something wrong here...' Diin says.

'You said the Rauks were warring beings, what is so odd about finding this one?' Aura asks.

'I feel another presence here. As Agonan said, I feel the Destroyer's hand has grown further beyond the realms of Aura. What we have here, is self-genocide! It appears the Rauks slaughtered each other, into annihilation...and it appears as though there are none left...maybe I'm mistaken...I hope I am.'

'So where are we to go? Agonan warned us...he said there would be no shelter here for us anywhere, and now that I see this place with my own eyes, I believe him.' Aura replies.

Diin remains silent, then speaks to the rest of them. 'Master Arctalus...when he was telling Nilta and I about Raukmar...he mentioned there is one place, over beyond the Lands of Gargoth...a sheltered, hidden place secret to all but the wisest of beings, and even they know not of the ancient Asyndian's lair...'

He looks at the puzzled faces upon them all. 'Yes, the black Asyndian Naumokron once kept an ancient workshop where he...experimented with, well...I'm not even sure what, but it is there, over beyond that far rim, beyond the plains of the ancient Rauk King the plains were named after, where once his fortress, so large and beyond all measure, could be seen from outside the vast spaces of the Galakaos...this...is where we are heading...to this secret place of Naumokron's.' Diin says.

'I'm not going there!'

'Nor shall I...'

'Neither are we...not to the place of the black Asyndian!'

The crowds shout out in protest and dismay.

'Those halls have been deserted for many eons...Naumokron has since lingered among the urchins in the Greywaste! There is nothing to fear there, only scrolls and writings upon a bloodied, recorded history scribed by the hand of the ancient one himself!' Diin retorts.

The Gormons, Civilians, and Asyndians were in an uproar for hours and hours, until Aura maintained them all and calmed them down, though the idea of going to this place terrified them, being outside the safety of walls and shelter was no better, and after an arduous affair, complied and followed along with Aura, Diin, and Nilta as they head off further north in the direction of the lands of King Gargoth.

Part XXVII:

Lands of Gargoth

~

Across these mighty planes, stretched outwards far beyond these deserts and desolation that lay before them, are a scattered range of mountains with no rhyme or reason, massive shards of boulders and natural citadels crumbled into heaps and piles some miles high.

Diin stops and the others look upon him, his head bowed and brows rise up, something troubles him. Nilta places a hand upon his shoulder, worried about her brother, for his legs begin to tremble, and she helps him sit upon the large rock nearby. Aura walks over to him, and kneels down next to him and Nilta, making sure everything is ok.

'My apologies, lady Aura, for dragging behind...but it's this place, this air is heavy...and tastes of war, and...and genocide...something happened here, a great war not so long ago...took place upon this ground, and these mountains, are not crags nor cliffs, these are the bodies of those who fought. These barbarians, the Rauks, they battled one another until none were left standing....I....' Diin goes silent, and looks around, the others look around with him.

'What is it Diin?' Aura asks.

'I, I hear something…' He falls down onto his knees, and listens into the dirt. '…I, there is a thud…the sound of something…beating, like a heartbeat!' Diin exclaims.

The others stay silent, the crowds are nervous, wondering what is going to happen next. 'Everyone please…we need to listen to know where this sound is coming from…please stay calm, we will be fine!' She tries to settle her people down the best she can.

'I feel it getting louder…' Diin places his hands over the ground.

Then, from out of the grey, decaying sky, a cry for help is heard. Aura, Nilta, and the vast crowds of Civilians, Gormons, and Civilians look above to see a young Asyndian heading for them. Aura recognizes him all too well, for young Hrend is heading in their direction, and not far behind, closing in, is the shadow of his father and the several other black Asyndians of Dregor, still in pursuit of him. Aura is terrified, for Hraʒon has already proven his power over her and the rest of them. Hrend lands and rushes to Aura's side.

'Lady Aura…I have nowhere else to go…I'm so sorry…I don't want to put you and your own in danger…please…I don't know what else to do!' Hrend clutches to her side in tears.

Aura grips tightly around the young Asyndian. 'Stay by my side Hrend…' Hraʒon and the Asyndians of Dregor land ahead of them, only ten feet away, and Diin follows the heartbeat over to one of the large rocks…where the sound is strongest…and he feels something begin to move. And the voice of Hraʒon…is making the quake become more intense.

'Coddle the child all you want! Because I'm going to kill all of you this time!' Hraƶon roars at the top of his lungs, as he and the other black Asyndians step closer and closer, until beneath their feet, the roar and rumble of the ground, stops them in their tracks, as the mountains above their heads, casts them over in shadow and large chunks of debris, crashes to the ground.

'It's alive...the rock is alive! Nilta, come help me!' Diin cries, rushing away, and Nilta helps pull him along.

'Everyone get back! Back over there!' Aura cries, picking up Hrend, and rushing away from the moving rock, and they all look back, gasping and crying in terror, as the rock takes on its true shape, and a huge being is formed, and upon the face, two huge black sullen eyes open and look down upon everything and everyone, the tiny beings that flee before him.

'My lady! What is it?!' One of the Civilian's cry.

'It is a Rauk, a titan of these lands! RUN!' Diin cries, and they get as far away as they can, only a steep drop upon the other side of them, keeps them from going any further beyond, and are trapped. Before them, the mighty Rauk rises up, higher and higher, some three, four hundred feet high, beyond the height of any mountain these Civilian Asyndian and Gormon eyes have ever seen. Only those of the ancient days long before have ever laid sight upon these huge beings of the rock lands in the north.

The Rauk looks down at Hraƶon and his Asyndians of Dregor with detestment and furrowed stone brows, he raises his large, titanic foot and slams it down upon the black Asyndians...crushing all, but one, for Hraƶon is seen flying away in the distance. The Rauk, roars with anger, and extends its mighty arm, and with its huge hand, grasps Hraƶon in its grasp, and crushes the Asyndian to pieces of bone, skin, and feather into an unrecognizable, mangled mess, and scrapping the remains away, off of the top of a nearby mountain.

'Dregooooorrrrr Fiiiilttttthhhhh...!' He roars, then turns his curiosity back to the frightened, tiny beings who were trying to flee from him. They watch as the roaring maw, turns into a slight grin, upon the Rauk's face.

'Hmmmm....my little ones...' He sniffs the air. 'You don't have...the smell of...Dregorrrr...upon you, there for...you have no reason....to be...frightened....those Dregor...are dead...now...' The Rauk spoke in long, drawn out sentences.

None dare to move, terrified of this beings titanic size, larger than any tower or citadel within the lands of Othetica, Fausengard...even larger than the obsidian fortresses in the south far beyond the Skahljah deserts. The Rauk kneels down to see the tiny beings better, and noticing their fear, holds out his long arm and fingers of solid stone and ancient dirt and minerals colored of a dull, ceramic marble.

Aura looks around at her people, terrified and afraid. One of the Civilian women screams at the large hand as it draws near.

'It means to smash us it does!' She screams.

The Rauk recoils back. Just as he gets up to walk away, he hears a tiny voice calls up to him. He looks down with curiosity to the miniscule Civilian woman. Aura tells Hrend to stay back with the others as she runs forward.

'Please! Please wait!' Aura rushes out to the Rauk.

'Hmmmm...hello...little one...I can't say I...recognize what you are...you appear to be...one of the ancient

Gooorrrrmooonnnn...but your much...smaller...' The Rauk spoke in long drawn out words.

'My name is Aura...I am a Civilian of Runegard...I understand you are a mighty Rauk...have you a name?!'

He looks carefully at Aura, his brows furrow curiously, then a wide smile curves across his stone lips. 'Hmmmm...I can't say that...I ever heard of a...Civilian before...Hmmm...' He furrows more, holding his finger to his brain, in deep concentration, trying to remember something, a long and ancient memory, a thought left far away back in the recesses of a time long past, separated by epochs. 'You...little friend of Urohgin...protector of these other tiny ones...you say your name is...Aaaaauuuurrrraaaaa...Hmmmmmm....I've heard that name....before.....sounds so....familiar....'

She looks at him wide-eyed. 'Ur...Urohgin? Is that your name?'

'Hmmmm...Yes...Aura... Urohgin in your...language...in old Raukish...it's a much...much...longer name...that takes days...and days to say...I, along with all the others...we arose from these...grounds...at the very beginning...the first ones...the oldest...' He ponders in his mind all the old memories his vast mind can still remember. 'Did you know...Aura...that Rauks were the first to see the sky...the sky when it was like an ocean...blue and endless....no clouds, just...blue...'

His voice begins to fill with grief. 'Then...the skies filled with fire, covered over by shadow and a shrieking roar from the jaws of some...beast or creature, a...being unlike anything...it was *HER*!...our lands charred...vegetation burned into...this desolation you see...that was when...the HEXAGUS...came forth...from that creatures maw...!' His roar shakes the earth around them. 'They conquered and destroyed everything...took my brothers and sisters as slaves to...build their fortresses and walls...made from corroded, black rock, a mineral I have never seen...a sickness they brought with them...!

For eons they ruled...they created their armies, the Dregor...marched upon lands of trees and wilderness, boiled oceans, killed and devoured everything...until...until that day came...the light pierced the sky and the flames opened up...the darkness was subsided...and from the outside...of space and time...twelve...twelve came...led by a mighty warrior in armor of gold and bright flames...his face shrouded by a helmet of...pure light...wings of a magnificent hawk or bird of some kind...that was when.'

Then, he remembered what he was trying to earlier. 'Auroras! That was what they were...!' He looks to Aura. 'Is...are you...are you little one...an Aurora! Come to bring...light to this...desolation as before?'

She doesn't know what to say. She only smiles at the Rauk, heart-felt by his tale. She bows his head to him. 'I...I wish I could be...such a figure that you speak of...but I have come to save my people, for we are refugees of our realm.'

The brows of the Rauk raise a little, his coal eyes seem to close a bit, as he nods in understanding.

'I regret I am nearly helpless of my own kind...and those who are by my side are those who remain loyal to the lands of Aura and the sacrifices of those who made it possible for us to get this far. I fear you and all of us...are one the same...we are all that's left of our kind, for our lands too, have been desolated.'

Urohgin nods in understanding, but rubs his chin in thought. 'Hmmmm...I feel what you...little Civilian named Aura...say is true for now....but...I have lived for...many...many...lifetimes and epochs...I...one who has...walked since the beginning...I have seen...many things...events...many curiosities...I feel...that you and your own...did not just come here...by chance...no...I think you were driven here...by another purpose...for it is...no accident you have come...I think...events have been set...in motion...

He lowers his head closer. 'Your people are loyal for their hope they see in you...for this world...it seems...has little to none left...for you who call yourselves refugees...little Civilians...Gormons...Asyndians...' He looks around at all of them, then looks up to the darkness that broods above their heads, then smiles down at Aura and the entire group. 'Take...heart little ones...it may not...appear as so...but I think...the skies have parted...once again...'

A faint smile, as fearful as they are in the presence of this mighty giant, comes over all the faces of the group, alleviating the sorrow just a little, as though a small glimmer of light has broken through to them. Aura looks up to the Rauk in awe, for she cannot help but love the enthusiasm of this gentle giant as he appears to be within his heart. Even though he is the last of his kind, he still keeps a certain positive attitude through all of this, even after being buried within the ruins of his brothers and sisters, brethren he had known since the dawn of time, who have perished around him by some looming darkness, no doubt influenced by the hand of the Destroyer, he still believes in that same piercing hope that was shown to him epochs ago, and she is amazed, that he sees such hope in so small of beings, far inferior in size and power compared to his own.

'And now, my lady Aura...how can I... Urohgin, last of the...Rauks...help you...?'

'We are heading over these plains, for there is a black colossus, a hidden fortress far beyond these rims that we must

401

reached...this place once belonged to a dark Asyndian...one who was once a...Dregor.'

'Errrrrrrr!' He growls at the name and the ground beneath them shakes once again. 'I...am familiar with...were you speak...a dismal place...kept in shadows...shadows that were once...my lands! Hmmmm....these plains are long, you and your company...would long perish before getting...half way across...you would not survive the heavy rain storms that persist eternally at the old fortress of our...once king...for the lands...are flooded into oceans...fathoms deep...so odd, there has been no rain for millenniums, until now...' He looks around at them. 'You will all fit in my hands...I will carry you there...to Na`bata...is its name...I have not been there in eons...not since this...horrific fighting...had taken place...'

Urohgin lowers down both of his wide palms, and they proceed onto the cold rough surface of his hands. They are lifted high into the air, hundreds of feet off the ground, close to Urohgin's chest so he can keep an eye on them and make sure nothing happens to them, taking great care as his fingers curl over top their heads high above.

They traverse over plains and continents, across miles and miles of land filled with jagged spires and ancient ruined fortresses of faded obsidian, once built for the dreaded Hexagus Lords. He trudges through the vast oceans, as they reach up his waist, the winds howl and blow wildly, as strong gusts shake the giant back and forth as he tramples across the miles and miles of vast seas, the lightning and thunder roars all about them ceaselessly, as they hurdle round each other under the cover of the Rauk's fingers that gives them shelter from these wild storms, unable to sleep haunted by the nightmares and shadows they feel swirling around them, haunting their thoughts and memories...their eyes still see the horrific gaze of terror within their thoughts of Hondor...a nightmare they will never forget...Aura still sees the chaos, the death and destruction...the slaughter...the abyss of the Great Divide...as the beast falls...falls deep into the yawning unknown. In her bitter sleep, she stands over the edge...she tries to step away...as the huge bestial hand lumbers up over her...grasping her...pulling her down, as she falls...falls...falls...

'NO!' She awakens screaming, as others watch on, startled by her cries.

'Aura...what is it?' She hears Hrend's voice, as he has stayed close by her side throughout the journey.

She looks around wide-eyed, relieved to be awake, yet the brooding sky above them, dulls her spirits. 'Hrend...I...I saw...him!'

'It was a nightmare...you've been asleep now for a good while.' Hrend replies, helping her sit up.

'Is everyone ok...have we reached Na`bata?'

'Not yet...it'll still be some time yet. But we did make it passed the storms ok, and over the oceans. You missed it though, we passed the fortress of King Gargoth, its spires reached far up over the water...a dreary looking place, covered in sludge and great chunks of it were crumbled away, but still, the architecture, at one time, would have been very impressive to witness, though it has seen better days I'm sure.'

She holds her hand over her head, feeling feverish and chilled by the storms. 'But everyone's ok though?'

'Yes, everyone's fine...some are a little nauseous by the water...but we're all well.'

Diin and Nilta walk over to her, Diin takes off his cape and hands it to Nilta to place over Aura. 'Here, take this my lady, you need it more than I. Are you feeling ok, you were having the most horrific dream it seems?'

'I'll be fine Diin, thank you.' She replies.

He leans in closer. 'It was about *Him*...wasn't it...Hondor...' He inquires.

She says nothing, only nods in agreement.

'Seems he's still terrorizing us still...for I've seen him too in my mind...'

She looks at him with sunken eyes.

'I have an uneasy feeling...something is twisting my gut into knots...I don't know how else to describe it...but I...' Diin goes quiet.

Aura looks closer to Diin, then turns to Nilta, who looks away. She tightens the cape more snug around the lady's shoulders. Aura reaches out and grabs Diin by the hand.

'What is it Diin...is...is he...!?'

'I don't know my lady...I just don't...'

'You do know! Tell me!' Aura insists.

Diin releases himself from her grasp and starts to walk away with Nilta guiding him. 'I will not trouble you anymore...try to keep warm...this eternal darkness seems to be getting colder...' And they both walk away to be alone, with Nilta's arm around her brother.

Hrend sits down with Aura. 'What was wrong with that Civilian my lady...he seemed very worried about something.' He inquires.

'It's nothing Hrend...we'll be ok, not to worry.' And she puts her arm around him. 'Thank you for your company.'

After some time, Urohgin calls down to Aura. 'My lady...you must come see this...have your Asyndian friend... bring you up to my shoulder...'

'Can you carry me up there Hrɛnd?'

He spreads out his wings with bold, strong fashion to stretch them out. 'I think so.' And he lifts her up under the arms and they fly up to the right shoulder of Urohgin. Here she looks out over the view, for miles and miles around them.

'This...lady Aura...this was once my...land...my home...Na`bata...is still a ways off...over there due...north...west...'

She takes in the silence and the serene wisps of wind that blows across her body and through her hair. 'It's so peaceful...I imagine it was once very beautiful...before all this happened.'

'Hmmm...it was...very beautiful...it was once...' His voice drops with sorrow. 'My land was...pure...everything...untouched by the filth, by the destructive force of those...beasts...those black beings of chaos! Everything...was so pure...before they came! Rauks are a war-like race...we always were...but...there was...honor...in our ways...take a look at all this...lady Aura...this is not honorable...this is...desecration!'

Part XXVIII:

Guardian of the Secrets

~

Within his mighty hands, the Rauk carries Aura, Diin, Nilta, and all the Civilians and Gormons within his grasp, while the Asyndians, led by Hrend, fly along among the wide strides of the hulking, lumbering colossus. Aura stands among the shoulders of the giant, looking out over the remains of the long lost and ancient civilization, if one can call a clan of such a war-torn beings a civilization, of these Rauk tribes and clans who once pummeled and battered each other, down into nothing more than fallen idols and piles of boulders and gravel.

'How much further is Na`bata?' Aura asks. She looks down below, into the palms of the giant, looking upon her tired and weary people, and the lost eyes upon their faces which either sleep or daze out into the nothing which surrounds them.

The Rauk replies in his slow, drawn out answer. 'We still have a ways…for Raukmar…our land…is vast, much larger than your home that you are used to…' He replies.

She seats herself upon a flat edge on his shoulder, her back against a large stone wall. The entire shoulder quakes and shakes as he takes each massive step, and the echo of his stomp thunders and thuds into the sky.

'If your people…wish to make camp…the dirt and gravel upon my palms…is very sturdy, my lady…' He adds to the conversation. 'They will need their full strength before the journey comes to its end…'

She calls up to Hrend and asks him to pass along the message to the others below. He carries away her orders on swift wings, soaring down the long column of the Rauk's arm, the size of a mountain cliff, and after a time, she can see the makeshift tents and fires being started.

'The flames do not bother you?' She asks.

He lets out a low chuckle. 'No…I can't feel such pain or fatigue. They…will be…fine…a fire will…do them good…for it is very…cold up here…beyond the Divide…' The Rauk replies to her.

The time feels to drag by as slow as the Rauk's wide stride, meanwhile Aura asks their traveler more questions, as she ponders with the darkening skies above them. She feels the chill upon her bruised flesh, the air is becoming painful.

'Sit within my ear…dear lady…then I will…be able to hear your questions better…your voices are so faint to me…and you will not be so…exposed to these winds…' The Rauk says.

Aura tries to take hold of the rocky steps and cliffs, but her hands are too cold, her arms too soar, as she struggles there is a voice above her.

'Let me help you, my lady.' And Hrend gently takes hold of Aura and lifts her up to the massive hole where the Rauk's ear is, and both of them duck down right inside.

'Are the others still up there?' Aura asks.

'A few…most of them have joined the others below…there's really nothing to see…just old rock for miles…'

'HMMMMMMM…..' Grumbles the Rauk.

Hrend panics, 'I'm…I'm sorry master Rauk…sir…I didn't mean…'

The Rauk laughs. 'It's perfectly…fine…I knew what you meant…' He replies.

'What does Na`bata mean, master Rauk?' She asks, rubbing her shoulders to keep warm.

'Hmmm…I don't know…Rauks…we have no language…we have to sense for words or…dialect…' He replies. 'It's an…Asyndian word…your friend…may know…'

She looks upon young Hrend, who has his wings wrapped tightly around himself as a barrier to the cold wind.

'Do you know what Na`bata means Hrend?' She asks.

'I was in the middle of my studies when everything happened…give me a moment…' He thinks for a second. 'It means…it's a secret place…yes, a secret place, so wherever we're going, was to be a secret from the eyes of others.

'How did you know about this place, master Rauk?' Aura asks.

'Na`bata…is within my old territory…Rauks…as you witness here…are extremely territorial…one morning, before the sight of the first star upon the horizon…a lone being…an Asyndian…he looked like your friend, he landed upon my head…and it awoken me…I attacked him, but…he was much too smart…and too fast…after many days of trying to smash this creature…I gave up…and in that moment, I could hear him…I know not exactly what transpired…but he spoke…he spoke to my mind…he said to me to let him stay here…I don't know what drew him to that place, but it was a large hill of granite and untouched by the corrosion of weather…but he demanded that spot…and he promised me…that if I leave him alone…he would give me…knowledge…the ability to speak…'

'Were you the only Rauk who could speak our language?' Hrend asks.

'Hmmm…yes, I think so…' He replies.

'Who was this Asyndian you speak of?' Aura asks, even though she knows, she wanted to understand what the Rauk knew.

'He never did…tell me his name…but his wealth of knowledge he shared…was incredible…I learned so much of my kind, and of all of your Gormons and Asyndians, no Civilians however…though I find your language the easiest to speak…the others I have forgotten, they gave me too…much…trouble…but that smell…' He grumbled. 'He had that foul smell upon him…the same as those…others!'

'What happened to him…this Asyndian?' She asks.

'He was here…for many…many years…eons…many seasons and days went by…I lost track…then, just before my brothers all fell to battle…the Asyndian left…and I never saw him again…'

'Do you know what he did or what he was doing?'

'Hmmmm…As I learned more thoughts and words…I began to inquire and watch…observe…he called the

409

word…because…with my new words…I was never allowed to question…but I watched what…he would do. He would often leave and return with strange and…unusual items…I know not…what these things were he brought…sometimes they were pieces of parchment…in books…or rolled…sometimes large…sacks…and bundles…he would bring living things…things that move, like you and me…'

'What of the other Rauks?' Hrend asks.

'I focused my time to…learn…and to…watch this Asyndian and…what he would do…while my brothers fought around my territory…I know not why…but they never…after he came…did come around my territory…'

'Fear…maybe…Asyndians were always performing experimentations and creating odd and unusual contraptions…I wonder what he was really up to?' Hrend replies.

'Perhaps we'll never know.' Aura says.

'Hmmm…perhaps…' The Rauk could not relate, because fear and emotion was not existent to him.

The tales fell silent, Hrend had drifted into sleep, and Aura was still awake for a time, then she to, fell into sleep. And the Rauk carried them on throughout the rest of the night. Then, there was a sudden halt, and she awoke. Hrend was gone, now flying around with the other Asyndians above, he could see them up ahead, circling around in the sky, around a large structure. She looks down and sees the Rauk's arms are outstretched like a massive bridge, to the opening of the massive granite structure, a large dome in shape carved out of the solid piece of mineral. The Gormons and Civilians walk across the fingers to reach the other side, with Diin and Nilta keeping behind.

'My lady…we have…arrived…' The Rauk says.

The remnants of the last remaining citizens of Runegard walk across the large outstretched hands of the Rauk in a large crowd, Aura walks behind them, along with Hrend, Diin and Nilta beside her. They walk along the way and come to vast, tall entrance, the guardian sentries, the stone idols of long forgotten Asyndian denizens have crumbled away, and only the large stone talons of their feet remain left at the base of the area. The mighty stone doors standing hundreds of feet high are ajar, and a powerful, strong and potent smell of must and decay pulsates in waves from the inside. The others cover their faces in sickness and disgust. They refuse to enter.

'I for one, will not go …it smells as though something still lives within these dank, decrepit halls!' One of the Civilians cries. 'We were better off back in that hole in the ground!' A Gormon shouts from among the crowds.

'Hrend, help me up to one of those platforms…' Aura asks, and the young Asyndian flies her up to stand upon one of the mighty bases of the crumbled statues. She speaks out to her people.

'My dear Civilians, Gormons, and Asyndians…you have been so brave thus far, and have been through so much…it is our union and all of us staying together, and seeing our situation through that has allowed us to come this far…you have never given up on me…and I have nor will I, ever give up on you! I understand your fears, for no one, not one of you, deserves what has happened, but we cannot change or undo what is done, and we must keep moving forward! This place, it seems, is to be our new home for some time, I know we have moved and moved, and moved, homeless like nomads, always moving on, as we watch our homes and our families die around us! You do not have to come with me, for I will go in myself, and see what is inside these ancient halls…I will not make you come with me!'

Hrend sets her back down upon the ground, the crowds of people surround her and hope for her return as she prepares to enter into this deserted colossus. Many cry for her, and many weep, many worry. Through the crowds, Nilta leads Diin by her side, and the two stand before her.

'Nilta and I are coming…' Diin says.

'I do not want you in their Diin…it could be treacherous, and…' Aura replies, but Diin cuts her off in mid-sentence.

'These eyes may be blind my lady, but my mind is not…I can sense even what the darkness cannot hide. Don't worry for me, Nilta is here…we can handle what's to come.' Diin replies, and Nilta nods in agreement to her brother's words.

'Very well… Hrend, I will need you to come with us.'

He stands at attention, 'I wouldn't do otherwise, I will gladly stand by the Lady Aura no matter what, you helped me escape from the grasp of The Destroyer, saved my life…and I will stand by you no matter what!' He replies will great enthusiasm.

Aura looks upon the great titanic Rauk, he looks back down upon her. 'My…Lady…'

'You have proven yourself to me to have great loyalty, and you would have no objection to looking over my people while I'm gone?' She asks.

'No…harm…shall befall them…' He replies in his slow grumble. 'May my joints and stones forever crumble to the surface of the world…and be one…with the dust…if I should fail you!'

She gives him a smile, for she has not smiled in many, many days, and is glad to see the Rauk upon her side. She looks back to Diin and Nilta, and the young Hrend. They may not be warriors, with exception to Nilta and her prowess and knowledge in a fight or battle, but she would not want to have any others by her side.

They proceed in with caution, through the narrow crack in the door, the faint flicker of torchlight guides them, but the darkness is so thick, it barely pierces the shadows ahead.

'Hundreds of years ago…I once heard that the famed Forgemaster…he created a special helmet, for the entire army of Othetica, that was able to pierce the blackest of night, the thickest darkness…' Diin says.

'What was the source of this mighty light?' Hrend asks, wide-eyed to hear the tale.

'My master once told me and my sister, that the light came from a sacred land, beyond Aura and Raukmar, far to the northwest, beyond the waters and seas…a land only the Asyndian knew of, where the craft of the builders and architects was beyond anything any Gormon or Civilian could ever conceive. It was these beings that helped instruct the Asyndians on creating and constructing civilization and establishing economy within Aura, a land that was, for a great many eons, lawless and barbaric, but as advanced these beings were, they were also blood-thirsty, and their punishments extreme…this was one of their many secrets, as to upholding law and order within our land…and the Asyndians took these ideas of execution, and implemented them for many, many millenniums. From what you told me Lady Aura, it appears…that Hondor, was the first attempt at an execution…in what must have been thousands and thousands of years, since Kar'durgra last felt the touch of blood upon its rocky soil.'

All fall silent at the thought of the voracious beast, the being of blood and slaughter, now falling for infinity down within the maw of the great divide, and there he will stay. Hrend breaks the silence and continues with the story.

'So how did the Forgemaster come across these sacred lights?' He asks.

'The Asyndians traded with these beings, and the lights would have been either a trade, or even gift of some kind from them...but as to how the Forgemaster would have got a hold of them...I don't know. I was told that he had many relations and connections among Gormons and Asyndians, so who or where and how he came about them, I don't know...nor does anybody else except him and those who gave them to him.'

'Who were these beings you speak of?' Aura asks.

'I don't know who they were, what they were, or if they even still exist...there was only a few mentions of them within scriptures and ancient writings, my master once told me that they were believed to be some colony of amorphous shapes that neither were born nor died, that they live within the deep subterranean realms that no eyes of anyone has ever seen before, deep, mighty caverns of citadels and oceans and mountain ranges, more vast and larger than what appears upon the surface of the world...Some say they are just like Asyndians and they live further up, beyond the clouds and space above in flying cities, much like Thylesian, only bigger and more grand.'

They look on in wonder, never knowing that a race could exist older than the Rauks and Asyndians.

'But all of this is speculation, and the writings are so old, it's impossible to say for sure what is real, and what the writers of the ancient world have altered and changed. many don't even believe the Forgemaster existed, but our master

414

Arctalus-Hon was there, he remembers what happened, he seen the events of the Second Grey Age take place, the collapse of Athilnovia, the Final War, the Hexagus walked upon Aura soil…the many Asyndians who made the long walk to the Great Divide, for they lost their wings and could no longer fly, so they…'

He stops himself, remembering the presence of the young Asyndian in their company.

'I am sorry.' Diin says, and Nilta guides him along, they have almost reached the end to this long tunnel of darkness.

They come to a mighty opening, a large archway entering into a vast room of darkness. Diin stops at the foot of the stairs that leads upwards.

Nilta looks at her brother inquisitively, knowing something is wrong, but she is unable to read his posture and his emotions upon his face, it's a twisted mesh of confusion with fear, yet awe, all at the same time.

'What's the matter…?' Aura asks.

'It's…it's impossible…there is something…alive in there!' He exclaims in a low tone.

They listen within, and soon enough…they begin to hear something, a low grumble coming from within, echoing throughout the room, the walls and the floor reverberate with the sound and the tremors of something large…something growling in the darkness.

They proceed up the stairs, and make their way, slowly, into the room. It is impossible to tell for sure, just how big this room is, but judging by the echoes across the walls and ceiling, it is massive.

They move along together, and come to a halt at the far end of the room, where they reach a large stone structure, the growling is all around them, and much louder as though it were right in front of them, but they keep a lookout around them, that seems to be some twenty or thirty feet across from tip to tip and twenty feet high. Across the front of the structure, there is, chiseled into the stone, a vast line of script, written in what appears to be ancient Asyndian.

'Hrend, are you able to read what this says?' Aura asks.

Hrend takes a closer look, though nervous to get near the growling stone slab. Aura holds the torch up to the lettering, and Hrend reads the words as best he can. 'This writing is so old, it's hard to tell, but I think it says'…and he follows her along the way, until he reaches the end of the sentence. '…beware of…the Guardian…Hiidum, has awakened, and blood will fill this room!' And as he reads the last of the words, a large claw, three times his size and width, with three huge nails at the end, hangs over the top of the stone slab, and reveals itself. The growling, which they now realize, was snoring, ceases, and the beast yawns, rattling the walls of this structure. Aura holds up the torch to a massive face that's almost Civilian-like, with whiskers upon the snout and yawning jaws like ivory claymores and long ears that slump over the sides of its head, one held back from laying on it during its sleep.

The beast looks down upon the horrified faces that look up towards it, and the creature lets out a low growl, as he sniffs the air about them.

'Hmmmm…you smell different, you are not the dark Asyndian…Hmmmm…what are you then? Intruders, come to steal the master's secrets? Come to take from the specimens…?' He falls silent. 'Then, you are welcome to them…for it has been…hmmmm…I don't know how long it's been since the Asyndian was last here. I feel, my guard duties…have long been done with, for I have not seen the master, oh for millenniums, maybe eons…I can't remember, it has been so long ago…'

He looks at how these visitors…these intruders, all look at the other, then at him in confusion, as though they did not understand a word he said, though he spoke in the common tongue of the Civilian.

'I apologize…if you did not understand, are you Gormon? You look rather small for Gormons, from what I understand, the Gormons are supposed to be large folk of great height, strength, and wisdom, though they speak in the common tongue of the Southern Lands, er…Aura you call it, yes. Shall I speak in ancient Fausengard, or maybe…maybe you are Asyndians perhaps? The young fellow there looks like one, though you do not cast the menacing eye like my master…as for the rest of you, I have never seen the likes of you before.

Aura steps forward to speak. 'I am a Civilian, my name is Aura, after the land of the Auroras that once ruled, this is Diin and Nilta, who are also Civilian…and this is Hrend, he is an Asyndian…'

Hiidum's ears perk up, and he looks at her in confusion. 'A Civilian…what is a Civilian…is there another species of being my master never told me of…have I been asleep so long?' He holds his wide jaws within his paw inquisitively and places the other along the slab, not moving from his place upon the large oblong stone monolith. 'I am intrigued, my little Civilian…please, I am curious, tell me more!' Hiidum grew more and more excited, as Aura and Diin told him their entire story, and Diin even went into more detail about the long history of the Civilians, he smiled at them with glee, bearing his jaws within his wide grin as they spoke.

417

They told him of the monster Hondor, and their flight from the land of Aura, the collapse of the bridge over the Great Divide, and Hondor's fall down into the darkness, along with the last Aurora, Agonan.

'So...that is why we are here mighty guardian, my people need a place to go, shelter from the terrors outside, until we can reestablish that which was destroyed, our once promising land of all Gormons, Asyndians, and Civilians.'

'You delight me with your tale, and your manners...little Civilians. I would be delighted to have you and your others among me as my guests of honor, for it has been so long since these halls had seen any life in them.'

They smile gladly, but Aura steps forward, carrying an authority about her.

'I will ask you this one question, mighty Hiidum, guardian of the secrets...my people have been through many hardships, many perils, have seen more death than any being deserves to see within our short lifespan...do I have your promise now, that you, a beast within my people's eyes, though as mighty and as honorable as you carry yourself, one who has been asleep for so long, and has not, I presume...had a feast himself I imagine for many eons past...I must have your promise, you will not touch nor harm, nor even look upon my own...as a potential feast...we have been hunted down long enough, and I have a position to uphold, within the eyes of my people and a responsibility of their trust in my position...for I am the only chance this world of ours has for survival...and to see us through into a new dawn...'

Hiidum holds himself up, puffs his chest with pride. He looks down upon the Civilian woman with a deep stare.

'My lady...you have my word, for my allegiance to my old master has long been broken...and I will swear, as long as you and your people are within these halls...then may none of them be harmed...for, if I may be so bold to say...I seek out larger game to fulfill my cravings...I have no interest, in your tiny, fragile bodies...' He bows his head as an oath. 'This, I swear by!'

Aura and rest of them bow to the great beast. 'I thank you, mighty Hiidum, on behalf of all those within the lands of Aura.' And Hiidum nods back to them.

'Please, bring your people...I am interested to see more of these...Civilians, and to see the Gormons again would be delightful...as well as the Asyndians!'

Aura prepares her people, and they enter into the great fortress of Raukmar. They stand in the now lit room, filled with the starlight of torches, within this vast and endless space, above and around them. They stand in awe and in fear of the great and mighty Hiidum, as he introduces himself to all these fascinating beings, all these new and interesting faces within his cat-like eyes.

'Greetings to all of you, and welcome into this sanctum...please make yourself comfortable...and I do apologize for the odor...'

The Civilians and Gormons look on, not sure what to make of this massive creature...for he and the mighty Rauk, have been the only ones not to try and kill them and eat them, and the manners of this beast, while welcome, they feel a need to keep their eyes on him...as does Aura, for she has been betrayed one too many times, and will not, if she can help it, be betrayed again, but she must do what she can and take what allies still remain in this bare, forsaken new world to all of them.

The company look about the area, finding old supplies, able to setup makeshift shelters and beds. Some of the

Gormons find an old food store deeper down, with enough dried food to last for a time, and this brings some feeling of fortune and happiness to the bleak attitude of all, but still they are without a home, and while a shelter over their heads is welcome, they still can't help but feel, unease…this is not a place they can call home, but they know that lady Aura has been through even more than them, and she has done what she is able, she has helped them escape captivity, guided them safely over this barren land, and have found them a place to stay, they do not want to question her rulership, she has stayed with them, she never abandoned them, though they all know, they can see that feeling within the eyes around them…they do not belong, they feel no rest, in these halls, upon these stone floors, and …the presence of this beast that calls himself Hiidum, he scares them…terrifies the children…even the brawn fierceness of the Gormons, they show uneasiness in his presence.

Aura and the others have been spending their time within a sectioned off room down the far eastern hall of the fortress, a smaller, sectioned off room that has had its secrets hidden away within for many eons past. She emerges every once in a while to check upon her people, to see how the young are doing, some of the elders among the group have fallen ill, and she brings strange liquids and powders within vials to them, ancient medicines and tonics she and the others have found deep within this room, and the ill are maintained, though the sickness of the loss of loved ones, friends, and the homeland…can never be cured. Many have inquired about what was in this room they have found, but she can say no more than… *"…we are looking for answers."* and then she will wander away, with that intent look upon her face, that glazed over determination in her eyes, the same look when…Hondor stood before them all, frantic and determined…that wonder, the why… and she would go away for a while. Until that day, she, Diin and Nilta, and the young Asyndian…they arose from the dark halls, with the look of determination upon her face, for she had found what she sought, but there was the gleam, the raised brow, for her business has not concluded, and she made her announcement, that she was leaving, she had to go elsewhere.

They did not want to see her leave, not here...not to leave them with the beast called Hiidum, for the people did not trust the Raumkat with the face of a Civilian, they did not trust that glimmer within its bright orange eyes.

She orders the young Asyndian to stay behind, that he is needed here to protect the Asyndians, Gormons, and Civilians, the last remaining survivors of Aura. She whispers into his ear, Hrend complies with a nod, and Diin and Nilta follow behind her, as she heads for the entrance to the fortress, through the large double stone doors, and the three of them vanish beyond the light of the outside. Several among the Civilians inquire about what is going on, and Hrend assures them, that Aura will return, for she has gone to find the source, a way to restore their fallen civilization that Hondor has destroyed.

What he could not tell them, nor would he know how to explain, that she must unravel further answers as to what they were dealing with, what the coming of Hondor meant to Aura's downfall and the further understanding, of the ages fading under skies of darkness, and the deepening, yawning abyss...that is fast approaching, for it seems, there's still, a deeper, darker day yet to come...or Hondor was the key, a catalyst, a tool used for Naumokron's sick purposes and deviant reasons...in hopes of capturing all-encompassing rule and darkness, over the realm, to be...reborn into a new universe, a new episode of epochs...as the one, supreme being, over a universe of his own creation...

Part XXIX:

Origin

~

They come to a large wall of ruins, once a mighty citadel of the ancient Gormon, before the divide, and they resided within the Fausengard territories of Northern Aura. Those that were left in Raukmar, would not have survived long thereafter. They have not acquired the writings of the Asyndian at this point, so it was the massive wall drawings upon their stone castles and halls that they drew upon, to tell stories, and most of all, warn other tribes of Gormon or the Rauks, Nilta looks over the massive caricatures with wide eyes of curiosity. Aura reaches out and touches upon one scene, that reaches nearly two stories high above her, and stretches out some distance to the left and right of the ruin. Diin sits nearby upon a large fallen stone jutting from the ground, buried in deep to the soil.

'This area…there is much energy here, in the air, in the soil, all around us…I can see a scene play out behind my eyes, but it's too dark, I can't quite tell what is happening.' Diin says.

The mighty Rauk leans down and kneels by the tiny beings, his mass shaking the dirt as his large knee and leg touches ground, he squints hard to read the drawings that are incredibly tiny to him, he then removes a large circular piece of glass from a deep pocket within the cloth tied around his waist, and holds the glass up to his eye, and the drawings are magnified by a thousand times so he can clearly see what they are seeing. He reads the drawing from left to right, starting with a large black smear off to the side, then to a grouped cluster of a many-serpent head, the serpent eats the darkness…he skims forward to the end, where all rest in some depiction of a pit or ocean of some kind. He removes the glass away from his eye, then speaks to the others.

'Yes…master Diin…this particular piece that lady Aura has found…this is an early depiction…of our realm's origin, how it was created…and how it will end…' The Rauk speaks in a long, drawn out speech. 'It is good we have these still around, for my memory is so old and so worn, I can't remember much of anything…anymore…' He continued.

'The end…how does it all end? Does this tell our future, is it accurate?' Aura cries up to the Rauk.

The Rauk lets out a roaring sigh. 'The end…nobody knows for certain what will be the end, nor when it will occur…we only know the end…when we reach it, when it…happens…' He sighs again, then rises up, walks over to a nearby mountain and sits upon the summit, resting his back upon the peaks rising behind him, as though the mountain were a throne. 'Your end? No…I don't think so…you're still aware, you still have your people around, there's still some chances left…maybe many, maybe one…I am no seer nor prophet…but I know I am at my end…I have reached the end, the future of my kind…which is extinction…I hid away like a coward…as we killed one another, becoming rocks with the dirt…I should have perished with them…but I'm still here lingering, I guess I was supposed to encounter you tiny…citizens of the Aura-Land…but this is the last chapter for me and my kind, I will not go further on into this darkness…but I'd rather perish with a little light left to pierce the sky, dome of Tundrok above us…'

He looks down to his massive feet, his arms hang down to the ground as the knuckles run across the top of the rubble and dirt, as he drags them around not knowing what to do with himself.

The Daughter walks over to the moping Rauk, looks up to the giant, then speaks. 'What exactly happens in those paintings…what is this ending of drowning in darkness, where did this all start…I wish to hear more of the story…from the beginning!' She cries up to him. The Rauk wipes the muddy tears from his eyes, then looks curiously at the tiny Civilian woman.

'Are you…sure you wish to learn of our making, for it is a foul, foul story…for I warn you, it's not a tale of wonder, but of darkness…and sickness…'

She nods with agreement. 'Yes…please go ahead…'

'According to the legends, of the ancient Gormon…'

'…A great cataclysm burst forth into a realm, a realm were nothing but darkness, an ocean of tar and murky depths consumed everything…the twisted mesh of Wom took form, the mother…who wanted to see beyond the darkness, to see if there beyond…anything existed. Her massive jaws began to tear away at the night, eating the darkness away…and that's when the light…for the first time…touched the Galakaos, what the Rauks call "Dark-Realm".

Wom ate away all the darkness, and the light brightened the Galakaos, what we call "Light-Realm" or as you say…Arla, but deep within her…the darkness was taking over, making her ill. She regurgitates the darkness into the *light, back into the Galakaos...but it was not just the darkness that emerged from her guts, also born were the many realms...including Aura-Land, and many others, there were also, the first beings, the First-Ones...the children of Wom, the Hexagus, born of the sickness...and the Aurora's, born of the light. They were to maintain a balance between day and night, darkness and light, but it was the Hexagus who wanted to cover all of the realms in darkness and the Auroras wanted to preserve the beauty of the light in the sky.*

The Hexagus...the lords of dominion and order under darkness...the Aurora's...the protectors of balance and peace through light...

The Hexagus were to keep order over the realms...for the mother to regain them...to...eat them, then she will be well again...and when Wom regains her realms...she will be whole...she will be well again...for it was the sickness of Wom that has twisted the minds of the Hexagus...whether she will...what will happen...it said that the realms will drown in a pit...an ocean...Wom's ocean of despair...deep within her guts...'

'And the figures there...is that the battle...the battle between the Auroras and the Hexagus?' The Daughter points and asks.

The Rauk nods.

'The Hexagus are still around and we still fight a battle against them...this is not over yet...'

'But the Aurora's are all dead...Hondor has taken the last of them.' Diin says.

'What is this...Hondor?' The Rauk asks.

'A darkness that the Gormon's anticipated could happen...a legend of death...brought to life...HôɳdoʀR...their word for the end, the last.' Diin's voice drifts off into his thoughts.

'I've never heard of this being before....although...I do recall...yes...the ancient Gormon who once...inhabited these walls...used to call this...this story they called *HôɳdoʀR* to them...in their ancient tongue... *HôɳdoʀR* was the *"Final-Darkness"...when all the light...passes to grey...and grey would fade away...into black*...and you say this being...his name is Hondor? Hmmmmm....it all makes sense.'

'That horrid beast destroyed and devoured everything! Our realm, our lands! My people...close friends! That bastard killed them all! And now the darkness has taken him!' Aura cries.

'It all seems to clear now...even to my blind eyes!'

Aura looks to Diin puzzled, not understanding what he means at first.

'It's so simple...everything that has transpired! Wom creates darkness, then the Auroras grant unto us the light, the light of all our realms...the ancient wars, the first and second Grey Age...and now...now Hondor...and this telling of Wom returning to reclaim that which she has lost, her power...and with her power reclaimed! Then darkness would cover over all and chaos would reign supreme once again!'

'It's some form of prophecy...' Aura replies.

'A prophecy? Or fate, my lady? For it seems that Hondor is indeed a catalyst...a catalyst for something that will happen, is going to happen...look at the sky and what do you see around us?'

Aura looks to the sky, covered in not night, but something darker.

'You see what I see...nothing, for it is all dark, is it not? The sun, the light, it no longer exists to us...I don't know for certain what fate has befallen Hondor, but it seems he paved the way...in a sense...emptied the lands...as he was intended to...and it won't be much longer now I'm afraid...' Diin lowers his head.

'You believe this...you think that this...Wom is coming? That she will, as some old paintings say...will swallow us?!'

'Hmmmm.....' Urohgin grumbles.

'How else could this darkness be explained? The light has faded, it's gone! The age of grey is passed...and now...now we are in a time of darkness...' Diin concludes his thoughts. Nilta walks over and tries to comfort him.

'It...it can't be...' Aura holds her tears, and struggles to keep back the stress of hopelessness from taking over, thinking of her people, the struggle of her and all the realms inhabitants, all that have died...she refuses to let herself think...that all this death, this destruction...of her own...has to be and nothing more.

'I cannot...I will not let some ancient paintings nor some old story let these bastards! These Dregor and their minions...have their way with us, all for the sake of fate's judgment...!' She looks to Diin and Nilta, 'Will you Diin, will you Nilta? Will you just let this happen? Do you not have your own fate to decide? Fate did not tell you to live when you would have or should have died with your master! No! You lived because you chose to, you chose to arise from the rubble and find your way! Fate did not let me lead my own to this place, I did...and I had help, help from all of you, all of us did this together, not fate, or prophecies...Urohgin, you lived because you wanted to, you knew yourself it was not your time to perish with your own! Fate does not control us! We control ourselves!'

She stands tall among them, a feeling of old, her once proud, commanding confidence fills her within. 'We are alive for a reason!'

'And...what reason...is that my lady?' Urohgin asks.

'You said to me Urohgin...that the Auroras came and brought light to this place once overcome with darkness...what about the Hero of Ages, how he defeated and drove back the foes of Hexagus, Hmm? They stood against the impossible odds and so will we...I will once again see to it, that light returns once more!' She cries with pride in her voice. And the others look on wide eyed and with awe.

'How can we against such a fiend? One who can swallow worlds?' Diin replies.

She walks over to Diin and Nilta, stands proudly by their side, placing her arms around them. 'I don't know...I just don't know, but if we keep together as we have, I know we can see this through. We're still alive in this darkness...at least, that's a little something to brag about, is it not?'

They give a smile, something they have not done for some time, almost hurting their chapped, sore lips.

'We are no warriors or sacred heroes, my lady.' Diin says.

'No, but we carry the hearts and perseverance, my friends. Will you stand with me? Will you help me? I asked you once...you followed me this far...and now I ask you again, will you follow me further?' She asks.

Nilta bangs upon her chest with her fist with pride.

'Yes Nilta, you do carry the heart, as well as the sword arm of a warrior...Diin, you carry the mind and wisdom...'

'And me, my lady?' Urohgin asks. Admiring the strength and determination of this tiny little Civilian.

Se looks up to the Rauk and laughs. 'It's always good to have a big guy on our side that can crush Dregor with one stomp!'

A smile creases upon his boulder face.

'Urohgin, take us back to Na`bata...I want to be with my people. I'm worried about them around Hiidum. There is something about him I don't trust.'

He lowers down his hands, and the three of them climb upon them, as they are raised up and carried back to Na`bata, and the lair of Hiidum.

Along the way back, they ride upon Uroghin's shoulders and take in the vast view around them. Diin turns to her and speaks.

'You know my lady, before I was blind, when I could look up to the clouds, and see the vast blue and the sun of Lota, and watch the stars at night, I kept track of them, and I noticed, as time went on, for many years, that there were less and less stars in the sky. And I pondered, I thought to myself, that...what if this darkness we face, as you describe it, is not an enveloping black around this once bright, seeing eye of our realm, but what if...as Urohgin has told us, that Wom is swallowing all these stars, devouring these worlds out there...and we are the last...the last light in the Galakaos?'

'Then I say to you Diin, that any light that shines, is better than no light at all...the last light will shine the brightest.' She replies. And the thundering steps of the Rauk echoes off into the darkness as he traverses across the wasteland of his domain.

Part XXX:

Cry of Phantasms

~

Through the dismal, yawning abyss he falls, deeper and deeper, yet no closer to the end of infinity's road, the tip of the nail, upon the finger of fates twisted hand. Into the black further, as black as the mind of this monster. Through his eyes, the shadows swirl round as the violent storm rages within his mind.

A fall of years, a fall of eons, who can tell, and down and down he goes, deeper and deeper still. Agonan has long passed from sight, swallowed away, taken into the abyss, vanquished by the eternal shadows which dwell in this deep dark.

The shadows cannot win, cannot overtake...what is far worse, far more darker and terrifying than them...for when Hondor falls...when Hondor falls, he will rise once again!

Even the Divide is not deep enough, to bury this creature's horrors, far away and deep within its eternal vaults and chasms into an endless drop. Hondor empowers the darkness, for he is darkness, Hondor fills these depths...for the depths of his slaughter and decimation, rain into an ocean of blood that reach down and down into endless fathoms, with waves that tower far above the skies and the fill the Galakaos, with the sensation of terror...terror that this beast inflicts upon realms, for Aura will be just a taste, a sip...a sip from the chalice of...all, and it will not be long, until he swallows his last, disgusting drop.

And deep within the beast's mind, Hondor's eyes pierce through the darkness within, lightning and piercing scourge with flashing lights, but there is not a sound, only the deafening silence...

***

Back in the past, in the faint memories and nightmares on the horizon of his being, black wings unfurl and cast shadows against stone and iron walls, riveted with bolts, thick and stinking of spoiled oil, as the maker stands before him in torchlight that melts the sickened green wax about the cluttered room, a room with shelves and desks lined with ancient manuscripts and scribbled notes, upon the walls hang diagrams painted in thick black ink upon crumbled parchment. He watches that damned Asyndian pace back and forth across the room, as the images become clearer and clearer, the lens within each eye in focus...

"KASTHAK...DOULLL!!!!" The Asyndian roars in these deep catacombs and dungeons, and from his palm held into the air, a jagged bolt of light rages forth in barrages as it strikes upon the flesh, and a scream races from the dark and pierces the scene of his memories, as they now stand in front of him, he is there...he can remember.

"KASTHAK...UUUNNNN....TOOTTTHHHAAAA!!!"

His flesh begins to boil over, and the skin runs down to the bone like wax, dripping down to the floor. He hears the *"drip...drip...drip..."*, looking down to see he is hanging over a yawning pit, now nothing more than a skeleton with some remaining internal organs, heart, lungs, and the wiring of arteries and veins strewn about his body in and out like snakes, as they pump vile liquids to and from the darkened heart beneath his ribs. Another bolt of energy surges through him, the pain is agonizing as he feels it rip away at what is left of him. He sees the shadows across the wall in the sparks of pale red light, he hears the creaking of chains and metal, as the links cast a silhouette to the wall, and there as well, are the shapes of massive hooks that pierce the bone within his bound wrists to keep him hung.

The Asyndian, the maker, ceases his assault upon the naked skeletal figure. Their eyes lock. *"It is almost complete...the flesh of what you once were...is gone! And now, my creation, the one who will conquer this world for my kingdom, my empire...who will build my fortress of the bodies by those you slay, and construct my throne...so that I may rule a new world, a new age...you shall encompass the powers of all you destroy, you will slaughter them, conquer them, and devour them, for their power will be your power! You will have no weakness, know no pain...and you have no fear...others will beware and flee your presence, and that's what makes you powerful...unstoppable! You, my creation...you are the darkness reborn under new shadows, and your shadow will spread over all, covering all in your malice, your hate...you will make them feel the pain you feel! You are their architect of hate! Therefore...you will destroy this foundation, and upon this realm, build this world, into a world of anger and pain!"*

"HôŊdoR....is the final darkness to conquer, before I...Naumokron, the ancient one! Shall return, and upon this blood-drenched world, I will reign!"

Naumokron, the maker, commands his powers to turn an ancient, rustic leaver over on the far side of the room to control the axel above the chains, and pulls the skeleton over to a large slab table. Hondor is lowered down onto the slab, as the blood and other foul liquids and melted flesh drips down the sides.

"Flesh...is but a coating, a fabrication...it peels, it bleeds, it cuts, its what's underneath it...you...crafted by the bones of eons long thought lost, once a ruler, a conqueror...and shall be once again...you shall be reborn. It's taken me lifetimes to exhume this long lost secret...the secret to extinction, of genocide...not even the Hexagus will be able to stand against you...for you will cut their flesh and tear out their insides to feast upon...all of them!"

"But you...oh no, no flesh for you, you will have a disguise...until you mature, become what you were always to be...and once you have conquered your exterior, rip away from it...you will be free to unleash upon this realm...a terror that has not been seen by any, the likes of which no one has ever dared to imagine!"

Throughout the longest hours, as year after year passes, Naumokron scorches, burns, shapes, and reconstructs his creation, as fire and smoke blazes across the creation, waves of energy and vast amounts of power, lash out and the weight pulsates against the stone walls of these rooms and tunnels, shaking the ground with massive quakes for miles and miles. One final blast and...

Down the far tunnel, Naumokron hears a shadow approaching, and the flock of wings getting closer. Naumokron ceases the torture of energy and power upon the figment of a being before him. He turns to his servants kneeling before him down upon their knees, bowing before his presence. Naumokron stares upon them with fierce blazing eyes.

"Forgive us, oh ancient one! But Kandarius is on his way, he's approaching the colossus this very moment!"

Naumokron hammers his fist down with intense rage, his black wings flare up in annoyance and anger. *"Damn! Why does he come now at this moment! Pests, these Civilians are!"*

He takes a black cover and places it over the slab and the being before him. He rushes about the room, gathering up notes and bundles of old parchment, hastily scrawled in black letters and symbols of the Athil dialect the Asyndians speak. He then proceeds to shove them into the arms of his servants. *"Here, I command you take these documents to the hidden fortress in Raukmar! Fly swift and unseen. Kandarius nor any Dregor must lay hand or eye upon these notes! And...if your weak minds get curious and betray me...I have placed an enchantment upon them, and if you break these seals...you will feel the wrath that will be unleashed...as the plague that will overtake you, shall rip the infidel to pieces! Am I understood?!"*

The servants bow, and they take the documents in their thinned arms of fleshy scale, their wide, pale eyes look to Naumokron in fear.

"And be cautious of Hiidum...I have not fed him for some time..."

The servant gulps. *"But...master...I thought the Guardian could go years without nourishment?"*

Naumokron laughs. *"Yes, that's what makes him loyal and unmoving from his duties...but he will not deny fresh meat if he can get his claws upon it...just tell him not to touch you because I said so!"*

They bow, yet their limbs tremble.

These are the last words they hear of their master as he storms down the hall, his wings rip about with the winds of a

435

raging hurricane, as he heads up to the main chamber to perch upon his throne, and wait for Kandarius.

They head out a secret entrance beneath the catacombs of the black colossus, into the desolation of the Greywaste, where outside they take flight and fade off into the distance as quick a pace they can go, to reach the fortress of Na`bata.

The ultimate fate of these servants...is unknown.

***

The shadows fade as his eyes witness the servants disappear over the horizons within black clouds, as his consciousness awakens by the glimmer of metal, across his eyes. He awakens, as his red gaze pierces the dark, and finds Agonan is still alive and is plunging blow after blow against him.

Hondor raises the axe, and deflects the swipes away, as the cuts across his gut and chest swell over and scar as they heal. He watches the Aurora raise the broken sword up, and goes to strike, but Hondor is faster and strikes first, as he lands the fatal strike of the living axeface into Agonan, deep into his chest. Agonan is stricken, and the sword falls from his hands, he can feel the pain as this weapon begins to eat away at his armor and flesh. Agonan grasps the chomping maw and with all his might, his strength failing fast, rips the blade away, and is able to gouge at one of the bright yellow eyes. The axe recoils with agitated pain, as Agonan flies in close, and grapples at Hondor, driving fist after fist into Hondor's face and jaw, but to no avail.

Hondor grasps Agonan's throat, and proceeds to squeeze the life of Agonan away, as the Aurora tries to remove the clawed, scaled hand and fight this beast off. But he has made the mistake and underestimate this monster, and he cannot budge the clawed vice away.

Hondor places more and more weight upon his crushing grip, and soon, he feels the neck begin to break, as Agonan feels his spine splinter, and releases a horrible, gurgling, choking cry of pain, as he feels the life being ripped from him.

There is nothing left Agonan can do, he is trapped, he has lost. And with a wrenching twist, and snap, Hondor cracks the neck away as sight is ripped from Agonan, and he sees no more, with one last gasp, and his essence ceases to be. Hondor releases his grasp, holds out the limp body of the dead Aurora, clenches his right hand into a fist, and breaks in through the ribs like a walnut, grasps the heart of Agonan, holding it up to the darkness around, then tosses the limp body away, to fall forever down into the abyss, for Agonan's tomb, is now the Great Divide.

Hondor lowers his hand, stares into the heart, as the beating clump of muscle and arteries pulsates within his grasp. He leans forward and with an animalistic hunger, bites into the heart with a single chomp, then swallows it whole.

Within him, he feels a rush of energy and strength, even greater than that which he possesses, fill his black arteries as the essence of this Aurora has given him additional strength and power, as he now possesses both the powers of the Auroras and the maliciousness of the Hexagus. He is unbeatable, unstoppable, unconquerable, but there is one...there is but one he must consume to become that perfect being that Naumokron had intended.

"You will be powerful...you will be unstoppable...but there is one who will complete you, one that will make you! Auroras...Hexagus...they give you more strength...but it is the Destroyer, Maz Dregor! It is he! He will be the final conquest...he will make you...IMMORTAL! All you must do...is obey me, your maker, your master, you will answer to me and do my bidding...for Hexagus will soon be summoned into this

realm in the flesh, and that...my creation...is when we will strike! You will devour them all, Hexagus...Auroras! You will slaughter them and feast upon them down to the bone, absorbing every last drop of blood and every piece of flesh, for every bite will make you all the more powerful...!"

A new burst of hunger rages within Hondor's boiling pit, he hungers for this new prey, to feast upon the flesh and blood of this destroyer! He soars through the darkness, tearing through the black with a sudden burst of energy as a shield of red surrounds him, as he dashes towards the far away cliff walls of the Divide ahead.

After what feels like gliding across centuries of empty blackness, he lunges forward, and his claws and axe strike upon raw, cold rocks and solid granite, for he has reached the boundaries of the Northern Divide.

Hondor begins and scales up the steep, eternal walls, to accomplish what no living thing has ever done...escape from the endless abyss that is the Great Divide, for once the darkness takes hold, there is no return...but...Hondor is the darkness, the empty pit of despair, of rage, of terror...of horror...for when Hondor returns to the surface...no living thing, will be saved.

Above, where the black clouds of storm and chaos swirl round, and the tongues of electric serpents char the ground and sparks burn the mountains into nothing more than heaping piles of ashes, a cold wind blows...Aura and the others can feel the chill crawl down their necks, a numbing feeling, a hesitation that something is wrong, the storms above them are becoming worse as they move closer towards Na`bata, where her people await her, left in an unsure, uneasy situation with this mysterious guardian who calls himself Hiidum. For their worries blind them from the legions of shadows that have followed them into Raukmar, the shadows soon to reveal themselves, as the cold eyes of the Dzjurger watches them from behind the worn rocks and boulders of these lands, waiting, for the moment to attack, with the ranks of the Dregor in wait and ready for their general's orders.

And...far behind them...a hulking arm rises up from the pits of the Divide, as the clawed hand of Hondor reaches outwards and grasps the raw soil, and the axe is brought down, wedged into place, and as the wind kicks up a haze of dust and debris of large stones, within the sheet of this dirt storm, a silhouette mounts the top of the ledge...as HE...has returned, HE...has come back...risen from a grave that could not keep this beast at bay.

"THUMP THUMP...THUMP THUMP..." A heartbeat echoes within earshot of Diin, thudding faintly, but getting closer.

'What is that? Can you hear it?!' He exclaims.

'Hear what Diin?' Aura and Nilta look at him closely, as they watch his expressions go from questionable...suddenly to fear, as a horror melts the color from his flesh, into a pale dead white.

'Diin, what is it?!' Aura inquires, and Nilta places a hand upon his shoulder. He walks away from them, heading to the tip of the Rauk's shoulder, looking out over the ridge, back towards the south.

'There! It's coming from over there...I hear a faint beating sound...like a heart...it's very faint, but its moving...fast...it's heading in our direction...OH NO!'

They look at him stunned with terror by the look upon his face. He turns in the direction of Aura, for silence has executed his speech, his throat is cracked and dry, as the band across his eyes dampens with perspiration.

'It's...IT'S HIM!'

A mad panic comes over Aura, a primordial fear clouding her mind and judgment, not knowing what to do or think. He's come back, somehow...this monster has returned. She begins to climb up closer to Uroghin's ear. 'We have to go faster! Can you take us any faster?!' She cries in desperation.

'Hmmmmm...I will...try my lady...what is the...matter?' He asks.

'I have to get to my people...they're in danger...!' She exclaims.

'We're all in danger!' Diin adds.

And they feel a sudden quake, as the Rauk tries to widen his stride and get them back to Na`bata as fast as he is able, for the desperation in Aura's voice, brings worry to this giant.

Part XXXI:

Confrontation

~

They have crossed into the boarders of Na`bata. The darkness above has spread, and the entire territory for miles around has been covered in the black, just as the lands of Aura have.

'Nearly there...my lady...nearly there...' Urohgin groans as he pushes himself as fast as he is able to go. Soon, the Rauk fortress is in sight, before a shrouding deep mist that has layered itself upon the land. Urohgin kneels down and lowers Aura, Diin, and Nilta onto the ledge, and the three race across the jutting causeway, hurrying blindly through the massive stone doorway.

They rush through empty corridors and tunnels, into the main area where she left her people under the watch of Hrend and Hiidum. The room is dark, with only the faint flicker of several braziers glowing a sick green flame. Immediately ahead of her she sees Hiidum sitting up upon his stone slab of a throne, and standing by his side, burns the red eyes and the black feathers of Duul`ak, or as Hiidum refers to him as, "Master Naumokron."

'Welcome back, Lady Aura...I hope my faithful servant had welcomed you graciously...' Duul`ak snickers with an evil, twisted air about him. His eyes look up to her as he looks over many notes and parchments within his hands, as he reads to himself.

'Where are my people!' She cries.

He keeps reading over his ancient scrawling, ignoring her. She hears whimpers coming from the corner of the room, she looks back to see the many faces of them peering out from the shadows as they are all huddled together.

'Help us my lady! Help us! He's been threatening to sick that fiendish monster on us! He's only waited for you to come!' Hrend cries, rushing forward to her side. 'I'm sorry I failed you my lady, he is too powerful...there was nothing I could do!'

She wraps her arms around him. 'Stay calm young one...I'm not going to let either of them harm us...we will protect you!'

Duul`ak laughs.

'Diin...Nilta...stay by my side.'

'We're with you my lady!' Diin replies.

'Hrend, stay with the others...' She commands, and Hrend stands by the side of the Gormon's, Civilian's, and Asyndian's men, women, and children.

'The Ancient One...that is what I was...but soon, I will be everything, I will be this world, it's current in a vast stream of the Galakaos! I will be the darkness brought down upon it...I was stopped once, only a minor setback, but I will not fail again! My creation has done the dirty work, and now I can begin my original plan and set into place my dominion over this realm, but there are still a few things that need taken care of...one of those things...is you, my lady! You and all your people...the last of Aura!' Duul`ak roars, clenching his fist, and raises it high above.

Aura feels a cold over her...a revelation...as she learns that this Asyndian...it is this Asyndian who is responsible for all this death, as this destruction, the annihilation, the death of all those around her, the cause of all the pain and suffering, the nightmares that will never cease, only until death releases them. It is this...Asyndian, who is responsible...for the wrath of Hondor. All the documents and all those scrolls and tomes they read and studied days ago...they were notes on the creation, the birth of that horrendous monster.

'YOU! It was you who did this! It was you who are responsible for...everything!'

'I wanted to create the ultimate warrior! Battle-ready, fearless, untouchable, unbeatable...immortal! A foe no one could destroy! He was to be the perfect killing machine, except, there was one flaw...he disobeyed me. So, like any servant or pet that will not obey...he had to be put down...and now the Divide has taken him into the abyss where he'll fall forever! And now that he has served his purpose, and I have no worries of that beast retaliating against me...I can complete the task at hand...' He pats Hiidum upon the head, as the beast makes a purring sound within its throat.

'You see, Hiidum here...has always served me faithfully, a patient and loyal beast he has always been...and for that, he is to be rewarded.

Diin and Nilta ready themselves for a fight. Aura tenses up, as she is not a warrior, but she will fight, she will defend those she loves, those she has fought hard to keep alive.

Hrend sneaks away to another room, rummaging around, until he finds what he is looking for. He grasps the items from an old chest he discovered earlier and runs back to the room, as Duul`ak comes to a close on his speech.

Duul`ak steps away from Hiidum. 'And now, my loyal Hiidum, guardian of my keep...I think you have earned your feast! Leave nothing left except for a pile of bones, so that I may lay them down, to begin the foundation upon which I will build my empire!'

Hiidum's eyes light up with a primal rage, as the hunger awakens, coursing through his gut, to feast upon these little morsels cowering in the corner before him.

Hiidum lunges forward, his stark eyes of hunger roar for blood and flesh. Hrend calls to them from behind, 'Lady Aura...here!' And he tosses the weapons across the vast room, two blades that still carry a rustic sting to them, and a spear, with the shaft broken at the bottom, though the point is still sharp and ready for its call to battle. The call has been heard, and Nilta rushes across the floor and grabs the spear in her right hand, she kicks the blades away towards Aura and Diin, who grab them quickly. Nilta holds up her hand warning them to stay back, distracting Hiidum's attention from the others.

Hiidum and Nilta circle around the room, eyes locked on one another. Nilta is crouched into a fighting stance, ready to move, ready to dodge and attack on a whim. Hiidum licks his jaws and jagged razor-front fangs that protrude from his gums, hissing at his foe. When he speaks, his vocals have dropped several octaves, not the friendly tone he had introduced himself with before.

'I guess I'll start with you then....rrrrrrrrr....'

They draw to a standstill. The room falls to a silence like death, only the faint murmur and whimper of Aura's people can be heard in the faint darkness of the corner, terrified. Duul`ak says nothing; he sits perched upon Hiidum's throne and watches with great interest at the battle about to unfold.

'I can feel your hands trembling silent one! The vibrations are thick in the air! I smell every bead of sweat of fear emitting from every pore in your body! You know you will die! All of you will DIE!' And he flashes a glance back to the frightened people. Nilta rushes at him while his head is turned, but Hiidum hears her footsteps, and turns back, clawing her away, slashing through the leather plate across her chest.

'How dare you?! Thinking you can attack me with my back turned...for that! I will take a life...' He laughs with madness, and rushes to the corner, grabbing an unsuspecting and horrified Civilian within his jaws. Hiidum carries the body into the middle of the room and proceeds to rip the Civilian to pieces, devouring them piece by piece. They watch in horror as the Civilian screams with pain, until there is nothing else but the sound of Hiidum's slathering, slobbering jowls crunching the bones.

Aura, in a fit of rage, charges forward with the sword raised before her, ready to plunge the rusted metal through Hiidum's black bestial heart. Hiidum raises his blood-covered whiskers and stares right into Aura's very essence, but she doesn't hold back, she keeps her force driving forward. Hiidum raises the blood-splattered paw, and slashes Aura away, the razor nails slice through her ribs and chest, as the crimson rushes from her pale flesh, staining her a burning red. She lies upon the ground screaming in pain from the blow.

Hiidum then rushes over and grabs another victim, a Gormon this time. The Gormon tries to fight back, though he gets his arm ripped off, and Hiidum makes a slaughter of him as well.

'Every mistake you make…I kill one of your cattle, your sheep you desire to protect!' He roars.

'Come on Hiidum, be done with this! I have no time for these games, just kill them and be done with it!' Duul`ak commands.

'But master, this fight against these weak pustules is uninteresting!' Hiidum retorts.

'You've proven yourself the superior, now just eat the rest of them and be done with it!' Duul`ak roars even louder this time.

Hiidum swallows the last mouthful of Gormon. 'Hmmm, very well…' He looks at Aura, then to Nilta. 'I said I would start with you…' He strides with wide feline steps over to where Nilta composes herself, holding her wounds, trying to stop the blood, when she sees the massive shadow looming across the floor and over her body. She looks up to the huge massive layers of jaws wide open, and the echoes of the dead scream out, of all the past devoured, who have been torn to pieces.

Then, as Hiidum is about to swallow Nilta whole, he feels something grapple upon his back, and then a stabbing, pricking feeling is jabbing into the back of his neck.

'Ahhhh…what is this…who dares?!' He roars, shaking the walls with his rage and anger.

Nilta looks up in disbelief, as Diin grapples around upon Hiidum's back, stabbing the sword repeatedly into the thick neck beneath Hiidum's mane. He clutches firmly upon the hair and fur to hold on as Hiidum jumps and bucks across the room, rattling and shaking his head and body, trying to get Diin, this nuisance off. He bites at his back, trying to find the tick that is biting and bleeding him, as streams of Hiidum's blood splash across the walls and floor as she tries to shake Diin away.

'Bug! When I get a hold of you...I'll crush you and rip your limbs off!!!' Hiidum screams.

Nilta, Aura, and everyone else watch with wide-eyes and nerves on edge as Diin grapples with staying upon the back of this beast, plunging the blade deeper and deeper in. They hold their breath...Diin raises up the blade to be plunged for the final blow...until...

Duul`ak lunges across the air, and grapples onto Diin from the behind, grappling him into a chokehold, wrestling with the blade in Diin's hand. Duul`ak grabs his arm and a pulsating shock of energy fries Diin's hand to a crisp, crippling the grasp upon the blade, as the splint of metal is thrown across the room, shattering against the wall.

Aura and Nilta gasp, as Duul`ak lifts Diin into the air, and throws him to the ground, where Diin writhes and grasps his arm in pain.

'Finish this Hiidum! Finish them off, destroy them all now!'

Hiidum lunges at Diin, and sinks his jaws into the blind-man's crippled body. Lifting him into the air, jaws sunk deep into his chest, thrashing his limp body around, then slamming him to the ground. A loud "CRACK" of Diin's skull pierces their ears, as eyes watch on in horror as Hiidum bleeds him away like a stuck rodent from the dunes of Isa in the east.

Aura staggers to her feet and shambles over towards Hiidum, with sword raised in her shaking arm.

'You bastard! Try some of me...finish what you started!' She yells. Hiidum raises his head, a piece of Diin's torn robe hangs from his teeth. He proceeds towards her, Aura begins to circle around and head towards Nilta, who has vanished back into the darkness. Aura now has her back against the wall of Hiidum's massive throne slab. Duul`ak swoops down and grabs Aura from behind to hold her, waiting for Hiidum to strike.

'Now I'll tear you to pieces...Lady Aura!'

Hiidum sees a faint glimmer of metal out of the corner of his eye, then a sharp stabbing pain jolts through his eye socket; now he sees no more. Nilta has launched herself from the shadows with spear in hand, and jabbed the piercing tip into Hiidum's eye socket, blinding the beast in one eye.

Hiidum leaps backwards, pawing at his eye, trying to remove the projectile from his eye. Tears and rivers of blood flow from the dead eye ball. His cries rattle the stone beneath them, he stomps around like a wild animal, no longer acting like the dignified beast they first met.

Nilta grabs Aura's sword, rushes across the room, waiting for a clean blow, Hiidum raises his neck up and Nilta strikes, slashing across his throat as crimson sprays across the area, covering Nilta in blood. Hiidum lumbers around, tripping over his feet, collapsing to the floor. He tries to crawl across the floor, but he gurgles his last breath, before his head slams to the ground, and his eyes roles back. Soon the breathing ceases. Hiidum has been slain.

Duul`ak looks on at the blood-covered woman in rage. He summons powerful pulsating lights of energy within his hands, ready to strike her. Energy pulses through Aura, singeing her body. Nilta looks back at him, ready to cut the wings from this black Asyndian that did this to her brother. She motions for Duul`ak to release Aura.

"C'mon! Fight me!" Her eyes scream, as the blood drips and runs down her face and body.

Duul`ak prepares for the attack, until the roaring sounds of battle outside reach their ears within. Duul`ak looks to the gaping doors, tosses Aura to the ground, and with vicious speed, he flies outside to see what is happening. Aura, Nilta, and the others hear it to, the loud, moaning grunts of Urohgin as he lands punches and blows down to the ground. There is a great struggle going on outside upon the wasteland.

Nilta rushes to Diin, holding him up to her, she tries to comfort him, tries to stop the bleeding. Before Aura can reach them, she lifts her brother up and carries him away.

Nilta carries Diin's body outside the walls and sets him down. Aura and the others rush out behind them as they witness the mass of shadows surrounding and attacking Urohgin ferociously. He swats at them like flies, but more and more pile on. He grasps a handful in his massive right fist and crushes hundreds of them all at once, but from a heavy looming shadow just ahead and closing, more and more Dregor rush forward.

'Bring the giant down!' A voice roars, as Dzjurger arises from the shadows, leading the Dregor into a frenzied charge, as rank upon rank rush forward towards the stronghold of Na`bata. 'Then, seize the stronghold! Kill everything that moves!' He cries to the tens of thousands of soldiers surrounding the area, as thousands and thousands more spawn forward.

Aura remains by Nilta as she witness the battle before them, their ears shatter by the roars and grunts of Urohgin as he fights the Dregor hordes off. The Rauk raises a fist high and slams into the ground, leaving a huge crater where hundreds of Dregor remain smashed, their black armor shattered into nothing more than fine grains of mineral. Nilta seems to take no notice, her attention rests only with the body of her brother.

'I won't leave your side Nilta!' Aura cries.

'My lady! We're doomed! There's Dregor everywhere, there's no way out!' One of the Asyndian's cries from above.

Aura looks out to the battlements, as the dark-thorned armor of Dzjurger pushes through the ranks, his pale dead eyes fixed upon the giant Rauk.

'The only way to bring down a mountain…is to break it!' And he calls back to the dark voids behind their lines and cries out in the black speech of the Hexagus.

"THŌṚNGA!!!" He yells, and the darkness of voids begins to ripple and pulsate. From the depths of some unfathomable plane, a shrieking, piercing cry more sickening than the deaths of millions, reverberates back through, crippling the senses of everyone hidden among the fortress.

Through the voids are heavy footsteps that shatter the ground beneath. The tip of a huge hammer reaches forward, the thick stone and obsidian blazes with fire within the carved-out head in the shape of a bestial monstrosity, then another hammer reaches through, this one spits from its stone maw a putrid, foul and corrosive acid that will eat and devour through anything. The two hammers are within the grasp of a single, titanic beast. It's hulking body lumbers out into the battlefield, covered from its head down to its hooves in scourged armor, every piece has been riveted to its pale green flesh, as dried rivers of blood remain from where the crimson once flowed down its limbs and body. The spikes upon its shoulder pauldrons and helm reach to the sky like skyscrapers, as this beast's height matches that of Urohgin, nearly scratching the tip of the skies. Thornga, terror of the black, has been summoned by its Hexagus master, and is prepared to destroy its foe.

Aura's people witness this new monstrosity and rush back into the fortress of Na'bata, screaming and horrified. 'My lady, we must get back inside!' One of the Gormons cries. Aura feels a small hand grasp hers, she looks to see Hrend still by her side.

'It doesn't make a difference…does it?' He says.

'No Hrend …no it doesn't. Because…if Hondor…if he…then it won't matter.' She replies, Hrend grasps her hand tighter.

'I'm scared…'

'So am I Hrend …so am I…jut stay near me.'

Within Nilta's arms, Diin coughs up more and more blood over his green robe, gagging on the fluid collecting in his throat, suffocating on his own blood, while the large slashes across his chest pump out even more blood. Nilta holds him closer, as his life fades away. The darkness is getting darker.

'Aura…Aura…' His voice is followed by the gagging, wheezing cough of blood. Aura lets go of Hrend's hand and rushes to Diin's side. She grasps his hand. Hrend follows.

'Diin…Diin you shouldn't be speaking, just hold onto your strength!'

'There's…(cough)   there's   nothing   left   to hold…onto…'

Nilta grasps tightly upon her brother, feeling his heart beat grow faint. Tears fall from Nilta's face upon his. 'No Nilta, none of that…I have to (cough) I have to tell you…Aura…'

'Yes Diin, I'm here!'

'Remember, I told you…there was a strong heartbeat coming from…the Divide…'

'Yes…yes I remember Diin!' Aura tries as hard as she can to hold back her tears.

'I hear it…again (cough) it's…it's getting louder, it's coming this way!' He starts to fade.

'Diin, Diin hold on!'

Nilta grasps upon Aura's arm to get her attention. Aura looks at Nilta as she mimes grasping her heart, cuffing her hands around her heart, and then holding it out towards Diin.

'What is it your trying to say Nilta?'

Nilta becomes desperate and frustrated, mimicking the actions over and over, tears now flowing like rivers as she becomes more and more anxious on the brink of her brother's death.

Aura watches Nilta carefully. 'Heart…heart…' Nilta grasps her heart. 'Heart…Her…love…LOVE!' Nilta becomes excited, and mimes transferring her heart to Diin. 'Love…you want to…you love…ok…' Aura turns to Diin. 'Diin, Nilta wants me to tell you she…'

A slight smile comes over his face. 'I…I know what she's saying…I love you too Nilta…(cough)' and more blood trickles from the corners of his mouth. Nilta holds her head down upon his.

Behind them, the bludgeoning hammers flail away upon Urohgin, cracking and smashing away at the Rauks arms and body, breaking him down more and more. The Dregor reroute their target and begin their march towards the fortress, as the titanic Urohgin is brought down to his knees. Thornga raises both hammers over Uroghin's broken body, and with a single blow, both strike at once, upon his back, driving the Rauk to the dirt, shattering him to pieces. Urohgin, the last of the Rauks, has fallen.

Aura stands and watches on in horror as now one hundred thousand, two hundred thousand, Dregor charge in their direction, guided by the shadows of the black clouds and shadows around, and the chaotic gaping voids follow behind. The monstrous Thornga lifts up both hammers and rests them upon each shoulder, and stomps towards the fortress, ready to abolish it down into nothing more than crushed pieces of broken stone and crunched bone.

'Aura...Aura!' Diin cries with what strength he has left. Aura kneels down to Diin's side and he whispers his final words to her.

'He's...he's here...' And Nilta and Aura watch as the last of Diin's life, escapes his scarred and broken body.

Nilta loses control and surrounds herself around Diin's corpse. Aura lets go and looks above her. Upon the broken spire above Na`bata's stone dome...the red eyes of Duul`ak pierce outwards to the horizon.

'So...you have returned.' Duul`ak growls under his breath.

A sharp, piercing terror rushes down her spine and into her guts, making her feel an excruciating sickness boil deep down inside her. She watches, past the hordes of Dregor, the hulking mass of Thornga, the lidless void of darkness, she looks past it all, because it means nothing. The footsteps rumble the dirt, trembles beneath their feet, and everything stops, time and all. Dzjurger commands all to halt, and they turn towards the far horizons, where thunder roars and lighting strikes ferociously, alighting the backdrop of the far southern skies.

*BOOM…BOOM…BOOM…*step after step, crushes into the ground, as upon the horizons, stands the silhouette of a massive armored shadow with the jaws of the axe of Blodaur Ror, within his grasp.

'No…no…!' Aura falls to her knees trembling, Hrend stands next to her.

Even the foulest of these Dregor can feel it, the cold terror sweep across the lands. In the shadow of this, one and true monster, there is a force to be reckoned with, a nightmare to be feared.

Hondor has come…and no one…no one will escape.

'So…it seems we meet again!' Dzjurger roars.

They feel the ground beneath them quake, and the darkness above, grows even deeper.

Part XXXII:

To the End

~

'Gather around me!'

Dzjurger roars.

'All legions reform!'

The hundreds of thousands of Dregor soldiers rush over the hills and from the valleys and gather around their general. From the gaping portals of the abyss, thousands more march through. Also among these ranks are a new breed of soldier. These new legions of blade and molten blood ride forward upon mechanical terrors, spitting fire from their razor jaws. Their claws stomp through the soil and rip the dirt to pieces. They scorch all in their path as they march across to the front where Dzjurger has called all to him.

Followed behind him, emerges several hundred horrific beasts of brute muscle and thick tangled fur; Trau`ls from ancient days. They carry huge clubs and hammers in their grip. They are armored head to toe in black armor, their jaws dripping a putrid black acidic liquid. They slobber for war, for battle, for blood.

Then, plowing through the lines, emerges the Grηndř, a machination that can only be described as, a propulsion engine of blistering steam from its haul, and a gaping maw containing thousands of rotating spinning blades, forged from the fires of the Destroyer's domain, the molten abyss of the Hexagus realm, deep within Wom's stomach. The blades of ebony and hardened obsidian churn and pulsate with a gurgling hunger for genocide.

Aura and the others look on as the despicable creations of the Hexagus pour forward and onto the land. But none, can eclipse the looming shadow in the distance, the shadow of Hondor, is almost upon them.

She walks over to Nilta. 'Nilta, let me help you get him inside…'

Nilta shakes her head wildly, pounding upon Diin's chest then holding up her fist with rage and anger. She points to the wide spread armies of the Dregor that lay before them. She wants to fight, to take them all on.

'No Nilta! No! We cannot stand against them! We have to get your brother's body inside…we must help the others!' Aura replies.

Nilta lays Diin down upon the cold stone walkway. She stands up pointing to him, and then to the armies. She holds her heart, then points to Aura's heart, then to her brother, and then back to the armies.

Aura shakes her head. 'No…No Nilta…there is nothing we can do! Diin would not want us to go storming into a sea of chaos with foes we cannot defeat!'

Nilta pounds on her chest furiously, then makes a motion, casting Aura away, insinuating Aura is a coward.

'You cannot beat them Nilta…none of us can! They will fight against Hondor and they will fall! We will fall! There is nothing we can do! I am scared of what is going to happen to all of us.'

There is silence between them for a moment. Aura looks back to the entrance of Na`bata, where her people look out in terror at what is transpiring. She looks back to Nilta.

'I feel…we will be reuniting with Diin very soon.'

Nilta lowers her head in sadness. Aura leaves her alone, there is nothing left to be said, for the end is nearer for them now. She turns back to the final stand against Hondor. She feels a tight squeeze upon her hand, as Hrend stands by her side.

The final line of troops emerge onto this realm. Above the skies of darkness roar, lighting and chaos scorches and fire begins to pour down onto the land. The world goes hot and molten, while the air is cold and frigid. Cyclones form in the distance in all directions; huge massive funnels miles wide, ripping apart land and ocean to nothing.

Duul`ak hovers in the skies above them, watching the armies as they plan to make their futile stand against the indestructible one.

'It seems…the second wave of cleansing…has washed upon this world, and it shall drag all back into the realms of nothing!' He cries then flies closer into the black.

The abyss of darkness spawned from the Hexagus Realm dissipates, and through the kicked up dirt and dust, the monstrosity of desolation emerges. Hondor has returned.

Within Dzjurger's mind, a distant vision plays within his memories. He remembers when his flesh was flesh, armor was armor, and not one the same in some meshed concoction of screaming creation. He remembers back to a time when there was less power in this world, and within himself.

He remembers the day on those fields, the ruins of Runegard burning in the distance behind him. He remembers the final stand for him and his troops. Then it was only him, those pallid, dead faces looking upon him with blank, lifeless eyes. Their limbs severed and scattered about by the cuts and blows of the double axes this beast carried within his hands. When he first confronted Hondor, it was a Gormon, a large being…but now, this beast has changed…it is something else. The armor and flesh are one, much like his own. The eyes pierce through the darkness beneath a helmet encrusted with scales and teeth. The figure is now triple the size…and the hunger…more ferocious.

'LEGIONS! Surround him!' He roars.

Hondor enters into the mists of his enemies…his prey and they encircle him.

The Axe of Blodaur Ror begins to glow and pulsate with energy, the eyes open wide, the jaws begin to drip and salivate.

The skies above roar even louder, and the darkness…grows even darker. Out there, beyond all the Galakaos, the realms have been extinguished. Their lights have become extinguished and faded. Something is coming…a faint roar gurgles beyond the boundaries of this realm. From these shades of former cumulus around them, shards of frozen, cold rain begins to pour down, as the soldiers churn dirt and water into disgusting mud, as Raukmar begins to flood and wash over this desolate place.

Dzjurger walks through the ranks and once more, stands face to face with Hondor.

'Here we are once more…you and I…but this time…I will not be defeated!'

Hondor stands motionless, facing the Dzjurger down, not flinching or looking around. Focused. The axe by his side licks its gums and incisors.

'Legions of Dregor, spawns of the Mother Wom, chosen of the Hexagus…CHARGE!!!'

Like black waves in a roaring ocean, thousands upon thousands of Dregor attack Hondor all at once in a free for all.

'It is futile…General of Maz Dregor!'

Dzjurger looks up to see Duul`ak floating above him.

'You cannot kill Hondor…he is indestructible, immortal, invincible! Hondor is the ending to all, the desecrater to life and birth…he is undying…he was once eventual but now forever and eternal! The Gormons called it Hondor, the end of everything, the death of all. And now…he is real, he is alive! And there is nothing…nothing any of us can do! The flesh of the Gormon was but a seedling…it was deep inside where the true essence incubated…and once it was released…'

Dzjurger looks back as Hondor cracks, slashes, breaks, slaughters, and pulverizes all the Dregor that attack as though they were paper crumbling in water. Their black blood of sludge splatters and spills across the land, mixing into the mud decaying the soil into a corrosive, sick substance. Dzjurger …A`deon…finds out that even the wicked can scream in pain.

'He will feed, and feed, and feed…he is never satisfied. And as he feeds he will grow, he will get even stronger.' Duul`ak laughs as Dzjurger watches his armies get cut down to size. 500,00…400,000…225,000…60,000…and the numbers decrease more and more and more, soon the land is covered in a deep, ocean of bile and sludge.

Thornga charges through the ranks…but Hondor slices and cuts him down into nothing more than steaks and chops. The Trau`ls…the riders and their creaking, shrilling machines…obliterated.

'Send forward the Grŋndř!' Dzjurger roars at the top of his lungs.

Grŋndř rolls forward, crushing all in its path with wide spiked wheels. Razor jaws chomping, and bludgeoning hammers pounding the ground into chasms and quakes. Hondor takes a battle stance, a deep churning roar grumbles from his throat, he dashes forward head-on at the Grŋndř. With a hacking slice, he chops away the right sledge from its arm, then he grasps Grŋndř's left sledge and breaks it apart into splinters. Grŋndř's eyes roll back from red to black, then red pulsates from the lenses, as its blood begins to fill within its pupils. Hondor jumps into the churning jaws of Grŋndř, the axe of Blodaur Ror hacks and slashes away, Hondor tears away the teeth and blades, then pulls apart the ribs and decimates the innards of this beast, drowning it from the inside out.

Grŋndř begins to slow its march, as all watch on, this churning beast get ripped to pieces. Blood and oils spit and splatter from its maw and hardened exterior. A massive explosion leaves a massive hole in the top of its back and spinal area. Hondor raises up the axe, then pulls himself from the carcass, covered in black sludge and bile.

Duul`ak laughs. 'What will you do now general…what will you do now?!'

Hondor leaps to the ground, shaking the bones of Raukmar, shaking and rattling the fear of Aura and the others.

Aura starts to turn back to Nilta, speaking franticly. 'Nilta, we must...'

She is gone, and so is Diin's body.

The entire realm shakes, and the roar of a darker threat is getting nearer. Something is coming.

'Nilta...Nilta!' Aura looks around in panic, wondering what happened to them.

'Where did they go my lady?!' Hrend cries.

'I don't know...I...I don't know where she went or what she is planning to do!' She looks back at Hrend, shaking her head, not knowing what happened to them.

Dzjurger stands face to face with Hondor.

'Maz Dregor thinks he chose a worthy general to conquer these lands, but he has failed as he will soon witness.' He glares down at Dzjurger, 'If you go up against Hondor, you will be destroyed as all these other slaves to the Destroyer...you are no different General A`deon...you are still weak, still a coward, built up by this armor on your skin and the power you think you wield within your hand! You think that shield will protect you? There is nothing to protect any of us now! This has become his world, and we shall be cleansed with all the others! Put down your weapon, and go cower over in Na`bata with all the others, make yourselves comfortable! Soon he will rip through the walls and bricks until he has reached the juicy meat inside!'

Within the blink of an eye, faster than a bolt of lightning, Dzjurger whips around and leaps into the air, strikes forward and then lands into the dirt. The blood flows down the blade, and Duul`ak falls to the ground, eyes widened by what has occurred. He reaches over and grasps the area where a wing should be, only grasping at a slashed nub, trying to stop the blood gushing from the mortal wound.

'What...WHAT HAVE YOU DONE!'

An ominous red glow encompasses Duul`ak's failing body, as the essence of Naumokron tries to escape its fate. A sudden burst of wind begins to drag all towards Hondor, as he inhales. The essence of Naumokron is wretched from Duul`ak's body, and the Asyndian's carcass turns grey as the eyes fade to white, then falls limp and lifeless to the dirt with a thud. Hondor draws the power deep within his chest, absorbing his master, as Naumokron lets out a wailing shriek of death, before he is engulfed. The two are now one. Electric pulsates in a shell of dominion around Hondor, as his strength increases tenfold. Creation has conquered over its master.

Dzjurger hears a voice within his head, his master speaks to him.

"It's almost time now...face him! Face this monster...you have showed your loyalty to me this far...falter now, and I will show you fate worse than what lays ahead!"

'Fate? What fate? Am I to be defeated by this creature...I will not be defeated again! You made me stronger, more powerful...then why? Why...!?'

The voice says no more. 'It does not matter, I do not need these weapons or this shield to show my true power! I'll tear you apart with my bare hands!'

Before Dzjurger can step forward, the shadow has engulfed him, he looks up into those blazing red eyes, just before the axe slices down, cleaving the general in half.

"RRRROOOOOAAAAAARRRRRR!!!!!!" A piercing roar, some other worldly dimensional catastrophe shatters the

chaos of the battle. Even Hondor turns away from his slaughter to look above, watching the sky grow even darker. The many shapes and soldiers now nothing more than objects shaded into night, blended silhouettes. Hondor resumes his slaughter, lifting up the slices of what's left of Dzjurger, and devouring them.

'What was... Hrend, go back inside! Go with the others!' Aura shouts.

'I won't leave y...!'

'Do as I say! I command you...there is nothing any of us can do now!'

'No! I'll face him, I'll defeat him!' Hrend soars out into the middle of battle, and lands right in front of where Hondor feasts.

'HRΣND!!!! NO!!!!!' Aura cries and as fast as she can, climbs down the rock face of the cliff and runs across the charred earth as fast as her broken body can take her, hoping to reach Hrend in time.

"RRRROOOOOAAAAAARRRRRR!!!!!!" The cataclysm grows closer now. Aura can barely see Hrend ahead of her, but she picks up her pace and moves faster.

'Hrend...get back here! Please, come back to me! Hrend!' She cries, tears rush down her face.

'I'm...I'm not afraid of you! Hey you! Face me!' Hrend shrieks. The terror reverberates in his voice.

'This is the end of you! Face me...I'm...I'm not afraid...' Hrend loses his composure and falls backwards, his feathers soaked and drowned by the pouring rain and the mud dragging him under.

"THUD THUD...THUD THUD...thud thud thud thud thud...." Hondor hears the increasing heart beat, the fear of this tiny little morsel, the fear increasing. He sniffs the air, sensing it, smelling the blood within the little Asyndian. He knows the taste and smell of Asyndian blood all too well, how sweet it tastes dripping down the throat and bubbling in the guts. Hondor looks down at the quivering, pathetic little shape. He approaches, stomping and sloshing in the mud. The rainfall increases, the waters are rising higher.

Aura kneels and takes Hrend into her grasp, holding him close, lifting him above the waters.

'I'm sorry my lady...so sorry...' He starts to cry, tears run down her arm.

She holds him tighter to her. They close their eyes, and Hondor reaches out his hand to grasp them. The axe licks its jaws, still not satisfied.

'Don't leave me please my lady! Don't go!' He clings to her tighter.

'I'm here with you Hrend...I'm here...I'm not going anywhere!'

They keep their eyes closed, as the shadows darken around them.

Part XXXIII:

Engulf (Wom)

~

'Hô∏doR…it's finally come! The ancient ones of Fausengard have predicted it would arrive…the end…the darkness encompasses all…and all fades to black! Hondor has swallowed everything!' From behind the shadows, an old Gormon whispers under his breath.

'Hondor? What is that other sound? That horrible roar in the sky…why does the sky grow darker still?!' An Asyndian woman cries.

'What are you blathering about back there?! Where is Lady Aura…that little Asyndian, what happened to them?!' A Civilian inquiries.

'It's too dark out there…I can't see what's going on!' Someone shouts.

'Nor can I!' Another exclaims.

'Something bigger is coming…something larger…can you feel it?! In the way the realm shakes and trembles before something monstrous! Something…is…coming!'

A few of the braver ones leave the shadows of Na`bata's dwelling, to walk out among the storms and the violent winds, they make the long walk across the long stone walkway out to the edge of the cliff. They vanish from sight of those that look out.

'Where did they go?'

'I can't see them!'

The brave group looks down over the cliff, an older Gormon with a graying beard looks down, his sharp eyes trying to pierce the darkness to see if he can find Aura and Hrend.

'Can you see anything?' An Asyndian asks.

'Nothing! I see nothing!'

'What good are your eyes then…I thought you Gormon were supposed to be able to see anything, even in the darkest places?'

The Gormon grumbles with agitation. 'Well these aren't normal circumstances now are they?! Why don't you use those wings and fly down and look?!' The Gormon retorts.

'Would you two stop fighting?!' A Civilian exclaims.

Then a burst of blinding energy throws them backwards, they are hurtled through the air and smash through the large stone doorway of Na`bata. Their bodies slammed against the far wall, behind Hiidum's throne. The others scatter from their hiding and rush over to help them.

Below, Hondor reaches for Aura and Hrend, until the blinding red lights break the darkness, and wave after wave of power pulsates across Raukmar.

'My lady...what is that light?!' Hrend screams, feeling the heat of the radiating waves burn upon his flesh. Aura adjusts her position and places her back towards the light, covering Hrend. She can feel the full force strike her skin, burning the clothing away, blisters forming across her back and shoulders. her hair singeing at the tips and follicles disintegrating. The grounds shake and cliffs begin to crumble. Aura grips Hrend and runs as fast as she can away from the blast. Hondor takes no notice, his back is turned facing the fiery lights.

Aura and Hrend rush to the top of a nearby hill of ash, now the charred remains of a once standing monument planted upon Raukmar's soil. Aura falls to the ground on her stomach in pain. Her flesh scorching from the blast.

'Don't worry lady Aura...I'm here...I'll stand by your side! Don't worry!' Hrend tries to reassure her.

Aura wakes in and out of consciousness. She gives Hrend a meek smile. 'You're...you're a good child Hrend...' She looks past him, towards Hondor and the light.

Hondor stands his ground, the axe of Blodaur Ror glowing within his grasp. The axe is ripped from his grasp by a powerful, unseen grasp, pulling the axe into the fiery voids.

A voice begins to speak to Hondor. It is the voice of *HE*, the Destroyer...Maz Dregor. 'You are powerful indeed...just as Naumokron had said. You slayed my champion, you have done much for me...you've washed these weak Civilians, Gormons, and these Asyndians from this realm...and for that, I thank you. The task is nearly complete, all will once more return to its place, and order will once more be returned to our world...our mother we serve...will be restored! She will no longer be sick, and for that I thank you!'

'I am sorry for taking your axe, but it does belong to us after all! Me and my kin…and our mother!' Maz Dregor laughs and his voice begins to fizzle away.

He takes a fighting stance, ready to charge. Maz Dregor's voice returns.

'I see you are angered…enraged…' The portal opens, 'If you want your axe back, then come and claim it from us…walk through the portal and become one with us! Take up my brother's axe and pledge yourself to us! Combine your power with ours…gain your full power that your maker intended! Naumokron could never realize how powerful you have…and still…can become. Just…step into the fire, into the darkness…!'

Hondor crouches, then pounces forward, charging with blind rage into the inferno before him. Aura and Hrend look on in shock in awe as the inferno closes up, and Hondor is gone.

Aura hoists herself up, struggling to her knees. She is in disbelief, the monster is gone.

The rain ceases. They look around them, into the skies, as darkness has reached its edge, and the line has been crossed.

And a deep, yawning gurgle rattles the skies and the ground beneath their feet, as they now feel it upon them, the ultimate blackness they have dreaded. The Asyndians feared it, the Gormons knew it, Civilians scoffed at and mocked the coming of the final darkness, and the suffocation of the realm of Aura. But the time has finally come.

'AURA! LOOK…WHAT IS THAT!!!' Hrend screams pointing at the sky. Thousands and thousands of bright moons are getting closer, they surround the realm of Aura within the Galakaos. Then a huge eye, more vast in size and larger than anything that can be described. The circumference is greater than the dimensions of the largest of planets and moons. The eye opens, a colossus orb of blood with a pupil, a pale sick greenish hue.

The eye turns away, and before them, before all of Aura and all the entire realm, thousands and thousands of huge razor teeth, millions of miles in distance from tip to mouth, open wide. The roar of this thing, this beast, and this terror is so loud, that all hearing is crushed into a deafening silence. Aura and Hrend grasp their ears, only hearing the pounding driving deafening gurgle from that vast, vast opened maw.

The others stand outside of Na'bata and look up in horror, their ears covered, their eyes shut, not wanting to see...they cannot look. Screams blare in bloody terror, but there is no sound, only the roar...the roar of Wom! The mother has come.

Aura watches in stunned horror. She cannot believe what is happening.

Hrend is terrified and does not dare to look. He stays close to Aura, as the two embrace, while the shadows and deepest of darkness closes around them. Wom's gaping maw takes the realm of Aura deep within its jaws. The mouth closes around them all, the roar echoes on and on for infinity, breaking apart the skies and ground around them. Just as the last of Aura's light is extinguished, she watches the ground crack beneath Na'bata. All within grapple and struggle to hang on. Their screams cannot be heard over the roar, as the cliffs snap and break away.

'No...please no...not my People!!!' Aura screams.

But it is too late, Na'bata falls from the cliffs above, and smashes into thousands of pieces of rock and piles of rubble. And beneath, rest the crushed bones of all Aura had left, all her people...demolished. She covers her face in agony, as sheer pain reeks and churns her stomach with sickness...*"All those people...all my friends...all those I had left...are...are gone!"*

Aura and Hrɛnd take one last look above. And the realm of Aura, the last realm of light. Is swallowed away. Final darkness has been reached, and the times of darkness, have now begun.

'Lady Aura...I can't see you...I can't see anything!' Hrɛnd cries.

'Shhhh...shhh...I'm here Hrɛnd...I'm with you.' She stands to her feet, eyes beginning to adjust to the darkness around them. 'Let's just take one step at a time Hrɛnd...we'll find our way through this...' She whispers to him. He lays his head upon her shoulder. His Asyndian eyes not adjusting very well to this darkness.

She stumbles along, tripping over rocks and holes in the ground, dropping Hrɛnd to the ground.

'What's the use lady Aura...there's nothing left...we're just going to die like everyone else! It's hopeless!' He holds his hands to his eyes. Aura kneels down beside him and removes his hands to look at him.

'Hrɛnd...Hrɛnd look at...look at me.'

Hrɛnd looks up, wiping his tears away from bloodshot eyes.

'Hrɛnd...I don't know what's going to happen to us...but I know we are still alive...we're still breathing...our light...is still alive in us, and that has to count for something...right?'

He says nothing, only holding out his arms to Aura. She wraps her arms around him and picks him up to carry him along.

'Come on Hrend…something tells me were not done yet…and I know we'll find something…we'll find something…and I think I have an idea of where we need to go…' She says to him.

Hrend begins to settle down, listening to Aura's words. 'Where's that…where are we going?' He asks.

'I'm not exactly sure…but I think we need to go in this direction over here…' She replies, and both of them head north, and then west for a while.

'There is no going back home…is there?' Hrend asks.

'No…no there isn't…we have to keep moving forward.' She replies.

Aura carries Hrend along. After every hill and every chasm and valley she trudges over and through, she keeps hoping, watching…looking for those lights that Diin told her about. Now, it's their only hope they have left.

Epilogue:

"...and all fades to black"

~

The realm of Aura,

is slowly drowning,

inside the pit of Wom's despair.

Flames of creation, fires of destruction,

Blood thick as oceans, from an endless reign,

Scales black as shadows, darkness in the age of grey.

Silhouettes of a realm, soon to fade away,

and all drown inside, the empty pit of Wom's Despair.

Ignite the furnace, for the final battle,

sacrifice life and limb, to keep the lights from extinguishing,

The blood of warriors, thicker than their armor,

their courage, stronger than iron or steel,

their battle is emanate, and their fate is sealed.

As darkness closes around them,

there is nowhere to run, no dignity in retreat,

they will stand their ground, and face what will be.

Victory or defeat, we have yet to see,

for the final battle awaits, there last stand they take,

yet as all fades to black....a spark of hope, awakes!

The Age of Black has begun...and the shadows are rising...

Continued in...
Wom

www.ingramcontent.com/pod-product-compliance
Lightning Source LLC
Chambersburg PA
CBHW060241030726
47493CB00024B/1453